The
Secrets
of
Flight

Also By Maggie Leffler

The Goodbye Cousins
The Diagnosis of Love

The
Secrets
of
Flight

Maggie Leffler

wm

WILLIAM MORROW
An Imprint of HarperCollins*Publishers*

P.S.™ is a trademark of HarperCollins Publishers.

HarperCollins books may be purchased for educational, business, or sales promotional use. For information, please e-mail the Special Markets Department at SPsales@harpercollins.com.

FIRST EDITION

Designed by Diahann Sturge

Library of Congress Cataloging-in-Publication Data has been applied for.

ISBN 978-0-06-242792-2

16 17 18 19 20   OV/RRD   10 9 8 7 6 5 4 3 2

For Katherine—
I'm so glad we're sisters.

The
Secrets
of
Flight

CHAPTER 1

Seeing Sarah

It was my eighty-seventh birthday when my sister Sarah walked into the meeting room of the Carnegie Library. Somehow she was still a young girl of about fifteen, with pale blond hair in a single braid down her back, just as she'd been when she scrambled up the climbing tree in the backyard and tossed apples to me on the ground down below. Of course, I knew it couldn't actually be my sister. Perhaps the Sarah-sighting was yet another side effect of aging. After all, the older I've become, the more everyone I come across reminds me of someone I once loved. I had no inkling that the girl with the braid might change everything.

The day had begun like any other, my birthday notwithstanding. When the doctor called about the results of my recent bone density scan, I was grateful for the tiny touch of humanity all the same. "So, it's official," I said, upon hearing the news. "You're saying I'm a little, old lady." The doctor chuckled before pushing another pill—this one for osteoporosis, which may prevent a hip fracture *and* cause sudden, irreversible blindness in certain susceptible people. "Frankly, at this point in my life, I would welcome a hip fracture—just so long as it's fatal," I replied. "Mrs. Browning, are you depressed?" the doctor asked, quite seriously, bless her heart. So, I fibbed a little and said to this kind young lady, who was probably about half the age of my son David, "My dear, much the way a youngster anticipates a birthday, I can't help but be a bit curious as to what exactly will be my end. You may have the luxury of distraction, but for me, death is my next big event." As the doctor grew silent, I waited for her to stop documenting our conversation into that godforsaken computer, waited for the gladness to arrive in her voice, when it might dawn on her that the date of my birth matched the day of her call. "Mrs. Browning," she finally said, "are you suicidal?" which was so far from the good wishes I'd been hoping for that I laughed. The joke was on me. I reassured her that I had absolutely no intention of ruining the surprise.

While the appeal of living forever was long lost on me, it wasn't as if I didn't value my existence. I had things to look forward to . . . or, well, one thing, which was my writers' group, a weekly gathering of senior citizens who struggled to write their memoirs. Herb Shepherd wrote about growing up in Pittsburgh, back when we played kick-the-can in the streets and had to bring all of our laundry in before noon, before our shirts turned black with soot from the steel mills. Victor Chenkovitch wrote heart-wrenching personal essays about his days in a concentration camp. Jean Fester wrote dreadful prose about her myriad health problems that hadn't—as of yet—been fatal. And of course there was the other Gene, Gene Rosskemp, who mostly seemed to show up for the women, or "young ladies" as he called us with a wink. No one had hopes of publication—no one, that is, except for Selena Markmann, who wrote novellas about domestic violence with "happy endings," wherein the attacker always appeared remorseful, bearing diamonds.

They didn't ask me to lead the group because I was a published essayist: none of them had read my book, nor could they find it anywhere since the publisher christened it *Miss Bixby Takes a Wife,* after my tongue-in-cheek essay about how men weren't the only ones who needed a doting partner to pick up after them. Even before it went out of print in 1958, the collection of essays never got much press apart from a handful of derogatory reviews claiming that it was a "lesbian manifesto" that "stole the angel in the house right out from under Virginia Woolf."

They didn't ask me to lead the group because they adored my writing: in fact, during the eleven years that I had belonged to the group, I had only turned in a single short story. Whenever I would pick up a pen to begin, it would rattle across the page in my shaky hand, leaving nothing of consequence behind. The real reason I ran the show every Tuesday from 6 to 8 P.M. at the Squirrel Hill library? I told them that in my former life I'd been the senior editor of a now-defunct New York publishing house.

It was an offhand remark I'd once made to Gene Rosskemp after he'd introduced himself in the mailroom of our high-rise apartment building. "Where're you from?" he'd asked, pumping my hand as I clutched my catalogs and bills, startled by the intrusion of this big-bellied, white-haired stranger in such a small space. Nevertheless, I appreciated the question. It was the first time since I'd moved back to Pittsburgh that someone had assumed I'd ever been anywhere else. "New York," I said, as he followed me into the lobby, and he said, "*Whoa,*" as if he'd expected me to say, "The North Side." Thankfully, he did not ask me how I'd ended up here, the question I'd been asking myself since my husband, Thomas, passed on the year before and I'd made the decision to move back to the city I hadn't called home in sixty years.

"What did you do in New York?" Gene asked instead, and when I said that I'd been an editor, oh, did his blue eyes get wide. "Magazine editor?"

I shook my head. "Book editor. Mostly novels. Some memoir."

When he exclaimed, "Mary Browning, you're just the girl I've been waiting for!" I felt like a young training pilot again, practicing spins and stalls in the air. "We got a group going—of writers! And between you and me, Millie ain't doin' so hot."

"Millie . . . ?" I asked, trying to rearrange my smile into concern, but it wasn't working.

"Millie Wisnicki, 'executive editor'—of the *Wisnicki Cousin Camp Chronicles*. You want the honest-to-God's truth," Gene added, leaning closer and talking behind the back of his hand— the mime of a whisperer, except that he was shouting. "If she had it her way, the group would turn into a knitting club!" Then he laughed and slapped his knee, and I didn't know what to think of this strange, loud man, except that he'd actually made me chuckle. I joined Gene for the next meeting, and the one after that, and every Tuesday for the next ten years. After the unexpected death of Millie Wisnicki in her carbon monoxide–induced sleep the spring before, Gene suggested the gauntlet be passed to me.

I took it seriously—or rather, took them seriously. This

notion of the Criticism Sandwich, two buns of praise to buffer each liverwurst of criticism, was never on my menu. If their prose happened to make me feel like taking my own life, I was compelled to tell them. On the other hand, if they stirred something up in me, some forgotten pulse of emotion—like surprise, or even hope—then I'd confess that, too. I wanted these people to write well. After all, it was for posterity.

My doctor never would've dreamed I was a woman with a passion. Nor my grocer Gary, a youngish fellow, mid-fifties and bald, who seemed surprised each week to find that I still had a pulse. My birthday, naturally, was no different, as he hassled himself with retrieving spices for me off the top shelf. He acted as if I hadn't signed up for Meals on Wheels just to spite him. The real truth was that, though my hands had a tremor, I still managed to cook—chicken soup and applesauce from scratch, and, when I was in the mood for something sweet, my own *rogalech*. I may not have driven in the preceding eighteen years, but I kept my driver's license updated, just for the sake of it. I still wore my stack-heeled, patent leather Mary Janes for a short walk to the library each week. I never feared death or cracks in the sidewalk. I did fear, in equal measures, protracted suffering and parallel parking, nearly all medication, and nursing homes. But my greatest fear of all was not having a voice of my own.

As per the ritual, when I paid for my cup of coffee and a bun and the few jars of spices for my pantry, Gary watched as I carefully counted out the change before he took the time to recount it—right down to the penny, as if, in the previous decade, I had ever once been wrong. "You are one amazing woman, Mrs. B," he said, the way he did every time, as he dropped the quarters and dimes into the register. I never once felt flattered. It was insulting, really, to have the ability to count be considered my great achievement.

Nevertheless, there were small benefits that the little old lady status afforded, I decided. Like at the Carnegie Library, where I could slip into the conference room carrying my contraband mug of coffee and paper bag of bread, and the security guard didn't so much as say boo.

Inside our dark paneled room, the group was already gathering in their seats, chattering about their adorable grandchildren, their fascinating travels, and their impending surgeries.

"How're the girls?" Herb Shepherd asked me, after showing me a picture of his great-grandson in a baseball uniform. "Josie and Hazel, right?"

"Wonderful. So grown up," I said, patting my empty pockets for footage of my own. I leaned toward him and whispered, "And Tyler got the job with Microsoft!"

Herb's eyes widened with delight, as Selena Markmann interrupted with a tap of her pencil on the table. "Good news, people. My great-niece—the one who is getting her PH.D. in psychology—is willing to type up any of our stories for a very reasonable hourly rate. So, if you've got something longhand or need a transcriptionist, she could use the work to help pay for books. Gene? Mary?" she added, handing out the information on Xeroxed pieces of paper, which I folded up and slipped into my purse out of politeness.

It wasn't that I didn't have stories to tell like the rest of them, but I certainly didn't want to run the risk of being *analyzed*. Whenever I toyed with the idea of penning my own memoir, I quickly gave up when confronted by the disquieting notion of telling my secrets. Years ago, after reading my one and only submission, they'd dissected my fictional heroine's character flaws like a roundtable of psychiatrists: "compulsive liar" and "clinically depressed," they pronounced. If I told the truth about my past, I could only begin to imagine what they'd think of me.

I decided, right then, not to mention my birthday. Gene would've wanted to run out and buy cupcakes, and that would've upset the other Jean, who had brittle diabetes. If anyone remembered, since the first year I let it slip and Millie showed up with a blanket she'd knitted for one of my great-granddaughters, I would do my best to keep them on the task at hand.

Except the task at hand that Tuesday night turned out not to be the writing at all, but instead the girl with the braid who walked into the conference room and looked around just as I was clearing my throat to begin. Her nose was not at all Sarah's nose and her eyes were more hazel than brown, but they were thoughtful like Sarah's and the girl carried herself with the same hesitant curiosity. After a moment, when no one appeared to claim her, I cleared my throat again and tweaked my glasses up on my nose, waiting for her to say she'd lost her study group and to make a hasty exit.

"Is this—the writers' group?" the girl asked.

"*Which* writers' group?" I asked, arching my eyebrow.

"The ad—the one in the paper." She held up a wrinkled clipping from the *Pittsburgh Post-Gazette* and read, "'Seeking New Writers! Talent and experience not necessary but interest in the craft a plus! Open to the public!'"

"I'm afraid you must be in the wrong—"

"That's us, honey," Selena interrupted me, her gold wrist

bangles jangling together against her purple sleeve. "I placed the ad a couple of weeks ago. We needed *someone* to replace Millie," Selena added, without even looking my way.

"You're in the *right* place—no pun intended!" the other Gene said, and the girl cracked an uncertain smile before taking a seat.

And then it was my turn to be baffled. I didn't give a hoot about Selena, who was obviously holding a grudge against me for not sharing her view that a wife-beater belonged in her "Hollywood Ending." No, it was the girl baffling me, as she slipped a notebook out of her backpack, took out a pencil, and chewed on it as she listened. I felt disoriented in her presence. Could this be a reincarnation of Sarah? Did she know my older sister, in some other life, how we'd shared everything—from clothes, to dolls, to a twin bed in the crowded apartment over my stepfather's dress shop? We even shared piano lessons: Sarah got the teacher, while I hovered by the door, memorizing her fingers on the keys. Or was it just coincidence, the way she and Sarah wore their hair identically and chewed on their pencils with the same revolting attention to the eraser?

"Well, who would like to begin?" Selena Markmann asked brightly, and I emerged from my reverie, feeling a mite foolish. Selena had just delivered my usual line.

Unfortunately, it was Jean Fester's night, an embarrassing showcase for the group. We were critiquing her bypass surgery.

"I found it a little hard to get through . . ." Gene gently remarked.

"That's because it was!" Jean snapped.

I kept watching the girl. Her manner was civilized: after all, we were not what she'd been expecting, but she stayed anyway. She even listened politely to the debate over whether or not it was a good thing that we all felt as if we'd been cut open by the end of the piece. And in her white blouse and khaki trousers— "Generals Pants," we called them in the service—her appearance was decent, too, as if she were waiting for a review from General Hap Arnold himself and the chance to pass from ground school into the air. But it wasn't her decency that shocked me; it was that she was there at all, like a birthday present I hadn't realized I'd been waiting for.

"Mary?" Herb Shepherd finally asked, when the room had gone silent, and I realized belatedly that Mary was me—still me, after all these years.

"I have to admit, Jean, it wasn't quite my cup of tea . . ." I began.

"Having my chest cracked open wasn't exactly my cup of tea, either!"

"Remember, we're here to critique the writing, not you." I smiled in the direction of her flaring nostrils and suggested that perhaps she'd rather read my suggestions. "I, for one, will be updating my living will to 'do not resuscitate,'" I added, and the other Gene laughed, as Jean Fester collected all of her feedback into a pile with a harrumph.

"So, you want to be a writer?" I asked the girl afterward.

She lowered her eyes. "Yes, well . . . my grandmother says that if you love to write, then you already are a writer. I'm working on a novel." I smiled, enjoying her quaky confidence. Looking up again, the girl glanced around the room. "Is this group just for . . ."

Those Not Long for This World? I thought.

" . . . nonfiction writers?" she finished.

"We welcome all writers, including those of fiction. What is your name, my dear?"

"Elyse," she said, shoving next week's submission into her backpack before zipping it shut.

Something caught in my chest. "Elyse." I smiled again. She smiled. "I am Mrs. Browning," I added.

"Nice to meet you, Mrs. Browning. And all of you," she said to the rest of the group. The men were smiling at her a little dopily, but Selena looked smug, as if she'd handpicked the girl herself.

"I do hope you'll be back," I said.

"Oh, I'll be back," she said, sounding vaguely confident.

When I got home that night and settled into my recliner, I was still thinking about the girl with the braid. The TV was on, tuned to a commercial for the prescription that had been offered to me that same afternoon. *This medication could cause blindness, coma, or even death. If any of these side effects should occur, call your doctor immediately.* I aimed my remote to make the screen go black again.

When I climbed into bed later, my heart was skipping beats. I thought about Elyse again. Maybe she would come back next week. Maybe she would write something worth reading. Maybe she would make me a writer again. Maybe I could tell her the truth about me. I shut off the light and waited. Something filled up my chest again, an unfamiliar vibration, and I regretted how cavalierly I'd spoken about My End earlier that day. With one hand over my heart, I inhaled and exhaled, imagining

Sarah watching over me, coaching me to breathe. The fluttering passed. I felt my shoulders relax. Maybe my heart wasn't stopping but expecting—like the moment I held baby Dave in my arms and knew he was the one who would make it home. Maybe this was just my life, starting over.

CHAPTER 2

23 Things About Me

By Elyse Strickler

1. When I was five, I wanted to be the first woman president of the United States, but my mother said the job was too stressful. "Oftentimes people will try to *assassinate* you—do you know what that means?" Mom said. So, I picked astronaut instead. "Oh, *sweetie*. Most of them blow up," she said. So, I chose writer—of novels, but Mom said it was next to impossible to get published, and that I would need a day job. So, for my day job I chose scientist. She said the PH.D. programs could be surprisingly cutthroat, and it was hard to get tenure at places like the National Institutes of Health. When I asked if I could be a doctor like Daddy, Mom said, "Absolutely! Honey, you can be whatever you set your mind to!" and Daddy said, "That's my girl!"

2. My mother's favorite phrase is "the Worst Case Scenario" as in, *Let's try and imagine, if not expect, ultimate disaster so*

that we might a) Never be disappointed when things go wrong and b) Occasionally experience the short-lived "pleasant surprise" when they go right. You might think she's an insurance agent, but she actually makes a living as a lawyer, representing the asbestos companies who are always being sued by the millions of people who are riddled with cancer due to asbestos. When I asked if she had "considered the Pros and Cons" (her second favorite phrase) of defending a substance that kills people, Mom said she wasn't actually *defending* asbestos, she was just making sure the right people got paid. Then she sighed and said, "It's complicated."

3. I have two little brothers, Toby and Hugh. Toby is two years younger than me and was selected to be in these Saturday classes at Carnegie Mellon for "Exceptionally Talented Youth" because he did better than I did on the PSATs, and he's only in middle school. My mother says that even if he's brighter than me, his social skills are lacking, and you can go farther in life with good social skills. I don't see how this is supposed to make me feel better.

4. I call baby Hugh "Huggie," which drives my mother crazy because it reminds her of changing a diaper. Huggie is the only person in the world who still snuggles me, usually while I read him books. Daddy stopped snuggling me when my breasts came in, and Mom will give kisses, but never just wraps me in her arms and lets me melt into her lap. Huggie is five now and is learning to read by himself, which means our Snuggling Days are numbered.

5. I've always wished I had a twin. One time, after Aunt Andie and I watched *The Parent Trap,* I told her my wish,

and she said, "You did have a twin. It died." Then she saw my face and said, "Oh, wait, maybe I shouldn't have . . ." Later I asked Mom for the whole story, and she said there wasn't much to tell: she had a miscarriage at twenty weeks. Daddy was the one who told me that my twin was a boy and his name was going to be Noah. Sometimes I like to imagine what my life would be like if Noah had lived. He'd probably play lacrosse. He'd introduce me to his friends and not let them date me. He'd tell me about sex instead of leaving pamphlets around the house—like Daddy and Mom did—with disgusting pictures of genitals falling off from sexually transmitted diseases.

6. Huggie almost didn't exist, either, because Daddy didn't want another child, he wanted to get a chocolate Lab, instead. When I was ten, I overheard them talking through the vent in my pink bedroom. My father was talking about how great things were with just two kids, one of each sex and disability-free. "But just imagine if something unspeakable happened to one of them—and then it would be too late for me to have another," my mother said, which was all Daddy needed to hear. As a doctor, he is all about preparing for the Worst Case Scenario, which must've been the reason Mom married him. I was relieved when the new baby turned out to be a boy. I hoped it meant that God had intended for Toby to be replaced, and I would be spared.

7. My best friend Thea and I made a pact that we are not falling in love with Holden Saunders this year, like all the other girls in school. Even though we're not falling in love with him, I always choose my hallway route between classes based on Holden's class schedule—I know,

for example, that if I linger at my locker outside of French, I'll see him going into Spanish, and that he always buys a can of soda outside the Choir Room before his fifth period English. Thea heard that Holden Saunders is actually dating this cheerleader Karina Spencer—aka Adelaide in last year's *Guys and Dolls*—and that she blew him on the first date, which is another reason we're not falling in love with him. Now that he's in our physics class, we can see him up close, and it turns out he actually does have some acne on his forehead, and the other day his left ear had a little honey-colored wax at the rim. We're also not falling in love with him because of his name. His parents must've thought they were the first people in the world to love *The Catcher in the Rye.*

8. Thea and I love to shop at the Salvation Army, which gives my mom hives. Thea got her favorite camouflage jacket there, which she pairs with combat boots and a miniskirt, black eyeliner, and her nose ring. Since I'm not allowed to go Goth, my fallback look is a twinset from Anne Taylor from Mom and a kilt from the thrift store. Which is my way of saying that even if we *were* falling in love with Holden Saunders, he's not falling in love with us—yet. Everything might change this year, because in psychology, Mrs. Desmond just announced that during the next month-long unit, we'll be paired off, two by two, with mock marriages. All I have to do is convince her to marry Holden and me, and the first domino will fall.

9. My mother doesn't know what it's like to not have guys drooling all over her. One time, Aunt Andie and I were looking at an old photo album and she pointed to a pic-

ture of an exotic-looking woman with full, dark eyebrows and long hair. "This is the woman who was almost your mother," Aunt Andie said. It was like she had no basic grasp of human genetics. "Your dad was engaged to this woman, Natalia, when he met your mom at a party in med school," she explained. "He called off the wedding to be with Jane." Then she saw my face and went, "Hold on, maybe I wasn't supposed to . . ." Later, when I asked Daddy about it, he just laughed and said, "I saw your mom and *boom*. She blew me away." That's how beautiful my mom was. She's still that beautiful now, when she smiles and laughs, which isn't so often anymore.

10. Two years ago, when I was thirteen, my parents called us into the living room for a Family Meeting. When Mom said they had big news, I thought they were getting a divorce. But then I remembered that they never fight, and that we don't have a housekeeper named Rocco with slicked-back hair and a hairless chest showing through his silk blouse, who would run away with Mom to California—like what happened to Thea's mother. So maybe it would be the Best Case Scenario for a change. "We're going to London?" I guessed, excited. And Mom said, "Daddy has cancer." When Toby asked, "What exactly is cancer, Dad?" his eyes were squinting as if the information he was about to consume would be delivered at light speed. And Daddy said, "It's when a group of cells in your body mutates and then proliferates—or reproduces—at an abnormal rate." My father held up a hand. "Hang on. Let me back up. Let's talk about normal cell death or *apoptosis*—" I interrupted to ask what the Worst Case Scenario was here. When Daddy

said, "I die," I felt like an invisible Darth Vader had just held up his hand and was choking me. As my mother insisted brightly that that would never, ever happen, I imagined us kissing my father's coffin before we lowered it into the ground.

11. Later we learned that the Cancer was named Pancreatic Neuroendocrine—or, "the good kind," if you ask Dr. Satinder Khaira—and after the surgery, it would make Daddy stay in his bathrobe and sweats and stop going to work for close to six months. But then Remission would move in, and Daddy would be known as a Living Miracle—at least by everyone at Fox Chapel United Methodist Church. Friends of the family just call him Really Lucky.

12. I still worry that something bad will happen to Daddy. And then I feel awful, because that means I have no faith or at least am part of the Ye with very little. When I told that to Mom she said she had no faith, either, but we had to pretend like we did. And I didn't know if she meant pretend for Daddy or for God, so that He'll keep giving us what we're begging him for.

13. Mom is petite, blond, and Jewish, and Daddy is tall, dark, and Protestant, and they decided to raise us with the holy days of both traditions so that one day, when we come of age, we'll be confused. I didn't grow up with Hebrew school, a Bat Mitzvah, or a church confirmation, but apparently, sometime after my birth, there was some sort of Baptism/Naming Ceremony involving a minister and a rabbi. It took a tumor to make Daddy want to go to church on ordinary Sundays, when it wasn't Christmas or Easter. One time after the service, I asked him if it was okay that

I felt like the minister was the Queen from *Alice in Wonderland* encouraging us to believe six impossible things before breakfast, and he sighed and said, almost to himself: "Maybe we should've picked one."

14. Sometimes when I'm falling asleep I see people's faces in my head, faces I've never met, and I wonder who they are, and if I will ever meet them. Aunt Andie says maybe they're lost souls, looking for someone to tell their stories. Mom says this explanation is just one more example of Aunt Andie living "in a fantasy land." Mom says Aunt Andie's lying to herself by thinking she's happy. When I said, "If she thinks she's happy, then isn't she?" Mom said, "It's a *deception*," as if Aunt Andie's "happiness" were somehow sinister. "No one changes jobs, changes cities, changes apartments every year 'just to try something new.'" Mom wants Aunt Andie to accept that she's actually *un*happy, so she can stop running away from herself.

15. I love that Aunt Andie only rents and never buys. I love that she calls herself an artist, even though she's never sold a single one of her weird paintings. I love that she still believes in Soul Mates even though she hasn't had a "viable boyfriend" (Mom's words) in years. Mom says if Aunt Andie would just lose thirty pounds, or maybe be willing to date "heavier" men, she wouldn't have had to borrow ten thousand dollars to freeze her eggs before her ovaries shrivel up. Mom lent Aunt Andie the money three years ago, and since then, the only conversations they have—when they speak at all—are about when Aunt Andie is going to pay her back. Mom doesn't know that I go to Aunt Andie's place after school sometimes or that we've met at

the mall for lunch. I don't care what Mom thinks: I still love hearing about Aunt Andie's hopeful First Encounters. She always says there's nothing more romantic than being able to look back at that initial meeting so you could figure out where it all began. It's the very reason I wanted to join the "Talent Not Necessary" Group.

16. My annoying brother Toby is the one who saw the ad in the *Pittsburgh Post-Gazette*. "Hey, guys, check this out: 'Writers Wanted—talent not necessary!' They're talking about you, Elyse!" Daddy said they sounded like a pretty desperate group of people, and my mom was worried about the part that said "Open to the public," which she thought was a euphemism for "Potentially Violent Wack Jobs." But I had this fantasy that maybe I'd open the door to the conference room and Holden Saunders would glance up and pause—mid-pencil-twirl—to tilt his head to the side, trying to place me. I'd be tempted to tell him that we've gone to school together for five years and that, in fact, when my family moved to the Regal Estates last summer, it actually made us neighbors. At the end of the session, before I could tell him any of this, he would walk up to me and say, half-squinting, "Elyse, right?"

17. Mom, as usual, wanted me to consider the Pros and Cons of attending the group. Such as, if I write more, then I will have more insomnia and then my grades might suffer. The only Con I could imagine was from that old movie, *Dead Poets Society,* where one of us might be compelled to commit suicide for the sake of our art.

18. The reason I can't sleep at night is because I am working on a novel about a group of four sisters who don't know

they're sisters, who end up at the same boarding school in England. I have already finished writing one hundred pages, which means I'll definitely finish my first novel before my sixteenth birthday, and hopefully be published before I graduate from high school!

19. When my mother read the opening of my novel, she told me that I shouldn't have set it in the 1940s, because I've never lived in the 1940s, and that I shouldn't have set it in London because I've never been to London, and that it doesn't make sense that one woman would have four babies with four different men and leave them in four different countries. She couldn't "suspend her disbelief" that they would all end up together at the same school in London, even if it was touted as the best girls' school in the entire world. She said *maybe* she'd believe it if I kept it to two sisters who didn't know they were sisters, but not four. Like it was that easy to say sayonara to Anastasia and Eliona. She told me to "write what I know," which would make a terrible story: here's me, going to school, and watching Holden in physics, and babysitting my brothers. The only way I would be able to have anything to write about is if I switched places with Thea, or if Daddy hadn't miraculously been healed.

20. Everything that I hate about my mother is everything I hate about myself. So it's really hard to hate her, and that makes me madder.

21. I have always wanted to save somebody's life. One time, before Daddy got sick, we were at McDonald's and a man inhaled a Chicken McNugget and was turning blue until Daddy did the Heimlich and saved his life. Toby watched

and said, "Awesome!" and two-year-old Huggie was sort of fascinated and said, "What happened?" but I watched the whole thing and wanted to cry. It's unfortunately how I react to any life-threatening situation, but I'm hoping that will change as I get older. Actually, I've never been in another life-threatening situation, but I have watched many on TV.

22. #21 is the reason I stayed when I discovered that the Public from the "Open to the Public/No Talent" group was just a bunch of senior citizens. I thought about turning around and pretending I was in the wrong room, but then I started dreaming for a moment. Maybe someone will fall out of his chair, and I could help him up. Or maybe I could do CPR on one of them, which I learned in a babysitting course. I wanted to be an unexpected hero. I wanted to be the kid interviewed on the *Today* show.

23. I thought about telling Thea that the group was elderly, but later, when she was asking me if there were any cute guys in it, something made my mouth say, "Just one. But he's older." When she asked if he went to Pitt, I said, "I'm guessing he's like . . . thirty," and she gasped, so I couldn't make my mouth say, "Times three." I thought about telling my mom that the group was not what I had expected, not in the slightest, but when she picked me up at the library and noticed I looked disappointed, she was worried that it was from criticism I might've received on my novel. "Oh, honey," she said, patting my knee. "It's not easy hearing painful truths from people who don't love you," she said. That's when I decided that I wanted something to happen to me that my mother couldn't protect me from.

PART 1

CHAPTER 3

Miri Wants

1938

The first secret starts with Elias Glazier, the wavy-haired lead actor from *Hamlet* whom my sister falls in love with in the winter of 1938. If it weren't for Sarah making me her accomplice—entreating me to go along for their dates at the diner, or to lose myself in the library while she visits him after the matinee, pretending to our parents, all the while, that she and I are together—their affair would've never taken flight.

The morning after my sister announces her elopement—"To an *actor*?" Mama screamed, as if he were a gentile—my mother tells me that she's made a decision: in two years, when I turn eighteen and graduate from high school, she's sending me to college.

"But that costs too much," I say, which is what Mama usually says about everything I want. Specifically, flight lessons at six dollars an hour, which we can't possibly afford, which I may not "save up" for because it's dangerous and frivolous, and Uncle Hyman says that girls don't belong in the cockpit of an aircraft. The path of my life has been laid out for me with the precision of a hemline: I'll live in the house on Beacon Street, and work in the family shop mending and making dresses. No one seems to care that I don't know how to sew.

"There are savings." Mama stops pacing to study her hand for a moment—at the chip of a diamond on her finger, which I realize she must be intending to hock. When she looks over at me, I'm surprised to notice the new wisps of white and gray in her dark hair that frames her face. "Just not enough for both of you girls."

"But then that won't be fair." Sarah is nearly twenty to my sixteen. If anyone should get the chance to go, she should be first.

"Sarah never cared about school. She spends her pocket money on *clothes*," Mama says with disdain, which is ironic considering our family livelihood depends on such consumerism, albeit cheaper frocks than the ones Sarah saves for. "She's a *dreamer*," Mama adds. "She picked a starving artist."

I think of Elias, with his equal penchant for scotch and comedy, particularly that of the Marx Brothers. "Emily, I have a little confession to make," he likes to say, being Hackenbush from *A Day at the Races*, as he wraps an arm around my giggling sister. "I'm actually a horse doctor. But marry me, and I'll never look at any other horse." His eyes are cerulean, his smile devilish, and he's nothing like the type of man we imagined, specifically Dickon from *The Secret Garden*, charmer of animals and healer of the lame, a character whom we both adored as girls. "He seems to really love her," I offer.

"Love!" Mama scoffs, throwing up a hand. "What do they know about love? They have no money and no education."

As my mother resumes her pacing again, I imagine starring in my own real-life version of a *Kitson Career Series* novel, the ones Sarah and I check out from the library where the young woman always moves to a new city to start a career, only in my story, it's not a man who's going to sweep me off my feet when I arrive. It'll be an airplane.

I'VE WANTED TO FLY SINCE WE LIVED BACK IN FREELAND, SINCE A pilot dropped into our backyard and stayed for dinner ten years ago. It was a Friday, which meant Mama was preparing for Shabbat, and Sarah was cooking up an adventure. "Meet me outside, by the tree. And don't let them see you!" Sarah opened our bedroom door a crack before inching it wider. Then she gave me a smile and slipped away.

Cradling my doll Molly and peering out the window, I waited in our room until, eventually, Sarah ran across the backyard in the fog. I saw her scrambling up the planks Papa had nailed to the twisty trunk of the apple tree. Then she climbed higher and her long legs disappeared inside the branches. I put Molly on the night table next to Sarah's copy of *The Secret Garden* and tiptoed downstairs. Unlike the workaday week, when Papa was out peddling crops from our half-acre garden, he was reading in the front room and smoking his pipe. I loved the smell of his pipe and just knowing he was home, relaxing—unlike Mama, who hit him with a dish towel and yelled, "Up! Up!" if she found him in his chair too long.

In the kitchen, Mama was braiding the challah on the counter. I could smell the meaty *cholent* in the oven. When her head whipped around, I was already crouched under the table. "Sarah?" Mama called. "It's time to help! Miri, come and set the table!" she added, yelling over her shoulder. Then she walked out of the kitchen with an exasperated sigh.

As soon as she was gone, I ran out the door and into the backyard. By then it was so foggy that I could barely see the apple tree on the edge of the yard. I thought of the evening when the mist rolled in so low and white that Papa called me into the backyard at dusk. "See, Miriush, now you can say you've stood in a cloud," he'd said. It felt the same that night, too, the hazy moisture on my face, as I felt my way up the planks and crawled into the tree.

"Mama's looking for us," I said, making my way higher until we were both completely shrouded by branches.

"*Sh*," Sarah whispered. "Let's see what happens."

All at once I realized this was as far as we were going; this was the adventure.

In the distance, the roar of a faraway plane grew closer, but I couldn't see it, despite the slowly lifting mist. Minutes passed that seemed like hours, and shadows began to lurk in the grass and the trees turned purplish. Through the window, I could see tiny flames flickering: Mama had lighted the candles. Still, no one came outside to get us.

I glanced back, away from the house, and saw a man falling from the sky. I blinked. Not fifty feet from my back porch, he landed without so much as a thud, like in a dream. Sarah inhaled, as she grabbed my hand and sat up straighter. Together we watched his parachute spread out on the field, watched him stumble, roll and lie still, and then, after a moment, he untangled himself from the mounds of white material, got up, and started walking. I squinted at the ghost in the fog wearing a flight suit and prayed that he wasn't squashing Papa's blueberries. "Come on," Sarah said, climbing down. The ghost kept walking right into our backyard and seemed headed straight for our back door, until we both jumped down out of the tree, startling him. It wasn't until the man gasped that I knew for sure he was real.

Somewhere in the dark, there was a high-pitched careening sound followed by a sudden, shuddering explosion. The pilot looked back, over his shoulder, and then at the lights of my house. "Are your parents home?" he asked Sarah, and she nodded, as I took him by the hand.

"There you girls are! Who is this?" Mama shrieked when we got inside, and we all got to hear the story of how the pilot, having lost his way in the fog with an empty tank, jumped from the plane. The fact that his blond hair and face were covered in blackish grit was nothing short of glamorous to me. He smelled like motor oil and cut grass.

Mama gave him towels, and the pilot, whose name turned out to be Charlie, washed up and joined us for the Shabbos meal. When Mama closed her eyes and sang the blessing, I snuck a look at the pilot, bowing his head, and then at Sarah, who was staring at him, unabashedly. She caught me looking, and we both smiled.

That night, Charlie slept on the sofa in the living room and the next morning Papa took me along to the crash site in the field a couple of miles away, so that the pilot could extract the mail from his plane and send it on by train to New York. On the car ride, Charlie told us that he first wanted to fly when he was my age. He saw an air show and was hooked.

"Were you scared last night—before you jumped?" I asked him, and he shook his head.

"Maybe for a minute. I just didn't want the plane to land on anyone."

"Looks like you did all right," my father said, pointing to the twisted pile of metal still smoking in the field miles from our house.

Driving back, I was still thinking about the pilot emerging from the fog with the calmness of an angel, when I said to my father, "Papa, when I grow up, I want to fly, too."

"You will then," he said, and I looked at him and smiled. "*Matuka sheli,*" he added, brushing my cheek with the back of his hand.

When we got home, Mama met us in the driveway, holding a letter from Papa's stepbrother, Uncle Hyman. He needed us to move to Pittsburgh *now;* there was no putting it off or he would fill the positions at his shop with someone else.

"Jobs for both of us and a real community," she said, and Papa sighed. I told Mama that Papa said I could fly, and she gave Papa a sharp look.

"When she grows up," Papa said. "If she wants."

"I want," I said, jumping up and down and clapping. "I want, I want, I want!"

"Oh, Rina," Papa said to my mother, when she threw up her hands. "Let her dream. Who's it gonna hurt?"

But not even two years later, in the winter of 1930, Papa was dead, along with my visions of flight. We'd moved to Pittsburgh by then, to the land of steel and honey, according to Mama, where we wouldn't need a Hebrew teacher to drive over once a week from Hazelton, because there was a Jewish school right in our new neighborhood. I remember walking back from the playground that day, how the house on Beacon Street was bustling with people, including the rabbi and all the men from the synagogue except for Papa, who I later found out was in the long box in the living room surrounded by all the little chairs. "There was an accident," Mama said and nothing more. It was eleven-year-old Sarah who explained in our beds that night that he'd slid off the third-story roof while chipping away at an ice dam after breakfast. I hugged my doll and whimpered with fear, until Sarah whispered in the dark that we must be strong like the Spartans of Greece, who never cried. At eight, I didn't know much about ancient Greece or what these Spartans had against crying, but from then on, I learned how to squeeze my face closed and let myself soundlessly shudder, imagining my tears deep inside, dripping off my organs.

All at once, Papa disappeared from our daily conversations, as if he never existed at all. At first I thought it was because Mama felt guilty for having ordered him to fix the leaky ceiling in the first place. Later, when I was ten and she married Papa's stepbrother Hyman, I wondered if she was always in love with him, a man whose neck hung over the collar of his shirt and whose face turned red at the slightest provocation. Later still, at thirteen, I noticed the way Mama and her lady friends gathered around the kitchen table to drink tea sweetened with jam and talk and talk, artfully avoiding topics of tragedy in front of the person to whom the catastrophe had struck. When I asked Mama about these conversational omissions, she told me that no one wanted to be reminded; no one wanted to risk crying and never being able to stop. I understood then that pain should only be briefly experienced in private, never to be mentioned again.

I cataloged all the things Papa missed—like the first blizzard of the winter, or the first Yom Kippur without him, or my first piano recital, or, when I was sixteen years old, the first country to be invaded by Nazi Germany—Czechoslovakia, followed by Poland and then Denmark, before Norway, Belgium, and Holland, and eventually France. He also missed his first daughter's marriage, but then again, it seems we all did.

THE MORNING AFTER SARAH'S ELOPEMENT, AS MY MOTHER CONtinues her restless pacing, I'm lost in a daydream of myself piloting an open cockpit plane—wearing a leather bomber jacket and a white scarf, tied jauntily around my neck—when Mama says, "You'll take a secretarial course and learn bookkeeping."

I look up, feeling disappointment crashing all over my face. "But . . . what about flying?"

"*Flying?*" Mama repeats, as if I mean trapeze artist. "Miriam, please. Be practical. I'm offering you an opportunity. The least you could do is show some gratitude."

Then she stalks out, leaving me alone with my guilt and some unnamable disquiet: *Sarah.* If she really is married now, I'm the only one left. What difference will a degree make if my world matches my mother's? At the sound of a tree branch scratching against the kitchen window, I glance over and sigh. Maybe she's right. Maybe my dream should've died when Papa did.

THAT NIGHT, I'M IN THE PARLOR LISTENING TO THE RADIO BY myself when FDR's voice comes over the airwaves. Uncle Hyman is still at the shop, and Sarah has already left with her things for the North Side, but I imagine Papa by my side, his blue eyes growing wide with wonder, as the president proclaims there will be a brand-new, federally funded Civilian Pilot Training program designed to build up the pool of available pilots. When FDR explains the four-month course will be offered through participating colleges, giving twenty thousand college students an opportunity to fly, I see Papa slapping my knee and exclaiming with glee, "Here's your chance, Miriush!"

Upstairs, Mama is on her knees, scrubbing the bathroom floor. When she doesn't stop to even wring out her sponge for a full five minutes, I say to her back, "I'm sorry for being ungrateful. I really do want to go to college."

She hesitates for just a moment before resuming her toil. "I already talked to Hyman about it. He says there's no point when you can learn bookkeeping on the job," she replies, her face turned toward the base of the toilet.

"But I want an education," I say again, and Mama finally twists around and looks up at me, her hazel eyes strangely vulnerable. "I'll get my secretarial degree," I tell her. "I promise. Please, Mama. Give me a chance."

AND SO, THREE YEARS LATER IN 1941, IN THE SPRING OF MY freshman year at the University of Pittsburgh, my double life begins as a secret student of the sky.

CHAPTER 4

Three Women and a Plane

The Sunday after my birthday everything changed all over again, when I returned to my apartment building after a walk and Gene Rosskemp cornered me in the lobby. "Mary! You gotta taste this!" he said, rather than hello, and then turned on his heel and disappeared down the hallway, past the wall of elevators. I sighed and clutched my purse to my bosom before following him down the corridor, past the nurse's office, and into the communal kitchen, a place I rarely ventured since not only was my own small apartment fully equipped, but the management had recently decided that the mentally ill and the aging were equally appealing tenants. To date, I'd been growled at by grown woman in pigtails and had possibly witnessed a drug deal just outside of the building. I was afraid to so much as heat up a bowl of soup in the microwave without being stabbed to death. Gene, obviously, held no such fear.

As my eyes adjusted to the flickering fluorescent light of

the grimy kitchen, Gene said, "Get a load of this, Mary—homemade cookies, right from the microwave!" He handed me a spoonful of melted goo, which I studied with a raised eyebrow. "For heaven's sake. What's in this?" I asked.

"Dark chocolate. Good for your heart."

Sampling the sweet bite, I glanced over at the table for a possible seat, which was when I noticed the *USA Today* lying there, specifically the Arts and Entertainment section, which featured a black-and-white picture of three young women and an airplane—its image like a lost memory. I coughed and sputtered on the melted dough.

"That bad?" Gene asked, rescuing the spoon before I could drop it.

"No, it's . . . quite good. Actually." I wiped my lip, still staring at the Fairchild PT-19, a plane I knew well, back when we were getting our wings. The three women were squinting into the sun: one smirking redhead, one shy brunette, and a short girl with curly hair, all smiling at something beyond the camera, quite possibly their future. They believed it was theirs to design. I picked up the paper, adjusted my glasses on my nose, and squinted at the newsprint. Congress, it seemed, was finally honoring the forgotten female pilots of WWII with the Congressional Gold Medal, "the highest civilian honor." According to the article, fewer than three hundred Women Airforce Service Pilots were still alive, but relatives were eligible to collect the medals of family members who served.

"BRING BACK MEMORIES?" GENE ASKED, OVER MY SHOULDER, and I jumped. I never even told the writers' group that I'd been a pilot during the war, not even when Gene invited me to go "flying" one day—model airplanes, it turned out, at a nearby park. As his little foam plane spun through the air above us and Gene expertly worked the controls, proudly showing off his snap rolls and lazy eights from the ground below, I thought, *How can I tell him that I made real figure eights in the sky?* "I mean of the time," Gene added, and I exhaled.

"It certainly does." I couldn't stop staring. How young they looked—and so happy, with their faces tilted toward the shimmering unknown. Beneath the three women and the plane was a caption: *Murphee Sutherland, Miriam Lichtenstein, and Grace Davinport, Women Airforce Service Pilots in 1944. Photo donated by the family of Grace Davinport.*

So, Grace is gone, I thought. At my age, when all of my friends were disappearing, I hadn't really expected otherwise. But would the rest of them be there? Murphee and Vera and—

"I saw this a while ago, back when it came out. Guess nobody likes to throw anything away around here. Funny how old pictures are—feels like you might know them, right? But in the summer of 1944, I was in France."

I studied the girl in the center, squinting into the sun. How naïve she was, thinking she was brave—naïve and reckless and stupid. It was no wonder Miriam Lichtenstein had disappeared in 1945. Yet here she was in a national newspaper sixty-four years later, *identified by name.* What could it mean? I finally turned and looked at Gene, realizing what he'd just said, *Back when it came out.* "Do you mean to say the medals have already been awarded?" I looked at the date of the article, two months ago this week, July 10, 2009.

"Doubt it." Gene pushed his readers up on his nose and stared at the photo. "Cute girls. I might've even dated one of 'em."

I rolled up the article and swatted him with it. "I'm quite certain you didn't, Gene Rosskemp."

"I mean, I would've wanted to," Gene called after me, as I left the kitchen, still clutching the newspaper.

Back in my room, I methodically locked the dead bolts and then the chain link, before dropping my purse on the table and sinking my creaky joints into the recliner. Then, with trembling fingers, I pulled out the newspaper and stared at the picture once again, at the girl in the center beaming with the joy of someone who is completely oblivious to her own end. "Miri," I whispered, as tears of disbelief filled my eyes. "Where did you go?"

THE FOLLOWING TUESDAY, AS WE GATHERED ONCE AGAIN AT THE Carnegie Library, my tremor was worse than usual. Perhaps it was because Herb Shepherd was inexplicably not present to discuss his own piece, and I had always liked Herb, our poetic voice of reason, who was either dead or severely incapacitated, I deduced, since he hadn't skipped a group in the last ten years. But more than likely, the shaking hand and the flip-flopping of my heart were simply side effects of the girl with the braid, who had shown up again.

I'd decided in advance that if she were present then maybe I would hire her to be my transcriptionist for the memoir I was too afraid to write. And if she were never to return, then it was just as well; life could carry on as usual. After all, why muck about with the past? The story belonged to the pilots in the newspaper, not me, Mary Browning. Except that young Miri had peered at me from the center of the picture and dared me to tell the story. Could I bring her back to life?

As soon as Elyse entered, slouching under the weight of her enormous backpack, I drew in a breath and felt my pen tremble in my hand. The girl was going to make me tell the truth, and she didn't even know it yet.

"Do you think we oughta give Herb a call?" Gene asked, glancing anxiously around the table. "He said he wasn't feelin' so hot."

"He *thought* it was just heartburn," the other Jean said, raising her eyebrow.

Then Selena Markmann burst into the room. "Herb's water heater blew up!" she said, breathlessly, flinging her bag down on the table. "His basement is flooded."

"So . . . he drowned?" asked Gene.

"He's waiting for a plumber, and he sends his regrets. We can mail him our critiques or save them for next week. But, since we're all here . . ." Selena added, with a nervous giggle, before proposing her new "Internet Initiative": Since the group was getting *younger,* she said suggestively, wiggling her eyebrows in the direction of Elyse, she thought we should "make a pact to go green," and save on Xeroxing costs by submitting our chapters via email. Once we were all online, we'd be able to contact each other in the event of an emergency, she pointed out.

"I still have a phone. Does no one else have a phone?" I asked. "And, forgive me, but which one of us is getting younger?"

"How many of us have computers?" Selena barked, and all but Jean Fester and myself raised a hand.

I glanced at Jean. "I don't believe Herb has a computer."

"He does," said Selena. "This was his idea."

"Let's leave the decision for a vote when we reconvene in a week," I suggested. "In the meantime, we need to select someone to hand out for the next meeting." It didn't matter whether you were undergoing emergency bypass surgery or were temporarily floating in sewage in your own basement: if you didn't show up, you didn't get another turn to be critiqued until the rest of us had been given a chance to submit.

"I could go," said a tentative voice, and we all turned to glance at Elyse, shyly raising her hand. "I mean, if no one else is ready."

Everyone loved the idea—everyone, that is, except for Jean Fester, who asked what a girl would write about these days, when she'd never had her freedom threatened?

A short while later, after the group had dispersed early and I had time to peruse the stacks and select a few novels for my night table, I approached the librarian, a woman in her midfifties, who looked at me kindly when I produced the *USA Today* article from my pocketbook, inwardly cursing my shaky fingers.

"A friend of mine flew planes during the war. I'm wondering if she wanted to attend the ceremony how she'd be found—if someone was looking for her . . ." The librarian scanned the article, her eyes narrowed with concentration. "I'm certain she couldn't just show up at Pennsylvania Avenue and expect to be handed a medal," I added with a laugh.

When the librarian finally looked up and smiled, I decided I must be wrong: she was not a day over forty-five. She just needed to smile more often. "Your friend must be amazing," she said.

"Not really, no. Just . . . an ordinary woman doing her part."

"Let's see what we can find out," the librarian said. I followed her over to a nearby cluster of desks, each one with its own computer. She pulled up a seat for me and then plunked her bottom down in front of the screen. "Okay if I drive?" When I nodded, mute, she started typing words onto a blank page marked with a rainbow of colored letters: Google. After a considerable amount of tapping and clicking, she landed on a university website. "Here we go. It looks like some folks at Texas Woman's University are verifying who the pilots were." She scrawled down a number on a small square of paper and handed it to me. I looked at the number and then back to her face. "I bet if your friend called this phone number, they could help."

"And if she doesn't have a birth certificate or other forms of identification? I'm fairly certain she said everything was destroyed in a fire."

"Oh, they have their ways. I'm sure if she just told them her name and Social Security number, they'd be able to verify that she was there."

"Of course. You're right. Thank you. I'll . . . pass this information on."

So, it was over before it had begun. Of course it was over. Had I really expected that I could just show them a black-and-white picture from the paper taken sixty years ago and expect them to recognize her? Did I even want Miri to be found?

On the way out of the library, I tossed the phone number in the garbage and then reached for the banister to steady my way down the steps, only to find Elyse sitting on the last two, down by the sidewalk on Forbes Avenue. Just coming upon her like that, lost in thought and looking like Sarah fiddling with her shoelaces, made my tremor start up again.

Elyse glanced over and smiled. "Hey, Mrs. Browning. My

mom won't be here for another hour. I should probably study, but the weather is so nice . . ."

"How about a cup of tea somewhere?" I suggested, forgetting that young people today only drink coffee. She hesitated, as if she were already committed to staying in that very spot of cement. "I have a business proposition to discuss with you," I added, deciding in that very moment.

We settled on Panera Bread across the street, which certainly wasn't the old-world charm I was looking for.

"So, tell me a little about your novel," I said, once we were sitting down in a booth by the window. I had already purchased our tea and Danishes and was still struggling to get the sugar packet into the cup without spilling it all over the table. Finally, I gave up and decided I like my Earl Grey bitter.

"The plot sounds stupid if I say it out loud," Elyse said, taking a sip from her mug.

"The best stories sound stupid when you say them aloud," I said. "Let's have it anyway."

"It's . . . well . . . there's this mom, Larissa, who kind of travels around, falling in love and getting pregnant by men in different countries, but she always leaves the baby behind, right after it's born." She set down her cup. "So, these four half sisters—Eliona, Anastasia, Cordelia, and Mathilda—end up at the same boarding school in London." She met my eyes. "Stupid, huh? Maybe it would be better if there were only two sisters?"

"It's a perfectly fine plot," I said, and her hunched shoulders dropped. "Look at *Ballet Shoes*: this archeologist stops collecting fossils and collects three babies instead who must earn money by dancing after he disappears for sixteen years.

It's just as far-fetched, but it works, as long as you can make your reader believe it. *But,*" I added, holding up a finger, "you haven't answered the single most important question."

"You mean, like, hasn't Larissa heard of birth control?" Elyse asked.

"No!" I said, accidentally raising my voice. "What *passion,* what *pursuit,* keeps her traveling so much that she can't possibly stay to raise her babies? What does Larissa have her heart set on?"

Elyse blinked at me, as if, in all her fifteen years, she'd never felt an aching desire to be anyone else, anywhere else, with someone else.

"I'll have to think about it," Elyse said, her voice thoughtful and intrigued.

"Well, think about it."

As she stared off somewhere over my left shoulder, there was a hint of a smile on the corners of her lips. Finally, she shifted her gaze back to me. "So, what's this business proposition?"

"Ah. Well. As you can see I suffer from a bit of a tremor," I said with a laugh, even though nothing about the tremor was funny to me. "It is quite hard for me to write these days, and I've been looking for someone to type my memoir."

"Is it written down somewhere?" she asked.

"Why surely," I said, tapping my skull.

Elyse smiled again, a lovely smile that made me feel hopeful and young myself. "So, like, you'd just talk into a computer mic or something? And I would, like, take the flash drive home and type it?"

"No. No, that won't do." I wanted to figure out if Miriam

Lichtenstein could ever exist again. For reasons I couldn't begin to explain, I didn't want to do it alone. "Perhaps you could just sit and listen to my stories and jot down some notes that might help me to organize my thoughts," I said. "You would be more of a collaborator, of sorts . . . and certainly I would pay you."

"It's okay. You don't have to pay me."

"Well, of course I would pay you. Isn't your time worth something? Don't ever give away your talents for free, my dear. Do you have an income now?"

"An income?" she repeated, her voice dubious. "I babysit my little brothers for, like, five bucks an hour, even though the going rate for sitters is ten."

"That's called 'earning your keep,' my dear. In my day, no one got paid for watching a sibling." When she looked down at her Danish, I wished I hadn't started a sentence with "In my day," which is probably why I said, "I'll give you fifteen."

"Per hour?" She looked up in wide-eyed delight. "Just so you know, I got a C in typing last year."

"I don't care if it looks like rubbish," I said. "Who's going to read it?"

The words were strangely liberating—what was there to fear if no one was ever going to see these pages? We arranged a time for Saturday afternoon, a week and a half later. I invited her to my apartment and asked her to bring her laptop. "I don't have one," Elyse said.

"Doesn't everyone your age have a computer?"

"I have a desktop. Which sits on my desktop." Elyse rolled her eyes. "I wasn't allowed to have a cell phone for emergencies until last year."

"Well, good. Teaching a girl to think for herself." When she shrugged, apparently unconvinced, I studied her for a moment. "So, Elyse, what do you want to be when you grow up?"

"A doctor and a writer."

Now, that made me smile. A girl who had plans! There was hope for her yet. I told her my simple rule, which I'd shared with the group: "Don't write because you want to be a writer. Write because you have something to say." She cocked her head to the side.

"My grandma Margot says that, too. She's a writer—she published a novel when she was twenty-six. *The Secrets of Flight.*"

"Sounds intriguing." I smiled.

"I've never actually read it." Elyse shrugged and took a bite of her Danish. "She moved away when I was ten."

"Well, I think any book written by a family member should be required reading—even if the author lives in Timbuktu." Elyse stopped chewing, as if considering this for the first time. "And medicine?" I asked, picking up my mug. "Where does that come from?"

"I'm probably going to need a day job," she admitted.

"My son Dave was supposed to be a doctor—just like his father," I said, a confession. "He was an early microbiologist, you see. At the age of seven he would pull the agar plates out of the incubator to tell his father which were group A strepto-coccal positive. But Dave surprised us by falling in love with music instead. We forced him to pick a dual concentration, something that might assure his parents that he wouldn't grow up to be a bum. So he picked computer science!" When Elyse smiled uncertainly, I thought, *Dear God, I've said too much.* "I fully endorse your plans for a dual career," I finally finished.

"Thanks?" She took a bite of her apple Danish, wiped her mouth, and then asked, "So what's your book about?" This time it was my turn for my face to cloud over. For a second I thought she meant my essay collection, *Miss Bixby Takes a Wife*, which had seen the light of day but just barely. But then I realized we were still talking about my "memoir." It seemed like such a ruse, when I wasn't even sure I could bring myself to tell the story.

"The book? Oh. Me, my life, the family secrets," I said breezily, and the corners of her mouth turned up as if she were intrigued. It was odd that I called them family secrets, when the family was long gone, and the secrets were important to no one but me.

THE NEXT DAY I RODE THE BUS OVER TO WALNUT STREET AND ambled down the sidewalk, peering in the windows of shops along the way. Headless mannequins wore silk dresses and precarious heels. Sarah, graced with good balance, strong ankles, and a tiny waist—even without a corset—would've been in seventh heaven among the racks. Meanwhile, the fruit in the window of the little grocery store looked like it might've been genetically engineered to look superior to any other fruit I'd ever seen.

The Apple Store was probably spectacular too, for someone of Elyse's age. There were display stations of computers and cell phones throughout the store and a line was forming at the front for the "Genius Bar." My son Dave—and I say this with only the smallest amount of bias—is smarter than all of those geniuses put together.

"So, is this a present for someone?" asked the salesman, a

sloppy youth with a mop of red curls, khaki shorts falling so low that I could see his undershorts, and a blue Apple T-shirt straining at a beer gut. Still, I liked his earnest smile.

I thought about saying the computer was for Elyse, but what would I call her? My writing colleague? And besides, the model I was looking at would cost me over a thousand dollars. It didn't matter that I had money to burn, money that it would be a sin to waste: the girl had balked about accepting payment for typing my memoir and was distinctly uncomfortable when I insisted on buying her a Danish at Panera. "The computer will be for me," I said.

"What kind of capabilities are you looking for?" he asked, and I blinked. "Email? Sharing pictures on the Internet?"

"I would like to type," I said.

"Gotcha," he said, guiding me toward a laptop on the display table. After he talked me through the "word processing" feature, I told him I'd take it. It was probably his easiest sale of the day. When he couldn't accept a personal check, I handed him my never-used-before debit card, issued against my will by the bank, and he slid it through a handheld device that turned out to be a cash register of some sort.

"You want to sign up for lessons to learn how to use the computer?" he asked.

"I have a little friend who can help me out," I said, and he nodded, punched a few keys on his device, and gave me back my card and a receipt.

So, that's what she is, I thought, leaving the store. *My little friend.*

Returning to my apartment, I made the unfortunate mistake of bumping into Selena Markmann just exiting the building in her usual purple splendor—wind pants and a jacket, which meant she was probably on her way to Jazzercise. She was always pestering Jean Fester to join the class to "get healthy," to which Jean would reply, full of venom, "Do you know what it feels like to have your internal defibrillator go off when you're not even having a cardiac arrest?" Selena eyed my Apple bag and said, "Well, well. Look who's joining the twenty-first century and going online after all. Mary Browning, the others won't believe it."

"Oh, this? It's for my great-granddaughter's birthday. My grandson Tyler and my son Dave are visiting with Hazel and Josie next week. Dave hates to fly and insists on driving all the way from Seattle," I added with an exasperated sigh. Selena's eyes turned to slits, reminding me of a very perceptive cat.

"Where are they staying?" she asked.

"The Sunny Ledge." The bus had zipped by the quaint little bed-and-breakfast that afternoon.

"The Sunny Ledge? They let children stay there?"

"Well, the twins are very well behaved. It's not as if anyone has to worry that they'll wreck the place. Josie's the only twelve-year-old I know who actually likes to *sew*," I added.

Selena brought a finger to her lips and screwed up her eyes again, as if contemplating other preteens with an interest in thread. "How on earth did I forget that they were twins? Because I had twins, you know," she finally said, as if I could've forgotten the tale of how Selena had single-handedly breastfed two babies, one on each side, when nursing was not the fashion, when, in fact, it was usually a sign of poverty. The only person who enjoyed that story was Gene Rosskemp, who said he never minded imagining Selena's "gazoongas."

"You should bring them to the group next Tuesday night," Selena suggested.

"They'll be gone before then. I really must go." Oh, how I wished that Dave had forgiven me, and that they really were coming.

"What was the name of that publishing house you worked for in New York?" she called after me. "I was trying to search for it online, and—"

"I already told you," I said, stepping onto the elevator, "it went out of business years ago." When the doors finally shut, I shut my eyes and exhaled.

Back inside my apartment, I set the Apple bag gently on the floor and fell into my recliner with a sigh, thinking that I used to be a better friend, back when I used to have friends, back when I was still Miriam Lichtenstein.

Reaching over to my little bookshelf, my hand found its way to the picture in *USA Today* of the three women and the plane. Just looking at it again made the old impulse rise up—the one that made me want to take a black, permanent marker and blot out the name in the caption, Miriam Lichtenstein, keeping her safe in her anonymity.

In the back of my bedroom closet, I pulled out an old shoe box before returning to the living room recliner once again. An hour passed as if a minute, as I rifled through the three-by-five photos inside: the one of Papa and Mama, leaning against his peddler's fruit cart—Mama smiling in spite of herself, as if she can't believe Papa's laughing when disaster looms; Sarah and Elias, looking like Hollywood royalty after one of his perfor-mances; Sarah holding baby Rita on the front steps of the house on Beacon Street; and the one that takes my breath away: I am in my Santiago blue uniform standing with Thomas—the picture I mailed to my mother only months before she cut me off. *Oh, Mama, did you have any regrets about me at the end?* I wondered, a pointless question after all this time. *Water under the bridge; such a stupid cliché,* I thought with a sigh. Especially in Pittsburgh, where the bridges are everywhere, each one arching over the water you thought you'd already left behind, your history always chasing you.

At last, I found the one I was searching for: one of the original photos of Murphee, Grace, and me in the middle, standing in front of Murph's Fairchild PT-19, taken sixty-five years ago on Ana Santos's Leica. I took the framed photo of Thomas and me in our later years—somewhere between grown-ups and grandparents—and swapped it with the fly girl snapshot. Then I set it on the shelf beside the one of Thomas, my son Dave, his wife, Carrie, my grandson Tyler. Miri was up there too, nameless but present. If Elyse noticed her, it was a sign to keep going.

After lining up the picture frames, I pulled back my hand and studied my bare fingers, gnarled by arthritis and wrinkled like the pages in the newspaper. None of us were getting younger, even Selena, fighting decay with her Jazzercise, even Elyse, who wouldn't recognize what it meant to be fifteen until it was all over. But, oh, to become the woman that Thomas might recognize once again, a woman running through the tall grasses and holding his hand. *Here I come, my love.* I closed my eyes for a little catnap in the recliner. *It won't be much longer now.*

CHAPTER 5

Fly Girl

This Saturday was my first meeting with Mrs. Browning since she said she wanted me to be the transcriptionist for the memoir of her life. Mom dropped me off at the Squirrel Hill library, so I could work on a "research project," and then I walked the three blocks to Mrs. Browning's high-rise apartment. If it had been Daddy driving, I might've told him about my new job as Mrs. Browning's assistant, but I didn't feel like hearing Mom say, "Should you really be taking on extra commitments when you only have one month left to design and create a bridge made entirely out of toothpicks? And if so, what about volunteering at the hospital, like we talked about?" Besides, it was kind of exciting, walking up the library steps from Mom's car and then sneaking out of the lobby as soon as she'd driven away. The way the security guard was eyeing me, like he knew I was up to something, made me wish I was up to something much, much worse.

In the lobby of the high-rise, there were wheelchairs against the wall and a small line of old people were waiting to have their blood pressure checked by a lady in pink scrubs, who was making them laugh. Once Mrs. Browning buzzed me up, I took the elevator to the sixth floor and got off feeling a little uneasy and wishing we'd decided to meet at Panera again. The hallway was dark and smelled kind of funny, like ramen noodles. I suddenly felt dread in my stomach, like maybe it was a bad idea to come here, especially if she wanted to dissect my novel again.

I had handed out the first two chapters to the group on Tuesday night, and everyone said that they loved them, and what a great job I'd done for someone so young, and I thought I could really trust them since they're so old. Old people usually have opinions worth listening to, unlike people my age who like to waste a whole English class—after reading *A Doll's House* by Henrik Ibsen—debating the possible influences on modern women's roles in society. I mean, that question could've been a topic for some graduate student's thesis; it shouldn't have been posed as a free-for-all to a bunch of kids, who say random things like, "Oh! Oh! I know a girl whose mom left on the back of a motorcycle for two years, but then she came back." And then Mrs. Kindling acts like this information is really useful to the discussion, when really she's just thrilled somebody raised her hand. Participation is actually a portion of our grade, even if the only thing you have to say is totally stupid. Sometimes I think, *If I had enough information about this topic I would destroy you, but since I know nothing, I won't say a word.* But it's different when people are old. I actually want to hear what they have to say.

Except that on Tuesday night at the library, they couldn't

come up with anything bad about the pages I'd turned in. Jean Fester actually said she thought it was "surprisingly sweet," which didn't give me a lot to work with. That's when Mrs. Browning kind of snorted and said, "I'm sorry—a woman gives birth to four different children by four different men and abandons them in four different countries, and you're calling it sweet?" Selena Markmann spoke up then: she said she thought it was handled very *whimsically,* that the author clearly wasn't *worrying* about the *psychology* of being left behind.

I didn't want to side with Jean and Selena, who seemed to be ganging up on Mrs. Browning, so I said sort of quietly, "I just liked the idea of being found."

"I would like to reiterate my point," Mrs. Browning said, which was that Larissa, the mother in the story, needs to have a passion that makes her run away. It had been two weeks, and I still couldn't come up with anything.

After I tapped lightly on the door to Mrs. Browning's apartment and waited, I heard keys jangling down the dimly lit hallway and then polyester parachute pants swishing toward me. "Elyse? Is that you?" came an astonished voice. I turned to see Selena Markmann, the one in the group with the blue-black hair, who was wearing a purple tracksuit. I smiled and waved hello, even though her eyebrows were scaring me a little since she'd drawn them on like black McDonald's arches. "What are you doing here?" she asked, but before I could answer, I heard the latch on Mrs. Browning's door, and we both watched it open.

As soon as Mrs. Browning saw who was standing next to me, her smile darkened. "Selena," she said, her eyes narrowing.

"Mary," Mrs. Markmann replied, looking like a detective who'd just cracked the case. "I was just asking Elyse what on

earth she could possibly be doing inside this apartment building on such a beautiful Saturday afternoon."

Mrs. Browning yanked on my arm and said, "She's helping
me move some furniture." Then she pulled me inside, slammed
the door, and sighed. "I don't mean to shock you, my dear," she
said, "but that woman drives me crazy." I said I wasn't shocked,
but maybe she could've come up with something better than
"moving some furniture," which made both of us laugh. And
just like that, I wasn't uneasy anymore.

Her apartment smelled normal, meaning it didn't smell like
much of anything at all. It was so small that the kitchen and
living room were actually one room with two different floors,
linoleum switching over to carpet. Everything on the rug was
squished together in a half circle: a love seat touched an end
table which touched an easy chair which touched another table
which touched a rocker which touched bookshelves and another end table. There were clocks on basically every surface
that didn't already have a book on it. While Mrs. Browning
put a kettle on for tea, I browsed around her shelves for a little
while. Most of the books I'd never heard of, except for *Franny
and Zooey* and *All of a Kind Family*.

Next to one of the clocks there was a black-and-white picture of a tall man in a dark suit who had a full, broad smile,
like somebody caught him in the middle of the greatest joke. It
was sort of hard not to smile back, which was weird, like he
was watching me discover Mrs. Browning or had even been
waiting for me to arrive. There was another color picture on the
wall of a shaggy-haired guy and a pretty blond woman leaning
against a VW bus. In her arms was the cutest, chubbiest baby.

"Is this you?" I asked, pointing to the pretty blond woman.

"Actually, no, that's my daughter-in-law, Carrie, with my son, Dave, and my grandson, Tyler. The other picture is of Thomas, my husband," said Mrs. Browning.

"Hey! Who is this?" I picked up a black-and-white photo of three young women standing beside a small airplane on a dusty-looking strip of land. They were wearing leather bomber jackets, baggy pants, boots, and, resting on the top of their helmets, goggles. When I glanced back at Mrs. Browning, she seemed to be holding her breath.

"That's me," Mrs. Browning finally said with a noisy exhale. "With Grace Davinport, my best friend from flight school during World War II, and Murphee Sutherland, another pilot. Grace is the tall one, on the right. We were fly girls."

I studied the picture for a few more minutes, trying to pick out white-haired, glasses-sporting Mrs. Browning in the smooth-skinned teenager squinting into the sunlight, with her dark hair blowing in the wind. It wasn't hard to figure out that she was the short one in the middle. I finally found her in the smile, a version of the one she owned now, except in the picture, her whole face was radiating joy. Grandma says she likes to imagine that when you die, you get turned back into your best self, and if I were Mrs. Browning, this is the one I'd choose. When I finally looked up, Mrs. Browning was standing in the kitchen studying me studying her.

"Murphee was a Chicago girl with orange hair, straight out of the bottle. Grace was from Iowa, so her worldview consisted of endless prairie and fields of corn and open sky, whereas almost all I'd ever known were steep hills and plunging valleys, winding rivers and at the heart of it all, the steel mills, turning everything overhead black."

"Wow." I snapped my fingers. "That sounds good. I should write that down."

Mrs. Browning smiled and handed me a tiny tape recorder off the end table. "Actually, I already started." My face must've gone screwy, since she added, "It's my husband's old Dictaphone for dictating chart notes. I was looking at some old pictures the other day and discovered this at the bottom of the box. So, I found some old tapes and started . . . remembering. You can listen later. But in the meantime . . ."

The kettle started to whistle, and we moved back into the kitchen, where the table seemed set for a special occasion: there was an embroidered tablecloth, a vase of dried flowers, a plate of lemon-ginger cookies, a china tea set covered in painted pink roses, and the real shocker of all: a sleek, white Apple laptop.

"Hey, where did that—whose computer is that?" I asked.

"I figured we'd need it for our project," Mrs. Browning said, looking a little sly. "Go ahead. It's yours to use," she added.

I ran my fingers across the lid of the MacBook, like it was the side of a Porsche. "Do you know how to use a computer?" I asked without thinking.

"Well, it's a Mac," she said, pouring me a cup of tea. "It just works."

"So . . ." I said, sliding a cookie off the plate. "Who were the fly girls?"

Mrs. Browning explained that while the men were busy flying planes abroad, dropping bombs on Germany and Japan, the women were needed to, as Mrs. Browning put it, "Protect the Zone of Interior." So she joined the Women Airforce Service Pilots, a group of civilian flyers trained by the military.

"Wait a second—my social studies teacher was talking

about this during 'Current Events'! Aren't you getting some award from the president?"

She nodded and smiled. "The Congressional Gold Medal. There's going to be a ceremony in Washington, D.C., next March. It's going to be quite an affair."

"Wow! Who's going to be there?" I asked.

"Heavens, I don't even know. It'll be a surprise to see who's still alive." She laughed lightly. "Dave and Carrie will fly in from Seattle, and Tyler and his wife and daughters will come all the way from California. So if nothing else, when the president shakes my hand, my family will be there to see it. Come, I have something else I'd like to show you."

We got up from the table, and I followed her into the little bedroom off the kitchen. "Now where is that thing . . ." she said, opening the door to her closet and rifling through the clothes.

I was kind of cringing since her hands were shaking so much with each swipe of the hanger. Finally, she found what she was looking for: her old leather bomber jacket. When Mrs. Browning touched it, she got a funny look on her face, too, like the jacket contained the greatest secrets of all.

"Who's the blond cartoon character?" I asked, pointing to the patch sewn onto the shoulder—of a little gremlin girl with blue wings and big, red boots.

"Fifinella, the patron saint of the fly girls. And she's not blond, my dear; that's her golden helmet. Go ahead, try it on," she added, holding out the jacket.

I hesitated for just a second and then allowed her to slip it over my shoulders. I pushed my arms into the sleeves. The jacket fit perfectly.

"Look at you," Mrs. Browning said, watching me settle into the jacket. "A real Women Airforce Service Pilot. It was always too big for me."

"Larissa should fly," I said, and Mrs. Browning laughed. I could just imagine that same thrilled burble coming out of her, back in the days of this picture.

"It would certainly give your main character a reason to leave her family behind. She wants to be pilot, not a mother."

But then I realized something. "The thing is . . . if Larissa's a fly girl, then I'd have to set the whole book in the United States instead of London."

"Oh, well, that won't work—you've probably never even been to the United States," Mrs. Browning said. And that made us both laugh.

"How'd it go, kiddo?" Daddy asked, when he picked me up outside the library at four o'clock. I almost told him what I'd really been researching, but he seemed preoccupied, like the only right answer was "Great!" and silence. He and Mom were going out to dinner, which meant that I was babysitting my brothers, which I do almost every weekend. After we ate left-over Chinese food, I read to Huggie for a while and let him fall asleep in his Batman pajamas, even though Mom said he'd worn them all day and had to change into something else. Then I made sure Toby was in his room fooling around on his desktop, before I watched *Be My Next Wife*. I was glad to watch the show without Mom, because she always feels bad for Thea's dad, who has to watch his older daughter as a contestant "fool around with a sex offender on national TV." And, "They've given a rapist his own show!" she always says. Then Daddy reminds Mom that the football star wasn't even convicted, but Mom always says that doesn't mean he wasn't guilty. The way Mom talks, you'd think Dr. Palmer had lost Stacey to drugs and prostitution instead of reality TV.

Afterward, I went back upstairs and checked on Huggie, who'd kicked off all his covers in his sleep. I covered him back up before going across the hall to Toby's room. "Stop surfing and go to bed," I said, nodding at the computer screen.

"I'm programming," he said, and I rolled my eyes. "Seriously. It's my homework." If the FBI were to show up and accuse Toby of hacking the president's email, it would shock everybody but me.

After closing his door again, I snuck across the hall into Mom's nook, which is this little office attached to her bedroom that has windows overlooking the backyard. The builder meant for it to be a walk-in closet, but Mom made it into her private little space, with a desk, a swivel chair, a chaise longue, and a wall of bookshelves. Mom likes to call it her Room of One's Own, as in, Get the hell out of my Room of One's Own.

It was dusk and outside the pool was still, and the sky was turning from purple into night. I craned my neck to the far right to see if Holden was doing his homework or talking on his phone, but unfortunately the Regal Estate McMansions are too far apart for me to catch a glimpse of him doing more than parking his green MINI Cooper in the driveway.

Then I snooped around Mom's bookshelves for a bit, trying to find Grandma's novel. Mrs. Browning was right—a book written by a member of the family *should* be required reading—but there was only Mom's fancy collection instead, the leather-bound classics with gold lettering on the binding, most of which she hadn't actually read. When I didn't see *The Secrets of Flight* wedged in her "used" book section—mostly law school texts and some paperback mysteries—I sat down and fished the old-fashioned Dictaphone from my pocket instead. After inserting one of the tiny tapes, I leaned back in Mom's swivel chair, put my feet up on her desk, and closed my eyes—until Mrs. Browning's voice crackled through the air, and I remembered I better get typing.

Half an hour later, I was fighting to stay on the home row while six-year-old Mary and her sister Sarah climbed an apple tree, when I heard the jangle of keys in the foyer and the beeping of the security system. Quickly, I turned off the Dictaphone, switched off the computer, and lunged for the light. The study went dark, except for the glow of Mom's bedside lamp from the other room.

Moments later, they were on the stairs. I heard Mom saying, "Lights out," to Toby, and then Daddy coming into the bedroom and heading straight for the bathroom, followed by Mom's footsteps a moment later. I should've surprised them then—Mom would yell at me for invading her private office and threaten to ground me—but something made me pull my feet up off the floor and hug my knees. Thanks to the strategic location of the trench coat hanging on one of the French doors of the office, they couldn't see me, but if I tilted my head a little to the side, I could see Mom slipping off her blazer and tossing it over the back of the chair. I hoped they weren't going to start making out or having sex with each other, but it didn't seem like that was about to happen, because they weren't saying anything remotely sexy. They kept analyzing the meal, how the halibut was "disappointing" and "gummy" and the butternut squash ravioli was missing "something vital—like more garlic or even a little cayenne to give it some life." It was the most boring conversation I'd ever heard and they hadn't even started analyzing the wine yet.

My parents are scathing when it comes to food. They are the exact opposite of my grandma Margot, who loves to make a show out of calling the chef out from the kitchen, just so she can say, "This is the best steak I've ever had!" which always embarrasses my mom. "You've said that about the last two steaks you've had, Mother," Mom always says, wincing.

Tonight, when I was in the fetal position in my mother's chair, I was hoping they wouldn't find me but this little part of me was kind of wishing they'd think to search—I mean did they really think I was already asleep by eleven? But Mom was asking Daddy why he hadn't finished his lamb, and Daddy was saying he had a big lunch, and just as I let go of my legs to give myself up, I heard Daddy say, "You'll never guess who I saw today. Remember Natalia?"

I hadn't forgotten Natalia—the "woman who was almost my mother," according to Aunt Andie—so I was sure Mom hadn't, either.

"Natalia?" Mom sounded puzzled. "From when we met?"

And Daddy came out of the bathroom and said that she's a widow now that her husband died of pancreatic cancer. Mom said, "That's tragic," and Daddy said, "I think you mean ironic."

"So, where did you run into Natalia?" Mom asked, unbuttoning her blouse. "Wasn't she in L.A. for a while, selling Viagra or something?"

"Well . . . that's the funny part." Daddy gave a heh-heh kind of laugh and swung his arms. "She's still out in L.A. but she came to town for a Pfizer conference and wanted to get together. She found me on Facebook. We've exchanged some emails."

My mom stood there in her full-length slip staring at Daddy. Then she asked, "When were you planning on telling me this?" the same line she always gives me when I make her sign a permission slip for a field trip to Boston that's going to cost five hundred dollars and I was supposed to have raised the money myself selling candy bars, but I forgot.

"Right now!" Daddy said, sounding a lot like me.

Mom wanted to know what exactly this woman wanted, and Daddy said, "To see me again," and Mom's voice got so low that to hear her I had to lean forward in my seat, almost exposing my head around the trench coat. I could see Daddy sitting on the bed in his boxers and undershirt, and I could see Mom facing him and I heard her ask him in a quiet voice what exactly he wanted from her, and Dad said, "To see her again."

I wasn't sure what was more awful about this moment: that Daddy wanted to see his old girlfriend or that I was trapped, eavesdropping. My heart was running so fast, it was hard to breathe.

"I see," Mom said, nodding vigorously. Then she asked if there were plans for other cross-country lunch dates? "Because—just for the record—I have a real problem with that."

"I knew you would," Daddy said, and then Mom laughed sort of bitterly and asked if he blamed her. Then Daddy looked up from his hands and said he didn't know what he wanted anymore. That he didn't know if he wanted to still be married. And then Mom exploded, "Must've been some fucking lunch!"

I pulled up my feet again and hugged my knees and decided I'd just wait for my parents to go to sleep and then maybe I'd crawl across the floor in the darkness. Tomorrow I would call Grandma and ask her what to do, just like I did when Daddy got cancer. Would Daddy want to move to L.A. where Natalia lived? California was so far away, although, relatively speaking, so much closer than heaven. Would he invite me to go with him? Could we take Huggie, too?

The conversation didn't seem like it was ending. Daddy was saying that it wasn't about Natalia. That he'd been thinking about it ever since he'd gotten sick. Mom said, "The cancer is gone!" and Daddy answered, "Yes. The cancer is gone." When I peeked around the coat again, Daddy was staring at Mom like she was a tumor still clinging to him. Daddy said since he had another chance at life, he wanted something different. He wanted a chance to be happy again. And Mom asked if he'd slept with her. Daddy looked sort of miserable when he shook his head and said, "I wanted to talk to you." And Mom asked, "To get my permission?" Daddy got mad then and said he wanted credit for being honest, and Mom said emailing your ex-girlfriend isn't honest, and Daddy said, "I think we should try some time apart." When Mom shouted, "So you can fuck other people and see how that feels?" I hid my face in my knees like a plane had just crashed into our house.

"You want everything to stay the same! You want the same job! Same life! Same restaurants! Same bottle of wine every time!" His voice was a furious hiss of a whisper, and I could feel all the exclamation points. "Life is short, Jane! And you're intent on living like it's a sentence."

"How long has her husband been dead—ten minutes?" Mom asked.

On the desk in Mom's office, the phone suddenly rang. I held my breath, afraid to move, as my heart drilled a hole in my chest. Two more rings went by. Downstairs, I could hear the machine pick up and Grandma's voice asking my mother *please* pick up, because she finally went to the doctor about that itch. "Jane? Please? It's important." After a long pause, she finally hung up.

Just then, Huggie started to cry—loudly—which meant that he had to pee. Huggie doesn't wet the bed anymore, but he gets deliriously pissed at the inconvenience of getting up to pee when he's trying to sleep. Sometimes my mom quietly guides him to the bathroom, other times we can hear her shouting, "Damn it, Hugh, we all have to pee sometimes!"

"I'll go," Daddy said, as the crying got more insistent.

"No, I'll go!" Mom snapped.

As soon as I heard her leave the room, my shoulders dropped. But Daddy just sat there on the bed, not moving. It almost looked like he was staring in the direction of the French doors, and I wondered if he'd heard me exhale. Finally, he got up with a noisy sigh and went into the bathroom. Once I heard water running in the sink, I uncurled my legs, slowly stood up, and softly unlatched the French door to Mom's office. As soon as I could see the bedroom was definitely empty, I flew across the rug, past the bed, past the dressing table, past the rocking chair, and kept going into the hallway, where, down at the far end, the kids' bathroom door was open. Mom was swaying slightly and hugging herself, while Huggie howled and peed into the toilet. Just as she glanced up at me, I turned the other way and ran, telling myself not to look back, thinking of the one line I'd seen on Mrs. Browning's instructions for night flying that she'd shown me earlier: "While solo do not look back at Runway before first turn is made." Back in my room, I collapsed on the bed, trying to erase my mom's blue eyes from the inside of my own lids. Her face may have been angry, her brows chiseled into a terrifying V, but her eyes were soft and vulnerable and heartbroken and . . . wet. And, now, so were mine. I couldn't really move to California and leave her alone. I couldn't really leave her ever.

CHAPTER 6

First Flight

April 1941

You ready for this?" my instructor Jim Newman asks as we sit tandem in the cockpit of the Piper J-3—or "the cub," as Jim calls it—waiting for one of the line boys to prop the plane for my first flight. It's been thirteen years since the pilot fell into my yard, three whole years since FDR announced the initiation of the Civilian Pilot Training Program, and six months since I matriculated at the University of Pittsburgh. Since only one in ten spots is available for a woman, I had to wait until this spring for a space in the program. It's been nine days since I finished first in ground school, beating out eighteen men, and another forty-five minutes since we walked outside the ready room and started inspecting the plane before takeoff.

"I've been ready forever," I say, and he laughs.

At twenty-five, Jim is six years my senior, but since he's taught me everything about how to ready a parachute and read a tachometer and altimeter, how to transition the plane from taxi to liftoff, how to listen to the sound of the engine to determine the tilt of the plane, and how to anticipate the landing, he may as well be sixty. I am so full of giddy anticipation that I haven't slept all week.

"Where's your wind coming from?" Jim asks now, and as I point north, I can't help smiling, thinking, *The wind is mine*.

At last, Hurly Stevens, blond and seventeen, arrives to get the propeller going. At his call, I turn the gas valve on and open up the throttle, while outside the plane, Hurly pulls the prop. The needles inside the dashboard dials spring to life as the engine catches. I shift my goggles down over my eyes, and Hurly backs away from the plane with a thumbs-up.

"Let's go, kid," Jim says, and I push forward the throttle and feel my heart, along with the engine, rattling harder as we barrel down the runway, gathering speed. The vibrations are so intense and the noise so loud that I can't help wondering if the whole plane might fall apart before we reach the end of the runway. Gently, I pull back on the stick.

"Not too fast or we'll stall out," Jim says, over my left shoulder, right in my ear. "Now feel the tail lift up," he adds, and I feel it swinging up, as I simultaneously pull back. *Bingo,* we're rising, climbing higher and higher into the dazzlingly blue sky—rare for Pittsburgh in the late afternoon. Glancing down, I catch sight of my gloved fingers clutching the stick and something inside me gives a little lurch. I am holding my own life—and Jim's life, too—in my hands. A terrifying realization until I remember Jim can put his own hands on mine at any time, and he can talk me through anything.

Finally, we level out at three thousand feet. The wind howls and the engine roars in my ears, while the rushing inside me grows quiet.

I'm doing it, Papa. I'm really flying.

From up here, Pittsburgh is a beautifully detailed, luxuriously green, topographical map of hills and valleys. Coal trains chug along the Allegheny River, the incline crawls up Mount Washington, and factories pour out black plumes of smoke that shift rapidly to the west in the wind. From this distance, even the steel mills are inspiring. We are making something: steel for planes, steel for tanks, steel for the war we're hoping desperately to avoid. I can see it all. And even though I've never been anywhere in my life, I've finally left home.

Once we've landed back at the airfield, and Hurly has arrived to service the plane, Jim and I unpack our chutes and sit in the lounge for a while, chatting about what to do in the event of an engine failure. Later, I'm marking my hours in the logbook when I notice the clock on the wall and gasp. "It's not really four o'clock, is it?" I ask.

"Nope," Jim says, checking his own watch. "It's more like four thirty."

I thank him and take off.

Half an hour later, after running all the way from the trolley, I'm nearly home when my knapsack breaks, spilling books across the sidewalk just in front of the house on Beacon Street. Frantically, I scoop them up, when a tall man in a tweed jacket stoops down to help me collect them, handing me first my math book, then geography, meteorology and navigation, and the Theory of Flight.

"You are very smart," he says with a thick accent, handing

me the last text, and for a moment I study the stranger with his angular cheekbones and slightly receding hairline.

"Wait—are you—'Cousin Tzadok'?" I say, remembering all at once that Mama said Hyman's newly emigrated second cousin would be joining us for Shabbat. I'm still juggling the books and the broken bag while trying to extend my hand. One paperback slips and hits the ground.

"Or 'Jack,' if you like. The name they chose for me at Ellis Island," he says, picking up the fallen manual. "*Civil Air Regulations?*" he adds, raising an eyebrow as he hands it back to me.

"Right. Thank you—I'm—so late," I say breathlessly.

"That makes two of us," he says with a smile.

Moments later, Mama turns from the stove, which is laden with simmering pots, and stares at me when I slip in through the back door. "You were supposed to be here hours ago! Tzadok will be here any moment." I don't tell her that he *is* here, that we decided I would go around the back, and he would ring the doorbell and pretend we hadn't already met.

"Your dress is black," she adds, as though I can control the emissions from the local steel mills. Although I suppose I could be more like Sarah, who lays out two outfits every day: one for the morning and one for later in the day, after the steel mills cover the first dress with soot. Squinting, Mama moves toward me. "What's that on your face? Dirt?" She licks her finger and rubs at the skin on my cheeks and forehead.

"Is it coming off?" I ask.

"Have you been wearing something on your eyes? There are marks . . ." she says, reaching for a wet dish towel instead. "And is this *grease* on your blouse? Miriam! Where have you been? Don't you dare let Uncle Hyman see you," she adds, before I can answer.

"Maybe I can sneak upstairs and take a bath . . ." I suggest, just as the doorbell rings.

"You have five minutes to wash your face, comb your hair, and change your clothes—then get back down here," Mama hisses, throwing the dish towel into the sink before moving out into the front hall to answer the door. I slip out behind her and head for the stairs.

ONCE I'VE SPLASHED WATER ON MY FACE, AND COMBED MY HAIR, and changed my frock, I rush back downstairs, where my uncle is introducing Tzadok to Sarah, who is back just for the occasion of his visit. Noticing me, Tzadok tips his head with a smile, before Uncle Hyman urges us all to take our seats. Then Mama waves the flames toward herself, welcoming in the Sabbath, and covers her eyes with her hands and begins to sing. In the flickering candlelight, I try to summon up my own quiet prayer. *Please let me do good things with the gifts You've given me.* I feel grateful for the warmth in the pumpkin-colored dining room, grateful for the bread we will soon be eating, and maybe even for the tight ball of anxiety inside my chest that released as soon as we sat down. I close my eyes and listen to the blessings, made even more holy to me by the fact that Sarah is home, and everything is better when my sister is here. Sneaking a peek at her to my right, I catch her peeking at me, and, heads bowed, we exchange secret smiles.

Later, after we've been to services and gathered around the table once again for Uncle Hyman to say the Kiddush and bless the challah, Mama emerges with the main course, chicken and roasted vegetables, and dinner digresses into conversations. I learn that Tzadok is eleven years my senior, that he left Germany in 1936 to stay with relatives in Belgium and then moved to England for further education. "Now that the Nazis are closing in on the English Channel," he explains, looking directly at me, "it seemed like a good time to leave while I could."

I can't help noticing that Tzadok frequently directs his remarks toward me, as if it's me, not Uncle Hyman, asking the questions. I may be a woman now, but I'm not used to the kind of attention usually reserved for my sister, who has always been striking, with her chiseled jaw and a regal nose, even before she cut off her braid for a stylish bob. Besides, at twenty-two, Sarah is closer in age to Tzadok than I am, although I suppose, as she is currently seven months pregnant with another man's baby, that might make her slightly less intriguing.

"What were you studying at the London School of Economics?" Sarah asks, spooning more potatoes onto her plate.

"Economics," Tzadok says, and I laugh.

"He was studying acting at the London School of Economics," I say, and Sarah gives me a good-natured shove.

"And you, Miriam?" Once again, Tzadok directs his gaze toward me. "What are you training for?"

My heart skips, thinking of the books he handed me back on the sidewalk, hoping he won't give me away.

"She's getting her secretarial degree," Mama says.

"How fast can you type now?" Sarah says, oh so innocently, and I glare at her.

"Yes, Miri, how fast can you type?" Uncle Hyman asks, turning red again.

"Thirty words per minute . . . ?" I guess, and this time Sarah's the one who cackles.

"Goodness, that's terrible."

"Perhaps Miriam has other things on her mind," Tzadok says, smiling at me, and I realize then that he's going to keep my secret.

"What about your family, Tzadok?" Uncle Hyman asks, passing the plate of *kneydlekh* and *meyrn tsimes,* my favorite honey carrots. "How are they?"

"I cannot say," Tzadok says, growing sober. "I encouraged them to leave when the restrictions against the Jews were starting, but my parents and brother wouldn't listen. They thought the Nazis would go away. Then there was Kristallnacht . . ."

I remember reading about it in the Jewish paper when I was sixteen: the night the Nazi mobs in Germany burned the synagogues and destroyed the Jewish shops.

"They took prisoners that night. My brother Oskar was captured and sent to a camp to do labor, and no one has heard from him since."

"But this was before the war?" I ask, and Tzadok nods, morosely. "What do you think happened to him?" I add, and Mama shakes her head almost unperceptively, a vibration of admonition.

"I fear that he's dead, Miriam."

THAT NIGHT, SARAH SLEEPS IN HER TWIN BED ACROSS FROM mine, just like old times since Elias has a show—a sin, according to my mother. "Performing on the Sabbath?" I heard her kvetching earlier. I watch Sarah tiptoe across the small pink rug, her white nightgown clinging to her pregnant belly, before she settles into the clean sheets that Mama is so particular about washing, even the weeks Sarah doesn't come home. Mama also irons the curtains, scrubs the floors, and airs out the mattresses every Thursday, making me certain I'll never be able to keep house one day, nor would I aspire to.

After Sarah blows out the candle, I ask, in the darkness, "Do you think Hitler will come here?"

"It's just a matter of time," she says.

I think of Roosevelt saying in his radio address that there are those who won't admit the possibility of the approaching storm. "So, what are we waiting for?"

"Everyone's scared. No one wants to go to war for the Jews. Something has to happen."

I imagine the Nazis marching through the streets, smashing the windows, setting fire to our synagogue, and burning down Uncle Hyman's shop, with my mother and sister inside. "If the Germans land here, we should hide. Or pretend we're not Jewish," I say.

I wait for her to tell me that they keep lists, they know who's who, they will ferret us out from under the floorboards and behind curtains in attics and that pretending to be something we're not is just wishful thinking. But instead her voice goes cold. "You can't turn your back on your own people, Miri."

"I just mean—if the Nazis were going to kill us . . ." I say, and the bed creaks as she rolls away from me and faces the wall.

"You're learning to fly for a reason," Sarah finally says, and it's only then that I realize she's been keeping my secret because taking flight is a responsibility—the power for change— and not just a whim.

I close my eyes, trying to push the images of Kristallnacht out of my mind and put myself back in the sky instead, flying high over Pittsburgh and beyond, across the ocean, farther than my fuel tank could carry me. I imagine myself piloting a B-26, dropping bombs on the Germans, the eruptions of light and fire below, while prisoners tear down the barbed wire, a flood of humanity escaping to freedom.

I have no idea that in just a few months, in June 1941, right after I've gotten my pilot's license and logged two hundred hours in the air, women will be banned from participating in the Civilian Pilot Training Program, and I'll have to wait three whole years to be given another chance to fly.

CHAPTER 7

The Sunny Ledge

I had assumed I'd see Elyse at the next writers' group three days later, except that she wasn't there—a good thing, too, I supposed, since we were dissecting Selena Markmann's tiresome romance novel about an adulterous wife and an abusive husband, who made love as frequently as they threw dishes at each other. Nevertheless, it was hard to participate in the group discussion when I was preoccupied by Elyse's unexpected absence. "See you Tuesday night!" she'd called on her way out the door to my apartment the Saturday before. Had something come up, or was she gone for good? Just so long as she wasn't dead. On Tuesday, I found myself perusing the *Pittsburgh Tribune-Review* for local tragedies and even scanned the obituaries, but there was nothing on her. And then, two days later, she surprised me with a phone call. I'd forgotten I'd ever given her my number. In fact, the phone rang so rarely, I'd almost forgotten I had a phone.

"I can meet this Saturday, if you want me to take notes for the book," Elyse said.

"Tomorrow? How about the Sunny Ledge for tea?" I suggested, an idea that struck me in that moment—and an idea that made her voice immediately lift, as she asked for the address and clarified the directions.

The next day, Elyse was twenty minutes late to the restaurant. Late enough for me to read the menu and order a cup of tea, but not so tardy that I was once again imagining her funeral. Just sitting there on the back patio of the restaurant in my favorite blue suit and squinting into the sunlight made me wish I were waiting for Thomas instead. He always loved me in Santiago blue, the color of my Airforce uniform.

A mother and her youngsters ambled by the outdoor seating area, and I watched as the little boy dutifully steered his baby sister's carriage right into an inkberry bush. Dave as a child came into my head then, the way Dave at any age had a tendency to appear since he'd stopped speaking to me. This time, he was six years old and swimming in the pool at the Scarsdale Golf Club, which had, only weeks before, made headlines for not allowing a debutante to attend a ball because her escort was determined to be of Jewish descent. "Mama, what's it like to be you?" he asked, treading water, his little blond head bobbing up and down. "I mean, I'm here and you're standing there, and I just want to know what's it feel like? Do you like being you?"

"I love being me," I said, crouching down—ready with a towel because his lips were already blue with cold. "Because I have you."

I blinked and looked around. The mother and her children were gone from the sidewalk, and my teacup was empty. Elyse had arrived, wearing her usual attire: khaki pants and a white oxford shirt. But she didn't look right—rather, she didn't look well. There were dark circles under her eyes, and she was hugging herself as if she were cold.

"Bus sick?" I asked, as she pulled out a chair and slumped into the one across from me.

She shrugged and nodded, glancing around. "This is nice," she said, and it was nice: the outdoor table, the breeze rippling the white cloths, the small vase of fresh cut flowers, the muted sounds of traffic down on Fifth Avenue below.

"How's your novel?" I asked.

"I haven't had time to work on it much lately." Her shoulders were hunched. "Sorry I missed the group on Tuesday night. My parents were—busy—and well . . . neither one would take me. But I'm thinking of making Larissa a spy," she said. I wondered what on earth a fifteen-year-old would know about espionage. "And of course she'll have to fly planes and stuff."

She seemed so downcast that I hoped she wasn't including a female pilot as a plot point to please me—or upset that I'd never paid her. "Here—for last time," I said, slipping some cash out of my change purse, since she'd left my apartment before I'd had the chance to remember the money in my wallet.

"Oh, you don't have to—I'm not finished typing yet—"

"My dear, I insist," I said, setting the money down, as a waitress appeared to ask us if we'd decided yet. Elyse barely peeked at the menu before ordering a cup of Earl Grey, but I went ahead and ordered the high tea, complete with scones and sandwiches and clotted cream and jam. After all, we were taking up a table.

"So what's the title of your book gonna be?" Elyse asked,

once the waitress was gone, and my bills were still lying beside her napkin.

"My book?" I repeated and then laughed belatedly. I'd been so busy thinking of her book. I thought a moment. "Maybe *The Forgiving Trees*."

"And what does that mean?" she asked, raising a single eyebrow.

"I don't really know," I admitted. "When Dave was five years old, he said he was going to write a book called *The Forgiving Trees*, and my husband and I thought it was delightful, although we had no idea where it came from. Nor did he. But that's what he said. Of course, he turned out to be a musician, not a writer."

"Well, you better ask him if you can use it now. Maybe he'll need it for a song."

"Oh, well . . . I don't think he'll mind . . ." I murmured.

Elyse leaned over and unzipped her backpack, producing the Dictaphone and tapes, along with the small, framed picture of Murphee, Grace, and myself standing by my Fairchild PT-19. I'd let her borrow the photo last week after she'd seemed so intrigued. It was a sign, of course: a sign that I should go on with the story.

"Where exactly were you in this picture?" she asked, sliding it toward me.

"The airfield in Sweetwater, Texas. 'Cochran's Convent,'" I said with a smile, as the waitress, bearing a tray, delivered a tier of scones and tea sandwiches, along with fresh pots of tea for both of us. "Please. Eat," I added, nodding at all the food, but Elyse just shook her head and picked up a lemon, as if she weren't sure whether to suck on it or squeeze it into the tea.

"So, why'd they call it a convent—it was, like, an all-girl campus?"

"Well, certainly there were some men. Many of the instructors were men. But it became a training facility for women, so the male cadets were specifically warned not to land there."

"Did your husband fly, too?"

"Thomas? Oh, no. He had terrible eyesight. But Grace was engaged to be married before she left for Texas at the age of nineteen."

"Did her fiancé mind when she left him for flight school?"

I shook my head. "He was a cadet himself, on his way to Camp Lejeune. And her family was very proud of her. There was a sense that we were contributing to the war. Everyone wanted to give a little bit."

"Did any of your friends get shot down?"

"We were ferrying supplies, and delivering ships from factories to air bases, not going to battle. Still, lives were lost."

"Weren't you afraid of crashing?" Elyse asked, reminding me of Sarah's daughter Rita, who'd asked me once if I was ever afraid of falling from the sky.

"Not really, no. I knew I had to be careful up there. But I just didn't think that was going to be how I would go."

"But . . . why did you want to—take that risk? Because of the war?" she added quickly.

"Because it was exciting!" I erupted. "It was the golden age of aviation. Everyone wanted to fly. And oh, those open-cockpit planes were romantic—the Eisenhower jacket, the helmet, the goggles—Hollywood all the way," I added wistfully, recalling my disappointment when I found out from my flight instructor that pilots didn't actually wear scarves like in the movies—the risk of getting the material caught in a propeller and strangling oneself was too great.

Elyse slumped back in her seat, hugging herself again. "So where are they now—Grace and Murphee, I mean?"

"Well, I don't know about Murphee. But Grace died—later on. After she'd lived long enough to have grandchildren." I'd learned that much from the *USA Today* article. I took a sip of tea and set my cup down with only the smallest clink. "We'd lost touch many years before. Right after the war ended, actually."

When I glanced up from my cup of tea, Elyse's eyes filled with tears. "That's just . . . so . . . sad," she said. "You called her your best friend, and you only hung out with her for . . . how long, exactly?"

"Well. Less than a year," I answered. I had only lived a fraction of my life with Grace—a *particle* of life in the vast scheme of time—but she was part of an era when I'd felt the most like the woman I was supposed to be. With Grace, I was the most carefree. "Embarrassing, really," I accidentally muttered aloud. "I'm embarrassed . . . to be this old."

Elyse surprised me when she started to giggle. "That's silly." She wiped her nose on the sleeve of her shirt.

"I just can't imagine what on earth I'm still doing here," I admitted with a sigh.

"Well, there must be a reason," she said, her voice full of naïve conviction. "And I think you look great for your age," Elyse added, finally reaching for a scone and stuffing it into her mouth.

"How old do you think I am?" I asked.

"Um . . . ninety?" she guessed, her mouth still full.

That made me laugh. "Ninety-one? Ninety-two?" she kept going.

"My dear, one should always go low. And a word of advice: no one ever wants to hear they look good for their age. It is implicit in the compliment that I would look frightening if I were twenty-one." Elyse laughed, such a hearty sound for someone so thin and small that it made me suspect she was capable of immense passion, even if she didn't realize it herself. "Do you want to be a great writer for your age or just a great writer?" I added, and she stopped laughing.

She reached for a triangle of salmon sandwich, finally realizing she was hungry after all, it seemed.

The truth of the matter was, Elyse was precisely that: an excellent writer for her age. And who could blame her for being fifteen? What had she experienced in her very few years on earth, aside from what she'd absorbed in books and movies? She had mentioned her father had been ill in the past, and when I'd suggested she write about that, she had said, "But then writing wouldn't be fun anymore." Elyse was blooming with imagination and a sharp sense of humor, that much was clear from the opening pages of her novel. But it was also juvenilia. Unlike Jean Fester and Selena Markmann and Herb Shepherd and the lot of them who coddled her efforts, I wanted to make Elyse better than her age.

"I've been thinking about your novel," I said. "About these four sisters with such complicated names . . ."

Elyse cringed. "My mom said their names are too weird, right? Especially Cordelia's. She said my characters should have ordinary names."

"I say, choose anything that spurs your imagination. I'm terrible at naming characters myself. Whenever I get stumped, I've been known to just plug in the name of someone I know, which is rather like cheating, don't you think?" I asked, and she smiled. "The real question, my dear, is what do you do with your characters once you've got them all together? They have to be united against something together, and it can't just be that they all hate math." Her expression turned thoughtful, as she tapped her fingers absently over the cover of her book. "Perhaps there's something sinister going on at the school that they slowly uncover?" I suggested. "The headmaster secretly—"

"Fights with his wife about wanting to cheat on her?" Elyse asked.

I blinked.

"The sisters could . . . overhear or something . . . and devise a plan to stop it?" Elyse picked up another scone and doused it with a spoonful of strawberry jam.

"Well, that's one avenue I hadn't considered."

"My parents might be getting a divorce," she added in a low, wobbly voice. "I heard them arguing the other night."

So that's what a fifteen-year-old knows about espionage, I thought. The teapot shook in my tremulous hand, spilling its contents on the tablecloth before I managed to set it down. "Sometimes disagreements appear catastrophic simply because you're there to witness it," I said, mopping up the tea with a napkin.

"My dad said he wants a divorce, and my mom was really mad, and neither one of them knows that I know." Elyse appeared to be struggling to swallow, as if the scone had turned to ground chalk in her mouth. "Do you believe bad things happen in threes?"

"Oh, heavens," I said. *Try nines.*

"Because first there was my dad, and now my parents. It makes me wonder what the next bad thing is going to be . . . People at church say it's a miracle that my father survived pancreatic cancer. But I don't know." She looked up at me. "Maybe he just had a good surgeon."

Sipping my tea, I gave a noncommittal shrug since I myself had never entirely believed in miracles, or at least, I couldn't fathom that one could happen to me. Then again, what was my definition of a miracle? A good marriage, for fifty years; a healthy child who grew up, reached his full potential, and kept a close relationship with his parents; a husband who died without suffering, surrounded by an extended family at the bedside? Most of that had come true. Perhaps I wanted too much.

The waitress was back, asking if we were ready for the check.

"Can I help with this?" Elyse asked, her hand vaguely gesturing to the detritus of our meal.

"The tab is on me. Take your hard-earned money, my dear."

"I didn't finish typing yet. And besides, you keep giving me ideas for my novel anyway." Her head snapped up. "Is it okay if I use—"

"My dear, you may use it all," I said with a smile.

CHAPTER 8

The Telegram

March 1944

M iriam Lichtenstein, *what is this?*" Mama shrieks, on the evening of the party, holding up a bag of sugar as if she's never seen one before. She sent me out this morning to trade food ration stamps with the women who meet for coffee each week, and now here I am, twelve hours later, with all the wrong ingredients. "I asked you to trade the meat and sugar stamps for *vegetables* and *eggs*. I didn't ask for sugar. We don't *need* sugar." She doesn't mean for this week, she means ever, or at least until the war ends—as if abstaining from apple strudel and knish, cheese blintzes and spice cake actually saves lives.

"Sarah needs sugar," I say, because ever since Elias was declared dead by the U.S. Navy two years ago, my sister, too sad to eat, has lost quite a bit of weight. She's just a slip of a thing now, with jarring cheekbones and a new cough that makes me shudder.

Mama must be silently worrying, too, because she goes ahead and puts the sack of sugar in the back of the cupboard without another word. I'll tell Sarah where it's been secreted, so she can make herself a good cup of coffee. It comforts me, imagining that maybe this is all it will take to make her better.

Elias left for war in the summer of 1942, just after his daughter's first birthday, and we gave him a going-away party then, too, like the one we're attending tonight for one of the neighborhood boys. I hate these parties, which always start out like a wedding and end like a funeral, all in one night. Behind every handshake and every lingering hug at the door, you're forced to acknowledge that Death is very near and imminent.

In Elias's case, he was declared missing, then dead, after a German U-boat blew up his submarine. It seems stupid and careless that it happened so close to home, just off the coast of North Carolina before he even got anywhere, but the world has shrunk as the war draws near. Ever since the Japanese bombed Pearl Harbor, we've been readying ourselves for potential invasions on the beaches of both coasts. At night the air raid sirens go off, because the steel mills are potential targets. We draw the blackout curtains and wait for the all clear. Sarah and I have figured out the precise distance a candle can be from the window without being detected by the air warden on the street below. It's nice to have her home again for these moments, but it feels like only a part of her is actually here.

Upstairs, I find Sarah staring out the window at our neighbors, the Byrds, whose gaggle of blond children are playing in the backyard of the house just across the alley. I've seen them running into the street when the iceman arrives, and sometimes playing some sort of keepaway game with the toddler. "Biting baby!" the older children scream, as she runs in circles and they scatter, avoiding the swipe of her teeth. We also find them mildly fascinating because they're the only Christian family on the block, still here despite the influx of Jewish families twenty years ago. If my niece Rita, three now and precocious as ever, were awake, she'd love to join them.

"Any news?" Sarah asks, noticing me.

"There's sugar. In the back left of the cupboard," I say, unbuttoning my grimy blouse and stepping out of my skirt.

"Oh, wow," Sarah says with a smile. "Coffee, again. And I meant, any *news*?"

"Nothing," I say, knowing we're talking about the Women Airforce Service Pilots.

Two years ago, when I was eighteen and my flight career seemed permanently stalled, my old instructor told me there was an "experiment" going on in Texas: pilot Nancy Love had created the first squadron of women pilots to ferry aircraft for the war—with a minimum flying age of twenty-one. That same September, with the permission of General Hap Arnold, aviatrix Jackie Cochran established the Women's Flying Training Detachment in Houston, where female pilots would undergo the same flight training as male army cadets. I applied immediately, but it wasn't until July 1943—the month the two training sites merged at Sweetwater—that I was invited to Cleveland for an interview.

Knowing better than to ask for permission, I told Mama I was going to visit a classmate for the weekend and then, to pay for the train, I hocked my pearls, the lovely little strand Papa had given me when I was eight. At the pawnshop, after opening the velvet box, I'd held the necklace gently on the pads of my fingers—marveling at the pinkish color of the pearls—and almost couldn't do it. The only way to part with them was to tell myself that Papa was buying me a ticket to fly.

In Cleveland, there were six other women waiting to interview along with me, each of us clutching our logbooks and pilots' licenses—me, additionally anxious about my age. But the assistant to Jackie Cochran told me not to worry; she'd seen my scores from flight school; Jim had written me a fine letter, and they would keep all my credentials on file.

I returned to Pittsburgh, bursting with hope and suspense, only to be met with nearly four months of silence. Fall semester started at Pitt, where I studied stenography and bookkeeping—and one Shakespeare class for Sarah—and bagged groceries at the general store on the weekends, until at last, another telegram arrived: *If you're still interested in becoming a Women Airforce Service Pilot, report to Indian Town Gap, Pennsylvania, for an Army Air Forces physical on December 18th, 1943.* Once again, I had to find my own way across the state, this time to stand in a line with a hundred men in their undershirts and skivvies—gawking at me, before the doctor slipped me behind a curtain—only to be told absolutely nothing. It's been ten weeks, five days, and nine hours since I passed my army physical—but I tell Sarah, "I'm trying not to think about it," as though I've been able to stop.

"Aren't you coming tonight?" I add, realizing she's wearing her gingham belted dress. The Old Sarah wouldn't be caught dead at an evening party in gingham.

"Someone needs to be here for Rita," Sarah says, shaking her head and coughing into her fist. "Besides, I can't go to a party alone. At least you have Tzadok."

"We're just friends," I say, and she gives me a look. "What?

It's true." Despite my parents' conviction that Tzadok is a good match, despite that I asked for—and he gave me, without hesitation—the ultimate favor of driving five hours across the state and back again, I've spent the last two years avoiding formal courtship. At times, I accompany him to family events, but I've never held his hand, never looked into his eyes and kissed him, nor has he ever made any such advances. On the way home from Indian Town Gap, I was even so blunt as to mention that I'm never getting married.

"You're too busy chasing your dreams, Little Bird," Tzadok said, using his pet name for me ever since I confessed the truth about what I was training for. "I admire you for wanting something so badly," he added, staring at the road, making me pity him for his own lack of ambition. "Sometimes I think, 'I will never speak German again.' There used to be more to my country than Nazis." He gave me a sad smile and, once again, I felt guilty for chafing against his gloom.

"You could do worse," Sarah says tonight, and she's right. He has a tiny apartment, a working vehicle, a formal education, and perpetual job security working for Uncle Hyman. But the only thing I feel when he looks at me intently is an urge to flee from his kindness.

"Remember when we both wanted to marry Dickon from *The Secret Garden*?" I ask, struggling with the zipper of my clean frock. "He could just blow his whistle and birds and squirrels and bunnies would come greet him."

"We're not living on the moor in England, and Dickon's not real. Here, let me help," Sarah says and, gratefully, I let her take over. She even lets me borrow her comb, since mine is missing. The joke is that for the few years she was gone, I didn't brush my hair once. "Tzadok will be mesmerized," she says, when I'm finished with my hair.

"You marry him," I say, and as soon as the words slip out, I think, *Too soon*.

Luckily, she sounds amused when she says, "But he only has eyes for you," and it seems, for a moment, the Old Sarah is back.

"Miriam!" Mama calls from the bottom of the stairs, making me hesitate.

"Be nice," Sarah says. "The man ruined his tires for you."

I come downstairs to find not Tzadok in the doorway, but instead a pimply-faced teenager in uniform handing my mother an envelope. She thanks him and ushers him out before turning to me with a question on her face.

"It's a telegram," Mama says, handing me the envelope.

After tearing it open, I read with Mama peering over my shoulder. It's an invitation, I realize, to come to Texas for the Women Airforce Service, dated March 4, 1944. *Signed by Jackie Cochran herself*. I yelp for joy and then clamp a hand over my mouth.

"Is this real?" Mama asks, snatching it out of my hand. "Jackie Cochran sent you a telegram? But how did she get your name? Hyman!" she shouts, before I can answer. "Jackie Cochran sent Miri a telegram!"

"Who's Jackie Cochran?" Uncle Hyman asks, coming into the front hall.

The answer tumbles out of me: "One of the greatest aviators ever—she won the Transcontinental Air Race—set the transcontinental flying record—"

"*That* Jackie Cochran?" Uncle Hyman asks, frowning, and I nod.

"How did she get your name?" Mama asks again, and I tell her that I applied—with recommendations—for the position last year.

"But why on earth does she think you can fly a plane?" Mama asks, and I hesitate and glance at my sister, Queen of Secrets, as she makes her way down the stairs. I think of when she told them she was in love with an actor. I wonder now, *Is it worse to know how to fly?* Sarah nods at me now. *Go on*, her eyes say.

"I learned through the flying program at the University of Pittsburgh—it was in the paper, you saw it . . . . The president thinks we need more pilots to win the war, so . . ."

"I heard they banned women," Uncle Hyman says, and from his voice, I can tell he thinks that was a good idea.

"That was before. Now that we're at war—"

"They're sending women into battle?" Mama asks, her voice rising.

"Not in America," I say, thinking of the Russian "Night Witches" flying bombing missions overseas, "but we need more trained pilots to help here."

Uncle Hyman grabs the telegram and shoves his glasses up on his head to get a better look. "Texas! You can't go to Texas! How will you get there?" When I say the train, of course, he barks, "On whose nickel?"

"What about school?" Mama says, her voice eerily quiet.

I tell her I'll take a leave of absence, which sounds much better than dropping out.

Uncle Hyman keeps rereading the telegram. "It doesn't look like Jackie Cochran is offering any compensation for travel—to or from Texas if you don't make it through the program."

"Can you try out for the Women Airforce Service after you graduate from college? It's just one more year," she adds.

"Mama, I have to go now. They just lowered the flying age," I say, and then watch as her face collapses into worry lines.

"How many girls applied for this position?" Sarah asks, her arms folded across her chest.

"I don't know. Twenty-five thousand?" I shrug.

"Twenty-five *thousand*?" Mama repeats. "And she picked . . . ?"

"Me. Yes, Mama. Me! Can you imagine?"

She *is* imagining it. I can see it in her eyes, which are growing more wistful than worried. Maybe she's thinking of what my father's reaction would be if he were here right now, or maybe she's thinking, like Sarah, that one of us should be able to leave the house on Beacon Street.

"Let me understand this correctly—you lied to us?" Uncle Hyman asks, his face tomato red. "You haven't taken a single course that I paid for?"

"I did. I took some—"

"Flying lessons!" he finishes. "At the university! And now you want us to buy you a train ticket across the country?"

"She has to go," Mama suddenly says, oh so quietly, it almost breaks my heart.

"Your mother and I need to talk," Uncle Hyman says.

"She's going, Hyman," Mama says, and I'm surprised and grateful. "You heard her: twenty-five thousand applied. They picked Miri."

I want to hug Mama, but before I can move, Uncle Hyman snaps at me to go to my room. "Both of you!" he says, jerking his head at Sarah.

I want to tell Mama I'm sorry for wanting so much and sorry for all that I've hidden, but Uncle Hyman is glaring so furiously that I run upstairs, light on my feet, with Sarah on my heels, and we close the door to our bedroom, and shut the shades, and we hug and scream and laugh and dance, all with complete, tiptoeing, arms-a-waving silence. What is it about being on the precipice of change that makes one capable of joy and fear simultaneously? As if she's read my mind, Sarah gives my shoulders a shake and whispers, "You can do it."

"But what about you?" I ask, suddenly worried.

"What about me?" she says, shrugging her thin shoulders. "I'm going to be fine." Then she shoots me her unforgettable smile and adds, "I already am fine."

CHAPTER 9

Mock Marriage

I kept hoping that Mrs. Browning was right, and that the fight between my parents was just a small shower on the weather map of their marriage that only seemed like a hurricane. But on Friday morning, Mom flew down to Key West for the weekend, which meant things were seriously screwed up in the state of the union if she was desperate enough to tell Grandma about it.

Five years ago, right after Huggie was born, and right when my mother "needed her most," my grandma Margot moved to Key West. Mom decided the best way to let Grandma know how much she missed her was to never let us visit Florida and to never call to say hi and to always let the machine pick up. Mom also couldn't get over that Grandma had a boyfriend, "this Ray guy," as in, "What do we really know about this Ray guy?" Mom's been suspicious of him ever since our one and only visit four years ago, when he took us on a kayak tour through the mangroves and pointed out rare species of birds and plants that my brother Toby later told us were not indigenous to Key West.

Mom got back from visiting on Sunday night, and the only thing she would say at breakfast on Monday morning was that Grandma "sends her love."

"Did she have any—advice for you?" I asked, my mouth full of cereal, as Mom spackled peanut butter all over the bread for our sandwiches like a tile guy who has to move quickly before the cement dries. "You know . . . helpful tips . . ." I said, and Mom stopped and stared at me, her face grave.

"There are things I need to tell you, but now is not the time."

Watching her shove all the sandwiches into Baggies, I stood there gathering all of my questions: *What if you tried to be more fun? What if you weren't such a hater? What if Daddy changes his mind?*

"Elyse, please get moving, before you miss the bus," Mom said.

I left for school kind of glum, especially when Holden Saunders drove by the bus stop in his MINI Cooper and didn't even look my way.

AT LUNCH, THEA CAME OVER AND PLUNKED HER TRAY DOWN SO forcefully her soda tipped over, and then she said, "Oh, shit!" as she mopped it up, like somehow I'd shoved her from across the table. I guessed she was pissed because Mrs. Desmond announced who our spouses were for the "Marriage Project," and I got Holden Saunders and she got Carson Jeffries, this kid who always wears shorts, rain, sleet, or snow. Although in some ways, they kind of look perfect for each other: there's Thea with her black hair and combat boots. And there's Carson in his nose ring and Converse sneakers and Hawaiian shorts. They're both kind of saying fuck you, I think: to absent mothers, reality show sisters, to winter. "You did the reverse psychology plan, right?" she asked, picking up her sandwich. "You didn't list him as someone you'd want to be paired with?" She didn't have to say who the "him" was.

My peanut butter kind of stuck to the back of my throat but I managed to say, "No, of course not," even though the truth was that I listed Holden Saunders twice, plus I put an asterisk beside his name and wrote at the bottom of the index card: "Holden is my next door neighbor, which would make it a lot easier for extracurricular projects."

The day got better after physics class, when Holden came over and said, "Hey. Elyse, right?" just the way I always imagined he would one day! And then he said, "I guess we have to plan this budget or something. What have you got going on sixth period?"

"Gym. My study hall is fourth period, but that's when you have Spanish," I said, and he looked so surprised that my cheeks started burning.

"How about the library right after school?"

"Don't you have lacrosse practice?" I asked, and he looked a little startled again.

"I've got mono. Not allowed to play for six weeks because I might rupture my spleen."

"That's great!" I said, a little too happily. "Two thirty it is!"

In the library after school, it took us a while to get started, because people kept coming over and saying hi to Holden, and he'd joke around with them and he wouldn't introduce me unless someone gave him a questioning look, and then he'd say, "Mrs. Desmond married us. She's my Psych 101 wife. This is our honeymoon, now beat it." Which I guess isn't a real introduction, but I didn't care, because it was thrilling to be called his wife in front of these people who'd otherwise never talk to me. Even Karina Spencer was at the library giggling at a table across the room with some other drama girls, and I saw her looking.

"So, like are you on the field hockey team?" Holden asked, after he'd opened a can of Coke stealthily, so Mrs. Jermaine, the librarian, wouldn't hear it. I was confused for a second until I realized he thought that the kilt I was wearing was part of a uniform.

"No, not field hockey. Not any team. I thought about doing cross-country . . . but then I didn't."

"I don't blame you. There's a reason you send people to do laps when you're trying to punish them," he said, and I laughed harder than I should have. I just couldn't believe that I was finally allowed to look into his green eyes without quickly glancing away, that I was saying words and he was saying other words back.

Then Thea walked by with Carson Jeffries. When she rolled her eyes at me behind his back, I just nodded and made a face, as if I felt her pain. Once they were gone, Holden nodded in their direction and said that it was too bad Mrs. Desmond hadn't arranged any gay marriages.

"Oh, I don't think he's gay. He just likes to wear shorts."

"Not him. Her. Aren't you two . . . ?"

"Gay?" A noise came out of me that was supposed to be a

laugh but sounded more like someone was strangling me. "No. She's my best friend. But we're not . . ." I shivered and glanced away from his face and somehow met eyes with Karina, across the library, who quickly looked down at her own book. Karina was wearing skinny jeans and a low-cut tank top and her hair was long and curly. All of a sudden, I realized how Holden saw me and I hated it. Hated myself.

"Is it true her sister's on *Be My Next Wife*?" he asked.

"You mean Stacey? Yeah. Why? Do you like her?" I asked.

"I wouldn't kick her out of bed for eating crackers." Thea always says it sucks, living in the shadow of a SILF.

"Eating crackers?" I said, confused.

"Forget it." He took a pad of paper out of his backpack and fished around in a pocket until he came up with a pen. "Did they finish filming, though?"

"Yeah, but all the contestants are sequestered in an underground bomb shelter right now. They can't come up until the final show airs." I said it so deadpan that Holden stared at me for a second before his face cracked open into a smile and then he laughed and that made my annoyance float away.

We finally got started on the budget. Holden thought it would be a good idea to figure out our monthly income before we totaled up our expenses. He asked what I wanted to be someday.

"A writer," I said automatically. Then my cheeks flushed thinking of Mrs. Browning saying, *Don't write because you want to be a writer, write because you have something to say!* I left out the doctor part—it sounded too intimidating, even to me.

"Aw, shit, seriously? Looks like I'm gonna have to be the moneymaker."

"What do you want to be?" I asked, even though the point of the exercise is to show us how much it costs to raise a baby when we're still in high school, not working on Wall Street.

"If it were up to me, I'd build houses. I helped my uncle gut a house last summer. That was cool. We had to demolish these old rooms and stuff."

"I hope there wasn't any asbestos in the walls," I blurted out, a stupid joke. Or not even a joke. Just me: turning into my fucking mother.

"Asbestos?" he repeated and laughed. "I-I don't know."

"Don't worry. I'm sure there wasn't. You'd have to wear special hazmat suits for that." *Oh, my God. Stop talking about asbestos*, I thought.

My face was hot, so I quickly looked down at the list he'd made of all the things we had to budget for, like clothes, books, food, cable, car maintenance, gas, and reminded him that he'd forgotten health insurance. "For my asbestos exposure," he said with a smile, and I laughed. "Guess we won't have to spend too much on clothes," he added, nodding at my outfit.

"Hey, I resemble that!" I said, a line my aunt Andie always says, from an old army show called *M*A*S*H*. But even though Aunt Andie always makes me laugh when she says it, Holden just looked at me like he didn't know what to think.

After looking back at his list, he asked if we were supposed to budget for the baby, and when exactly we were being issued this sack of flour that we would have to feed and clothe and provide child care for? I told him not for another two weeks, and that we'd have to agree on a name. "We're making it a boy," Holden said.

"We don't get to pick the sex, remember? 'Just like in real life.'"

"In real life, you get to choose your spouse," Holden said.

"What if she gives us a sack of flour with disabilities?" I said suddenly, and then mimed Mrs. Desmond offering us a swaddled infant: "Congratulations! Your baby is just a torso!"

Holden choked on his mouthful of Coke and sprayed it all over the table. Then he kept laughing and coughing, and I was laughing, too, and Karina Spencer and the girls at her table were watching us, and I felt like I finally existed. The librarian came over and told us we had to leave. In the corridor, on our way out of the building, Holden offered me a ride home. Then he added, "Maybe next time we can meet at my house," and my face hurt from smiling so much. "Hey, aren't you in my physics class?" he realized, and I nodded. When he asked if I had a partner yet for my toothpick bridge, I told him I didn't, even though I was supposed to go to Thea's that weekend to work on it. "Maybe we can be partners," Holden said. It was suddenly, definitely the best day of my life.

AFTER SCHOOL, I ASKED HIM TO DRIVE ME TO AUNT ANDIE'S SO the ride would last longer. We listened to music as he zigged and zagged around traffic on the bridge, but I wasn't really paying attention to anything except for Holden's hands, tapping on the steering wheel, and his jeaned thigh on just the other side of the emergency brake. I thought of Mrs. Browning's stepcousin Jack driving her five hours out of his way to Indian Town Gap and wondered if love was proportional to the distance traveled. If I were Mary and Holden were Jack, what secret would I ask him to keep?

When he pulled up outside Aunt Andie's condo, Holden put the car in park and said, "Well, wifey," and I laughed so hard I almost forgot to get out of the car, until I realized Aunt Andie was tapping on the passenger window. Her frizzy brown hair was barely contained in a clip, and she was wearing a skirt and sweater instead of her usual painter's overalls.

"I was just on my way out," she said, as I stepped out of the car and onto the sidewalk. "I have to return a mattress today or its mine forever." I knew, without asking, that this had something to do with the hot sales guy at Brookstone. Aunt Andie had been buying and returning an inordinate amount of pillows because he'd laughed at one of her jokes.

I introduced Holden to Aunt Andie, whose eyebrows went up as soon as she heard his name.

"S'up?" Holden said, leaning over the gearshift to wave.

"S'up?" Aunt Andie repeated, with an exaggerated head nod, making me cringe. "You're coming to the mall?" she asked me, and I nodded.

"While you're there, buy her some new clothes," Holden called.

"What are you talking about? I think she looks *fab-u-lous*," Aunt Andie said, exaggerating the word, which made me cringe again. "Later, G!" she called, before shutting the passenger door.

" 'Later, G'?" I repeated, once he'd driven away.

"Do people not say that?"

"Maybe they do," I said, my self-loathing returning. How would I know what people say, when I'm just the girl wearing the fucking kilt?

AT THE MALL, WE LEFT THE MATTRESS SAGGING OVER THE TOP OF the car like a maxi pad for the roof, ready to absorb the rain, and headed for Brookstone so Aunt Andie could ask the hot sales guy to help us carry it to the store. "The only problem with the hot sales guy is that his name is Blane. I don't know if I can ever truly love a man named Blane."

I halted, midstride. Just across the expanse of marble tile was the clothing store H&M, whose windows were filled with plastic Karina Spencers, wearing just the right thing.

"Do you think . . . ?" I hesitated. "Could we maybe try on some clothes first? Just to see what they have?"

"Oh, *dahling,* I would love to," Aunt Andie said.

So we looked, and I tried on, and I was surprised to find out that some of the skinny jeans were actually comfortable. Aunt Andie kept gushing that I looked amazing, but I wasn't sure any of the clothes really seemed like me. "Isn't this too . . . revealing?" I said, squirming in the fitted maroon shirt and jeans, in front of the mirror.

"Honey, just because you are an old soul doesn't mean you've gotta dress like one," Aunt Andie said. "What exactly are you afraid of?"

"I don't even like most of the girls in my school—why would I want to look like them?" I asked.

"It's called assimilation," Aunt Andie said, which reminded me of my mother telling me the other day after church that *of course* she was still Jewish. Then I thought of Mrs. Browning and the gold cross that dangled from the chain around her neck and the story I was typing about her Jewish family. Would she, like my mother, consider herself "highly assimilated"?

"We all do it to get by," Aunt Andie went on. "It doesn't have to change who you are on the inside."

I stared at myself in the mirror. Would I get used to looking like someone else, eventually preferring skinny jeans and Uggs to Salvation Army poodle skirts and flats? What would Thea say if she saw me now? What would *Holden* say? Just thinking of that made my heart do a weird thing in my chest, like it was trying to fly away. I caught Aunt Andie watching me, and I quickly pulled the shirt over my head to take it off, so she wouldn't see me blushing. Just as I was squirming out of the jeans, the saleslady asked through the dressing room door if there was anything she could take up to the register. Aunt Andie raised her eyebrow at me.

"All of it, please," I said.

IT WAS AFTER FIVE THIRTY WHEN WE GOT BACK TO MY HOUSE. I barely had time to get out of the car and head down the stone walkway, when Mom appeared on the doorstep. Her work clothes were rumpled, and her hair was going every which way. If she were a painting, it would be called *One Long Day*.

"What's going on? Where've you been? Haven't you gotten any of my texts?" Mom asked, all in one breath.

I slipped my phone out of my pocket. "Oh . . . whoops."

"She wanted to tag along while I returned a mattress—or tried to," Aunt Andie explained, handing me my backpack. "I can't believe it. I'm one day late, and the Brookstone guy won't let me return it. I've bought and returned five pillows. I thought we had a bond."

"That's Blane for you," I said, and Aunt Andie shot me a wry smile.

"I don't understand." Mom's blue eyes were darting back and forth. "You drove to Elyse's school and took her . . . where . . . ?"

"She showed up at my condo, " Aunt Andie said. "Then we went to the mall. Now we're back. Got your new things, kiddo?"

"Got 'em," I said, a mumble, only Mom kept staring at me, until I finally went ahead and showed her what was behind my back—a shopping bag from H&M—before she managed to set it on fire with her laser beam vision.

"Early Christmas present," Aunt Andie said as Mom rifled through the outfits like a customs agent, making me cringe. If Mom had bought me the clothes, she'd make me model them for her and Daddy, while Toby pretended to be sick and Huggie clapped as if he were really at a fashion show.

"We don't need these," Mom said, shoving the clothes back at Aunt Andie.

"Yes, we do!" I said, my voice a shriek, as I ripped the shopping bag out of her hand.

"Aunt Andie *can't afford these*," Mom said, enunciating as if I could only lip-read. "She has *credit card debt*. She owes us *thousands of dollars*."

"You're really going to do this, Jane? You're going to keep this grudge going when Mom's dying?"

"Wait—what?" I said, startled.

Aunt Andie and Mom looked at each other. "Oh—God. Your mom didn't want me to—Elyse—Grandma's—um . . ."

"Grandma has cancer," Mom said.

I blinked. "Like Daddy?"

"Yes, but this is a different kind."

"Better or worse?" I said, looking to Aunt Andie since, when she wasn't painting, she worked as a radiology technician.

"Um—I—according to her doctors—well . . . geez . . ."

"We don't know," Mom told me.

"The only thing she wants is for us to be normal again," Aunt Andie said, and my mother laughed, meanly.

"She also wants you to stop putting all your resources into one dream, but I don't see you giving up the eggs in the freezer anytime soon. Which would be fine if you could *afford the rent*." Aunt Andie winced in the spray of Mom's words, as if she were spitting. "I heard what she said—that you'll never be able to commit to any man, because you're not committed to reality," Mom added.

"Grandma said that?" I asked, startled.

"She says what she wants now," Aunt Andie said, her voice grim. "No filter. 'It's *my* deathbed,'" she added in a singsong just like Grandma would, if she were actually on her deathbed.

"Wait. Her *deathbed*?" I repeated. Suddenly Mom's last-minute trip down south made sense. But Grandma walked miles on the beach before breakfast, and sang loudly in the evenings on the dock, and cackled with her head tipped back at dinner. It couldn't be true. "And you didn't tell me?" My voice was doing that shrieking thing again.

"Honey, she's *okay*," Mom said. "I spoke to Rabbi Horowitz *and* Pastor Stan and told them we want everyone on this. Pastor Stan's got three different churches praying for her—what?" she snapped, since Aunt Andie's smile was sudden and sort of rueful.

"It's just a strange side effect of status, where you can farm out your greatest needs—someone to cook your meals and scrub your toilets and shop for your groceries and now, someone to pray for your miracles. When does the delegation stop?"

Mom stiffened like she'd opened the door for a FedEx package and found a Jehovah's Witness instead. "Thank you for bringing my daughter home," she said, all businesslike.

"And for the clothes," I said quickly, still clutching the bag. "We're keeping the clothes."

Mom glared at me before turning her death beam back on Aunt Andie. "In the future, if you want to shop for Elyse, you can write me a check, and I'll take care of it."

"Mom—"

"Elyse, go inside."

"Wait—I'm sorry," Aunt Andie said in a breathless, urgent rush. "It's great that everyone's praying. Maybe it'll work. Jeez, I hope it works. But whatever happens, I just want us to be okay, Jane," she added, and it hurt me to hear the pleading in her voice, but Mom didn't seem to be moved.

"Good night," she said, before closing the door, and then whirled around to face me. "We're not finished."

"Yes, we are," I said, stomping up the steps, only the carpet was so plush, my feet made only an unsatisfying, muffled thump.

"Elyse, wait—get back here!" she shouted.

I could've waited to hear what she had to say—about Grandma, and Daddy, and even Aunt Andie—but it was much more satisfying to walk away, knowing that she was suffering, maybe even more than me.

CHAPTER 10

Sweetwater

March 1944

The train station in downtown Pittsburgh is loaded with servicemen and women, the cadets and the WACs and the WAVES, and women traveling with small children—families en route to extended relatives, while the men are at war. The Red Cross is there, too, handing everyone in uniform a pack of cigarettes or a hot cup of coffee. It's too hectic to worry about how I'm feeling or fret about the fear in Mama's eyes whenever I glance over my shoulder to make sure she and Sarah are keeping up. Instead I press on toward Platform 6, trying not to clip anyone in the feet with my bag. I'm grateful when Tzadok slips the suitcase from my hand and lifts it high overhead. "We must get you on this train, Little Bird," he says, expertly weaving through the throngs of humanity.

It's cold outside on the platform, and my breath hangs in the air, but the crowd keeps me warm in my thin, wool coat. Before long, the train pulls in and the bodies on the platform push forward, as if we're all going to the same place. There's hardly any time to say goodbye, which is probably a good thing, since Mama, crying openly now, is killing me with her tears. It's like the end of the farewell parties for the servicemen, only I don't even have a photograph of myself in uniform to leave her with for the mantel.

"Do good things, Miri," Sarah whispers in my ear, giving me a quick hug and slipping an envelope into my pocket.

"I hope you find all you are seeking," Tzadok says with his German accent, handing me back my bag and, despite his formal speech, I know that he means it.

"Go," Mama says, pushing me away before I can hug her one last time. And even though she's insisting—or maybe because of it—I have this strange feeling that nothing will ever be the same between us.

It takes five days to get to Texas. I spend the first leg of the ride sitting on my suitcase at the end of the packed car trying not to think about Mama—not of her naked finger where her diamond ring used to be, or how she was scrubbing the toilet when I'd asked her to send me to college in the first place. The night before I left, Sarah and I were both curled up on our sides, facing each other, when I whispered across the tiny space between our twin beds, "What if she never forgives me?"

"She wouldn't let you go if she thought you shouldn't do it," Sarah said. "Mama probably wishes she could fly away, too."

"But what if—"

"Stop," Sarah said, and in the yellow light of the candle her face was soft and shadowy, like a memory. "Now is not the time to doubt."

As the crowded train lurches along, I close my eyes and exhale, recalling how safe I felt in my sister's gaze. Then I remember the envelope in my pocket and take out her short note, which is actually a quote by Virginia Woolf from *A Room of One's Own:*

> If you stop to curse you are lost, I said to her; equally
> if you stop to laugh. Hesitate or fumble and you are
> done for. Think only of the jump, I implored her, as
> if I had put this whole of my money on her back; and
> she went over it like a bird.

Think only of the jump! My sister wrote. *I know you'll fly high for both of us.*

At last, after a mass exodus in Chicago, I'm finally able to scramble for a seat to myself before the crush of passengers embarks. I end up facing a bespectacled older man wearing a yarmulke who smiles at me as if we're kindred spirits when he notices the Star of David hanging from my neck. Focusing out the window, I try to make my mind as flat and blank as the landscape passing by, trying not to think of Mama's teary eyes, or how thin and breakable Sarah felt when we hugged, or even Tzadok's expectations for when I return. The other day he said, "It is good for you to do this now, before you make your life." Does he think this is something I just need to get out of my system before I come back to marry him?

In the dining car, I use the pocket money from Uncle Hyman to buy dinner: a small piece of bread and cheese, green beans, and a tiny portion of meat. When the serviceman in front of me gets twice as much food on his plate, I can't help wonder-

ing if I got less because I'm a woman or because—like my seat
mate "the Rabbi," with an equally sparse serving—I'm Jewish.
Then another cadet slides up to the counter, and I watch as
the steward smiles before loading up his plate with extra meat.
"That's enough. Really," says the soldier, as the steward heaps
more food on his dish. Then I realize it has nothing to do with
race or religion or gender: it's the uniform. Rations don't apply.

The train pulls into Houston at six in the morning, and then
I take a bus to Sweetwater, still swaying like I've been on a boat
the last five days. Besides some tumbleweeds blowing across
the airfields, a control tower, and the barracks, surrounded
by a chain link fence, there's not much to see, except for the
planes—*oh, the planes!* As soon as I hear the discordant roar
of a hundred propellers, stopping and starting, growing distant and drawing near, something wakes up inside me, as if I'm
finally coming to after a three-year slumber. There's an open-
cockpit PT-19 taking off with level wings and a perfect pitch,
and here's a BT-13, "The Vultee Vibrator," coming in for a noisy
landing. Meanwhile, six women in flight suits and parachutes
make their way to the field where the Texan AT-6's are parked.
They look so assured, like women warriors, and I wonder if one
day that'll be me. Mesmerized, I stand there, following each
plane's departure and arrival, praying I haven't forgotten how
to fly.

My bunk is nearly empty when I get inside: just six lonely-
looking cots and footlockers all in a row. Except that one person
is already present, a girl with brown curls, who quickly runs
her arm across her nose and bleary eyes. "Oh—hi! Sorry to—
I'll just . . ." I say, as if I've wandered into the men's shower.

Quickly choosing the cot in the far corner, I hoist my suitcase on top and keep my head down.

"I've just gotten some awful news," the girl blurts, and I glance behind me, as if she may be confiding in someone else, someone who deserves to be privy to this information. I'm not sure I'm ready for naked emotion from a complete stranger; in fact, I'm not even ready for roommates. The physical space seems smaller than the room Sarah and I share at home.

"My mother sent a telegram," she goes on. "My uncle's dead. At least, that's what the U.S. government says."

"I'm so sorry," I say, feeling a rush of genuine concern. "Do you have to leave?"

"Well, we aren't having a funeral, not until we know for sure. He's been missing in the Pacific for a year. Besides, even if we were certain, I wouldn't go home. It took me three days to get here. I've been preparing for this for the last four years." The girl looks at me. "You must think I'm a horrible person."

"No, I . . ." I trail off, thinking of Mama warning me that you can't trust anyone who isn't related to you. *Why cry in front of people who don't share your blood, who would betray your confidence in an instant?* While I don't necessarily believe this, I must've taken it to heart, because the girls I've grown up with in school are more like acquaintances than friends. I didn't tell any of my old classmates that I was leaving for Texas. I couldn't imagine anyone would care.

"If my mom sent a telegram that my uncle died, I wouldn't even cry," I confess now, because this far from home, trusting seems more like an instinct than a risk. After all, this pilot with the earnest brown eyes probably gave up everything to be here, too. "When my dad died, I wished like anything it had been my uncle instead," I go on. I'd thought of this many times, how things could've been so different for all of us, even Mama. Because Papa was the only person to nudge her grimace into a smile and her smile into a startled laugh, as if she was surprised by the sound. "Everyone would've been so much happier if Uncle Hyman had been the one to die," I add, almost wistfully.

"Well, everyone except for maybe . . . Uncle Hyman," the girl says, deadpan, and just to hear his name on the lips of this stranger sends a smile shooting across my face. She grins back and stands up to extend her hand, which is when I see how tall she is, six feet, with long, model legs. "I'm Grace Davinport."

"Miri Lichtenstein," I say, humbled by her height. Nevertheless, after we shake I go ahead and move my stuff over to the footlocker next to hers. She's in Sarah's spot now. "Where's home?" I ask, snapping open my suitcase.

"Iowa." She tells me she's logged more than twenty-five hundred hours back in Ames, thanks to her family of farmers who pitched in to keep her flying after the Civilian Pilot Training Program at the University of Iowa ended. "I just had to promise to bring them along as passengers."

"You're lucky. I haven't been able to fly for the last three years." I don't want to admit that I couldn't afford to continue lessons that weren't federally funded, but she can probably figure that out, the same way she seems to know that I want her to tell me I've got nothing to fear.

"You'll be fine," Grace says. "They're going to reteach us everything anyway—we're learning the 'army way to fly,' right?"

"I hope so," I say, taking a deep breath and thinking of Sarah. *Now is not the time to doubt.*

AFTER UNPACKING MY SUITCASE, I STOP OFF AT THE BATHROOM, where a dishwater blonde from Tennessee, who introduces herself as "Louise," is inexplicably scooping up a family of cockroaches to set them free outside. I feel as if I'm witnessing some sort of grotesque circus act.

"If you're not going to kill them, don't you think they'll crawl their way back home?" I ask, watching her shake them off her hands, outside.

"Aw, look at you," Louise says with a grin. "Already calling this place home."

Back at the bunk, I'm introduced to the rest of the women designated by God or Jackie Cochran and with whom I'll be spending the next ten months. There's Vera Skeert, from Baltimore, who keeps clutching her very big binder as if it's a flotation device. "That's a *vera* big binder you've got there," Murphee Sutherland from Wayne, New Jersey, says with a wink. Vera is worried because she's spent the last three months singing on scholarship at the Peabody Institute instead of flying. I glance over at Grace, whose brown eyes meet mine. *See?* They seem to be saying. *You're not alone.*

"You'll be fine. It's like riding a horse," says Ana Santos from Chicago.

"Except if you fall, pull your rip cord," Murphee says, and Vera Skeert hugs her "Vera big binder" even tighter. Murphee has orangey-red hair from a bottle, and Mama would probably call her "a crumb," but I like her already.

Ana Santos studied art at the University of Chicago ("Mostly still lifes—of food" she says, eating a candy bar) and actually slipped a box of paintbrushes and paints into her footlocker.

Just as I'm doubting there'll be any free time for that, we're called out to the flagpole and lined up in formation with all of our classmates to take an oath. According to our commanding officer, Captain Digby, a man with a surprisingly slight physique for such a gruff bark—"If you think you know what you're doing, think again! If you believe you don't have more to learn, go home!"—we'll be up at six tomorrow and running two miles before breakfast.

Then comes the paperwork—signing my life away over and over. Yes, I understand the risks of flight. Yes, I am fully aware that, in the event of disaster, the government will not be paying for my funeral. I'm issued my books for ground school—"Is it okay if I feel like vomiting?" Vera says, balancing the stack on top of her binder—and then, at the next window, a leather flight jacket and sweater, and finally, at the last window, a jumpsuit for flying.

"Size?" the man barks from behind the counter.

"Small?"

"We've got forty-four, forty-six, and forty-eight," he says.

"Forty-four?" I guess, and he hands me an enormous bundle of olive material.

Back at the bunk, Ana shakes out the so-called zoot suit and we crack up at its enormity. We've been issued the men's flight suits, I realize, unfolding my own, which looks big enough to fit Uncle Hyman. Murphee pulls on her own suit and flaps the sagging sleeves at us, like a small child playing dress-up. When she turns around, showing us the billowing material whose crotch ends halfway to her knees, we laugh harder.

"How do they expect us to fly planes in outfits that don't fit?" Vera asks. "This isn't safe."

"Why don't you complain? See how that works out for you," Murphee says.

"I wish I had a camera," I say, still laughing despite my unease. On my five-foot-three frame, I have to roll up the sleeves and cuffs eight times so as not to trip.

"I've got one," Ana says, pulling out her Leica from her footlocker.

We go outside into the blustery cold sunlight and pose in front of the barracks in our comical flight suits—Murphee, Grace, and me in between—as Ana snaps our pictures. Giddy from outfits and maybe even just from being here, I glance over and see Captain Babcock, one of the military instructors, walking by the far end of the building—still close enough for me to catch the disapproval on his face. I wonder then if this is part of my military training: to be presented with absurd expectations and to take it on with a straight face. I can't help feeling as if, by laughing out loud, I've already failed the experiment.

THAT NIGHT, I AM COMING BACK TO THE BUNK FROM THE SHOWERS when I look up and am awed. At Avenger Field there are no lights of the city, and no steel mills, either, so the void of space looks more like a blue-black velvet curtain, studded with diamonds. It's the loveliest thing I've ever seen. Taps plays at ten o'clock, but the lights are out sooner this evening due to the high winds rustling the power lines, so I write my sister by flashlight, before tucking my pen and paper into my footlocker and crawling into bed.

The wind stops. I listen to the sudden stillness, eerily quiet, except for the sound of crickets and waiting.

The important thing is that I have arrived.

CHAPTER 11

Confessions

Elyse's arrival at the writer's group on Tuesday night was marked by a minor commotion. In the single week since we'd seen each other last, she had acquired some new clothes, that is to say, clothes that other girls her age were commonly wearing: fitted jeans with a jersey shirt and clunky suede boots that looked perfect for space walking. She looked like my sister Sarah masquerading as a twenty-first-century teenager.

"Elyse, my word!" Selena Markmann gaped beneath blue-black bangs, the first to notice the girl ambling into the conference room. "You look so grown up."

"Whoa," Gene Rosskemp added, surveying her new look. "Who's the lucky guy?"

"Huh? Oh." Elyse pulled out a chair. "My aunt just took me shopping." She may have shrugged coolly but the little smile, playing at the corners of her mouth, gave her away.

"Whoever he is, be careful." Jean Fester held up one of her

red pens like a can of Mace. "Give him the milk, and he's not going to want to buy the cow."

"I always say, you gotta let the guy taste the milk, so he knows if the cow's worth payin' for," Gene said, and then laughed loudly and slapped his knee.

"Both of you, please. Leave her alone," I said, and finally, Elyse made eye contact with me before sliding two packets of typed papers in my direction: one titled "The Telegram" and the other, "Sweetwater." Just to see my own words typed on a page made me feel as if the oxygen had been swept from my lungs.

"Here are your chapters," Elyse said, and I quickly shoved the pages beneath Herb Shepherd's story. I hadn't even envisioned my vignettes as chapters; I certainly hadn't considered giving them titles.

"Mary Browning, are you finally writing something for us?" Victor Chenkovitch asked, with his hands folded on his big belly as he leaned back on the special chair cushion he'd used ever since his back surgery.

"Heavens, no," I said, feeling my cheeks flush.

"It's a memoir," Elyse said, and when I stared at her, shocked, she said, "Well, it is."

My heart clanged at the betrayal. Hadn't I mentioned it was a secret? Unless . . . I hadn't.

"I volunteer Mary to submit for next time," Herb Shepherd said, and I suddenly despised him for the perpetual crumbs in his mustache.

"Yes, do, Mary," Selena said. "I can't *wait* to hear all about your time as a New York editor."

I exhaled, berating myself for the little white lie that had slipped out when I first met Gene Rosskemp in the mailroom all those years ago—reinventing myself in a single moment—and the lies that had followed since, creating less a tangled web than a dark, muddy grave. Mary Browning as a New York editor? Small potatoes. They didn't know about the four babies I'd lost, or that I never wanted the war to end because the day they said I had to stop flying I thought my life was over, or that the last time I spoke to my son Dave we argued, and it was all my fault. And why should I have told them? So I could feel the catch of loss in my throat in the one place I felt blissfully forgetful? I wanted to be happy for just a little while. They didn't know that the thing I missed the most was not my penmanship, which used to be lovely, or my husband, who was also quite lovely, but in fact was my future. So many promises and hopes I had for myself were wrapped up in to-morrow, and the greatest loss of all was not having more to look forward to.

"Then see how it feels when we rip you to shreds," Jean said, still waving around her red pen, now a bloody scalpel. Honest to God, I'd never seen her smile like that, her craggy yellow teeth reminiscent of a ghoul's.

"Maybe she just wants to get through the first draft," Gene said, rescuing me, and I looked at him gratefully.

"Yes, I'm not really sure where it's going yet . . . but eventually, yes . . ." I demurred. "But let's get back to the task at hand. Herb's piece is up for discussion. 'The Steel Mill Summer'—a lovely title."

"But what about the main character? This 'Bert' guy? I had real a problem with his likability," Selena said.

And we were off.

AFTERWARD, I FOUND ELYSE SITTING AT ONE OF THE STUDY CAR-rels hidden between the bookcases and laid a fifty-dollar bill next to her pencil. She looked up at me in surprise. "Take it. It's yours. And I'll need my Dictaphone back," I said.

It was exactly the opposite of how I'd imagined sharing my story, yet ever since she and I had started talking, memories would pour out of me at odd hours. Since Elyse didn't have compatible equipment, I lent it to her for the transcribing.

"Oh, right. Sorry," Elyse said, and I watched as she scrab-bled around in her pack on the floor until she came up with the little recorder. "I wanted to ask you—how come you didn't use your real name?" she asked, and my eyebrows shot up in surprise.

"On the tapes," she said, standing up and handing me the Dictaphone. "I mean, it seems kind of weird that your Jewish parents would name you after the mother of Jesus."

I startled and glanced around, as if one of Hitler's infor-mants might be hidden in the stacks or, worse, Victor Chen-kovitch, who'd actually suffered in a concentration camp and would surely resent my desertion. It was true; I couldn't bring myself to say Miri Lichtenstein's real name aloud. It made her—me—too vulnerable. So I stuck with Mary.

"I mean, you might not think anyone will ever read it, but lots of people could be interested in your story, and frankly, it just doesn't sound authentic," she said. "Do you want to bring a tape to the next group or should we meet on the weekend again?"

"I think—I will likely need to take a step back from the memoir." I nodded to myself. *Definitely, pull back, before it's too late.*

"O—kay . . ." Elyse's forehead crinkled. "You never said it was a big secret. The book."

"Well, now you know." My hands were clasped in front of me. "I'll need my tapes back, too." Just watching her dig around in her pocket before dropping the miniature tapes into my palm one at a time like dice, I couldn't help noticing the fit of her new jeans. "You're nearly unrecognizable today."

"It's just jeans and a shirt and some boots," she said with an exasperated sigh.

"If they're comfortable, by all means—"

"I don't see what the big deal is. It's easier not having people look at me like I'm a freak all the time. I *prefer* blending in," Elyse said.

"I understand—that desire. Truly," I said. "I'm sorry."

She stared at me for a long moment, as if debating whether to gather her things and bolt or believe me.

"What happened to your family?" she asked, and I startled again and searched the stacks, but we were still completely alone. "I'm right, aren't I? You changed your name and your religion?"

"That's a complicated question, my dear," I said, and she waited. "And this is probably not the time or the place for a complicated answer."

"So, let's go to a coffee shop or something," Elyse said. "I have another hour until my mom picks me up."

The sudden laugh that burbled out of me surprised us both. She actually thought I'd feel safer baring my soul at a Starbucks.

"I WAS NEVER ESPECIALLY RELIGIOUS, AT LEAST, NOT IN THE WAY my parents were," I said, back at my apartment, the best place

I could think of for a cup of tea and conversation such as this one. "And I felt insecure knowing that just across an ocean, scores of girls exactly like me were being murdered simply for being Jewish."

"I thought no one knew what was going on until the end of the war," Elyse said, reaching for noodle kugel, something I'd been in the mood for last night and baked, never dreaming I'd have company to share it with.

"Oh, we knew—maybe not the extent of it. But there were more than whispers about the mass extermination of Jews. So, from the time I was in my early teens, I was frightened knowing it was only by luck of our geographic location that we weren't marched away at gunpoint."

"When I read *The Diary of Anne Frank,* I felt that way, too—like it was only chance that I was born here and now. I'm half Jewish," she added, her mouth full of kugel. "My mom's side."

"And how were you raised, may I ask?" I said, helping myself to seconds. The spoon shook, scattering clumps of noodles on the tablecloth.

"On a little of both, but not enough of either." Elyse shrugged. "What's Dave say about your history?" she asked, and I blinked. "That's your son's name, right?"

I thought of the last time we spoke, the way he shouted at me before I hung up on him. "Dave doesn't know," I admitted, and I watched as her thick eyebrows dropped.

"For real?" Elyse asked.

"He was brought up Lutheran." I hesitated. "And I always made him wear a gold cross outside his shirt collar, even after he complained that boys don't wear necklaces." This reminded

me of the awful afternoon when he disappeared in a line at
Yankee Stadium as a young boy, ending up in the custody of a
security guard.

"Mama, what exactly does it mean to be Jewish?" Dave
asked me later in the car, once we'd been successfully reunited
and were on our way home. I stared at him in the backseat
through the rearview mirror. He was cheerfully swinging his
legs and wearing Thomas's perpetually inquisitive expression,
even at the age of five. "The security guard asked me."

"The security guard . . . did what?" I repeated, startled.

"When I asked if I could buy his bottle of pop off him for
a penny. He said to the other guard, 'Will ya look at this kid,
trying to chew me down?' Then he looked at me and did that
thing where you close one eye and said, 'You're not Jewish, are
you?' I said I didn't *think* so, and then he laughed."

"Next time, just say, 'no,' you aren't Jewish," I'd said, bris-
tling. In the moment I'd thought it was at Dave, for having
what I so desperately wanted to protect—his innocence. But
beneath the ripple of irritation was a tide of rage at the security
guard for using a slur in front of my child.

"And what does it mean if you chew somebody down?" he
went on. "Like you chew them up into tiny bites—"

"That man was ignorant, and I don't ever want to hear you
speaking that way," I'd said, glaring at him in the mirror. "Let's
leave it at that."

"But you never told me, what's it mean to be Jewish?" Dave
had asked again, and then my fury was replaced by guilt.

"How could you not tell him?" Elyse asked.

"It never really—came up . . ." But it did, of course, because from then on, I pushed him out the door and into the

world wearing a cross. Every afternoon, he'd return with it in his backpack, until the day he said he lost the necklace in the creek.

"What made you ask?" I picked up my teacup with a tremulous hand.

"I don't know." Elyse's voice grew strangely glum, as if she knew about the breach between Dave and me. "I guess because everyone keeps things from me and when I find out, it makes me so mad that they think I didn't deserve to know. Like, Mom didn't tell me that my grandma is sick. Seriously sick. Deathbed sick."

I set down my cup.

"Grandma went to the doctor about an itch, and it turns out she's got cancer. Which is just so hard to believe because, well, Grandma looks really young, and she's in great shape—or at least, she was. She moved away a long time ago; my mom only let us visit her once in five years."

Disheartening news aside, I couldn't help but feel relieved by the shift in topic—for now, at least, my betrayal was forgotten.

"How old is your grandmother?" I asked, and Elyse shrugged and pushed her plate away.

"Maybe . . . sixty-eight?"

"Well, she *is* young," I said. "What does your grandmother say about her condition?"

"Every time I call her, her boyfriend Ray answers and says she's resting. I don't know what's going to happen next," Elyse finally said quietly.

I wanted to reach out and give her hand, clenched into a fist on top of the table, a reassuring squeeze, but refrained, for fear it would make both of us uncomfortable. It occurred to me then that it had been years since I had been touched by another human being who wasn't under the direct auspices of a Hippocratic oath. "What's going to happen next is that you must visit your grandmother," I decided.

"I can't right now." Her eyes, meeting mine, flashed with sudden panic. "I have to wait. I have to wait until she tells me to come. I'm not just gonna barge down there."

She was afraid. Of course, she was afraid. "Well, when you're ready to go, you must go," I said. "And if you can't pay for it, I will." The words were sprung from my lips before I even realized what I was offering. For heaven's sake, she wasn't even one of my great-granddaughters. But, then, why not spend the money?

"What about your memoir?" she asked, and when I hesitated, she added, "I think we should keep going. And when we're done, you should give it to Dave. It could be your apology."

Tears filled my eyes, threatening to spill over. "Some things . . . aren't worthy of forgiveness."

"That's not true. I'd forgive you," she said.

Somehow, I managed to swallow. And then I did reach over and squeeze her hand.

ONCE ELYSE WAS GONE, I CONTINUED TO MULL OVER THE EVENTS of the evening, as I paced around trying not to vomit. After polishing off the kugel I'd suddenly felt ill, with niggling abdominal pain, cold sweats, and intractable swallowing. But I still didn't expect to vomit, considering I'd nearly conditioned myself to suppress the reflex, the way I'd trained my inner ear to keep me upright even when I was spinning through the air. And yet, as I staggered to the toilet and flipped up the lid, it occurred to me that only a few weeks before my bed had shaken and my building had swayed because of an *earthquake* in *Pittsburgh,* which hadn't seemed likely then, either. Woozy, I leaned over and waited for the earthquake inside me to pass.

Here was what I would've liked to explain to Elyse over tea: that while I never set out to change religions, something curious happened to me once I had. When your family has decided that they never want to speak to you again, suddenly the idea that someone could love you no matter what you've done, no matter how you've let them down . . . Well, it moved me. And later, when you wonder if you're being punished for not honoring your parents, since your own babies won't honor you with the gift of survival, you think, *Is this God smiting me with what I deserved?* But no, it's not a punishment, you decide, it's life, and the only way to get through it, the only way to hold on, is to believe, and believe, and believe again.

Once the war was over, while other Jews were working hard to preserve our heritage here in the States, I still wasn't brave enough to claim my own history. I wish I'd been braver. I wish I hadn't let my sister down. I wish I never let that little girl go.

A sudden spasm gripped my belly, before I retched again and again, until at last the pain was gone. After mopping my face on a cold rag, I flushed the toilet and then made my way back to my bed. *That's better,* I thought with a sigh. *Not quite as awful as I remembered.*

PART 2

CHAPTER 12

The First Day of the Rest of Your Life

April 1944

It's astonishing how quickly life has fallen into a routine: up with the sun and out into the wind, line up for breakfast by the flag, then lecture all morning. After ground school and lunch, we report to the flight line, and I don't see my bed again until after dinner, sometimes not until eight in the evening. By then I'm almost too tired to shower, but my back is aching from carrying around a thirty-pound parachute all day so the hot water—when there is hot water—feels divine. The weekends are for recovery, for walking instead of marching, for Ping-Pong in the mess tent. This particular Saturday, I'm playing as if the war—or maybe just my sister's life—depends on it.

Just two weeks after I'd gotten here, a letter arrived from home:

Dear Miri,

They are sending me away for a little while, just until I am well enough to come back home. I've lost a bit of weight, which makes Mama say, Eat, eat, eat, all the more. I am trying to eat, when I can catch my breath. The doctor and nurses at the TB sanatorium are very nice, and at the very least, I'll be able to rest between the treatments. Still, I can't bear leaving Rita, my clinging koala-bear, my remora-fish, who can grab hold of me and never let go. Mother thinks she's my other half. Why do I love her so much? Because she's my flesh and blood, or because she could be a better me? Oh, I could cry for a while. But it's not just Rita; it's this place, so desolate that it lends itself to tears. Is this really my home for the next however many months? I'm so lonely. Have I ever been lonely before? I'm beginning to associate it with the heat. Each morning that I wake up the room is filled with this sultry fog, and it makes me feel like I'll never get to the other side of the day. Crazy that there was a time when we were all crammed into the little house, you and me and Papa and Mama and Aunt Rebekah and Uncle Hyman and Bubbe, and I read A Room of One's Own *and wanted nothing more than the chance to be lonely. Now it's painfully clear that loneliness and being alone are completely different.*

Oh, Rita. You never knew that when you were born, you would walk around with my heart inside you. You couldn't feel it the first day when I left you off at school, as I watched you tottering up the stairs, praying like crazy that G-d would keep us safe—you, and the part of me inside you. And you can't feel it now either, when I'm so far away.

*Keep sending me your stories, Miri. I love to think of you
in the air, flying high for both of us.*

Oceans of Love,
Sarah

The same day the letter arrived, I ate lunch in the mess hall
across from Grace from Iowa—or "Corn," as Murphee likes to
call her—and told her I may have to leave. She set down her
forkful of powdered eggs and stared at me, eating my biscuit. It
was so hard to swallow the mixture of carbohydrate and grief
lodged somewhere between my mouth and stomach.

"Even if you were at home, there's nothing you could do,"
Grace said, which wasn't quite true, when Rita needed to be
tended to.

"What if Teddy were in the hospital?" I asked, meaning
Grace's fiancé, who'd shipped off with the army four months
ago. "Wouldn't you leave?"

"Teddy wouldn't want me to. He'd tell me to stay."

I thought of Sarah. *Now is not the time to doubt.* If I quit the
program, she'd be the one feeling guilty—or worse, furious
with me. "So, I'm not a horrible person?" I asked, my voice
meek.

"Well, let's not go that far. You *did* want to kill off your
uncle," Grace said.

I broke off a piece of my biscuit and threw it at her.

SINCE THEN, I'VE BEEN TRYING TO WORK EVEN HARDER THAN
before. I skipped a night out at the Blue Bonnet with the girls
from the bunk, and a dance in a neighboring town, which Mur-

phee guaranteed would have loads of "handsome cadets." I'm not sure if I'm trying to turn myself into a supreme pilot or merely punish myself for being a bad daughter for not being there.

Grace, at least, is content to stay in with me—even if it means playing Ping-Pong on a Saturday night.

The ball hits the table inbounds and whooshes by Grace's shoulder. "Yes! Ha!" I scream and watch the confusion settling onto her face, watch as she lowers her paddle and salutes with the opposite hand. I glance back and realize there's a uniformed cadet standing next to me and that—*darn!*—this may mean a do-over.

"Miriam Lichtenstein?" the cadet says, after I quickly salute. "Jackie Cochran wants to see you in her office."

My heart revs up like a propeller starting, and my ears start to ring. *Sarah,* I think.

I swallow and nod, even manage to smile for Grace, who looks utterly worried, as if the cadet just handed me a pink slip. *No one gets a private meeting with Jackie Cochran when they wash out,* I tell her with my eyes, but she knows this, too; she knows it's a telegram from home.

I'VE BEEN IN SWEETWATER, TEXAS, FOR FIVE WEEKS, AND EVEN though the reason I am here in the first place—flying as a civilian under the auspices of the military—is almost entirely this exceptional woman's vision, I've never actually seen Jackie Cochran up close. As soon as we're face-to-face in her office—she, red-lipsticked and blond-bobbed; me, hair-matted and ragtagged—I can understand why she's known as the "blond bombshell," and why I've never had a man so much as look in my direction—Tzadok not withstanding.

"Miriam Lichtenstein? Oh, good," she says, dismissing the cadet and gesturing for me to take the seat across from her desk.

"Is everything all right?" I ask, my heart banging away in my chest. It's highly possible that I will actually pass out on the floor in front of my aviator idol.

"Everything's fine. Relax, relax. I was just reviewing your file. Mr. Hendricks writes that you're an exceptional pilot . . ." Ms. Cochran says, referring to my flight instructor, who told me not to salute when we met. "Put your hand down, Miss Lichtenstein, I'm a civilian like you."

"And Captain Digby says you passed your first check ride," she adds, referring to that first harrowing military test required after logging twenty hours in the air—where, after grading my takeoff, my spins and stalls, loops and chandelle, Captain Digby reached under the instrument panel and turned off the gas six times during the flight just to see how I would react. It was a test of alertness, I later learned, to see if I'd panic when the engine quit. Six times in a row, I simply turned the gas back on.

"They must've taught you well back in Pittsburgh." Ms. Cochran folds her hands on her desk and leans forward as if conspiratorially. "Tell me, Miss Lichtenstein, are you happy here?"

My eyebrows are knit together, as if I'm standing in front of a blackboard filled with differential equations. "I—of course. I'm always happy when I'm flying." *When is she going to show me the telegram?*

"Many of the women like to go off the base on the weekend. Go to church or to a dance or to dinner," Ms. Cochran says.

"Yes, ma'am," I say, wondering if she thinks I was part of Murphee Sutherland's group who didn't make curfew last Saturday night. Does she expect me to rat them out? *Is there even a telegram?*

"But not you," she says. "You're Jewish." I cock my head to the side, even more confused. "Miss Lichtenstein, it's been brought to my attention that there isn't much of a Jewish community in Sweetwater. In fact, there isn't even a synagogue."

"Oh?" I ask, shifting in my seat. Did Mama find out about my Friday night flights and make some calls?

"We may be in the Bible Belt of America, but there's no reason you shouldn't be able to worship as you please," says Jackie Cochran. "Your flight instructor, Mr. Hendricks, has a family friend in Abilene who has offered to take you to services next Friday."

I blink, bewildered and even a bit guilty. I've been too exhausted to pray lately, just these pitiful little petitions whenever I toss a coin into the wishing well and kiss my Star of David on my way to the airfield. *Please don't let me wash out. Please let Sarah be okay.* I haven't let myself think about Shabbat or the synagogue, because it'll only remind me of everything else I'm missing, too. "Abilene?" I say instead.

"It's forty miles away. They'll be expecting you for dinner and evening services."

The phone on her desk rings and she quickly picks it up. "Jackie Cochran."

I sit there, uncertain, until she catches my eye and waves at me to go. "Just a minute," I hear her say when I'm at the door. When I glance back she is covering the mouthpiece of the phone. "And Miss Lichtenstein, don't forget—you'll be representing your country when you go. Make an effort." By this I assume she means, *Wear some lipstick.*

A WEEK LATER MY FLIGHT INSTRUCTOR PICKS ME UP ON BASE IN his old Ford for the ride across the prairie. Mr. Hendricks has blondish hair and a boyish-shaped face for someone so old— thirty, I think. With his combination of flight skills and congeniality, it would be easy to fall under the spell of romance, if I were silly enough to be prone to crushes. When I apologize for taking him so far out of his way, Mr. Hendricks tells me he's a local boy, born and raised in Abilene. "The army training site at Camp Barkley is the best thing that ever happened to the economy in this town," he says, and I stifle a yawn, thinking that Mr. Hendricks—like most aspects of my life—is more fascinating up in the air. "They even built a new synagogue to accommodate everyone. Probably see a bunch of cadets there," he adds, and I glance over, a tiny bit interested.

EVENTUALLY WE PULL OFF THE HIGHWAY AND STOP NEXT TO A shop on the main drag of town: Rubinowicz's Pharmacy. There's a SORRY WE'RE CLOSED sign in the window. Outside, a dark-haired man in a suit and yarmulke stands smoking a pipe in a patch of grass that needs to be mowed. The sight of him looking like the elders of my childhood temple suddenly makes me miss everything I've left behind: Pittsburgh, my family, even my religion. I think of my father, who held my hand in the backyard when we stood in a cloud, and a tear—so unexpected that I think it's been caused by West Texas dust—pricks the corner of my eyes. But no: it's him, this man. I can imagine Papa sharing a smoke with him and asking for his advice.

When we first got to Pittsburgh, Papa sought quite a bit of counsel from the rabbi, about which I could only guess. He never liked the city, or being beholden to his stepbrother, but he did grow to love the rituals of our new community. "Your mother was right, Miriush," he told me one day, as we walked hand in hand down Murray Avenue toward Beth Shalom.

"Right about what?" I asked, quickening my stride to keep up: two of my small steps equaled one of my father's.

"About everything. She's right about everything. Remember that," he added with a wink.

And maybe Mama *is* right, I think now: maybe I do need a community beyond the women in my bunk. Maybe the only way to practice my faith is to be surrounded by others doing the same. I climb out of the passenger side and smile at the man, who squints with each puff. When he notices me, he lowers the pipe and waves.

"Mr. Rubinowicz, this is Miriam Lichtenstein, the pilot I was telling you about," my instructor says to the man.

"I see, I see—welcome," he says with an accent—Eastern European rather than Texan. I watch as the two men shake hands. "How is your father, Stephen?" Before Mr. Hendricks can answer, Mr. Rubinowicz says, "Go inside, my dear. Sol's in there." I must look confused because he adds, "My son, Solomon—he's just finishing up. Then we'll walk to services." I hesitate but he says, "Go on, go on."

I enter the shop with a jangle of bells. The place reminds me of the pharmacy on Murray Avenue back home, only smaller.

There are bins of candy at the front, swivel stools, an ice cream counter, a soda fountain, aisles of canned foods, and, of course, medicines. Just as I'm gingerly stepping toward the one, lit aisle, I see him: a blond, bespectacled young man in a yarmulke inspecting each bottle of medicine before displaying it on the shelf. Then he glances up, and our eyes meet, and he smiles—a huge, broad grin that makes me look behind and check that it's actually for me. *It must be the uniform,* I decide: air force–issued, Neiman Marcus–designed, wool gabardine with a little black tie and matching beret. It would make anyone who wanted to win the war smile. But then he takes a step toward me, crashing into a couple of boxes on the floor, and I think, *No, it's the lipstick.*

"You must be the pilot," he says, hand outstretched.

"Miriam," I say, moving toward him before he trips again.

"Sol," he says. We shake and smile and let go.

"Ah, look," Mr. Rubinowicz says, entering the store. "You found each other."

A few minutes later when we file out, Sol holds open the door for me; I look up to thank him and notice he's still blushing.

WE HEAD TO SERVICES AT TEMPLE MITZPAH, WHERE I SPEND AN hour wedged between Sol's mother, a big-bosomed woman in a belted housedress, and his little sister Hannah, who is all of about twelve. I can actually see Sol across the synagogue but don't even glance in his direction for fear the cantor will see that I am only intermittently paying attention. I should be praying for Sarah, but all I can think about is him, and how we walked here together, side by side, behind his father, as the cirrus clouds painted the sky in ribbons of darkness. Every now and then the backs of our hands would accidentally touch, which was both thrilling and terrifying.

Afterward, the Shabbos meal is served at their house, a tiny ranch with a front porch shrouded by mesquite trees. There's gefelte fish and grilled salmon and rice, all prepared by Sol's mother. Next to Hannah sits "Uncle Leo" a recent émigré of my grandparents' generation, I decide, noticing his white hair and the brown spots on his wrinkled hand when he waves. When they seat me next to Sol at the table, I can't help wishing there were a *mechitza* hanging between us. It's hard to concentrate when my heart is so full of questions: *How old is he? What does he like to read? What are his dreams? How on earth did he end up in Texas?*

"*Amain,*" I say belatedly, when Mr. Rubinowicz has finished the blessing over the wine, and everyone has begun eating.

"Where are you from, my dear?" Uncle Leo asks from across the table. His spectacles have a line etched into the glass right across horizon, cutting his view of the world in two.

When I tell him Pittsburgh, his eyebrows furrow and he holds a hand up to his ear until I repeat myself, louder. "Steel," he says, triumphant, and I smile, thinking of Murphee's nickname for me. With Sol to my right, I am anything but Pittsburgh steel; I am palpitating and flushing, liquid and limp.

"And you?" I ask him and in the same moment imagine my mother scolding me: *We don't ask people with accents where they've come from, Miriam. Especially when they most certainly have escaped.*

"Odessa," he says, the corners of his mouth drawing down,

and as I'm trying to dazzle the old man by recalling the primary export of Odessa, all at once I remember something about the massacre of Jews in the overtaken Ukrainian city just a few years back—Sarah had read me disturbing excerpts from the article in the Jewish paper, and I'd begged her not to go on. Now I can't help wondering if he made it out beforehand, or if he lost loved ones.

"So, this 'women's air force,' " Mr. Rubinowicz suddenly says, gesturing with his fork, and I wonder if he's deliberately changing the subject. "What exactly are they training you for?"

"Moving airplanes and ships to different bases—"

"How do you move a ship?" Sol asks, his voice incredulous.

"It's attached by a cable to the bottom of the plane," I say, and his eyes widen. "Or we'll be trailing targets for the cadets to fire at for practice . . ."

"Holy moly," Sol says, impressed, and I flush.

"We read about the crashes in the paper," Mr. Rubinowicz says, as his wife spoons more kugel onto Hannah's plate. "Don't these girls know what they're doing up there?" he adds.

"They're guinea pigs!" Mrs. Rubinowicz erupts. "They fly planes the men are too afraid to try."

"We're going through the same program the male cadets go through, except for gunnery. There haven't been any accidents since I've been here." *Not counting Ana,* I think, who got ejected during a spin recovery when the floppy sleeve of her coveralls caught on the seat belt lever, unbuckling it and sending her flying. Luckily, she pulled her parachute cord and landed in a field, five miles off base. *I wish I'd had my camera,* she said of her descent. "I just want to fly. There's really . . . no other way."

"But this is all only temporary," Mr. Rubinowicz says. "Until the war ends."

"Not necessarily," I say. "General Arnold just introduced a bill in the Senate to make us part of the air force officially. We're going to be part of the military. It's what they're preparing us for."

"The military?" Uncle Leo repeats, the natural timber of his voice quaking, unless that's disbelief. "Why should a woman volunteer for the service?"

"She wants to fly, Uncle Leo!" Mrs. Rubinowicz enunciates and shouts. "Solomon wanted to fly, too, but they won't take him," she says, looking at me now. "Not with his heart like it is."

"My heart's fine," Sol says.

"What's it like?" Hannah asks me, and I like her for her quiet shyness. She reminds me of my niece, Rita.

"We march a lot," I say to her, and she giggles.

"The food must be terrible," Mrs. Rubinowicz says.

"No, it's really delicious," I say and then regret it, knowing what her next question will be.

"Kosher?"

I think about my answer for too long before half-nodding, half-shrugging. The truth is, I haven't tasted gefelte fish in months, and I haven't missed it a bit.

"So, what does your family think about this?" Mr. Rubinowicz asks.

"They think—" I stop abruptly. "Well, my sister, Sarah . . ." The kugel sticks in my throat, mid-swallow, when it spasms. My eyes tear up, and I cough and cough. Sol's parents look up, vaguely alarmed, and then glance at each other.

"Water! Get her some water," Mr. Rubinowicz snaps.

I shake my head and wave at Sol to sit down, but he's already gone. There's a clang of glassware, a rush of water, and then a glass is banged down on the table in front of me with a small splash. I've stopped choking by now, but I drink quickly to be polite. "I'm sorry . . ." I clear my throat. "My sister was just diagnosed with TB. She's quite sick."

There's a brief pause, a drop of concerned eyebrows and shuddering shoulders, and then Sol speaks: "They're close to a cure, you know." I look at him gratefully. It feels like such a relief—both the words that he's saying, and that I'm actually allowed to make eye contact. "Streptomycin. They discovered it last year at Rutgers University. They're trying to get approval to do a study with actual patients."

"Solomon wants to be a doctor, but he can't get in," Mrs. Rubinowicz says. "Which is a great mystery, because his father and I have met plenty of idiots who are doctors."

"Thanks, Ma. Inspiring words," Sol says.

"It's the Jewish quota. They only let in a few every year," Mr. Rubinowicz explains. "He can't get rid of the *H* for 'Hebrew' on his application."

"That's how it starts," Uncle Leo barks, so maybe his hearing is not so bad after all. "First the quotas, then your basic human rights, then your *home*. It's difficult to be a concert pianist without a piano," he adds, looking at me, and I nod, big-eyed and solemn.

"Sol's trying for the last time," his father goes on, "and if they don't let him in this fall, he has some important decisions to be making."

"Right, Pop. I know." Sol puts his napkin down on the table.

"Classes start in August," Mr. Rubinowicz says, peering at

his gold pocket watch as if it were a calendar. "If they wanted him, he should've heard by now."

"What time is curfew on base?" Sol asks with a noisy exhale, and I realize belatedly he's talking to me.

"Ten o'clock."

"How will you get back?" he asks, and I feel my face heating up again.

"Oh, I think—Mr. Hendricks is coming for me," I say.

"I can't leave the shop to anyone," his father goes on. "Sol handles everything. All the purchasing. All the books. What's gonna happen when I go?"

"Frank, leave him," his mother says.

"The United States may look very different by then," Uncle Leo says. "Who knows what's going to happen to any of us?"

"You have a point, Leo." Mr. Rubinowicz sighs and leans back in his chair, finally looking at me with such kindness in his brown eyes, I am once again reminded of Papa. "Miriam, is this too much trouble? Coming all the way to Abilene for Shabbos with us?"

"Not at all," I say, glancing around the table, at everyone except for Sol, because I can't stop blushing. "It was a really wonderful meal."

"She'll come back," Mrs. Rubinowicz says, a verdict.

"Maybe next time you don't wear the uniform," Mr. Rubinowicz adds.

LATER, HANNAH SHYLY TAKES MY HAND AND LEADS ME INTO the backyard to show me "Papa's Tree of Life." I blink at the green branches, laden with inexplicable, tiny melons and watch as Mr. Rubinowicz reaches up and cuts one down with a sly wink, instead of waiting for it to fall.

I look at the fruit in his hand then back up at his face.

"Mango," he explains. "I've been cultivating this little tree for years. Every time I thought it was dead, it came back to life."

We take it back inside and I peel and eat my first mango— eat it all the way down to its core. It is, by far, the most delicious piece of fruit I've had since the war began—the most delicious piece of fruit in possibly my entire life, which reminds me of Papa and his vegetable cart. "You should sell this," I say, mango juices still dripping down my face, while, in the front room, Uncle Leo plays the piano in a rapid tinkling of high notes that reminds me of soft rain coming across the blueberry fields, punctuated by booming chords that sound like soldiers storming a concert hall. He plays and plays as if he's making a desperate plea, and Mr. Rubinowicz only replies, "I can't sell a miracle."

IT'S DARK AND DRIZZLY WHEN MR. HENDRICKS DRIVES ME BACK to base. "It must've felt good to finally get a chance to worship," he says. "And they're such a nice family—the Rubinowiczes."

It's so strange, the things I never cared about, silly things like kissing. *Who needs it?* I always thought. There's Sarah, falling in love with a starving actor, and here's Grace, who worries sick if she hasn't heard from Teddy in a few weeks, because who knows what's happening on the shores of France, and just when I am one hundred percent certain that I never want to clutter my mind with anything but avionics, I am suddenly equally certain that I want to be kissed. I want long, I want slow, I want fingers in my hair.

"Yes," I finally agree, after a moment of silence, save the slap of the windshield wipers, back and forth. "Nice family."

CHAPTER 13

The Marriage Project

Tuesday morning at breakfast, as Mom was frantically slapping peanut butter on slices of bread for all of our lunches, Toby asked her what the deal was with Dad. She stopped for just a second as if debating whether to lie and say he had an early morning surgery. "We heard him leave last night," I added, when Toby glanced at me.

"Dad's fine," Mom said, squirting some jelly onto each open sandwich. "He just wants to spend some time by himself, thinking about things."

"Thinking about what things?" Toby asked levelly, but Mom reminded him he was about to miss his bus. "Why didn't Daddy say goodbye to us?" he added.

"It was late, and he thought you were asleep." Then she scooped up Toby's cereal bowl, even though he wasn't quite finished. "I have a deposition today, so no one can miss the bus. *Hugh Strickler? Where are you?*" she added in a piercing shout, just as my baby brother appeared from the living room holding up his Lego creation, some sort of half-car, half-boat, equipped with missiles on the side.

"It's the Generator Sixteen Thousand Thirteen. Can I take a bath with it?" Huggie asked, which made Mom start shrieking again about getting dressed for kindergarten.

I waited until the boys were gone to ask her where Daddy went when he left to go "think about things."

"Daddy is staying in the very nice apartment that he decided to rent while I was in Key West—it's fully furnished," Mom added, like I'd been worried he was using milk crates for chairs. I hoped that didn't mean Natalia was staying there, too. "He'll be back, but in the meantime, I'd really prefer that no one in the community know about this yet. We're still trying to reconcile the situation. Oh, and Elyse? Can you clear your dishes, please?"

I sighed and picked up my bowl and carried it to the sink.

The thing is, when I thought about who I wanted to call about Daddy leaving, it wasn't Grandma, because I didn't want to worry Grandma when she was sick. And it wasn't Aunt Andie, because Aunt Andie was the last person Mom would want to know. I did think of calling Thea, but Thea had been acting weird with me ever since I got paired up with Holden for the marriage project. Just as Mom was saying, "It's really no one's business that Daddy is gone," I knew I would tell Mrs. Browning. She was like a safety deposit box for secrets.

But just as I was planning on getting dropped off at the library before six and then sneaking over to Mrs. Browning's high-rise, Mom asked me if I could babysit after school, since she would have to work late and Daddy wouldn't be here to watch Toby and Huggie. "I have my writers' group tonight," I said.

"Please don't do this to me," Mom said, which really pissed me off, even though her voice was kind of quaky when she said it. I wanted to tell her that *I'm* not the one who wants to spend some time apart and maybe have sex with other people. But it seemed better to lie and say that I had handed out my next chapter for critique and that everyone was counting on me to be there so they could discuss it. We were actually discussing Gene Rosskemp's story about being a captain of the truck brigade in World War II. You wouldn't expect it from a man like Gene, who swears like crazy and makes such stupid puns with an exaggerated wink in case you missed it, but he actually wrote an amazing story about rescuing a truckload of wine during the Nazi occupation of Paris.

Mom sighed. "Never mind. I'll figure something out."

LATER THAT MORNING, I WAS STANDING IN THE SCHOOL LOBBY waiting to file onto the field trip bus with the rest of Mrs. Kindling's English class and thumbing through emails on my phone when I looked up and saw Thea, who was weaving her way through the crowd. Her face contorted in surprise or repulsion, it was hard to tell which.

"Hey, thanks for the ride," I said, meaning later on—from writers' group. After Mom's mini-meltdown, I'd texted Thea from the bus about picking me up from the Squirrel Hill library that night.

"What the hell are you wearing?" Thea asked, nearing me. A couple of kids turned to look. If they hadn't already noticed my new skinny jeans, they were now.

I could feel my face getting hot. "Just . . . clothes."

"You so look weird," she said.

"Well, that's nothing new, right?" I said, and Thea still didn't smile.

"We're partners for the toothpick bridge, right?" she asked. "Because I heard Holden telling one of his dick friends that you were his partner."

"Well, he did kind of ask me, and it's not like we started yet—"

"But we did start!" she said. "We started when we planned to be partners! You can't just go switching now, when it's due in three weeks."

Mrs. Kindling started shouting at us to form a line for the buses. We were on our way to see *Our Town,* the play by Thornton Wilder that we'd read earlier in the year.

"You know he's going to want you to build it for him, right?" Thea said, backing away from me. "While you're blowing him."

"Well, that would be difficult . . ."

"Maybe you can have a threesome with Karina Spencer—now that you're twins."

"Thea—" I started, but she was already gone.

After the buses pulled up at the Public Theatre, we filed off two by two. I was worried I'd end up stuck next to Carson Jeffries until the AP class mixed with the regular English classes in the lobby, and suddenly Holden and I were side by side, which made it easier to forget about the fight with Thea. Inside the theater, he let me go into the row first, and then he sat down next to me—he even stayed there after some of his lacrosse buddies were waving at him to move down where they were sitting. "This is my wife," he called, pointing at me, and I tilted my head back and laughed so loudly that one of the parent chaperones turned around and glared at me. Then the lights dimmed, and the actors brought out two tables and a couple of chairs and started miming their morning rituals as the Stage Manager explained them, and Holden leaned over and whispered, "Is that supposed to be the set?" and "Where're the props?" which made me so giddy that for the whole first act, I could barely do anything but contain my spasms of laughter.

Even after the intermission, when he might've found his way to a new seat, Holden stayed by me. He smelled good, too, like maybe he was wearing his father's cologne or a really spicy, masculine deodorant. Somewhere, during Act II, Holden kind of shifted in his seat and straddled his legs a little, and I must've been sitting funny instead of crossing my own, because suddenly we were touching, calf to calf. My face heated up, but I didn't pull my leg away; I just stared straight ahead and pretended I couldn't feel the pressure of Holden Saunders's jeaned calf against my own. Onstage, the actors were pretending to slog through the rain and mud on Emily and George's wedding day, and all I could think about was that we were finally, finally touching.

When I'd read the play by myself for school, alone in my pink bedroom, the end had actually made me tear up, and I wasn't even sure why except that when Emily wants her mother to stop and look at her—to realize that nothing bad has happened yet, and they don't even know it—a terrible sadness welled up in me when I imagined the future, terrifying and tragic, unfolding without my control. But in the theater, when the cast took their seats and stared straight ahead, expressionless, and Holden whispered in my ear, "Are they supposed to be dead?" my shoulders shook with silent laughter. The Stage Manager was saying, "We all know that *something* is eternal. And it ain't houses and it ain't names, and it ain't earth, and it ain't even the stars . . ." and I suddenly thought of Grandma, inexplicably suffering so far away, and of Daddy, moving out without saying goodbye, and laughing-tears kept squeezing out of my face, until I realized I was actually crying. Luckily, a few minutes later, when George collapsed, weeping at Emily's feet, Holden pointed out that the actor had a big string of snot coming out of his nose, and then my grief turned back into giddiness again.

After school, I asked Holden if he could drop me off at the Squirrel Hill library for writers' group. I couldn't go home, because even if Mom had found another babysitter, she probably wasn't authorized to drive me across town to the library right at dinnertime. Holden shut the door to his locker and glanced down the hall. "Um, sure," he said, and I followed his gaze behind me, where Karina Spencer was rummaging through her own locker. I wondered if it was true that they'd broken up.

"We're getting issued our flour baby on Monday," I said. "So . . . that'll be interesting. I guess we have to keep it 'alive' for two weeks?"

"Uh huh." He zipped up his letterman's jacket, still staring somewhere over my left shoulder. When I glanced back at Karina again, she looked me up and down before slamming her locker door shut. Then she flipped her curly hair over her shoulder and walked away in the direction of the gym, where the cheerleaders were warming up.

I felt like the emperor in his new clothes.

AFTER HOLDEN DROPPED ME OFF, I ENDED UP ACROSS THE STREET from the library in Panera with two and a half hours to kill before the meeting, so I bought a bagel and some coffee—which I'm actually not allowed to drink until I'm eighteen, according to Mom—fit the headphone jack into Mrs. Browning's Dictaphone, and pressed PLAY. She'd let me take her laptop with her last time so that I could keep working on it, since typing each sentence took forever.

Just as Mary was arriving in Abilene to meet Sol for the first time, Mom called, but I didn't answer it. Instead I texted Thea and asked her if she was still coming to pick me up outside the library at eight thirty. She texted back: "Ask Holden." I groaned. He'd actually already told me he had a student government meeting that night. "I told him we need to talk," I wrote instead and then went back to typing. Fifteen minutes went by without a message except from Mom: "Where are you?" Suddenly, it was three minutes after seven, so I silenced my phone, quickly gathered up my trash, and reloaded my backpack. Outside, the clouds were hanging low and gray, and I rushed across the street, uneasy about Toby and Huggie, just because Toby always gets headaches on cloudy Tuesdays, and Huggie was upset last week because he'd accidentally wet the floor during rest time at kindergarten. But then I felt mad at Mom for always making me feel like another mother, so I ran up the steps of the library two at a time instead of calling home. I hoped Mrs. Browning wasn't going to be upset that I was six minutes late. She never specifically talked about the importance of punctuality, but she didn't have to. Whenever somebody straggled in after seven o'clock—usually Gene Rosskemp—she'd just pull down her cat lady glasses and give him a look.

But when I got inside the conference room, the group was already assembled around the long table and two plastic chairs were empty, one for me and one for Mrs. Browning. I slipped into the seat next to Selena Markmann and whispered after a couple of minutes, "Where's Mrs. Browning?"

"The hospital," Selena said in a normal voice, even though Herb Shepherd was in the middle of announcements. "They took her by ambulance last night. I saw the paramedics taking her away on a stretcher."

"Did she . . . seem okay?" I don't know what I expected, except maybe something like at a football game, when the sacked quarterback waves as he's carried off to get his head scanned. But Mrs. Markmann only gave me a palms-up shrug, like, *Who knows?* I spent the rest of the hour wondering what had happened to Mrs. Browning and how I could find out. I wondered if I could visit her, or where they took her, or if her son Dave had been called in from Seattle. It seemed hard to believe this was the same glorious day that Holden and I finally touched, but then I thought of dead Mrs. Soames from *Our Town* saying, "My wasn't life awful . . . and wonderful."

Just in case Thea was going to park and walk in to scope out any cute guys in the writers' group, I left a few minutes early to stand outside the library. I kept getting a weird, fluttery feeling inside every time I worried that she wouldn't show up at all, but I shouldn't have fretted, because I'd only been standing there for a few minutes when her dad's Subaru station wagon appeared in the line of traffic snaking down Murray Avenue. He'd probably insisted on coming, too, since it was already dark. I liked Dr. Palmer, a radiologist who worked with

Aunt Andie at Magee Women's Hospital—I secretly wished that they'd end up together.

When Thea finally reached the curb and parallel parked like a pro, I quickly opened the back door and hopped in. "Hi, Elyse," said Dr. Palmer from the front. Mid-tug on the seatbelt, I paused, realizing that he was in the driver's seat, and Thea wasn't even in the car.

"Thea says to tell you she's busy." Dr. Palmer swiveled around and added, "All buckled?" and then waited until my seat belt made a reassuring click before facing forward again, leaving me staring at the bald spot on the back of his head.

"Is she working tonight?" I asked. Thea had a job at the movie theater, saving money for tattoos, but I already knew the answer to that.

"No. No, she's not. She just . . . wouldn't come. Which is too bad because I was looking forward to riding over here with her. Q-T time, right?" He put on his blinker and inched the car forward to ease back into traffic.

If Thea were here, she would've rolled her eyes and snorted: "That's redundant. Quality time time?"

"Right," I said, and then, in a quiet mumble, "Thank you for picking me up anyway."

"Well, I told her we couldn't leave you stranded in the city after dark. Getting ready for the toothpick bridge?" he added, and our eyes met in the rearview mirror.

"Oh, um, yeah . . ." I trailed off. And then, because I couldn't stand the silence any longer, I said, "Sorry you're missing *Be My Next Wife*. I think Stacey's going to get a garter tonight."

Dr. Palmer winced and jerked his head back, as if I had shot him at close range.

WHEN I GOT HOME, THE HOUSE WAS EERILY DARK, EXCEPT FOR IN the kitchen, where Mom was wiping down the stove by a single light. She didn't turn around even after I said hello. I thought about asking if Toby got a migraine or if Huggie stayed dry during naptime, but instead I leaned against the kitchen island and asked her how the deposition went.

"It didn't," she said, scrubbing even harder. "I couldn't get a sitter, so I had to leave work early."

"I'm sorry, Mom."

"How did Daddy seem?" she asked finally, which confused me for a second until I realized she must've thought Daddy brought me home from writers' group. When I told her Thea's dad came and got me, Mom whirled around. "You asked Gordon Palmer to pick you up?"

"Well, no, I asked Thea, but she's only got her provisional license and he doesn't like her to drive after dark."

"How could you do that to me?" Mom erupted, throwing the sponge into the sink.

"Do . . . what to you?"

"Embarrass me by asking your friend's father to go a half hour out of his way rather than calling your own father, who could have easily—"

"I didn't know I could call Daddy! I thought he was . . . *thinking*! And I saw Thea, so I thought I'd ask—"

"At the group? Thea's in the writers' group now?"

"Yes," I said with a sigh, deciding it was easier to lie. "He was picking both of us up."

Mom exhaled and told me that the reason she'd given me a cell phone was for emergencies, that I couldn't just turn it off and not let her know where I was. Then she turned around again to start rinsing a pot this time.

"Why did Daddy leave?" I asked her back.

"Your father thinks he's unhappy."

I thought of all the times Mom said that Aunt Andie only thought she was happy. "Well, if he says he's unhappy, but he's not unhappy, what is he?"

Mom sighed. "A fucking idiot."

I went upstairs to my room feeling antsy and worried— about my mom, about Daddy, about Grandma, and maybe even about me. I tried to call Mrs. Browning, but of course there was no answer at her apartment. Then, because I wanted to find her, I decided to turn on my computer and Google her. I don't know what I was thinking—like maybe she'd pop up with a blue GPS ball, blinking her hospital location? But her name was right there on Amazon, Mary Browning, the author of *Miss Bixby Takes a Wife*. The used book was selling for ninety-nine cents and the condition was listed as pretty good. If I had a credit card I would have bought it. Instead, I closed out the window, which is when I saw "survived by . . ." in another link, so I clicked again, which led me to an obituary from the *Seattle Times*. The article was about David Browning and his wife, Caroline Browning, who were killed with their toddler, Tyler, in a head-on collision with a drunk driver on August 15, 1983. Included in the short list of whom they were survived by was *Mary Browning of Scarsdale, New York*. Out of all the Mary Brownings on Google, I knew this one was mine.

I climbed into bed and pulled the covers over my head, feeling sadder about her loss than about my own, or maybe sadder because of all of those things. It seemed silly to worry about wearing skinny jeans or not wearing skinny jeans or bridges made of toothpicks or even falling in love, when for one second you can be having a cup of tea with someone and in the next, you're alone at the table with one white cloth fluttering in the breeze. I lay awake for a long time after that waiting for what happens next.

CHAPTER 14

Steel in Love

May 1944

I'm alone in the ready room watching planes take off and waiting for Mr. Hendricks when Captain Babcock walks in, a short, stocky guy with a reputation at Cochran's Convent for failing pilots simply for the error of being women. I quickly turn back to the window, thankful I got my military check ride out of the way weeks ago and won't have to worry about him now.

"*Miz* Lichtenstein?" he asks in a slow drawl around a wad of chewing tobacco. I straighten up, startled, as he checks his clipboard and curls his top lip. "Is that a Jewish name?"

"Yes," I say, remembering Grace telling me that this man must not have been hugged as a child, and Murphee deciding that he must have a very small penis.

"German?"

"No, sir. I'm from America."

"I meant the name." He rolls his eyes and motions for me to follow.

"I thought—is Mr. Hendricks coming?" I ask, jumping up and trailing after him. I'll take any one of the civilian instructors, because the only way to get assigned a second military check ride is if you're failing out.

"We're short staffed today. Therefore *you* are assigned to *me*." As we walk out toward the field, Captain Babcock spits a mouthful of tar on the ground and adds, over his shoulder, "I'll have you know that I don't like women, and I sure as hell don't like women pilots."

This must be very hard for you to be here, I think, skipping to keep up.

Reaching the flight line, I place my chute on the left wing of the plane before going through a cursory inspection. With his hands on his hips, the captain keeps puffing out his cheeks and shaking his head, as if impatient to get a move on and fail his next victim. Quickly, I look the plane over from left to right and tip to tail.

"Ready yet?" he asks, aggravated, as I'm kneeling to check for anything leaking from the fuselage.

"Ready," I say, even though I'm not.

Once we're strapped in, the lineman comes out to prop the plane, and with one last check of the control tower, I strap my goggles on over my helmet and push the throttle slowly forward on the Stearman, the open-cockpit biplane of my childhood dreams. Propeller buzzing like a saw, and the engine vibrating the soles of my feet to the top of my spine, we bear down the runway into the red grit. Liftoff is positively graceful, the way the tail lifts and we rise through the rocking winds. The noise is deafening but reassuring—a declaration of power—as we make our way across the sky toward white islands of clouds that look like glaciers and snowbanks. Spring may have come to Texas, but at one thousand feet, it's still blustery winter. As my nose drips over my chapped lips, I can't help marveling that there's nothing but a square piece of glass separating me from all this glory.

Grading my banking and navigational skills, Captain Babcock sits behind me, and each time I take us for another round of spins and stalls, my stomach flutters like we're on a roller coaster. Then, just as I'm pulling up from a snap roll, I look out across the expanse of blue sky and see a band of approaching darkness, black dots in the distance dipping and diving, collapsing and rising like a cloud of bees. *Birds,* I realize, catching my breath as we draw closer, a great big flock, wuthering to and fro. For a moment, I'm mesmerized by their fluidity and speed, the way they travel like schools of fish in the sky. With a rush and a graceful *whoosh* they dart, en masse, down and then up and across. *If only you could see this, Papa.* When another wave of them hurtles toward us, I inhale sharply.

"Lower!" Captain Babcock orders, but he's too late—the wave of birds is crashing into us—or maybe we're crashing into them. First comes the jagged sound of the propeller chopping the air and all its inhabitants, and then wings and decapitated feathered bodies rain into the open cockpit. I duck as a crow careens toward my head, and from somewhere behind me, Babcock screams.

Adjusting my hand on the stick, I level out the horizon, which isn't so easy when my windshield is now splattered in blood. I think of flight lessons back in Pittsburgh, how I was taught to estimate the attitude of the plane simply by the sound of the engine rather than checking my instrument panel. Except there's an eerie silence, save a quick whisper of wings that swoops past my ear as the remaining flock soars off, untouched, before the whir of the propeller putters to a stop.

"We lost the engine!" I shout, turning the key, trying to get it to catch, except there's only grinding and the howl of wind streaking past the cables that hold the biplane together. "Captain Babcock?" I glance behind me, just able make out his goggles, which are covered in blood as if he's been shot in the face. "Sir? Are you . . . ? *Sir?*"

More silence passes, as a math problem forms in my head: *If a man is traveling at one hundred and twenty miles per hour going east, and he's struck by a one pound bird going west . . .* A noise escapes my chest, something between a laugh and a gasp—Is Captain Babcock *dead?* Then I remember the engine definitely is. I can't hesitate just because my plane now happens to be a glider. To our right, there's the dusty prairie, and above, the looming cloud islands, but how am I going to get us all the way back to Avenger without an engine? *Aviate, communicate, and navigate,* I remind myself. *A cornfield will do.*

After radioing back to base, I check the straps on my parachute and start looking. At least the dust has settled, and the sky is calm, as gravity takes us lower, two hundred feet, then another hundred more. Peering over the side, I spy the perfect field, except that we're too high for the approach, so I jam my foot on the right rudder pedal, which yaws the nose to the right and sends us banking to the left, creating the drag we need to descend.

"What the hell are you doing?" a sudden voice barks from

behind—concussed Captain Babcock, returning to consciousness.

"Landing the plane, sir," I say, trying not to think of the feathered carnage at my feet.

"Start the engine!" he orders.

"It's dead, sir."

This is just a complex work equation, I tell myself as we dip lower still, thinking of ground school. Gravity is the force, wind our displacement, and it's up to me to solve for the angle between the two vectors. All I need to do is stay in control, to hit the ground at a forty-five-degree angle while avoiding that water tower, and those power lines, and this tractor . . . It's physics and luck now.

When we hit the field moments later, the Stearman bounces and rolls on the wheels, flattening knee-high stalks of corn. I clamp my feet on the brakes, and we come to a controlled stop not far from a blue-jeaned man, whose straw sticks to his gaping mouth. I let go of the stick and exhale, my heart still flying in my chest. Behind me, Captain Babcock groans as he unhooks his seat belt and stands up, swaying. Meanwhile, the farmer clutches his shovel in the middle with two hands, like a tightrope walker steadying himself with a balance stick. "Hoe-Lee shit," his lips are saying.

Captain Babcock staggers out first, and then I unbuckle my seat belt and climb down from the cockpit. It's not until my own feet hit the ground that I realize I'm trembling.

"You folks all right?" the farmer asks, approaching us as I peel off my goggles and helmet with shaky fingers. My flight suit, I see now, is completely washed in blood. "Why, you're nothin' but a girl," he realizes.

"She landed the plane," Captain Babcock says, rubbing his head, either in disbelief or pain, and I smile, hoping this means I've passed despite steering us into the birds in the first place. If we were back at Avenger right now, the girls would be jumping into the fountain, zoot suits and all, to celebrate. Grace is probably already there, splashing around. Instead, we're in the middle of a breezy cornfield, with a big sky above and the endless prairie stretching beyond. In my head, I'm already writing a letter describing it all to Sarah—if only it wouldn't take weeks for our correspondence to crisscross the country.

Captain Babcock asks the farmer if we can use his phone, and he nods, still gawking at me and scratching his head with bewilderment.

"Sorry about your corn," I say.

THE NEXT DAY IS SATURDAY AND MURPHEE SAYS SHE WANTS TO go dancing—wants us *all* to go dancing. "Come on, ladies. Enough with the 'I'm just here to do a job; I can't have any fun.' We all passed our check rides. Miri landed a goddamn plane without an engine *and* almost killed Captain Babcock. We deserve this!"

Vera looks up from her very big binder and says, "I'm not paying a thirty percent tax on a night out, thank you very much," referring to the new tax on big bands, alcohol, dancing, and fun of any kind. I'd read about it before I left home and, never being in a position to have fun of any kind, didn't give it a thought.

"I know a little guy who'll make sure we won't have to pay any tax on the drinks." Murph holds up a flask and winks.

"Does he have a name?" Ana grins, showing her deep dimples.

"Yeah. It's Jim. What do you say? Corn?" Murph adds, turning to Grace, who's in the middle of kicking off her boots.

She falls back onto her cot. "I just don't see the point when Teddy's not here."

"Oh, Teddy, Teddy, Teddy," Murphee says with a sigh.

I foolishly feel the same way myself—about Sol, who wrote me a postcard two weeks ago: *Dear Miriam, It was a pleasure to meet you! I hope you'll find a way to join us again for Shabbat sometime. I will be thinking of you whenever I see a plane fly by. Yours, Sol.* I've reread it over and over, just to imagine his hands forming the words on the page, and can recite the postcard from memory. With the rations on gas, Mr. Hendricks couldn't take me back to Abilene for services, and despite my fantasies, Sol hasn't appeared to whisk me away. Maybe I should stop waiting for something to happen.

"I'll go if Miri goes," Grace says.

"I could go," I say slowly, and she sits up and stares at me in disbelief.

"But it's your Sabbath!"

"Just until there are three stars in the night sky," I say.

"And then anything goes," Murphee says, snapping her fingers and swinging her hips.

I OPT FOR THE NICEST THING I OWN, MY AIR FORCE UNIFORM, until I turn around and notice what everyone else is wearing: Murph, orange hair blazing against the black of her knee-length dress; Ana in a belted, tan frock; and Grace in a gray, short-sleeved number that makes her brown eyes look hazel.

"Is that the best you've got, Steel?" Murphee asks.

I think of my beige dress, crumpled at the bottom of my footlocker. "It might be hard to dance in my flight suit," I say.

Grace snaps open her trunk and hands me a dress. "Here, Miri. Try this."

I gasp at the deep, rich red, a dye color I haven't seen since the war began, and unfold the rayon material. "Where did you get this?"

"Oh, ages and ages ago."

"You never see red like that anymore," Murphee says, admiring the fabric. "Except maybe on the black market."

"I need some black market shoes," Ana says with a sigh, holding up her rationed leather pair of kitten heels with a visible hole in the toe.

I slip on the knee-length, V-neck frock, and Grace zips up the back, so the faux sash hugs my waist. The short sleeves have the slightest flip, and my neck—encircled by a gold chain with the Star of David—is completely exposed. It's the prettiest thing I've never owned, and I want to keep it forever.

"Steel, you look like a young Joan Crawford," Murphee says, and Grace tries to find a tiny makeup mirror so I can see myself.

"I don't have any nylons . . ." I say.

"Easy peasy," Ana says and then stoops down and draws a makeup line up the back of each of my legs. "Now you do."

LATER, WE ARE AT THE DINER, SQUEEZED INTO A BOOTH—ANA, Murphee, Grace, and me—when I see a man just outside on the sidewalk, a man with blond hair and glasses who is absently tapping on himself as if his chest were a drum and his fingers the sticks. I blink. Forty miles from his home in Abilene, Sol Rubinowicz is peering at the menu taped just inside the window.

"What's up?" Grace asks, when I gasp.

He's a breath away from me, but I'd have to lunge over Murphee to rap on the window. *Look up, look up, look up,* I think instead, and his eyes glance up and then linger on my face. I smile and hold my breath, afraid to move and afraid to break his gaze for fear he'll disappear if I blink again. We stare at each other through the window. Then he smiles and points to the entrance. *Meet you over there?* I nod and feel my face crack open with joy. *Yes, yes, definitely yes, meet you—here I come!*

"What about dessert?" Murph calls after me, as I move past the waitress who is carrying a tray of ice cream floats toward our table.

"Go ahead without me," I say, opening the door with a jangle of bells.

Outside on the sidewalk, Sol stands there, staring at me with baffled amazement.

"Sol?" I say, letting the glass door fall shut behind me. "What are you doing in Sweetwater?"

"It's kind of a funny story." His laugh is sheepish, as he runs his hand through his hair. "I wasn't allowed to take the truck because it might break down, but then I took the truck, and then it broke down."

"That happened to me yesterday," I say. "Only it was a plane. I landed in a cornfield." When something furry brushes up against my ankles, I yelp and side step, startled by a tabby cat.

"Well, I'm glad you're okay," Sol says, stooping to pet the scraggly thing, whose back is matted with tufts of dirty fur.

As I watch Sol's strong and capable hand cupping her nuzzling head, I'm struck by a thought: *I want to be that cat.* My cheeks flush with embarrassment, as if Sol can read my mind. "Is she yours?" I ask.

"I think she's a stray. Want to sit?" he asks, jerking his head toward a nearby bench, and I nod and follow him over.

"So, what are you doing in Sweetwater?" I ask again, once we're sitting, the cat still intermittently brushing up against the rungs of the bench. The evening is warm and breezy, the lamps just flicking on over the sleepy side street. From out here, the inside of the diner has a golden glow and bustles with activity, as if it's the stage, and we're in the dim theater seats.

"I wanted to see if you were free for dinner tonight." He smiles and nods at my dress. "But you look like you've already got plans."

"Going dancing. With my friends." I glance at the diner window again, where they're all watching over ice cream floats. Ana's dimples are cutting divots in her cheeks, while Murphee is grinning and saying something obviously inappropriate, because Grace is blushing, one hand covering her mouth. "You should come, too."

"They were able to patch the tire on the truck. It's almost ready, and I've got to get it back. When I called to tell them I needed money for the tire, well . . . it wasn't pretty. Hey, buddy," Sol says to a cocker spaniel, straining on its owner's leash as they pass, and I think, *He's Dickon, Sarah, straight from* The Secret Garden, until I realize the dog is actually lunging for the stray cat.

"Have you thought of being a vet?" I ask, and he laughs.

"I'm more partial to helping humans. Adult humans. Well, anyone who can talk. I was in the hospital once—"

"Because of your heart?"

"There's nothing the matter with my heart. It's just a murmur from when I had rheumatic fever as a kid. That and I have an extraordinarily slow pulse." Sol holds out his hand, and nervously, I move to shake it. "No, feel. My pulse."

Fumbling around on his wrist like a guitarist learning the strings, I can't believe I'm actually touching Sol Rubinowicz in public, when two weeks ago I couldn't even make eye contact at the dinner table. At last, the slow, steady beat of his blood pumping half the speed of my own bangs against my fingertips. "Are you alive?" I ask.

"Very much so."

In my entire life, I can't think of a single human being who has gazed at me the way Sol is right now. Tzadok comes to mind, but he always makes me feel like a small child who has managed to delight a sad, old man. Sol and I stare at each other for a long moment, until I hear the bells from the diner door, followed by Murphee's voice: "Steel, we're going. Is your friend coming, too?"

"Is my friend coming, too?" I ask Sol quietly.

"I can't right now. But I'll find you again."

WE GET TO THE CLUB, WHERE THE BRASS BAND IS PLAYING GLENN Miller and the entire dance floor is filled with Army Air Forces servicemen and women. Suddenly, I wish I had worn my own uniform—anything to give me confidence right now. The truth is, besides the Hora, I've rarely ever danced. I certainly can't *swing*.

"You should be wearing this," I say to Grace, after turning down yet another close-cropped cadet who wants the chance to spin around the lady in red. *It's not because of me,* I think, *it's the dress.* Besides, what's the point in being here, when the only person I want to be dancing with is Sol?

"Give someone a chance," Grace says just as another uniformed man comes up to offer his hand. She glances back at me and shrugs, as he leads her onto the floor, leaving me standing beside Louise, the blond pilot from Tennessee who holds a special affection for everything, including roaches. She's not in our bunk, but we march together, and eat together, and now, apparently, avoid dancing together.

"How do they make it look so easy?" I say, as we stand back, taking in the crowd with their gyrating glee.

"Flying looks easy, too. From the ground," she says, and I glance at her and smile. "I heard about what happened to your plane," Louise adds. "You've gotta inspect it extra carefully before takeoff—don't count on the mechanics to do it. You never know what kind of sabotage they'll pull. Some of those airmen can't stand that a woman can do their job."

"It was a bird strike," I say, and she shakes her head, reminding me of Captain Babcock, who'd been perplexed by the engine failure himself afterward, but not convinced an investigation was in order—perhaps too ashamed of his concussion.

"With the size of that prop and that engine? The birds would be chewed up—not vice versa," Louise insists. "Seriously, watch your back."

Unsure if she means in flight or right now, I glance over my shoulder to see Murph, who pushes a gangly guy wearing a green army uniform right into me, making me stumble. "Miri, meet Jeremy. Jeremy, Miri!"

Jeremy is tall with shaved black hair, so there's not much to distract from his enormous ears, except for his smile, which is nice enough, if just a bit bewildered. I wonder if she's picked him out for me because she thinks he's Jewish.

"Want to dance?" Jeremy asks.

"Um . . ." I say, as Murph shoves me toward him. Louise gives me two thumbs-up and off we go, into the sea of bodies grooving and hopping, swinging and swaying.

When I tell him I don't know how to dance, he says, "It's like a waltz, only faster—just do what I do and leave the rest to me," so I let him push me away and pull me back, and spin me around and spin me back, all in time to the music. Soon enough I realize I'm laughing, enjoying myself, even if Sol's not here, and I can't do the dress justice.

We shout-talk over the brass band, which is how I find out that Jeremy's from the Bronx, New York, that he's a Reform Jew, and that he hasn't found a temple since coming to Texas.

"There's one in Abilene!" I say.

"Have you been?"

"Three weeks ago!" I mention the Rubinowiczes then, "old family friends" who wanted to see me as much as possible when they heard I was stationed in Texas.

"If I can borrow a car from my CO, can I give you a lift there sometime?" Jeremy asks.

"That would be wonderful!" It's only after the words are out of my mouth that I realize I've just made a date with a man to see another man.

After a few songs, I excuse myself to find a bathroom and afterward discover Ana, Louise, and Murphee at a table drinking water—or possibly vodka by the way they are collapsing on each other, Murph laughing so hard mascara is dripping down her cheeks. I follow her gaze onto the dance floor, and my mouth gapes when I see Grace swinging over her partner's shoulders, and shooting underneath his legs, then whipping up in the air with a scissor-kick of her legs.

"Good God, Corn, was that a backflip?" Murphee asks when Grace gets back to the table, panting. "Does Teddy know you can jitterbug like a Cotton Club dancer?" Grinning, Grace slumps into a chair and reaches for the pitcher, just as Jeremy weaves his way through the crowd and approaches our table. "Have a seat," Murphee says, kicking out a chair for him to sit down, and he does, right next to me.

"So, how am I going to reach you?" he asks, looking at me, or at least, glancing furtively back and forth between my eyes and curls. Is he checking out my dry scalp or does he want to brush away a stray hair that's fallen out of my bobby pins?

"Um, Miri?" Murph interrupts, clicking her tongue, and I glance over at her. "Seven o'clock," she adds, and I swivel around to see Sol, making his way toward our table. With his plaid tie, tweed jacket, and unshorn hair, he looks out of place among the servicemen.

"You made it!" I say, standing up, as he approaches.

"I made it." Sol says, his voice both wry and relieved. "Apparently just in time."

There is a beat of silence, as the band pauses between songs, and I realize that Jeremy has stood up as well. Both men are staring at each other. "Oh, Sol, this is—Jeremy. Jeremy—Sol."

"You're Sol? Miriam says you've known each other forever," Jeremy says, and Sol looks right at me when he answers.

"That's right. Forever." My face heats up, and I glance at the floor as "Smoke Rings" begins to play.

"So, when are we going to Abilene together?" Jeremy asks me, and Sol's eyes widen as the corners of his mouth go up.

"I don't think—I'll need the ride after all. But thank you," I say, quickly turning away from Jeremy's crestfallen face.

"Want to dance?" Sol asks, holding out his hand.

We walk out onto the floor among the other couples swaying to the slow music. It seems too intimate to cling to him the way Ana drapes herself over her partner, so I position my hips at a right angle to Sol's torso and straighten my arm as if I'm leading. "This works better if we're facing each other," he says, placing his hands on my waist and shifting my pelvis toward his. "Relax this arm. See? We fit."

"I see," I say, except that it comes out a strange little whisper.

"That's a pretty dress," Sol says, drawing me closer.

I have to work hard to keep my voice even and measured. "Oh. My friend Grace lent it to me."

"Well. Jeremy liked it," Sol says, and I laugh, in spite of my guilt.

Then he leans in so close to my ear that I almost think he's going to kiss me. "I like it, too."

WE DRIVE BACK TO BASE UNDER A FULL MOON, JUST SOL AND ME, *alone at last.* Just thinking those clichéd words makes me think of the romantic novels Sarah used to sneak out of the library and hide beneath the bed so Mama wouldn't see—novels with sappy endings, unbelievable coincidences, and the worst offense of all: declarations. "Like all a woman needs is to have a man make a declaration," I once said to Sarah, who retorted, "Would that be so bad?"

"So, you never finished telling me before—why were you in the hospital?" I ask, pointing out the road back to Avenger Field.

"I cut the tendons in my hand on a table saw when I was fourteen and had to get surgery. I still have very little sensation in the tip of my right pinky finger." He lifts it from the steering wheel and wiggles it. "The army didn't like that, either."

"I can't imagine flying a plane with numbness in the tip of my right pinky."

Sol shoots me a smile, so he must know I'm joking. "I paid attention as the doctors made their rounds. That's how I learned to map out the location of organs and their conditions by percussion." I must look perplexed, because he adds, "Normal lungs sound one way and lungs full of fluid sound completely different when you tap on them—that sort of thing. It seemed like I was being shown this window into medicine for a purpose. They won't let me go to war, but at least I can help some other way."

It's quiet for a moment, save the sound of the engine, until I finally ask, "What will you do, if you don't get in again?"

"I'm not working in my father's shop the rest of my life, I know that." His voice is firm, almost hardened, but then he sneaks me a look. "You must know how I feel. It's why you fly, isn't it?"

I think of his father's tree in the backyard and the juices dripping down my chin the other night. "Flying makes me feel as if I'm sucking out the mango of life."

"Exactly." Sol grins and then chuckles. "Although, Miri,

you do know . . . No, of course, you know . . ." He shakes his head.

"Know what?"

"That it's the marrow of life? 'I went to the woods because I wished to live deliberately . . . and not, when I came to die, discover that I had not—' "

"Right," I say. "Emerson."

"Thoreau. And it was marrow of life," Sol says.

"We'll see," I say, folding my arms across my chest.

" 'We'll see'?" he repeats, and then laughs—a great, big booming laugh, which makes me join in. There's so much at stake these days—a cure for TB, Hitler's next move, my sister's survival, Thursday's check ride. *If I can spend the rest of my life laughing beside this man, I'll be happy,* it occurs to me then, and the thought is so urgent, it feels like a prayer.

When we get back to base it's nine fifty-two and the moon is shining like daylight. Sol pulls up just before the gate and pushes his glasses up on his nose. "What . . . *is* that?" He's pointing to Fifinella, the red-booted, blue-winged Walt Disney creation decorating the sign over the gate.

"That's Fifi, the good gremlin—she keeps the bad gremlins out of the planes."

"Ah," he says, cutting the engine. Then he faces me with a smile. "You asked that guy to bring you all the way back to Abilene just to see me again."

I can tell in that sentence it's the story we'll toast at our wedding, the story we will tell our children one day: how, once upon a time, Miri Lichtenstein tried to dupe a serviceman into taking her all the way from Sweetwater to Abilene for Sol Ru-binowicz. *Oh, no,* I think, *that won't do.*

"Not quite," I say, and his eyebrows shoot up. "I told him we were family friends, and that I wanted to go to temple. You, meanwhile, couldn't stop thinking about me. You went to the trouble of *stealing a truck*. And when all hope was lost, suddenly there I was in the window of a diner. It was the first time in your life you'd ever conjured anyone right out of your head."

Sol tilts his head back and laughs, loudly, and I'm thrilled once again. It's a wonderful sound, and I caused it. *There it is*, I think. *The Declaration*. "Is that how our story goes?" he asks.

"That's right." I play with my necklace. "Get it straight."

"And what happens next in the story? Do I kiss you in the moonlight under that gremlin?"

"You do."

As he opens his car door and makes his way around the car, I can see his shoulders are still shaking with laughter. I quickly jump out of the passenger side before he can reach the handle. "I've got it," I say, slamming the creaky door of the truck behind me.

"I guess you do," Sol says, watching me coming toward him. We meet in the headlights. Giddy with anticipation, I think of Murphee saying, *You can't smile and pucker at the same time, honey*, which makes me want to laugh, until he leans down, brings his hands to my face, and pushes back my hair. Then I close my eyes and our lips meet and meet and meet again. His kisses are gentle but firm, inexperienced yet expert. Moments or days later, we finally pull apart.

"Goodness," I say, as the first notes of Taps begin to play.

"You are," he says, and I squeeze his hand, back away, and then turn on my heel and run. "I want to see you again!" he calls after me.

"Yes!" I say, jogging backward for a moment, just long enough to see his quick smile.

LATER THAT WEEKEND, I WASH THE RED DRESS AND RETURN IT to Grace, part of me wishing it were mine forever, and part of me knowing it doesn't really matter anymore. *He kissed me!* I think, and everywhere I look I see color, rich, vibrant, and bright.

CHAPTER 15

Miri, Lost

The Saturday after I got out of the hospital, Elyse surprised me with a phone call. Despite the fact that I wanted nothing more than to crawl into bed and rest longer, despite the fact that I hadn't gotten out of my nightgown for an entire day and had almost forgotten how to reconstruct my top curl with bobby pins, I told her that of course I would love to see her. She showed up that evening cradling a sack of flour in one arm and holding a Tupperware of chicken soup and dumplings in another. When I exclaimed, "How wonderful!" and asked if she had prepared it herself, she said, "Oh, no, Mom did. These are leftovers. But it seemed like getting-better sort of food." It did look like getting-better sort of food, just so long as I stuck to the plain broth and never let an ounce of fat cross my lips again.

"Do I look the same?" I asked tentatively, because I'd spent four days in that godforsaken hospital, with interns and residents asking me the same questions over and over, and entire teams of surgeons visiting my bedside and pushing on my belly. "Exactly the same," she said, and her tone was not one of relief but encouragement. She seemed to know that I needed to hear this, for perhaps if I appeared unchanged, the same might hold true for my life.

I can't say that she looked the same, however. "You've cut your braid!" I realized, with a bit of sadness, I must confess.

"I have to blow it dry now with a special brush, which is kind of a pain," she said.

"Well, it looks lovely," I said, and I meant it. Her pale blond bob suited her heart-shaped face, but she didn't look like Sarah anymore.

"Oh, I almost forgot—your chapters," she said, rifling in her backpack for the next two packets of papers: one titled "The First Day of the Rest of Your Life," and the other, "Steel in Love."

"It's interesting, reminiscing like this," I mused, touching the sheaf of papers, still surprised, once again, to see my life neatly typed and collated, with a chapter heading, no less. "It's as if not a day has gone by. I still feel the same on the inside, and then I look in the mirror and see an old woman staring back. It's . . . disorienting." I looked up at Elyse's smooth skin, realizing she wouldn't know her own beauty until it was gone.

"Sol would still recognize you," she said, with such passionate naïveté that it made me wonder if she'd slipped down the rabbit hole herself. Maybe love is like a check ride, I thought, the test to see if you can keep a clear head when you're falling and still manage to put the plane down gently.

"Oh my dear, it was all a very long time ago." When I leaned back in my chair, my stomach growled.

"Should I heat up the soup in the microwave or"—she suddenly glanced around—"on the stove?"

I told her I wasn't ready to eat just yet, that I'd save it for later. I didn't want her to see me picking out all the dumplings. Besides, I still didn't have an appetite. I thanked her for the soup, and the sack of flour—

"Oh, this is our baby—Henry!" Elyse said, giddily turning over the paper sack so I could see a smiley face drawn on the side. "We got married in psychology class, and now we have to share babysitting duties for the next two weeks." I gave her a small smile, too tired to let her know that when one is nurturing and caring for one's own child, it is no longer called babysitting.

"And who, pray tell, is the father of this lovely sack of flour?" I asked, and Elyse's cheeks bloomed an even deeper shade of crimson.

"Holden Saunders," she said, a shy confession. It occurred to me in that moment that Elyse Strickler would not be a young girl for much longer. How so much could change in a matter of a week. "This flour has my teacher's autograph on it, so at the end of the project we turn in the same baby," she added. "But I can buy you more. Send me to the store with a list, and I'll pick up whatever you need."

As I sank into a nearby kitchen chair, I realized with some dismay that, if I never wanted to see the likes of a Meals on Wheels volunteer darkening my doorstep with his specter of grossly inedible food, I would probably have to take her up on that. The whole effort of preparing for Elyse's arrival—the shower, the dressing, the top curl, and now standing for five whole minutes—had already tired me out. I glanced up at her and smiled: like any good fly girl, she was standing at attention, waiting for her instructions. "So, it seems that my gallbladder has been giving me trouble," I said, before explaining that the first attack hit after the noodle kugel, followed by the big one two days later, after I had a craving for eggnog and Boston cream pie, followed by four days of intravenous antibiotics before I left the hospital against medical advice.

"Against medical advice?" Elyse said, her eyes growing wide. "But why?"

"Well, first of all, I was there too long. One day is too long, when it comes to the hospital. And second, they wanted to remove my gallbladder—at my age! They said with the infection, it would be at risk of rupturing and causing me tremendous complications, all of which were possibly fatal. And I figured, what do I have to lose?" As soon as the words had floated from my lips, I regretted them. Presumably, Elyse's grandmother, struggling with cancer of some variety, wanted desperately to live, and there I sat, ready to crumple my own life up in a ball and toss it away.

"I think you should do what they tell you to do," Elyse said. "I know someone, too—a really good surgeon. He's a friend of my dad's."

"Yes, well . . ." I sighed and smoothed down the edge of the tablecloth from where I was sitting. "How is your grandmother?"

Elyse glanced down at her folded hands and shook her head, as if she couldn't bring herself to say it aloud. Finally, she looked up at me. "Did you really mean what you said about sending me to visit her? Because I'd pay you back—I'd type your whole memoir for free."

I hesitated, and not because of the cost. "What's your mother's story?" I asked. "Why won't she send you herself?"

"She said I can't go until Christmas break. But Aunt Andie says Grandma might not make it that long. Mom says that Aunt Andie's being a melodramatic pessimist."

There were risks to optimism, I knew. It had led me to believe the doctors, when they said Thomas would get better after his stroke. Perhaps if I'd feared the worst, I would've been at his bedside to kiss him goodbye.

"Does your mother know that you come here?"

"Mom's not really aware of anything right now," Elyse admitted. She told me about the other night, when her younger brother Hugh was wheezing, and she'd come upon him in the kitchen, sitting on the counter and squeezing his liquid asthma medication into the nebulizer for a treatment—all by himself. "I mean, he's five; he's had asthma since he was two, but still. She never even noticed his cough."

I thought of how I'd been not too much older than Elyse when I left home against the wishes of my parents. I thought that if I were dying and my grandson Tyler were alive, I would've given anything to see him one last time. I thought that if Elyse's grandmother didn't make it until Christmas, surely her mother would wish she'd sent Elyse, and then it would be too late. "My dear, I always mean what I say." I reached over to lay my hand on top of hers. "Of course I'll pay for the tickets."

After she'd walked me through the baffling process of purchasing airplane tickets online, she wrote down a surgeon's name and number with specific instructions. By the end of her visit, I knew I would call. It wasn't just that I didn't want to let Elyse down when her own grandmother was dying, or even my ever-present worry about who exactly would find my body should I succeed in passing away on my own terms. I realized that for the first time in years, it mattered to someone whether I lived or died.

OF COURSE I WOULD RUN INTO SELENA MARKMANN THREE DAYS later on my way out of the high rise, when, after the hulla-balloo of sirens and paramedics last week, I wanted nothing more than to slip anonymously out of the building. It was only three thirty on a Tuesday afternoon, but Selena's purple eye shadow met the arch of her eyebrows, as if she were ready for a night out Flamenco dancing. "Mary Browning, what *happened* to you?" Selena said loudly, despite the fact that the lobby was full of people. "Jean and I were saying you'd never missed a group meeting, so we knew it was *serious.*" I told her that it was nothing of the sort, that I merely dropped the leg of a coffee table on my foot, and I couldn't walk myself down to the ER. "But . . . you were wearing oxygen," she said, baffled. I flipped my hand as if waving away a mosquito and said that, according to my husband, the late Dr. Thomas Browning, if a patient is over a certain age and she passes wind, she receives a colonoscopy; if she hiccups, an EKG gets ordered stat; and if she clears her throat, an oxygen mask is applied. Selena just blinked and looked down at my feet, which were clad in my usual Mary Janes. "They gave me a boot, but if it's not frac-tured, why bother? And who has time for crutches?" I added, moving quickly away from her and out the door. At least I re-membered to limp. When I glanced back, Selena was just stand-ing there in the lobby, holding her packages.

I RODE A BUS OVER TO SHADYSIDE HOSPITAL AND THEN CROSSED the street to the doctor's office. After giving the receptionist my name, I took a seat in the waiting room and wasn't even halfway finished with the first page of forms when the nurse called me back.

"But . . . is there a gown?" I asked, after following her down the hall to an office with two chairs facing a desk, rather than an examining table.

"Oh, he'll speak to you first in here. Stay dressed," the nurse said with a smile, and I sat down with some relief, thinking that I already liked his old-fashioned style.

Just as I was wondering if the doctor was "older"—nearing retirement, but young to me, of course—the door opened and he entered.

There were two things Elyse hadn't mentioned when she recommended the surgeon: the first, that he was quite handsome. Dr. Khaira was tall, with warm brown eyes and smooth cinnamon skin. The other thing, of course, was his nationality. Perhaps because I'd been imagining my husband's friend from residency, Dr. Peter Kara, a redheaded Irishman, it hadn't occurred to me that this doctor might be Middle Eastern. At least Dr. Khaira's accent was undetectable, as he told me that he'd reviewed my CT scans and the good news was that I didn't have cancer.

"Was there a rumor that I did?" I asked.

He explained that someone must've thought so, because my primary care doctor had suggested that I see him, a surgical oncologist—that he was used to removing tumors wrapped around people's organs. "Thankfully, you just have run-of-the-mill gallstones."

I reminded him that I was only there on the recommendation of Rich Strickler, whose name had worked like magic to get me a next-day appointment.

Dr. Khaira snapped his fingers. "That's right! Now I remember. How do you know Rich?"

"Well, I don't really. But I've gotten to know his daughter through my writers' group." *Well enough to fly her out to Key West on Friday morning*, I might have said.

"Elyse is such a great kid," Dr. Khaira said.

"Oh, yes," I agreed.

"How's Jane?"

"I believe it's a difficult time for her," I said to the surgeon, and he nodded slowly, as if a bit perplexed, and then looked back at the computer that contained my hospital reports. I cleared my throat. "Tell me, do you really think surgery is necessary at my age?"

"Well, you just had acute cholecystitis. You've got a seventy percent chance of having another gallbladder attack with more serious complications every time. You're lucky that you pulled through with the antibiotics." He looked over at me and smiled. "There's no reason that you shouldn't do well with surgery. You've got no other major medical problems, and you look about ten years younger than your stated age."

There it was: the doctor compliment. I reminded him of how hospitals had a way of rapidly aging everyone—from the young patient to the old. Hospitals even took their toll on the people who worked there, especially those who rendered the most difficult decisions. *Except for Dr. Khaira,* I thought to myself. Judging by the diplomas on the walls, he was very experienced, and yet, he appeared to be a happy-go-lucky man who hadn't known a sleepless night. Could I trust him? I cleared my throat again and asked him if, since he specialized in oncology, I would have to find another surgeon.

"Of course not. You're a friend of the Stricklers. I'll be happy to do it," Dr. Khaira said, and there was an unspoken *It'll be fun* in his smile. I could guess, pretty easily, that a simple case like mine could provide him with great satisfaction after all the malignant tentacles he'd fished out of people's bellies. I wondered if he was one of those surgeons who believed all miracles occurred by the grace of their own hands, or if he answered to a higher power. *Could he be Muslim or Hindu?* I suddenly wondered, but of course, I knew better than to ask.

"Where are you from?" I asked instead, thinking, *Iran? Iraq? Pakistan?*

"San Francisco," Dr. Khaira said, and I told him I meant originally. "Well, I was conceived in Buffalo."

"And your parents?" I asked. "Where were they from?"

"Why? Are you familiar with small towns in India?" he asked, raising an eyebrow. "And what about *your* parents?" he added, with playful irritation in his voice.

Maybe it was because I had inadvertently insulted him, and I wanted to show him that we had something in common. Or maybe I was thinking of something I'd said to Elyse the other day: *Every family has secrets and they're usually only important to the people who are keeping them.* "My parents were from Germany—German Jews," I found myself saying to Dr. Khaira.

He glanced at the name on my chart and gave me a quizzical look. "Well, that is unexpected."

For one strange moment, I wanted to confess my real name—to give it to him like a present, and see if he might forgive me. But then I thought of Jacob wrestling with the angel all through the night, and how, in biblical times, one never revealed one's name to a stranger, for fear of surrendering one's power. I couldn't tell him when Elyse didn't even know my name. But I wanted to.

Thankfully, Dr. Khaira didn't seem to be waiting for any great confessions. He simply picked up his pen again and twirled it like a mini-baton between thumb and index finger and then launched into taking the rest of my social history—had I ever smoked, used drugs, drank alcohol? "Retired?" he added, when we'd been through the list.

"Oh, yes," I said and gave him the brief but true history of me: World War II fly girl, mother to one son, English teacher, and published author. Obviously this was Dr. Khaira's final appointment on an evening when he had no pressing plans, because he leaned back in his chair and asked me what on earth had prompted me to write a book. "My husband," I said and told him how I had been upsetting certain well-to-do people at dinner parties in New York by spouting off my feminist opinions on the subservient nature of traditional wifedom. "If you have something to say, maybe you could try writing it down," Thomas had gently suggested in the car on the way home, never suspecting that I would do exactly that—*and* sell it to a publishing house. Dr. Khaira laughed. I added that Thomas had died of a stroke, but that we'd been married fifty years before that.

"Fifty years. Wow. What's your secret?" Dr. Khaira asked, giving his pen another spin.

"Open communication," I said, remembering Dave as a young man, bragging to his then girlfriend Carrie about how

Thomas and I had invented a "secret love language," when Dave was a boy. We'd given it up by the time he'd reached junior high, but he'd never forgotten. "My parents just spoke in pig Latin until we figured it out," Carrie had said with a laugh.

"A daily dose of laughter," I went on. "Democratic decision making. And three little words. Well, one word, repeated three times." And then I told him the silly phrase Thomas and I would use: *Dubba dubba dubba.* It was a great way to end a fight: you got the last word, even if the last word was complete and utter nonsense.

"Are you married, Dr. Khaira?" I asked, as he glanced over my living will, which I'd brought with me.

"Not anymore." Dr. Khaira looked up and said rather wryly, "I guess I failed my husband training."

He glanced down at the papers on his desk and seemed to remember what we were both there for. "So, about your living will here. It says you don't want to be resuscitated, you don't want to be on a ventilator, and you don't want IV antibiotics. But I'm going to need you to reverse your code status just for the surgery." I could feel my eyes dilating, as he rushed to explain, "You're going to be on a ventilator during the surgery, right? That's general anesthesia, my friend. And we might even run a bag of IV antibiotics while you're open. I need to be able to treat you for the simple stuff—postop infection, pneumonia, whatever. Then, after the discharge, your living will can go back into effect. Let me just get you through the postop period, and then you can go home peacefully." *And die however you please,* his tone said. He asked me about decision makers, and I wondered how awkward it might be to ask Gene Rosskemp—or any other of the writers, for that matter—to act as my medical power of attorney. "Brothers, sisters, children?" he added.

I let myself dream for just a moment. I imagined if Sarah had lived. I imagined that her daughter had grown up with my son, and their children knew each other, and we met on Friday nights for dinner. Oh, how I'd loved the warmth around the table, the comfort in knowing we were all there, our heads bowed in the candlelight. I imagined if Thomas and I had raised Rita like our own, and Dave would've had the sibling he'd always wished for. I blinked and realized Dr. Khaira was still staring at me, waiting for an answer. "I'm afraid my family is all gone now," I said.

"But you have one son?"

"Dave and his wife and child were killed by a drunk driver," I said, and then I startled myself when tears filled my eyes, and I started to weep.

"Oh my God. When was this?"

"Not recently," I admitted, still crying despite the foolishness of it. "In fact, quite some time ago. But there hasn't been a day since that I didn't wish it had been me instead." *So much potential, wasted,* I thought, for his full life and my own joy.

That afternoon in the doctor's office as I continued to cry, Dr. Khaira just sat there watching me, respectful of my sorrow, I felt. Finally, with shaking fingers, I reached for a tissue on his desk. It embarrassed me to do so: the tissues were here for the people who had to hear that despite the surgery, the cancer was back. Not for me. "Please, I'm sorry." I blew my nose and wiped my eyes. "What more do you have to ask, Dr. Khaira?"

"Please. Call me Satinder," he said.

"Satinder, I'm sorry that I asked about your parents."

"Asked me what?" he said and then smiled back. "See, I already forgot."

OUTSIDE THE OFFICE, THE DAY WAS BRIGHT, AND I HADN'T BEEN waiting very long when the bus pulled up at the stop. Once I'd swiped my bus pass and was safely in my seat, the driver snapped off his hazards and we were moving once again toward Squirrel Hill. My mind was drifting back to another place, right after the war, when Sarah was consumed by her own worries of who would raise her daughter.

Sarah, how can I explain? I thought. *I didn't understand what I was giving up, until it was too late. If I could do it all over, I would've tried harder; I would've convinced him that I made a promise for both of us. I just wasn't given a chance.*

The bus lurched to a halt at Forbes Avenue, and I quickly gathered up my purse and shakily made my way down the steps. As soon as I'd made it off the last one, the driver slammed the doors shut and peeled away, making me feel as if I'd been spit out on the sidewalk. I couldn't help thinking that I probably deserved it.

CHAPTER 16

Miami

Grandma's boyfriend Ray picked me up at the Key West airport, saying, "Change of plans, little buddy. We have to go to Miami tonight."

"Miami," I repeated, slipping my arm through the other shoulder strap of my backpack. I had just come through Miami. I had run an all-out sprint to reach my connecting flight, which was on this tiny little commuter plane sitting on the runway in the wind. I ran so hard to catch that flight that I overtook a beeping cart carrying an old woman with *two* canes and an even older man who looked like he might've been dead. I ran so hard that I think I passed the pilot, too, a tall blond guy, jogging out of the restroom with a little carry-on. And now we had to go all the way back? "What for?"

"There's a problem with Margot's bag. How was the flight?"

I told him it was fine. I didn't tell him how the pilot warned us it was going to be a bumpy ride due to the imminence of Hurricane Claudette, and that I felt queasy the whole way from worrying my plane would crash, just to make Mom right: something bad was definitely going to happen since she hadn't approved of the trip. Or maybe I'd made myself sick thinking about Thea, who hadn't sent me a single text in the week since I ditched her for the physics bridge. I also didn't tell him that Mrs. Browning had actually flown me first class from Pittsburgh to Miami, that the seats were wide leather armchairs, and that stewards had brought me warm towels like at a Japanese restaurant, and cranberry juice in a wineglass. I didn't tell him because then he'd probably ask me who the heck Mrs. Browning was. This morning, when Mom freaked out, I'd lied and told her that Daddy had bought the tickets. It was only after I said it out loud that I realized if I had asked him, he probably would have.

Ray put a hand on my back to lead me out of the air-conditioned lobby and into the balmy dark of the parking lot, where palm trees tussled in the breeze and the soft air felt like it was actually caressing my face. *A problem with Margot's bag* didn't mean much to me, and I wondered just for a second if shopping for a new one would be involved. When it looked like Grandma wasn't waiting in the car after all, I thought of Mom going, "What do we really *know* about this Ray guy?"

But Grandma was in the back of the topless Jeep after all, just curled up in a sleeping ball, looking sort of like a child. When Ray reached through the air where a window should've been to give her shoulder a shake, Grandma slowly sat up and stretched. "Hiya, baby cakes," she said to me with a yawn. "Just taking a little snooze, since your plane was late. Wow— look at you, honey!" she added. "I'm loving your hair. It makes you look so different."

I blinked. Grandma looked different, too, just like Mom had

warned me, except that in this case "looking different" was a euphemism for "bald" the way "big-boned" meant "fat," and "not feeling well" meant "about to die." Grandma must've seen it on my face, because then she said, running a hand over her slick scalp, "Oh, sweetie. Jane didn't tell you about my new do, did she?"

I shook my head. When Grandma had first moved down to the Keys, replacing her cardigans and blazers with pink shorts, halter tops, and dangly earrings, Mom had grumbled that she'd looked different then, too. I'd vaguely imagined that Grandma was finally going to get gray hair and maybe some knitting needles or something.

"I shaved my head when the chemo made it fall out in clumps. Your mom probably expected me to wear a wig or one of my scarves the entire time, but they tend to blow off in the Jeep. Did Ray tell you the plan?"

I nodded and then shook my head again, wondering if I'd forgotten to pack all words, or just the right ones.

"We're off to Miami, so that I can have a little procedure done first thing in the morning," Grandma said, pushing the front seat forward so she could hop out on sandaled feet. She was wearing a linen jumper, which covered her knees and most of her calves as well. "Kind of an emergency deal, or I'd have waited until after you left."

It was hard to imagine what kind of emergency could still allow Grandma to smile so warmly, but I made the corners of my mouth go up in return. Then we hugged, and everything felt right again, at least until we stopped at an Exxon miles up Route 1, which was when I saw in the fluorescent light of the bathroom that Grandma was actually yellow.

WE STAYED AT A HOTEL RIGHT ON MIAMI BEACH IN A ROOM with two queen-size beds. When Grandma climbed into bed next to me, I saw the bag filled with putrid green fluid attached to her side and I wished that she had chosen to buddy up with Ray instead. When she checked to make sure I'd called Mom to let her know I got here safely, I said I'd already called, which was true—except that I didn't specify where "here" was, since Mom would've been even more furious, no doubt, "on so many levels." Mom could never admit to being angry on just one level. It wouldn't *just* be because I'd flown all the way down to Key West, only to have me retrace my steps in the backseat of a topless Jeep, driven by a suspicious man, who knew nothing of Key West flora and fauna, much less about how to care for a bald woman with bag problems, or *just* that he slept in the next bed wearing nothing but boxers and a white T-shirt, but mostly because an emergency trip to Miami meant that Grandma was very, very sick, and Mom didn't want to believe it. She didn't want me to believe it, either.

The next morning, Ray looked a bit worried when he dropped us off at the hospital after breakfast. "Are you sure you'll be fine?" he said, hesitating.

No, no, no, we're not, I pleaded with my eyes. I'd just found out in the car that the bag on Grandma's side was actually connected by a tube to her biliary tree—not an actual tree, but "little ducts connecting things together," she cheerfully put it. The ducts were clogged with cancer, and the bag wasn't filling right, and a radiologist was going to have to put in a stent— "kind of like a fancy straw," Grandma said—to open the tree back up again. "Will there be blood?" I asked, feeling suddenly queasy, but Grandma said that all we should see was "more yucky green stuff."

And then Grandma linked her thin, yellow arm through mine and told Ray to beat it. "Elyse can take care of me. Go sell your boat." That was the other thing they forgot to tell me until then: that Ray had already planned to meet a man from Michigan about a sale. Once Ray was gone, we sat in the hallway, waiting for Grandma to be called in by the radiologist. On my lap, I held my PSAT book of a thousand questions.

"So," Grandma said, stroking the curled ends of my new haircut. "Who's the lucky guy?"

I felt my face flushing as I told her about Holden Saunders and the marriage project and how he'd given me a ride to the airport that morning. I left the part out before it, where Mom was screaming at me for making plans without consulting her. Holden already knew about my trip, so when I called him on his cell phone before school, he said of course he'd take me. He seemed to like the idea of an adventure, if it meant cutting class. We got stuck in the Fort Pitt tunnel traffic, and I almost didn't care if I missed the flight, because it was me in the passenger seat of his MINI Cooper—me, who had passed all the other girls waiting in the cold at the bus stop. Once we got through the tunnel, Holden drove like a maniac, weaving in and out of traffic, and I was holding on to the Jesus bar above my window when an old Smiths song that my dad loves came on the radio— "And if a ten-ton truck, crashes into us, / To die by your side, would be a heavenly way to die . . ." For just a second, I felt like that would be true. When we pulled up at the airport, Holden popped the trunk, grabbed my little suitcase, and then ran around the car to hand it to me. "Now don't worry about Henry this weekend," he said, and I laughed. Then he bent down, and I kissed him, somewhere between his lips and his dimple, before he finished the reason for his leaning, which was to pick my backpack up off the ground. Blushing wildly, I slung it over my shoulder, and he grinned and said, "Come back safe."

I told Grandma about the kiss. Under the circumstances, I left out the part about the heavenly way to die.

Grandma laughed and said, "You remind me of me!" Then she told me more about the boy that she loved when she was fifteen, Jonathan Byrd. Jonathan had grown up next door to her in a four-story house with six brothers and sisters. All the children played instruments—Jonathan was a trumpeter—and his mother played the guitar. "One summer we took a trip to the countryside," Grandma said, and her face had a faraway look, like we weren't actually sitting in the hallway of the hospital, watching patients being wheeled by. "We all piled in to the Volkswagen bus for the forty-five-minute drive from Pittsburgh to Yough Lake, and the whole way there, none of them stopped singing—it started with hymns but eventually digressed into 'Peggy Sue' and 'That'll Be the Day,' so I could join in. When we picked up a hitchhiker, we serenaded him, too, butchering Buddy Holly all the way down the highway."

I laughed, and she smiled. A janitor came down the hallway, mopping the floor, but Grandma didn't seem to notice.

"Would you want to see him again?" I asked.

"Jonathan? Oh. I would love to. But not like this." She swept her hand over her checkered blue gown. "Certainly not bald."

A middle-aged man wearing a suit and tie and only one shoe crutched his way toward us. He seemed mad at the crutches, swearing with every swing step. Behind him, one of the transporters was wheeling a little old lady with white hair and glasses who reminded me of Mrs. Browning. I wondered if she'd made the appointment with Daddy's friend Dr. Khaira and, if so, would she actually listen to him? Then I thought how weird it was that I knew so much about her, and she wouldn't even tell me her real name. Even weirder that there was so much I didn't even know about my own grandmother. She was a writer like me, or at least, she had been. We probably had a lot in common.

"I'm sorry I never read your book, Grandma," I said, as another man was pushed by on a gurney, wearing the same thin, checkered gown that Grandma had on. She turned and looked at me. "The novel you wrote when you were twenty-six?"

"Oh, honey," she said with a laugh, "of all the things I'm sorry about, that's not one of them. I'm sorry I didn't get to see you more. I'm sorry your mother was so hurt that I started a new life after Grandpa died. I'm sorry that Jane and I . . . weren't closer."

"Were you upset when she married Daddy?"

"Because he's Christian? I might've worried a little about how the children would be raised. But for the last four years I've been with Ray, who's agnostic. Your mother was in love, and your father's a good man, and that's all that really mattered to me."

When I thought of Mom and Daddy, my eyes felt wet with tears, which I quickly swiped away with my fingers, but Grandma must've noticed.

"Jane thinks I don't know something's up at home," she said. "She thinks I don't know that she's keeping things from me. No one wants to worry me, or upset me, or give me any more bad news. I guess it's just part of my disappearing act."

It seemed like I should make some sort of honest confession right then. So I said, "Daddy moved out two weeks ago. He says he wants a divorce. And Mom's been worried about her job. She feels like they're looking for an excuse to fire her since she canceled a deposition and lost a client. She's kind of a mess right now." Grandma listened and nodded, and her face looked so crumpled with concern that I almost regretted telling her the truth. But then the radiologist finally called her name, and she lowered her shoulders and stood up with such dignity, that I was awed. From where I sat, I could just see the edge of the cold, steel table that awaited her. The sign on the wall said INTERVENTIONAL RADIOLOGY but the room looked like a morgue from a *CSI* show. Watching Grandma walk through the swinging door, I held my own back a little straighter, pretending my PSAT book was balanced on my head, not my knees. Then I waited and watched the traffic of gurneys in the hallway.

When they finally pushed Grandma out of the room, she was on a stretcher. I stood up and shut my book.

"Hi, Grandma. How did it go?"

"It went," she said with a wince. "Apparently feeling 'pressure' is a euphemism for 'intense pain.'"

I followed the stretcher into the recovery room, which was filled with a line of other gurneys. A nurse connected Grandma's IV to a bag of clear fluid, stole a glance toward my book, and asked what I was studying for. I told her that I wasn't, really . . . The nurse laughed. Grandma said, under closed lids, that I was going to be a doctor and a writer, that I'd decided that when I was five years old.

"Wow—good for you," the nurse said, and I could tell by her voice that she didn't believe it. I didn't believe it, either.

When Grandma reached out her hand, I slipped it in my own and bent close to listen to her quiet voice. "Elyse, about writing—wait as long as you can before you put yourself out there. You don't have the luxury that we did forty years ago: you can't just disappear."

"Okay." I squeezed and she squeezed back. "Can I still read your novel?" I asked, and she opened her eyes.

"It's not very literary." I started to protest, and she said, "But I will make sure to get you a copy."

After that Grandma napped for a while on the stretcher, while I sat in the chair next to her bed and watched the ebb and flow of the recovery room. At last, the nurse came back in, checked Grandma's vital signs, along with the output on the bag, and said we could go.

We walked out through the automatic doors of the hospital into blinding sunlight. I squinted at the sky, wondering if it had ever looked so blue in Pittsburgh, wondering how it was possible that people were sunbathing and windsurfing and Rollerblading while other people were dying. Beneath the flapping palm trees, a landscaper was spraying a white cloud of gas, some kind of fertilizer I guess, across the bushes and grass, and I tried not to inhale the toxic fumes.

"God, I hope that stuff doesn't give me cancer," Grandma muttered.

I glanced over at her and, without thinking, let the breath that I was holding on to turn into a mouthful of laughter. Grandma met my eyes with a sly smile, and I laughed even harder, especially when I remembered that I'd left my review book in the recovery room, and I wasn't going back for it.

CHAPTER 17

Hard Landing

June 1944

I am flying through the night—without a plane, without an engine—over the Texas prairie, whose endless sky is full of shooting stars. I could gaze at them forever until it occurs to me my parachute hasn't been deployed; in fact, I'm not even wearing one. I'm falling fast, accelerating through space and time toward impact, my heart peaking in the back of my throat, when Murphee Sutherland suddenly barks, "Come on, ladies. Up and at 'em." I open my eyes, briefly disoriented, and then exhale. Grace groans as she pulls herself out of bed and reaches for her boots, and Ana wonders if there will be powdered eggs for breakfast again, while Vera warily reminds us that today's the day we fly the Texan AT-6—the claustrophobia-inducing, closed-cockpit plane with the narrow landing gear. "Six hundred horsepower engine," Ana reminds us with a grin, and Murph says, "Oh, baby." As we pull on our clothes and lace up our boots and step out into the wind, sunlight is just making its way over the horizon. It's marching time.

We are four months into our required flight hours, through primary and basic ground school and moving to the advanced phase of instrument flying, where we'll learn to rely only on the dashboard in the plane to guide us. At the end come two solo cross-country trips, one five-hundred-miler, in the Stearman—without a radio, without flying in formation—and a thousand-mile flight in the AT-6. If I pass, I'll get my silver wings at graduation in October before we receive our official orders, scattering us to air bases across the country.

That's the plan, anyway, until Captain Digby, a whistle dangling from his lips, hands me a letter after calisthenics. I recognize Mama's neat handwriting on the outside of the envelope. *I need you at home,* she's written. *Consider quitting the program.*

"The doctor says Sarah's not responding to the treatments," Mama says later, after I beg a favor from Mr. Hendricks and use the telephone in the instructor's lounge.

"What are they giving her?" I ask, shivering in my government-issued shorts and T-shirt, still sweaty from the morning's PT.

"I don't know. I'm not there."

"Is she—going to be okay?" Tears fill my eyes as the last word gets lodged in my throat.

"Of course, she'll be all right, but it would cheer her up, Miri, just to see your face," Mama adds. "And I can use your help in the shop and taking care of Rita."

Through the ready room window, I see the women heading out to the flight line, the first time we get to fly with a classmate. Today's mission will take us a state away, to Oklahoma, where we'll stay overnight at the officers' quarters, and then ferry a different aircraft back to Sweetwater. "I can't just up and leave. There's a war going on."

"The war is not in Texas," Mama says, her voice sharp. "And you sound awfully happy these days," she adds, making me wonder if Sarah's been sharing the letters I've written just for her.

"Do you want me to be unhappy?" I ask, a silly question, Sarah would say. As if happiness mattered to Mama. Were Abraham and Isaac and Jacob and Joseph really worried about feeling happy?

"What if something happens to you, Miri?" she adds, her pitch climbing. "You can't pretend it's not dangerous."

"Mama, I know what I'm doing," I say, and she is quiet for such a long moment that I wonder if we've been disconnected.

"Finish the job you've committed to," she finally says. "Then come home."

LATER THAT AFTERNOON, MURPHEE AND I ARE AT THREE THOU-sand feet, flying in formation toward an air base in Oklahoma, when a thick fog rolls in and completely shrouds the AT-6. I blame my mother for this sudden shift in the weather.

Behind me, Murph studies the instrument panel, while I'm the "safety pilot"—the extra set of eyes up front to make sure we're not following a false horizon. Except that in every direction, all I can see is white.

"Let's try to get underneath it," Murph says, so we dip down five hundred feet, only to be met with endless, choppy white and more blindness.

What if we collide with another aircraft—the one carrying Ana and Grace flying parallel to us only minutes ago? My gloved fingers are numb, and my heart surges as if I'm back in the dream, on the verge of falling to earth just by the realization of my own weightlessness.

"The fuel gauge is dropping," she adds, as the plane lurches violently in the wind. "There must be a leak."

She radios our coordinates, and as we wait for a reply through the static, Mama's fears, Uncle Hyman's disapproval, even Captain Babcock's disgust floods the engine inside my chest. Suddenly, the fact that I am here at all, barreling above the earth at twenty-five hundred feet, seems like an audacity. Gravity has to catch up to me sometime.

A voice comes over the radio, giving us the location of Altus Army Airfield, the nearest military base, one hundred miles north.

I turn the mixture valve, hoping for that ideal fuel-to-air ratio that will make the gas last a little longer, when the engine starts to make an ominous rumbling sound.

"Careful. You're running it rough," Murphee says. "We're gonna stall out."

"There's a storm from the east," I hear Ana say over the radio from one of the other planes. "Visibility is zero."

At last, new coordinates arrive: a civilian airfield not twenty miles away, in Vernon, Texas. All three of our planes are instructed to land when able.

As we level out at a thousand feet, the fog dissolves into gray pockets of heavy rain. Below us, the plains come into view and then at last, the grid of small-town streets.

"There's the strip," Murph says from behind me.

"That's a road," I say. "With cars on it."

"We're nearly out of gas. If we stall out over a house—"

"I can make it. Just—hold on," I add, spying the airstrip to the west. I'm not sure if I'm coaching Murph, the plane, or my mother, whose voice keeps lingering in my mind like a curse: *What if something happens to you?*

At five hundred feet, I lower the landing gear, lock the wheels, and give the throttle some juice until the air speed indicator reads 95 knots. If the fuel gauge is accurate, we could lose the engine at any moment. Beginning our cross over loop, perpendicular to the direction of the wind as well as the strip, I radio: "Aircraft 6537 on final, gear down and locked," and we make our approach for that final turn that will put us in line with the runway. Except that I make the arc too shallow—or maybe I just haven't accounted for the wind pushing us the opposite way and the fact that I can't back off the throttle so quickly in a storm—but suddenly we're flying off course.

"You're going wide!" Murph shouts, as I jam on the right rudder to yaw the nose back in the direction of the runway.

"Come on, come on," I mutter, clutching the stick in my sweaty palm as we descend. If I break the glide of the plane too low, we'll hit hard and bounce, so I wait and wait and then right as we're nearing touchdown, I pull back on the stick, hard and fast. Instead of landing, the plane lifts up, rising skyward like a doomed balloon.

For a single moment, as the ground grows farther away, it's silent in the cockpit, save the strain of the engine on empty, the patter of rain against the hood, and the buzz of my self-doubt. *What if I can't*—I think and then stop, remembering Sarah.

Now is not the time. There's no choice but to fly higher and circle around again.

"Steady!" Murph shouts over the engine. Between the whipping wind from the west and the diagonal sheets of water from the east, it's hard to keep the wings level and maintain speed at 75 knots as we cross over for another pass. One hundred fifty feet below, the ground is green and lush, beckoning and dangerous; it can save us or take us.

Sweat drips down the back of my flight suit. I think of the movie we watched in ground school, where cadets were advised to have a "light but firm touch" on the stick like "taking a pulse," and realize I'm strangling the patient. *Let go, Miriush,* Papa says in my mind, and I ease up my grasp and exhale.

This time when I make the turn parallel to the runway, I get the approach right, descending in a straight path for the wet, grassy landing strip. The front wheels and back tail of the plane are perfectly aligned on all three points, and my feet are stable on the deck. At the precise point of touch down, I cut the throttle, remembering the Ten Commandments for Safe Flying, specifically number five: *Thou Shalt Maintain Thy Speed Lest the Earth Arise and Smite Thee.* That's what it feels like, too: an assault from the earth, as the right tire explodes and we find ourselves skidding in that direction. I jam hard on the left rudder but the tail wheel is already shooting out like a weathervane seeking the wind. My feet dance on the rudders, left and then right and then left, trying to compensate for the shifting tail, which sends us into a dizzying ground spin and makes my brain feel like its torqueing inside my skull. We skid one hundred and eighty degrees and then finish the length of the runway backward, as I ride the brakes with all my strength, despite how many times we've been told to go easy on them. Just before slamming into the hangar, the plane comes to rest.

Toppling back in my seat, I gasp with relief. There's a high-pitched ringing sound in my ears, along with rain quietly drizzling against the hood.

"Well," Murph says, peeling off her helmet. "That was fun."

ONCE THE OTHERS ARE SAFELY DOWN, WE USE THE AIRPORT phone to call back to base for instructions. Jackie Cochran gives us a name of a local hotel within walking distance and says she'll send an army bus to pick us up in the morning. "You'll get vouchers for the rooms and meals, and whatever you do, stick together and don't tell anyone who you are." We know the drill: women pilots are an experiment. There are no insignias on our flight jackets for a reason.

After making sure the planes are securely chained down to the metal loops on the ground, we wait for the rain to let up and then walk back toward town, a conspicuous group of six women in pants. "What if we get picked up by the sheriff?" Grace asks. We've all heard the story of the women in a class ahead of ours who were arrested under similar circumstances for wandering out to look for dinner—arrested on charges of solicitation simply because they were wearing pants and there weren't any men with them.

"Fine by me—just as long as he drops us at the nearest restaurant," Ana says. "I could eat a horse, and I'm sick of walking."

"To hell with 'em," Murphee says. "If they arrest us for wearing pants, Cochran will bail us out."

We find the hotel easy enough, a narrow, three-story establishment on the main street of Vernon, which looks like a town from the set of an old western movie. Eyeing us nervously, the owner slips us the keys to our rooms, as if this is a holdup. I have a suspicion that he wouldn't have let us check in at all if Jackie Cochran hadn't called ahead. Ana asks him about where we might get some grub, and he points to a swinging wooden door—the entrance of the hotel restaurant. The moment we walk through it, wearing our pants and flight jackets, conversations trail off and utensils stop clanging against plates. I feel like we're the six Lone Rangers.

It's a tiny, ten-table establishment with sprigs of flowers and flickering votive candles on the tables. Grace points to the sign, which says, SEAT YOURSELF, and so we do, taking it upon ourselves to push two tables together. I quickly rescue the centerpieces, as everyone continues to watch us.

"Welcome to Vernon, ladies, what brings you to town?" the waitress asks, handing out menus once we're seated.

We glance at each other. "The storm," Grace says.

"I could sure use a drink," Murph adds, and then orders a double. "What?" she says, after the waitress leaves. "It was dicey up there."

"Too dicey," I mutter, feeling like Vera.

"You sound like me after my first fight with Teddy," Grace says, amused. "Spooked."

"I thought you two never fought," Ana says.

"Not with an ocean between us. But that's how you get stronger," Grace says, looking at me, and I glance up from my menu and exhale.

"I just—hated to have to land."

"We all gotta come down sometime, somewhere, so why not

here?" Murph asks, perking up as the waitress returns with a tray of drinks and a basket of rolls, still warm from the oven.

"Here—keep this to yourselves," she says quietly, releasing a tiny handful of cubes near the breadbasket.

Vera gasps. "Is that—?"

The waitress holds up a finger to her lips and then gives us a conspiratorial wink before she walks way. Grace tosses one foil pat of butter to each of us.

With happy anticipation, I slather the rationed butter onto my roll, barely noticing that one of the patrons, portly and red-faced—reminiscent of my uncle Hyman—has approached the table.

"Excuse me, ladies," the man says, thick Texan accent, and we all look up. "Sorry to interrupt your meal. My wife and I have been taking bets, and I think I'm right. Are you a baseball team?"

Murphee coughs so hard on her roll that Vera has to swat her on the back.

"That's right," Ana says, "we're a baseball team."

"Because my wife here thought you were German spies, and some other fellas over there thought you might be prisoners of war." The man hitches his pants up, reminding me of Humpty Dumpty.

"Nope. No, sir. We're a baseball team. Here to entertain the troops."

"Isn't that right? I knew it, honey!" he turns and calls over his shoulder.

We are one of the best-kept secrets of the war, and we don't even know it yet.

LATER, I CURL UP ON CLEAN SHEETS AND USE SOME PAPER FROM the hotel nightstand to pen a letter to Sarah about the events of the day. I leave out the part about getting spooked in the storm, and how the whole plane could have flipped over and crushed us during the ground spin. Instead, I tell her about what happened after we landed and the goons in the restaurant who think we're just here to entertain the troops.

"You're always writing," Murph says, running a towel over her wet hair. "And you're not even the one with the fiancé," she adds, jerking her head toward Grace, who grins through a yawn in the comfy chair where she's reading an actual book instead of an aviation manual.

"I just want to remember it all," I say, feeling sheepish, because when I'm not corresponding with Sarah, I'm writing letters to Sol. He writes me back, too, pages of longhand about his past and our future. *I'll set up a medical practice out of our home, so whenever you return from the sky, you'll know that I'll be there.* I love that in Sol's dreams I can still fly when the war ends, no matter what decision is reached at the hearing later this month. I can even envision our someday family: a little blond boy with his arms outstretched at the top of the steps waiting for me to scoop him up. Or in Sol's arms beside the runway after the air show, waiting to greet me as I climb down from the cockpit.

"What are you reading over there, Gracie-Grace?" Murph asks, combing her orange locks.

" 'The Open Boat'?" Grace says, looking up from her pages. "Stephen Crane. I read it ages and ages ago, but I didn't really appreciate it until now."

I think back to my high school English class. "Something about a captain, a cook, and a correspondent who are trapped out at sea?"

Grace nods and smiles.

"Sounds like flight school," Ana says.

I decide then that Murphee Sutherland would be the Captain, the way she barks at us to get cracking each morning— our beds made for inspection, our boots tied before we march out to formation. Meanwhile, Ana Santos is the cook, who keeps cheerfully bailing out the boat and asking about what we will eat when we make it to shore. And I am the correspondent.

"Wasn't there another guy? An oiler?" Murphee asks. Grace says the only thing she can remember about the oiler is that he ends up dead in the shallows.

THREE DAYS LATER, BACK IN SWEETWATER, THERE ARE SIRENS ON the airfield in the evening, and I run out of the mess tent to see fire trucks and an ambulance screaming toward a plume of smoking metal hidden somewhere beyond the trees, several miles away. Dust and grit sting my eyes, and I can't stop watching the commotion and panting with panic. When I finally get back to the bunk, Grace is already there, huddling on her cot. "Oh, thank God it wasn't you!" she says, letting go of her knees when I walk through the door and rushing over to hug me. Her eyes are big and brown, matching the fear in my own.

"Who was it?" I ask, but Grace doesn't know, and so I take off my boots and zoot suit and slump on my own cot, my heart turning somersaults in my chest as we wait. One by one, pilots return from the field, ordered to ground by Captain Digby.

"Who was it?" Vera asks, the moment she steps across the

threshold of the barracks, her arms strangely empty without her behemoth binder.

"Who was it?" Ana asks, forty minutes later, and we shake our heads.

Another half hour goes by and still there's no sign of Murphee.

"Where the hell is she?" Ana says, pacing back and forth.

"You know how she likes to talk to people—she's probably getting the scoop," I say, only I'm not quite confident. Murphee likes to take unnecessary chances and has already risked a pink slip for her wild abandonment of precision flying.

"Did you see it?" Murphee asks, finally bursting into the room. Grace bounds up from the bed and hugs her, and tears of relief prick my eyes. "I watched it fall. The plane lost its engines and just dropped like a meteor—Louise Hayes," Murphee adds, before we can ask again. "No survivors."

"Oh my God," Vera breathes, and Ana starts pacing again.

The falling feeling sweeps over me again. *Louise, I just went dancing with you. You were a wallflower with me. How can you be dead?*

"But there wasn't a cloud in the sky, and her takeoff was perfect," Grace says.

"Sabotage," Murphee says, slamming the door to her footlocker.

I think of Louise warning me to carefully inspect my plane and doubting that the birds were responsible for my engine failure that day in the Stearman. "But . . . sabotage how?" I ask.

"Sugar in the gas tank," Murphee says. "The plane can still get up, until eventually the carburetor quits and the engine just conks out."

"Come on," I say. "Who would do such a thing?"

"You'd be surprised. Some men go crazy by the idea of women 'invading the cockpit.' Of course, the military will probably call it 'pilot error.'"

I think of the last crash investigation, for the WASP at Camp Davis whose plane went down when her engine was hit by a shell from the gun crew trying to qualify for overseas duty. Jackie Cochran had flown to that site, too, but left it to the military to sort out the paperwork. "Pilot error," they claimed again, despite the fact that the pilot had radioed she'd been hit by the flak from the antiaircraft guns the guys were shooting during tow-target duty.

"What's Jackie Cochran going to do? Make a stink and have them scrub the whole program? We're on thin ice as it is," Vera says, reminding me that the congressional hearing to militarize the WASP is coming up at the end of this month.

"Jesus," Grace says. "Someone should pay for this."

"No one will pay—and certainly not the goddamn government," Murphee says, her voice bitter. "They won't so much as give her a flag for her coffin. We're just civilians, remember?"

There's a soft knock at the door, and Mildred Winter, another pilot, pops her head into our room. "Someone's here for Miri. And Captain Digby wants us at the flagpole in ten."

No one asks who's here for Miri. Nobody catcalls and tells me they'll see me k-i-s-s-i-n-g in a tree; no one has the energy for that now. In the silence, I pull my boots back on and run outside and into the wind. Inside the gate, Sol is there. Just seeing him like that, clutching his fedora in his hands, makes my heart lurch with relief. Finally reaching him, I let him hold me for a long moment, thinking how strange it is that I was ever afraid to touch him.

"I heard a plane went down," he whispers into my hair, before kissing my forehead and then my cheeks. "I was afraid it was you."

"It was my friend Louise," I say, the words choking in my throat, and he hugs me harder, for a long time. Engines are roaring, planes are landing, and the wind is still howling in my ears. "You came all the way from Abilene?" I finally say.

"My father—he's the one who heard someone talking about it at the shop. He gave me the keys to the truck and told me to go make sure you were all right." I feel a swell of love rise up like a wave, and I don't know if it's for Sol or his father. "There's something else . . ." Sol slowly adds, a flicker of worry crossing his face. "I got a call today from a school in New York. They accepted me for the fall class."

"Medical school?" I gasp and pull away. "You got in? Sol, that's—wonderful."

"Sort of. Maybe. The timing is bad . . ."

"You've been waiting for this your whole life!"

"I know, it's just . . ." His head sags, almost guiltily. "I don't want to leave you."

I place my hands on his cheeks and tilt his head up until our eyes meet again. "This is your calling. You have to go."

THAT NIGHT, LOUISE'S BUNKMATES TAKE UP A COLLECTION TO send her body home, and we all pitch in what little money we have. We don't talk about how she wanted to be a vet, or that she thought flying was easier than swing dancing. She's still very much in the present tense, still scooping up the cockroaches in the bathroom to set them free, because to dwell on her in the past tense means we'd have to dwell on ourselves. We are shaken but silent. I can't sleep again, my mind awash with plane sabotage and Louise's flagless coffin. I think of Sarah, lying in a TB sanatorium, and Mama making dress after dress after dress in Uncle Hyman's store, and of Sol's face, twisting with worry, despite all the promises for the rest of our lives. Is he afraid to say goodbye because he knows it might be forever?

The rest of the week goes by and while things are not exactly back to normal, it's the military, which means the routine is always the routine: marching, breakfast, marching, ground school, marching, lunch, flight line. Planes go up, planes come down, and while I might cast a quick glance over the man servicing my AT-6, I push away the fear before it can disable me, the same way we push away the topic of death at dinner. The truth is, none of us wants to think about things we can't change. If I worry that maybe I'm next, I'm already done for, so instead I wake up each day and tell myself there's a reason I'm here.

On June 26, we're at the bunk after PT and changing into our flight suits, when Murph rushes in from the field. "They're shutting us down!" she says, and I stop lacing my boots to regard her standing there. "They're shutting us down!" she repeats, like a wild-eyed, orange-haired Paul Revere, and there's a sudden constriction in my chest, making it hard to speak.

"They can't do that," Grace says.

Murph hands us each a mimeographed paper like a pilot dropping an evacuation flyer—and we are civilians in a town about to be wiped off the map. It's a letter from General Arnold informing us that as of December 20, 1944, the Women Airforce Service will disband. Effective immediately, the program will no longer take new pilots.

"What about the petition to Congress?" I say at last.

"You heard the lobbyists—we weren't meant to replace them, we were meant to *release* them for combat," she says bitterly. "The men are coming home and they want their jobs back. The bill sunk. We're not part of the military, and we never will be."

I imagine this news reaching the house on Beacon Street, as Uncle Hyman reads the paper and drinks his morning coffee—turning redder by the sip—and Mama rinses the dishes. At first she's annoyed when he begins to read aloud—*can't he see how busy she is?*—but then, as he's pontificating about how women should never have been allowed to fly in the first place, she snatches the paper away and scans the print herself. *Disbanded*, she sees, and for the first time in four months, Mama exhales. But then I think of Sarah, alone in her dreary room, searching the sky through her hospital window. *You're staying,* she says, and in my mind, and it's an order, not an option. I have six months to fly—possibly for the rest of my life. "I'm staying," I say aloud, and Murph looks at me with surprise.

"Aren't we all?"

CHAPTER 18

The Visitor

In the forthcoming days after my appointment with Dr. Khaira, I approached my gallbladder surgery as if I were awaiting execution. At night, it was all I could imagine: the steel operating room table, my prone body frozen under the bright lights, the sharp instruments slicing me open. It wasn't Dr. Khaira's skill that I doubted, only his optimism: whenever I thought of undergoing general anesthesia, I couldn't imagine ever waking up again.

So, I went shopping for books to distract me, for a new soft nightgown and sheets, for fat-free frozen yogurt, since I'd promised Dr. Khaira not an ounce of Häagen-Dazs would cross these lips until after the surgery, knowing it could precipitate another attack. In fact, just as I was leaving the little corner store, with my bag of carefully selected, nutritionally tasteless items, Gary the grocer called out, "Oh, Mrs. Browning? You're a nickel short." It must've been the shock on my face that made him wave his hand and tell me to never mind.

"No, no, no—you need your money!" I insisted, fumbling in my change purse and setting down five single pennies with shaking fingers. The last thing that I wanted was the charity discount for senior citizens who'd forgotten basic addition.

Still flustered from my mistake, I rushed from the store, whose bells jangled on the door, before sidestepping an older man on the sidewalk going the opposite way.

"It takes a bullshitter to spot a bullshitter!" the man called, which made me hurry on, until the same voice said, "Mary Browning, there's not a damn thing wrong with your foot," and I whirled around to see Gene Rosskemp standing there. He was wearing jeans and a flannel shirt under his jacket and in his hand was a stick, the end of which contained a stuffed horse's head. The head was bright white, the mane absurdly pink and purple.

"I beg your pardon?"

He waved the horse's head in the air, streamers and all, and said, "Come on now, *pony* up. What the hell happened to you? Selena said you left on a stretcher by an ambulance because you stubbed your big toe."

"It spontaneously and miraculously healed," I said, and would've tap-danced to prove it, but at this point, having given Gary the grocer the wrong change, I was now officially afraid of the cracks in the sidewalk. Instead, I asked him why on earth he was holding a pony.

"It's for the newest member of the Rosskemp clan—we finally got ourselves a little girl! Thought I'd send a gift, although I don't know how the hell I'm gonna ship this thing."

"Maybe you can wait and give it to her when they visit."

"Eh." Gene waved his hand in the air. "They live in California. They'll never visit. I get a Christmas card each year. Birth announcements. A thank-you letter if I send a gift." He took out his wallet and then slid out a picture and handed it to me. I peered at the lovely little blond boy wearing a conductor hat and sitting in a large toy train.

"Beautiful boy," I said, handing it back.

"That 'beautiful boy' is a professor of linguistics now at UCLA. He's the one whose wife just had a baby girl. I don't blame him for not keeping in better touch. His dad and I had a falling-out along the way. Can't say I exactly know why." Gene glanced to our right and steered me out of the path of foot traffic and over toward the bench on the edge of the sidewalk. "My grandson does his best to keep me in the loop. And I do my best to make sure they remember me," Gene added, patting the horse on its head as he sat down.

It occurred to me then that maybe I was wrong about the writers' group. It had been ages since I'd listened to the stories between their stories, ages since I'd heard anything but the loud pulse of my own losses and regrets. But they must have been suffering, too, suffering and struggling to find something to feel hopeful about.

"I know a secret about you, Mary Browning," Gene said, dropping his voice.

"Oh?" I said, flushing with fear.

"A little birdy told me at the last meeting that you flew planes during the war. You acted all impressed with my model airplanes, and you never even told me you were the real deal!"

"Well, I-I wasn't *acting* that day. It was marvelous watching you fly . . ."

"Aw, Mary, don't patronize me," he said, even though I

wasn't. I'd loved feeling the sunshine on my face and the small thrill of standing next to a man who wanted nothing more than to show me his passion. "I was waiting to hear what was wrong with my story, when you didn't show up the other night," he added, even quieter then. "Waiting to have my ass handed to me, looking forward to it, really."

"I have to have my gallbladder out, and I'm terrified," I blurted, feeling foolish by my own irrational fear—after all, the other Jean had had her chest sawed open the year before and lived to write horrid prose about it. I plopped down on the bench next to Gene and heaved my packages onto my lap. It felt good to sit.

"Oh, I had mine out after the war, and it was no big deal," Gene said. "These days they just pump you full of gas and slip a tiny camera inside you, snip, tug, and it's out—piece of cake. Was for me and they sliced me open all the way from here to here." He drew a long, invisible line across the top right corner of his belly. " 'Course, just a few years ago, I started to get some right-sided pain again, right? And I go to the emergency room and they run tests, and after a while, the doctor comes in really shocked—and the last thing you want is to have something that makes a doctor practically speechless, right? And he says, 'You're not going to believe this but somebody left a metal clamp inside of you sixty years ago.' He slaps up an X-ray on the light box and I see with my own eyes, plain as day, the handles. Looks like a pair of scissors! And doc says it must've shifted or something, which caused my pain. So, they took me back to the OR to remove the clamp." He smiled at me. "But that's not gonna happen to you."

"Good Lord," I whispered.

"Relax, Mary. The more you worry about shit going wrong, the more you open yourself up to it. Don't get stuck in your own head. Bad place to be—unless you're writing or something."

"I liked your story very much, Gene," I said, suddenly reminded. "In fact, it actually surprised me."

A smile spread across his face. "Surprised you?"

"You actually made me care about an inanimate object—a truckload of wine! I cared about whether the wine would make it past the French police. I cared when it looked like the bottles might be broken. I wanted the Seventy-Fifth Squadron to succeed in the great rescue. And when you and your wife shared a bottle on your anniversary? Delightful."

"Mary Browning, are you feeling okay?" Gene said, and I could tell I'd made his day, possibly his month. "Is this the bad gallbladder talking?"

I laughed, until I realized that the woman in a purple tracksuit striding toward us—fists pumping, weights swinging from her ankles—was actually Selena Markmann. She would have kept powering on by if Gene hadn't whistled like the construction worker that he once was.

"Mary Browning!" Selena exclaimed, as if I were the cat-caller. "There you are! I just had the pleasure of meeting Tyler's nephew. How wonderful for you!"

I stared at her. "Who . . . ?"

"Your grandson *Tyler,* who works for *Microsoft*?" she reminded me. "His nephew is visiting. He said he's a cousin of the twins? Your great-granddaughters?" It was quite strange: the woman sounded utterly serious.

I blinked. "Oh?"

"Yes, he's here. Well, not here here. He's back at the high-rise. I asked how long he was visiting for, and he said he lives in the area. How nice for you to finally have some family nearby."

"Oh, yes. Very nice. My. I had almost forgotten he was coming," I said, woozily rising to a stand and collecting my packages.

"Well, he's up there," Selena said.

"He is? Still?"

"Sitting outside your door on the floor, waiting for you. I gave him the fiction for next week's meeting. You'll be there, won't you?"

This Tuesday's writers' group was exactly one week before my surgery. I would dissect fiction one last time before Satinder Khaira would dissect me. "I'll be there with bells on," I said.

Gene smiled and said, "Thatta girl, Mary. You'll be *horsing around* in no time!" he added with a wink, waving around that silly horse again.

I quickly walked the single block back to the high-rise and then took the elevator to the third floor. Sure enough, in the shadow of the hallway, I could see a boy sitting in the hall, his legs stretched out across the floor, and a laptop open on his knees. I thought of Dave and my scalp began to tingle.

"Mary Browning?" the boy asked, when I stopped in front of my door.

"Hello," I said, eyeing him. He had reddish hair, very fair skin, and a smattering of freckles across his cheeks and nose. "And you are . . . ?"

"Toby Strickler." He shut the lid of his computer and scrambled to his feet. "You know my sister, Elyse?"

"Oh, Elyse! Yes, of course. Come in, come in," I said, quickly unlocking my door and ushering him inside before Selena could return. "How is she?" I added, after shutting the door and setting my packages down on the counter.

"I don't know how she is. She left." Toby put his backpack on the linoleum floor before sliding his computer onto my kitchen table, right next to my own. I couldn't help wondering why he was in possession of a laptop computer when his older sister was not. I was about to inquire, when he asked, "So, how do you know my sister?"

"Well, we met at the library—at the writers' group. I believe you met Selena, earlier, who is also a member?"

"Oh, yeah. Here." Toby stooped down to unzip his backpack and rummaged around until he came up with two packets of collated papers: a short story by Victor Chenkovitch about the Holocaust, which would probably be more uplifting than the next chapter from Jean Fester's memoir: we were finally at her partial colectomy. Before I could thank Toby, he stood up and added, rather sternly, "You bought my sister a plane ticket to Key West?"

"Yes. Why?" I asked, startled. "Is everything all right?"

"Well, she's fine. But my mom got called into her boss's office because of it."

"Because Elyse went to Key West? I'm sorry; I don't follow . . ."

"My little brother was sick, and Mom needed Elyse to watch him. I could've stayed home all day, but Mom didn't trust me to be in charge for ten hours. And my dad wasn't around, and Mom didn't have any help, so she canceled this really important deposition again and got in trouble with her boss."

"I see. Well. Goodness, I'm awfully sorry." I pulled out one of the kitchen chairs, intending to offer it to the boy, but sank into it myself, since he seemed intent on standing, hands on his hips.

"Mom was really mad at Dad because she thought he bought the tickets for Elyse, but he said he didn't know anything about it. Mom said she didn't believe him, because Elyse told her the tickets came from him, so they got in a bigger fight, and now they're getting a divorce."

"Oh, dear." I massaged my head.

"And, you know, she's under age eighteen. She can't just go flying off to—wherever," Toby said, playing an excellent mimic of his mother, I presumed.

"Excellent point, sir." I thought of myself, long ago, leaving home for the sky, and how my mother and Uncle Hyman had said more or less the same thing. "As I understood it, your grandmother is very ill."

At least that got his shoulders to drop. "Mom doesn't really know what's going on."

"And how did you figure out that it was I who bought Elyse the tickets?"

"I hacked her email," Toby said with a shrug. "She has the easiest passwords. And there was a confirmation email from Travelocity. It had your name and address, and the price of the tickets and everything."

"My credit card number, too?" I asked, alarmed.

"Just the last four digits." He was watching me, waiting now, but I wasn't sure for what. "So?" he prompted.

"So . . . ?"

"So, why would you pay a thousand dollars to send my sister to Key West?"

That made me laugh, because really, how could I answer that? It was, indeed, a very good question. Because she looked like my sister Sarah? Because she reminded me a little of me? Because I had quite a lot of money and no one to spend it on? "I guess the best answer is that I can afford it. And it seemed like a good idea at the time. Perhaps I may have overstepped my bounds."

"Just seems like a lot to spend on airfare. During hurricane season."

"It is a lot of money. But there are times to save and times to spend." I sighed. "Is your mother aware that I was the one to send Elyse to Key West without consulting her?"

"I didn't tell her yet."

"I see. Well . . ." I searched my brain for something I might offer the boy to keep his mouth shut, until the answer struck me: "Would *you* like to go visit your grandmother in Florida, too?" A flicker of confusion crossed his face, followed by a slow smile, and then a laugh of obvious disbelief. It was a lovely sound, and I knew, in that moment, he wouldn't tell a soul.

"Elyse is in big trouble. I don't want to be in big trouble, too."

"No, of course not, you're very right. You're a bright young man. You can't just . . . as you pointed out . . . come and go as you please." I hesitated and then asked him what he wanted from me.

"I don't really know," he finally said. "I just want things to go back to normal."

I nodded in complete understanding. Since old age had settled upon me, I'd been feeling the same way. "Is there anything I can do?"

"Do you have any food?"

And then it was my turn to laugh, as I creaked to standing and headed over to the kitchen cabinet, which I flung open so he could see my selection of cereals. He picked Honey Bunches of Oats. With tremulous fingers, I handed him the box and then went to retrieve a bowl from the drawer and milk from the fridge. Toby thanked me politely and took a seat across from me. I sat back down and watched him, watched his furrow of concentration as he steadied the milk and then the smile as he crunched on his first mouthful. Then I leaned on my hands and watched him some more and thought that his mother did not know what she was missing.

"Where does your mother think you are right now?" I asked finally, once he was halfway through the bowl.

"Piano. But I called up and canceled this morning, so my teacher isn't expecting me. Then I walked over." Toby reached into the box with his fingers, grabbed a handful of dry cereal, and crunched on that, too. I wanted to figure out how I could possibly help, but instead I found myself asking about Selena Markmann. What could have possibly given her the idea that Toby was related to me?

"She was being kind of nosy—wanting to know who I was and how I knew you and why I was waiting here. So, I said I was your nephew, and she said she thought I must mean your *great-great*-nephew, so I said, Yeah sure, and she said, Are you related to the twins? And I said, They're my cousins." He shrugged. "It seemed easier to make up stuff to get her to go away."

"Bless your heart," I whispered.

CHAPTER 19

Goodbye Forever

July 1944

It is the end of July when Sol shows up at the gate outside of Avenger Field for our last date. I watch his face stutter through various emotions—confusion, surprise, and wry amusement—when he realizes I've brought along the women from my bunk, minus Vera Skeert, who stayed behind for church this morning and to study her aviation manuals this afternoon. "Oh, wonderful. You've brought . . . bodyguards," Sol says.

"Hey, Sol!" Murphee says, with a mock Texas twang in her voice, as she hops into the back of the Ford pickup. She's wearing cutoff shorts and a plaid shirt tied at the waist. "Thanks for letting us tag along."

"Where am I taking you all?" he asks, genuinely curious.

"Inks Lake! We heard the waterfall is supposed to be gorgeous," Murphee says, flipping her orange hair. "Ana even packed her paintbrushes. And Grace wants to see a golden-cheeked warbler. Come on, ladies!"

Grace gives me a smile and a shrug before climbing into the back.

"It's our only day off," Ana says, by way of explanation. "And we're heathens."

"They know it's on the other side of the state?" Sol asks me.

"They know. They like hiking."

"And men!" Murphee calls. "Take us to your friends."

"I WISH YOU DIDN'T HAVE TO GO," I SAY, ONCE WE'RE ON THE highway and heading southeast. At least I get to sit next to him for the long ride, while the rest of the ladies are in the truck bed. In my side mirror, I can see Murphee tipping her head back and laughing. "Someday, I'll visit you in New York," I add, reaching over to give his hand a reassuring squeeze.

"Miri . . ." he starts, taking a deep breath, and I hear the gloom in his voice and pull away, thinking, *This is where I find out we were only in love in my imagination.* "The thing is . . . I sort of fudged my application."

"To medical school?" I say, confused but relieved. *Med school. Not us.*

"It was sort of an experiment . . . at least, in the beginning," Sol says, shifting his eyes between the road and me. "I knew they kept rejecting me because of the quotas. And why should my religion matter to a public university? So, this time I applied everywhere as 'Solomon Rubinowicz,' except for a school in the Bronx, where I called myself 'Thomas Browning.'" He grips the steering wheel harder and glances at me. "They accepted me. They don't know I'm Jewish."

I can't help shuddering when Murphee lets out another cackle somewhere over my left shoulder. "But what happens when they find out you are?" I ask, dropping my voice.

"They're not going to." He tells me that he knows a man who knows another man who makes extra cash by altering documents in the basement of his printing shop. For no small fee—two months of Sol's salary at the drugstore—Sol got himself another name, another birth certificate, and another chance to enter medical school. "If you marry me, you'll be Mrs. Thomas Browning."

Marry me. The words fill my head with an unexpected rush, unless that's just panic. "But . . . what would it mean . . . exactly?" I ask.

"It means they can't discriminate against us," he says. "It means we can make the future whatever we want it to be."

I hesitate. Back home, Squirrel Hill is a largely Jewish community, and while it's recognized that there are clubs and schools that we aren't permitted to attend, I've always felt more held back by being a woman than by my religion. "We can still be Jewish," he adds. "We'll just . . . have another name."

"Give it time, Rina," Papa used to say to my mother, when she wanted to leave Freetown. "More Jews will move here, and we'll build a synagogue. Until then, we have our faith, our girls, and our bit of land. What more do we need?" he'd repeat like a mantra to Mama. Was Papa right? Could Sol and I be unmoored from the fold and still keep our faith? Was it enough to rely on each other?

"What will your parents say?" I ask, thinking of his father.

How can Sol betray the man who gave his only son the keys to the truck and told him to go find me? And how can I betray my mother who has given me everything, always?

Sol inhales and reaches for my hand across the gearshift. "I care what you say."

Of all the scenarios I could possibly imagine for the rest of our lives, I never imagined this one.

HOURS LATER, WE REACH THE FALLS, OR AT LEAST APPROACH striking distance, after a long drive in the heat, a quick snack at a general store in Eden, and one stop at the apartment of Sol's friends. Murphee is still disappointed that "the men" consist of one Matthew McAllister, a freckled law student who can't stop sneezing into his hankies, and Jack Koppleman, another bookish mate who quickly dropped his pencils for a truckload of women pilots. When we finally park the truck in the dust, we're a thirsty, sweaty, sunbaked lot, almost too tired to set off through the wildflowers as the sun begins to descend in the sky. Trailing behind the others, I wonder if I dare tell him not to do it—not to go away. But then I think of how I felt when women were banned from the civilian pilot training program just after I'd made it through—and when the good ol' boys in Congress voted against us last month. *If all I needed was a new name to fly,* I think, trudging through the tall grasses, *I'd give myself a new name. But how can I deny my religion, my family?*

"Are you okay?" Grace says quietly, falling back to join me. "I knew we shouldn't have crashed your last date."

I nod and then shake my head, belatedly. "No, no—it's fine. I'm fine."

But I'm back in the fog again, searching for a way out. Is this goodbye for now or goodbye forever?

At last, we reach the shade of the woods and listen for waterfalls to guide our way, which invariably turns out to be wind rippling through the junipers. Finally we find ourselves in a lush alcove: a blue-green pool, surrounded by cliffs of rock.

Murphee immediately strips down to her skivvies and takes the plunge into Devils Water Hole, screaming and shivering. Sol goes next, whooping and cannonballing into the lake. I'm feeling more tentative, balancing on the wet boulders near Grace and Ana and the law students. *How can you have written me such long letters and never bothered to mention this social "experiment" against institutionalized discrimination?* I think. But I know the truth, that it was never an experiment but a means to an end, the only way to fulfill a dream. Who am I to ask him to get another one? At last Sol climbs back out, scoops me up in my one-piece bathing suit, and throws me into the freezing water. Coming up for air, I feel like a child, being born—the slap and chill of reality. I have to choose: life with Sol or life with my family.

We haven't been treading water very long when Murphee decides things are getting boring—it's not enough that we have a can of tuna, saltines, and four apples to feed the lot of us, that the sun will go down and we're probably miles away from wherever we parked the truck. "I dare y'all to jump off the top of that boulder," she says, pointing to the tallest rock rising above the water, which appears to have been placed there by a giant.

"Let's all do it," Murphee says, beginning to climb the rocks. "What're y'all, chicken?"

"What's with the accent, New Jersey?" Ana asks.

"I'll try," Sol says and then turns to look at me. "What about you, Miri? Are you in?" I feel as if he's asking me everything about our future.

I think of what Mama would say, and then, just as quickly, what my sister would say. *Keep sending me your stories, Miri. Keep flying high for both of us,* she wrote. I have to do it for the same reason I have to do everything right now, like flying, like marching, like running, like hiking, like breathing: I have to do it, because Sarah can't. "Of course, I'm in," I say.

I'm terrified—clamoring up the boulders, with shaking arms and legs. And once at the top, I can't stop shivering uncontrollably. Even Grace is smarter than I, hunkering down in the pool below and cheering us on the higher we get. Murphee is the first to go, screaming the whole way down. I watch and wait for her head to bob up again and am relieved by the sound of her cackling. Then goes Ana, who screams obscenities and then laughs hysterically when she resurfaces from the lake.

"I can't," I say weakly, as we stand at the edge, even though, after climbing so high, it's the only way down. I'll never manage the rocks in reverse.

"But you're a *pilot*," Sol says.

"Without a plane!"

"Come on—it's easy." He grins and reaches out for my hand. "Breathe and fall. Breathe and fall, that's all we have to do."

I think of my beautiful nightmare. "I can't change my name. I can't—lose my family."

"Then I'll stay in Abilene."

"You have to go. It's—what I would do. But Sarah's sick, and Mama needs me. I can't let them down," I say, my voice cracking.

"Oh, Miri, don't cry. Not on our last day together." Sol pulls me toward him and then kisses me, until my teeth stop chattering and my lips warm up again and my tears stop falling—until Murphee is shouting something about getting a room. "I don't have to be Thomas Browning forever," he adds, still holding me close. "Can you wait four years for me to be me again?"

"I don't know," I say, bewildered.

"Jump!" Grace shouts from the pool below.

"Jump!" Ana screeches.

Sol's palm brushes down my arm until he finds my hand again and squeezes. "Ready?" he asks.

I look down at the drop and then up to his reassuring face and nod. Together we take a flying leap off the precipice. It's over quickly: the rush of the fall, the wind in my ears, the flail of my arms, and then a graceless splash. We find each other underwater and then come up for mouthfuls of air and laughter, lots and lots of laughter, and that's when I know that the right thing to do is to say goodbye forever, and that I'll never know joy like this again.

HOURS LATER, WHEN WE GET BACK TO BASE, THE GIRLS PILE OUT of the back of the truck bed and traipse off toward the barracks after thanking Sol for the lovely day. I wait until they are out of earshot to tell him I can't go with him, not now or in four years from now, or ever. "I can't give up everything for the sake of your future."

"Our future," he says, squeezing my shoulders. "I'm not giving up *you*."

"But you are," I say, willing myself not to kiss him one last time. "And I need you to go." I back away, knowing that once I cross under the gate of Avenger Field, he can't follow me. "Please, don't—write to me," I add. "Don't try to keep in touch. It'll only hurt me more."

When I glance back from the dusty path that leads to the bunk, he's still standing in the same spot outside the gate, absently percussing the borders of his heart. I remember the Spartans of Greece and keep walking.

PART 3

CHAPTER 20

Toothpicks

I got back from Key West on Sunday night, and the only thing Mom said when she picked me up outside the airport was, "Well, how did Grandma seem?" I finished stuffing my bag in the backseat before I climbed in the passenger side and told her about the emergency procedure to make Grandma look not so yellow. Mom blinked, turned back in her seat, and put the car in drive. She stayed silent for a while, long enough for us to leave the road around the airport and merge onto 79.

"Am I grounded?" I asked finally.

"I don't think so," Mom said slowly. When I glanced over, she was wiping a tear off her cheek. "Just as long as your schoolwork won't be compromised," Mom finally added, her voice stronger.

"I got all my assignments from Friday. I'm not behind in anything."

Except for the toothpick bridge, which was due in five days. I couldn't believe six weeks had slipped by since Mrs.

McClure first gave us the assignment—and that it had been over two weeks since Thea stopped talking to me. Maybe if we were still partners, I would've created something more than a shaky drawing of a bridge by now. But if we were still partners, Holden Saunders wouldn't have come up to my locker on Wednesday morning, three days after I got back, and said, "Yo, wifey, my house, after school?" When I nodded, beaming, he added, walking away, "And bring some toothpicks!"

The house was empty when we first got there, and I watched as he turned off the alarm, tossed his backpack on the counter, and offered me a drink. I set Henry, our flour baby—just a few days shy of his two-week birthday—down on the table and stood next to Holden as we peered inside his parents' Sub-Zero fridge, which was pretty well stocked. "How about a beer?" he asked me.

"I don't see any beer," I said.

"My parents keep it locked up in the basement fridge, but I know where they keep the key."

I just laughed and said, "No thanks—but the lemonade looks good."

We stood there for a few minutes leaning against the counters and self-consciously drinking our lemonade. The house seemed so quiet, which made me a little nervous when I thought about what my mom would think if she knew I was here instead of at Thea's. Especially when Holden kind of looked me up and down and said, "I hope you didn't buy all new clothes for me."

"*No*," I said, insulted, because I didn't want to be the sort of shallow girl who'd buy new clothes for a boy, even if I am that sort of girl.

"Well, it looks good," he said, staring at me, which made my face heat up and my breath get stuck in my chest, so I looked into my lemonade and gulped the rest of it down.

We talked a little longer in the kitchen—about how Kurt Metzger got sent to the principal's office for giving Mr. Edmund the finger in gym, and how Mrs. Royal, the French teacher, was in love with a man in Tennessee, and how Herman Melville is overrated. We'd just finished reading *Bartleby the Scrivener* in Mrs. Kindling's AP English class, where this guy, Bartleby, takes over the office and locks himself inside and when they ask him to leave, he just repeats over and over, "I'd prefer not to." Holden asked me if I was going to Homecoming, and I said, "Not yet," kind of hopefully, but he didn't ask me. I almost wondered, since he's so hot, if he expected me to ask him.

After that, we took off our shoes—Holden's mom's rule, since all the carpets are plush white—and went up to Holden's room, which was surprisingly neat and sparse, except for the electronics—he had an iPad and an iPhone and a MacBook and a flat-screen TV on the wall. There were vacuum marks in the rug, and the blue comforter on his bed didn't have a wrinkle in it. I put Henry on the dresser next to all of his "father's" lacrosse trophies, while Holden carried in a chair from the other room, so we could both sit at his desk. Then we took out our notebooks and compared the drawings we each made of the bridge we were supposed to build. Holden laughed when he saw mine, which looked complicated and elegant, like the Hulton Bridge straddling the Allegheny River. "Are you crazy? This thing has to hold thirty pounds," he said, and then he showed me his drawing, which looked sort of like a crude box, but I guessed it would do a better job of holding weight, and besides, it looked a lot easier to build. Except that when we finally started to work, the toothpicks just kept clumping together with glue and sticking to our fingers. It was impossible to create anything but globs of toothpick goo, and it was making me anxious, every time I thought of Mrs. McClure going, "Well, you guys should be putting the final touches on your bridges by now, if you're not already finished."

"Fuck," Holden said, for about the thirtieth time. "Are you sure you don't want that beer? 'Cause I could use one." I was feeling pretty much doomed as far as getting an A in physics went, so I said okay.

We crept back downstairs and then all the way to the basement, where the locked fridge was. Holden winked at me when he came up with the key, which had been tucked away in one of the drawers of his dad's workbench. Then he unlocked the fridge and we both chose a beer—Newcastle brown ale for him, a Sierra Nevada for me, exotic *and* a favorite of my dad's. My chest was full of nervous electricity, but I smiled at Holden as if I had done this before.

We drank sitting at his desk by the toothpick debris. The beer tasted terrible, which kind of surprised me, like Eve might've felt if the apple turned out to be a mealy Jonagold. I must've made a face, because Holden asked me if I'd ever had a beer before, and I shook my head. He told me it helped if I chugged it, so I kind of held my breath and drank it as fast as I could get it down. When we went back to work after that, the fact that the toothpicks wouldn't stick to anything but our fingers just seemed sillier and sillier, and we couldn't stop laughing. Suddenly, Holden asked if he could kiss me. My head felt swimmy and fizzy, and I said, "Oh yes!" so readily that he started to laugh. We moved over to the bed, and it was the best first kiss of my entire life, even if his fingers were a little sticky on my face, and I kept wondering if he might be getting glue in my hair or if I was going to get mono from him. His lips were soft compared to my chapped ones, and I wasn't quite sure what to do with my tongue when he put his in my mouth, so I just swirled it around and tasted peanut butter. After a while, he gently pushed me backward, and I could feel his erection pushing into my crotch, which freaked me out a little when I realized what it was. I liked it, but mostly I was scared of liking it.

"Hey," he whispered. "Want to go to Homecoming with me?"

"Yes!" I sat up on my elbow and said, "But I just have to make sure I'm not volunteering at the hospital that night." It seemed better to lie than say I had to check with my mom, who won't let me date until I'm sixteen.

"Volunteering?" Holden repeated.

I don't know why I picked that verb except that I was thinking of how Mrs. Browning was having her surgery next week—Gene Rosskemp had emailed to tell me after Mom made me skip writer's group the night before—and how Mom had said that if I wasn't doing a fall sport, I should at least become a hospital volunteer, to beef up my college applications and ultimately get into medical school someday.

"Well, if it's voluntary, can't you volunteer another night?" Holden asked.

"Yeah, sure. I just have to see if I can get out of it." I kissed his earlobe. "I'll let you know by tomorrow." I would ask my dad first; that was the answer.

We went back to kissing again, and after a while, he

reached up under my shirt and started squeezing my breasts like he was trying to milk them, which reminded me of Gene Rosskemp and Jean Fester comparing me to a cow. I sort of stiffened because 1) I was afraid his mom would get home and walk in on us; 2) I hate my breasts because they sort of jut out like two cones; and 3) I didn't want to be thinking about senior citizens. Except that every time he would ask me if I was okay, I would tell him that I was definitely okay. Because this was Holden Saunders! Kissing me! Nuzzling me! Giving me mono! He unzipped his jeans then, so his penis stuck out of the hole in his boxers, the one Huggie always calls "my penis hole" instead of "my fly," and when I touched it, I was amazed that a penis could be that big, compared to my little brothers'. One time in Key West four years ago, I saw a penis hat in the window of a shop on Duval Street, and I thought, *What's that supposed to represent?* because I'd never seen anything so big and long and erect, but apparently the hat was supposed to represent Holden Saunders's dick. "Want to suck on it? That way we don't have to worry about one of those," he added, jerking his head toward Henry, on the dresser, whose smiley face was looking sort of dopey and clueless.

"I'd prefer not to," I said. When Holden blinked, I wondered if he'd ever had a girl say no to him before. "I'd prefer not to," I repeated.

Suddenly, he cracked up. "Who are you, Bartleby the Scrivener?" he asked. Pretty soon we were both laughing, until we heard the alarm beep from the front door, and we jumped up from the bed. Holden zipped up his jeans and I was tucking in my shirt when his mother yelled, "Holden?" from downstairs.

We both went out to the carpeted landing, which has a railing that overlooks the downstairs marble foyer.

"What are these shoes doing here?" she asked, standing there with groceries even though it hadn't looked like their fridge could hold a single thing more. "I could've tripped and killed myself!" Holden's mom had brown hair with perfect curls at the end, and her eyebrows were thin and arched, like she might've been surprised instead of angry. "Who's your friend?" she added. Holden introduced me and said that we were partners for the toothpick bridge in physics. When she asked how it was coming, he shrugged and said, "Slowly."

"Would you like to stay for dinner, Elyse?" his mom asked.

I did want to stay for dinner, because a girlfriend would stay for dinner, but Holden's hands were in his pockets and his eyes weren't meeting mine, and I got the feeling that maybe he thought his parents might be embarrassing or maybe he didn't want me to hear him getting in trouble for the missing beer bottles, or for not newspapering the desk in his room before we started using glue, so I told her I had to get home. She seemed surprised to hear that I lived next door and could walk myself home, and confused when I came downstairs lugging a sack of flour, even after I reminded her that it was our psych baby. I realized then that all those times Holden wrote in the babysitting log that he'd left Henry with his mother, probably the only thing watching the baby was the little gold man on top of his MVP lacrosse trophy.

As I walked the acre across Holden's yard into my own, it was windy, and leaves were blowing down all around me and sticking to my feet. I hunched my shoulders and zipped up my jacket and held Henry tight against my chest, wishing he were something real and warm to protect.

THE NEXT DAY, BEFORE I GOT THE CHANCE TO RUN INTO HOLDEN to tell him I could go—figuring I'd worry about Mom's reaction later—Thea walked up to my locker and asked if I'd heard that he was going to Homecoming with Karina Spencer. It was the first time I'd heard her voice in two weeks.

"No, he's not. He's going with me," I said, realizing all at once that my arms felt uncharacteristically lighter since I'd accidentally left Henry on my desk during geometry—two periods ago. "He asked me yesterday."

"Well, she asked him this morning. And he said yes."

I shut my locker and said that couldn't be true, but that I had to go—I had to get back to math and on to English before the bell rang.

"Finished your bridge yet?" Thea asked, as I backed away from her into the sea of students, and I shook my head. "But it's due tomorrow!"

Rounding the corner past the gym, I bumped into Holden and he stumbled backward, laughing with surprise. "Whoa, easy," he said, chuckling and steadying me. He looked so kissable in his jeans and sweatshirt, and I was thrilled that his hands were touching my shoulders, and so for a second, I started beaming, too.

"Have you seen this?" Holden added, still laughing, as he handed me a sheet of creased notebook paper. At the top of the page someone had drawn a picture of a cube labeled "All Purpose" with an X through it and at the bottom the words, *Pay or The Torso dies.* It took me a second to realize that what I was reading was a ransom note, for Henry. "Rob Parker found our flour when he showed up for Calculus," Holden explained. I sort of panicked then and said if something happened to Henry, we'll fail the project.

"Stop calling him 'Henry,'" Holden said, glancing around, like he didn't want anyone to find out that we'd actually named it. "Listen, about Homecoming—"

"I can go," I blurted.

"Karina Spencer asked me this morning, and I said okay. Since you weren't sure."

"But I am sure!" My heart was pounding, and my face felt hot. All around us kids were rushing to beat the bell, except for at the end of the hall, where a couple of guys were hooting and laughing. Holden turned and grinned, which is when I realized that these were his lacrosse buddies, and what they were laughing about was Henry, whom they were volleying back and forth between them like they were running a football drill. They neared us, trailing flour.

"Listen, Elyse, you're really cool, but—"

"Aw, look!" one of them interrupted, noticing me.

"'I'd prefer not to,'" Rob Parker quipped, and they broke up, laughing.

Holden winced, as I stared at him, tears gathering somewhere in my throat.

"No, *I'd* prefer not to," his blond buddy replied, tossing Henry higher. "What about you, Saunders? What do you prefer? Fellatio? Or do you prefer not to?"

"Okay, you guys. Shut up," Holden said, but he was smiling when he said it.

"Watch it!" Rob Parker said, lunging for the flour. I watched as the lacrosse player tipped the bag before it hit the floor in an explosion of flour. "Fumble!" the blond guy yelled, and even Holden was laughing. When I turned and ran, he didn't even call after me.

AFTER SCHOOL, I WAS JUST GETTING BACK FROM THE BUS STOP when a horn honked from a BMW turning around in our driveway. It was Dr. Khaira, leaving, and I waved back, wondering if he'd been looking for my dad, wondering if Mom considered him part of "the community" or if he was allowed to know the truth about the divorce.

"Hey, buddy," he said, after rolling down his window.

"Hey," I said, hiking the strap of my backpack up on my shoulder. And then, because he looked so very sorry, I asked, "Is everything okay?"

He shook his head. "I think you better go inside."

I DUMPED MY BOOKS AND SHOES IN THE MUDROOM AND WALKED into the kitchen, which was empty except for the same breakfast dishes crusting in the sink from this morning. In the family room, Toby and Huggie were watching *SpongeBob SquarePants*, and Huggie was already in his Batman pajamas, even though it was only four o'clock.

"Where's Mom?" I asked.

"Upstairs talking on the phone. Grandma died," Toby added, glancing away from the TV.

"No, she didn't," I snapped.

"Ray called. He said she was 'septic.' That's like an infection in your blood that kills you. Ask Mom," Toby said, since I was just standing there, slack-jawed, while SpongeBob danced around celebrating dental hygiene.

"But I just saw Grandma. I saw her *four days ago*. She was fine."

"Ask Mom," Toby said again, before turning back to the TV.

Upstairs, Mom was in her bedroom, so deep in conversation with Rabbi Horowitz that she didn't notice me until I stood next to her, flapping my arms. "Five minutes," she mouthed, covering up the mouthpiece. I listened for a second but as soon as I heard her talking about "flying Margot's body back to Pittsburgh," my heart switched from beating to vibrating, and it was suddenly hard to take a deep breath.

"I know, I know—*shocking*," she said. "We didn't even know she was sick."

No, you *didn't know*, I thought. *Maybe if you'd listened, she'd still be alive*. "Clueless," I hissed, my voice trembling with sudden rage and something else—panic, maybe. Panic that Grandma could be gone just like that, as if her life meant nothing at all. But Mom just furrowed her eyebrows at me and shooed me from the room.

Across the hall, my dolls and stuffed animals and pink rug looked like relics from another era of me. I wanted to call Thea and tell her the impossible news that Grandma was dead but I couldn't call Thea, because Thea wasn't speaking to me. I wanted to tell Daddy, but I couldn't tell Daddy when he wasn't even living here anymore. I even wanted to call Grandma and tell her, but then I remembered and started to cry. Had I actually sat here last night, drawing a new mouth on a *sack of flour*—which only made its smile more misshapen and slightly evil—imagining myself as Holden's girlfriend, when a deadly infection was multiplying in Grandma's blood? I was the clueless one.

Ten minutes later, Mom was still on the phone when I walked past her room again, my eyes raw and my head still swimmy with tears. "Devastated," I heard her say, which made me want to hurl a toothpick bridge at the wall just to watch it shatter, until I remembered I hadn't even built one. My limbs were still twitchy with dread, as if they were conducting electricity. Thumping back down the steps, I accidentally knocked over Huggie's Lego tower in the process, which wasn't the shatter I was going for, thanks to the carpet on the landing. Gently, I scooted the remains out of the way with my foot and then kept going to the mudroom, where I emptied everything from my backpack except for the toothpicks and slipped my arms through both shoulder straps.

In the garage, I untangled my bike from the rack and considered my helmet for half a second before snapping the chinstrap in place with a sigh of self-loathing. What the hell was wrong with me that I couldn't even run away without taking basic safety precautions? *Charles Darwin applauds you*, Grandma said in my mind, which made my throat tighten when I thought of how, from now on, Grandma's voice was just a construction of my imagination.

In the windows facing the driveway, I could see Huggie leaning his head on Toby's arm, as they shared a bowl of microwave popcorn in the blue glow of the TV. For a second, it was hard to pedal away, especially when I realized it was thirty-two degrees, and all I had on was a sweatshirt. But eventually Mom would be looking for me, and scaring her to death, even briefly, was a satisfying thought. Besides, there was only one person I could think of who would know how to build a bridge out of toothpicks. Unfortunately, I kind of wanted to kill him, too.

DADDY ANSWERED THE DOOR AT HIS NEW APARTMENT LOOKING bedraggled in a T-shirt and jeans. His mouth gaped for a second but he immediately pulled me into a hug and asked, "Elyse, are you all right?" He must've seen that my nose was red, my eyes were puffy, and that my teeth were chattering after riding five miles to his place. My helmet was still dangling from my fingers, and I resisted the urge to slug him with it. "I'm sorry about Grandma," Daddy said, his chin in my hair. "I loved Margot, too. The whole thing is kind of a shock. I'm so sorry she's gone."

"I'm so sorry you *left*," I snapped, startling myself, which made him step back, as if struck by a power line. "I mean, I get that Mom's annoying. But what about me? What about Toby and Huggie? You didn't even say good-bye!"

"I'm sorry," Daddy said, sounding more bewildered then apologetic.

"How could you just leave?"

"It's kind of hard to explain. Even to myself." He sighed. "Does your mother know you're here?"

I nodded, even though I hadn't even received so much as a frantic text yet. "I need help with my physics project," I added, almost belligerently.

"Sure, sure. Let me just straighten up a few things." He turned and walked into the bedroom, while I set my helmet down on one of the chairs and glanced around. He had a nice view of the Allegheny River, where the red and gold trees were reflecting across the water in the setting sun. The place was compact. The kitchen island was a quarter of the size of the one we have at home, but instead of the clutter of school papers and mail there was only a single pen, decorated with the letters of a drug company. I picked it up and studied the letters for a moment in my palm: *Pfizer*, they spelled. I thought of Natalia, the Viagra rep "who was almost my mother."

"Elyse?" Dad called from his bedroom. "Have you eaten?"

"No," I said, following the sound of his voice down the hall. He was just finishing making the bed, and the room was mostly neat except on the floor was an open duffel bag.

"Are you hungry?" he asked, tossing the last pillow by the headboard, and I shrugged, too afraid that if I mentioned the women's silk pajamas hanging out of the bag, I might start screaming. "Well, I am," he said. "Let's get a pizza."

I waited until we were back in the kitchen and Daddy had hung up the phone with the restaurant to ask, "What's the deal with Natalia? Is she your girlfriend now?" It was scary: my voice sounded almost like Mom's.

"I—it's complicated." He faltered. "I'm not moving to California. And she lost her first husband to pancreatic cancer. She thinks she'd be stupid to date a guy with the same thing."

I felt my eyes get big. "Wait—the cancer's back?"

"No, no, no. You just . . . never know in life."

There was something so depressing about the way he said it, like he'd fully resigned himself to the eventuality of death and the notion of never seeing me again. I didn't mean to start crying again, but I couldn't help it. When Daddy wrapped his arms around me, I let him, thinking that one day even this moment would be a memory, which made my face feel like a sponge, wringing water all over his T-shirt. I wished I could go back in time to when my parents laughed at each other's jokes, and Daddy could swing Huggie onto his shoulders and still have a hand for each of us, or back to last weekend when Grandma and I were cracking up outside the hospital, or even back to yesterday when I stood on the edge of the lawn in the wind and watched the leaves floating down all around me and knew that Holden wanted me, too.

"Remember Noah?" I suddenly said, wiping my snotty face with my hand, and Daddy's pupils kind of dilated. "My twin who died?"

"I—don't remember telling you his name."

"Well, you did." My voice was wobbling again. "Sometimes I wish he'd lived, so if anyone treated me like shit, Noah could kick his ass." I didn't mean to swear in front of Daddy; it came out before I even realized I'd said it.

"Elyse," Daddy finally said, his voice cautious and grave, "whose ass do I have to kick?"

"Nobody." I wiped my nose on my sleeve. "I just want things to be different."

"Me, too." His shoulders sagged. "I'm sorry I left without saying goodbye."

LATER, WE WERE SITTING AT THE BAR IN THE KITCHEN EATING pizza when he asked me about the physics project.

"I have to build a bridge. Out of toothpicks. Here's what I have so far," I said, reaching into my backpack to pull out ten boxes of toothpicks, which I carefully stacked on the table in a neat little tower, next to my water glass. "It's due tomorrow," I added, blotting my pizza with a paper towel.

Daddy looked at the boxes of toothpicks and looked at me. Then he started to laugh, and laugh, until his eyes were tearing. His giddy disbelief made me smile, even though I hadn't planned on smiling at him ever again. Since he was handling the news pretty well, I figured I might as well take out the drawing of the bridge that I'd been imagining all along, the one that couldn't possibly be constructed. "Here's what I had wanted to build," I said, handing him the picture, complete with five arches and crisscrossing cables and a separate, parallel foot path. "But I think we're going to have to come up with something a lot easier."

Daddy sobered up, as he inspected my drawing. "It's beautiful," he said, and when he looked up at me, there was excitement in his eyes that I hadn't seen in a long time. "This is the one we should make."

"But it has to hold thirty pounds."

"This is the one we should make," he said again, tapping the picture, and I gave him a watery smile, imagining myself walking into Physics the way that Grandma had walked into the interventional radiology room to meet the cold steel table— chin up, back straight—and with my bridge, soaring.

CHAPTER 21

Beacon Street

1945

In the beginning, he sent updates every few weeks—student housing was depressing, the subway system confusing, his coursework daunting, and he missed me, missed me, missed me—but either Sol's overwhelming schedule or my complete silence have made his letters fewer and farther between. I focus on flight instead and the growing anticipation of where my orders might send me after October's graduation. There are one hundred and twenty possible air bases I might be stationed at—one hundred and twenty places to forget Solomon Rubinowicz.

In late August and September of 1944, I make two solo cross-country flights, the first from Texas to Delaware in the PT-19, the open-cockpit, wooden plane covered in fabric that we initially trained on, and the second at night, a round-trip from Texas to New York in the AT-6. There is something about hovering over the earth at 208 miles per hour in the dark that makes every thought disappear except the single question: *What does the plane want?* I feel myself becoming one with the craft, anticipating every rattle in the engine, every dip and spike of the instrument panel, every light in the distance, every cloud in the sky. The constant alertness and repetitive adjustments to stay aloft become almost meditative, so that the sound of the engine is no longer deafening, and the vibrations of the plane nothing more than a hum.

In October, we are commended for being safe and dependable pilots who fly "the army way" and honored at graduation with our silver wings. We receive our orders with a caveat: in light of the imminent disbanding of the Women Airforce Service in another two months, it's okay to leave now; we've already done a great service to our country. Not one of us, not even Vera Skeert, considers going home early.

I end up in San Diego, where I spend the next two months test-piloting B-26 bombers, massive, twin-engine aircraft that come back from the Pacific in pieces. Crews patch up the steel fuselage, riddled with gaping holes, overhaul the engine and repair the landing gear, and then leave it to our all-women crew to fly the beasts to make sure they really work. Each time we land at a new army base to deliver "the Flying Coffin," we are met with bewilderment from our male counterparts, who seem shocked that we can handle two thousand tons of steel in the air—or even, where it's most crucial, on the landing, where many pilots have stalled out and crashed. Or maybe they just can't get over the pants. ("You girls should be in skirts," says a cadet, embarrassed to have accidentally called me "sir" until I removed my helmet. "You try strapping on a parachute over a skirt," I say.)

The Soviet Union has invaded Germany, and the United States has landed in Iwo Jima, and soon the soldiers—including Grace's Teddy, if he can just hang on—will be coming back home. We fly back to attend the final graduation of the last class of women pilots, which takes place on a bright, cold day in December. Sitting in a row between Murph, who's been towing targets at Camp Davis, and Grace, who's been ferrying planes from Andrews Air Force Base, I glance at the rows upon rows of uniformed women pilots and can't believe it's all coming to an end.

"Listen up, ladies," Grace says in a whisper. "You're all invited to the wedding next summer."

"We'll be there with bells on," Murphee says.

"I hope Teddy has some single friends," Ana says with a grin, leaning forward on the other side of Murph.

"If I take a train from Baltimore, would anyone be able to pick me up in Des Moines?" Vera asks, her voice doubtful. "Otherwise I'll have to look for a bus from the train station, and if the church isn't close to the reception—"

"Can we worry about the logistics later, Vera?" Murphee asks.

"Invite Sol," Grace quietly urges me. "I know that he'll change his mind. You were meant for each other."

At the mention of his name, my face heats up. I never told Grace I was the one who broke it off and certainly not the reason why. "He can't think about marriage; he has to focus on medical school," I said, because to admit more would betray him and all that was at stake for his future. Besides, I couldn't imagine she'd really understand his dilemma, although maybe I should've given her more credit. After all, we were, each and every one of us, about to get our dreams snatched away forever.

Moments later General Arnold takes to the podium, and we crane our necks to see him, a white-haired man, with rounded cheeks and a well-decorated uniform. After giving us a history of how the WASPs came to be, he congratulates all of us for our hard work, for the service we've done. Nevertheless, we've completed our mission, and the Women Airforce Service is officially over.

That night, we go out to dinner at the Blue Bonnet and secretly spike our sodas and toast the rest of our lives. Afterward, when the cattle wagon never arrives to bring us back to base, we stumble through the empty streets of Sweetwater on foot, our arms slung over each other's shoulders, our breaths clinging to the chilly air. Leaning on Grace, I look up at the sky and wish I weren't fuzzy with rum, because I need to memorize these constellations before I never see them again.

"I feel like we're being kicked out," Ana says, on my other side.

"That's because we are," Murph says, slurring slightly. "You heard General Arnold. 'Each and every one of you is ordered to leave the premises by December twentieth.'"

"Everything we've been through, and everything we've risked has been for nothing," Vera mutters.

"Not for nothing," Grace says. "The men were always going to come home one day."

"I just really thought—we'd proved something," I say.

"We did, damn it," Murph says, sending the line of us off-kilter when she lurches forward.

"I hate goodbyes," Ana says, with a strange, barking sound, and when I look over I realize she's not laughing at all, but crying. And then we're all hugging each other in the road and promising to keep in touch forever, promising we'll never forget what we did, even if everyone else does.

Three days later, we're scattered back to our old lives: Murphee Sutherland back to waiting tables in New Jersey, Ana Santos back to painting still lifes in Chicago, Vera Skeert back to training for the opera in Baltimore, and Grace Davinport back to Iowa, to finish planning her wedding.

I land at the Sixth Ferrying Service Detachment in Pittsburgh, realizing as the wheels of my plane touch down that this is it—the AT-6 may go up again but not with a woman in the cockpit, and certainly not with me. Still reeling, I get a ride from the airport to the looming TB sanatorium on Leech Farm Road. Except that it's closed to visitors when I arrive, and Sarah's nurse sends me away until tomorrow. So I take the trolley back to Squirrel Hill and then walk to Beacon Street from Forbes Avenue. Still wearing my dress blue uniform, I catch smiles and waves from neighbors shoveling snow and children playing hockey on the icy streets, which makes me grin and wave back, despite the ache of loss inside me. Never have I felt so American and simultaneously betrayed. How could the lobbyists have rallied against us? Why couldn't General Arnold have done more to make us part of the military?

I've been home for all of ten minutes, sitting in the kitchen with Mama as she kneads the challah, when she tells me that she's glad I'm back, because they desperately need another seamstress in Uncle Hyman's shop.

"I can't replace Sarah," I say, glancing through the window at the gaggle of blond children playing in the alley. Is it possible that in the ten months since I've been gone the family next door has added more children to their impossibly large brood? They're everywhere, laughing and screaming and swinging their hockey sticks. "I'm terrible with sewing."

"If you can be taught to fly, you can be taught to sew." Mama's hands move quickly over the dough, pushing, pulling, and pounding.

"Maybe there's something else I can do to earn money . . . something at the airport . . ." Even as I'm saying the words, I can't really imagine it. What would I do—become a Pan Am stewardess after I've flown a B-26 bomber? And besides, I'd have to become certified as a registered nurse first, which means more school.

"Miriam, your flying days are over," Mama says, and the words feel sharp and heavy in my chest.

My niece bursts in through the back door then and stops short when she notices me at the kitchen table. "Come in and get warm, Rita. Take off your coat. Not on the chair; put it on the hook. And say hello to your aunt," Mama says, as my niece paces through her orders, never taking her big brown eyes off of me.

"Hi, Aunt Miri." She comes to stand in front of me, a smile playing at the corners of her mouth. Rita has dark braids and eyes and though her wrists look like twigs you could snap, I can tell she's strong and scrappy. "Do you like flying planes?" she asks, and I nod. "Are you ever afraid of falling from the sky?"

"Never," I say automatically, and she smiles. "Was that you outside, playing street hockey in the alley?" I add, pinching her cheek, still pink from the cold.

Rita grins and tells me she just likes to watch the big kids. "Want to come upstairs and see my doll?" she adds, tugging on my arm.

"I would love to see your doll," I say, letting her pull me to a stand.

"It was her mother's." Mama's voice is terse as she washes the flour off her fingers.

"Her name wouldn't happen to be Caroline?" I ask, and Rita gasps in surprise.

"Take off that uniform," Mama says at my back, and I exhale. "You're home now."

UNPACKING MY DUFFEL IN MY ROOM, I FEEL AS IF I AM COMING back from another planet and touching earthly objects once again. The carpet is pinker than I remember, the painting of a little girl dressing her doll over the bed childish and quaint. How is it possible that I left only ten months ago, when everything feels so different? The first thing I do is take a bath, and afterward I stare at myself from many angles in the mirror, wondering if my future has already been written or if someday, sometime, I might bloom again. Without flying and without Sol, it doesn't seem possible, which is probably why, an hour later when I am across the dinner table from Cousin Tzadok, and he is smiling at me with kind brown eyes and saying with his thick German accent, "Welcome home, Little Bird," I remember how he drove me all the way to Indian Town Gap and think, *Maybe I could love you.*

Despite Mama's orders to hang up my uniform forever, I wear it the following day when I go to visit Sarah alone. Outside, sycamore trees extend their leafless branches over the sidewalk that leads to a hulking brick building. Treading carefully on the ice, I think, *Well, isn't this collegiate?* Inside the building, where the patients and nurses whisper in the corridors rather than speak, I pretend that this is actually a library, or a convent—anything but a TB sanatorium.

At the end of a sea-foam-green hallway, I find Sarah lying in bed, propped up on two pillows, wearing a white nightgown. The room is empty except for her bed, a desk with a washbasin, and a chest of drawers. At least the tall windows still manage to fill the room with light.

"You're back! Oh, Miri, you're back," Sarah says, and I'm startled by her hazel eyes, how big and hollow they are, but on her lovely face is the same wide smile.

"I'm back," I say miserably.

"What *happened*? Mama said the women's airforce disbanded," Sarah says, and I love her for exactly this: thinking of me right now when we should only be worrying about her.

"It's over," I say, shaking my head. "They don't need us anymore."

"But what about the petitions to Congress?"

"The men lobbied against us. They didn't even let Jackie Cochran speak at the hearing. General Arnold did all he could but . . ." I shake my head. "He had to go fight a real war."

"Oh, Miri, I'm so sorry. I loved your letters. I reread them again and again. It made me happy to know you were out there living, while I've been stuck in here. Is that all for me?" Sarah adds, nodding at the clutch of books and cards and papers—all the news of the outside world—in my hands. I awkwardly hold out newspapers from Mama, and the cards Rita made out of construction paper, which makes Sarah's eyes well with tears when she opens them.

"Oh, I miss her. You can't understand how it's killing me to be here," she says, and it's true, I don't entirely understand, but the evening before when I hugged Rita, and she touched the buttons on my blazer and beamed up at me, I felt a surge of longing that wasn't for the sky.

"Well, at least you've got a nice view," I say instead, nodding at the huge windows facing the street and the snow-covered lawn.

"Don't," Sarah orders, which makes me look away from the window and stare at her. "Don't pretend it isn't horrible."

"I'm sorry," I say, pulling up a chair by the bed. I want to reach for her hand, but I'm still afraid. Mama told me she'd been coughing up blood the day they took her away.

"All I can do is lie here, or sit up and read. This week I'm allowed to wash and sit up for an hour. Last week, they collapsed my lung, to give it some rest, and I had to take all my meals in bed. I look for you in the sky, though," she confesses with a sheepish smile. "Whenever I see a plane, I imagine you're the one flying it." She shifts in bed, her hand moving up to her lower ribs. "Tell me about Sol, Miri. I never understood why it ended between you two just because he left for New York."

I let go of the breath I've been holding since touching down in Pittsburgh. "He changed his name to get into medical school."

Sarah's eyebrows knit together, and at first I think she didn't hear me.

"He's not Solomon Rubinowicz anymore," I say. "For the

next few years, he's Thomas. Thomas Browning. Which is not that unheard-of, I suppose—authors use pseudonyms to get published. And when Tzadok came through Ellis Island, he changed his name to Jack."

"They *gave* Tzadok a new name."

"What's the difference?"

"They forced him to assimilate. You have a choice." Even as Sarah's voice becomes softer, it grows more insistent, and her breaths are becoming rapid. "Doesn't Sol know what we've been fighting for? If he becomes one of them, then Hitler wins." When she starts to cough, I shudder and glance away.

"He's not becoming anything but a doctor. And I miss him. I've missed him every day for the last five months," I confess.

She finally stops coughing and lies back to look at me. "Our ancestors died for their names, Miri. Sol may not understand that, but you do."

But how can it be wrong to hide behind a name when the only reason we haven't been tortured and murdered ourselves is by luck of our location? Only I can't possibly ask this question of someone who meets her own suffering every day and has no ability to run away.

"Listen to me, Miri. You can't live in fear about the possibility of what they might do to you," she says, and tears prick my eyes, because she's right—for all my bravery in the sky, I am a coward. "I need you to raise Rita," she adds.

"You're going to get better," I say.

"Promise me you'll stay who you are, and raise her the way she was meant to be raised."

"I will, Sarah. Of course, I will," I say.

"Promise," she orders. "I can't have you running back to Sol—or whatever alias he's going by."

"I promise," I say, and it feels like the truth. Again and again, when I think of this moment, of Sarah's face and my words and the way we are holding each other's gaze like it is a covenant in itself, I know it has to be the truth.

THE WINTER OF 1945 DRAGS ON UNDER PITTSBURGH'S SOOT-filled skies that turn the snow black and leave my hopes carbon-crusted. The heater is broken in Tzadok's old jalopy—has been broken since the war began, and can't be fixed until they start making car parts again—so each morning when he picks me up to ride to Uncle Hyman's East End shop, Tzadok tucks wool blankets around my lap and knees. "Smile, Little Bird," he always says, and each morning when I make the corners of my mouth turn up for him, it feels like a mechanical exercise. In January, Grace writes to say that Teddy has been killed in action, and I tamp down my tears for the wedding that would've been, for our reunion lost, and for my own hopes killed in action. Despite the tragedy, despite the fact that the sun won't shine again, the papers are full of heartening news from the war front. The Soviet Union has liberated Warsaw and Auschwitz and marched on toward Berlin; meanwhile, the United States begins bombing Japan, first Kobe, then Tokyo, and when the Soviet and the American troops meet on the River Elbe in Germany in April 1945, we know we are closing in on the end.

It quickly becomes apparent that I can't so much as make a straight hem or iron a mended dress without burning it, so

Uncle Hyman moves me over to the bookkeeping, where I work side by side with Tzadok going over the numbers. He seems to want to make me happy, that much I can tell. One day, he asks me what I miss about flying, and because I can't bring myself to say *the power, the exhilaration,* I simply tell him "the view." So, after work, he takes a detour to Mount Washington—or at least, he tries, but before we reach the top, the engine in the car overheats and we hold up traffic as we wait for it to cool down. "Maybe after the war, when I have a better engine, I'll take you," he says after turning around, and I don't tell him that we could just as well have taken the incline, because I realize this is his grand romantic gesture, and I'm uncertain if I want to be present for its execution. I spend the winter trying to convince myself that when Tzadok smiles, his angular face is actually quite attractive, and maybe, just maybe, if he has to kiss me then I can get used to that, too. For the first time in my twenty-three years, I'm intent on marrying, because otherwise, I may be bound to the house on Beacon Street forever.

At night I try not to think of Sol's lips on my wind-chapped cheeks, or the Texas sunshine making me squint, or cloud is-lands billowing in the bright sky. I am restless and depressed, aching to be free, until more and more news leaks about the horrors of the concentration camps, bodies upon bodies upon bodies, and I realize that I am not a prisoner at all but simply an ungrateful child who wants too much.

One night, when Tzadok and I are bent over the books in the back room of Hyman's shop, going over the inventory and the payroll, I turn my face up to him, willing him to look into my eyes. Finally, shyly, he puts his pencil down and kisses me. The kiss is fumbling and awkward but really not so bad, I think, reaching up to caress the bones in his face. Maybe I can convince him to grow a beard.

Citing the doctor's advice, Uncle Hyman won't allow Sarah to return home, and Mama busily pretends, despite all evidence to the contrary, that death is not upon us. In some ways, it's easy to forget. One moment during visiting hours, Sarah and I are sharing a conspiratorial laugh over the way Uncle Hyman looks when carving a roast chicken—sweaty, red-faced, and vaguely short of breath, as if he's actually killing it right there at the table—when Sarah suddenly asks, "You don't believe it's really happening, do you?" and I automatically shake my head, knowing that it's her own end she's talking about. "I don't believe it, either," she confesses. "I feel like me, but"—she holds up her arm, as thin as Rita's—"I'm not me." Two weeks later, on May 3, 1945, Sarah is gone.

Shiva begins, seven days of mourning where we sit on tiny stools in the living room while the community files in to pay their respects and feed us. I'm not supposed to lift a finger, not to prepare foods or wrap up the leftovers or clean the dishes, or even myself, but just sit and be still and pray and receive. All I want to do is fly away, and Rita's an easy excuse—someone has to run after her as she crashes about—except that Mama's clucking friends quickly intercede anytime my niece needs a snack or a tear dried when she skins her knee. At nearly four, Rita's too little to really understand what this means, that her mother, who's been gone for almost ten months, is never coming back.

Or maybe I'm the one who doesn't get it. For the first day, I can't even cry, not even when I'm sitting *shemirah*, reading psalms through the night next to her closed coffin in the living room. As a candle burns in the dark, we take turns—Mama, Uncle Hyman, and me—keeping watch over her body, but I can't believe Sarah's actually in there.

It isn't until the following evening, after the burial, that I notice Rita's missing and find her on the floor of my closet—Sarah's closet, too, I remember belatedly. Curled up in a pile of her mother's clothes, the little girl isn't crying, but her mouth is pulled into a wobbly frown, and I wonder then if Sarah taught her about the Spartans of Greece, too.

"There you are," I say, stooping down to crawl into the closet next to her. It's musty inside, making me cough. I reach up to pull the cord on the lightbulb, which glows yellow and warm somewhere above us. Rita doesn't move at first, until I reach over and rub her back and caress her hair, and then she crawls into my lap, still holding Sarah's red sweater like a blanket. "Are you hungry?" I ask, channeling Mama, a firm believer in the power of comfort food. Rita shakes her head. "Can I . . . read you a book?" I offer, and slowly, she nods. "Well, go pick," I say, and she crawls off my legs and over to the little bookshelf beside Sarah's old bed. After retrieving one, Rita plops back down on my lap again. I know the light is better in the bedroom, but I don't even suggest moving. It feels right to sit on the wood floor in our cocoon of clothes, the faint scent of Sarah wafting around us.

Rita's picked *The Runaway Bunny,* by Margaret Wise Brown, the story of a little bunny who wants to run away and his mother won't let him. As soon as I begin reading, my voice begins to quake. At first it's because *I* am the bunny, obligated to stay, but then I read the line "If you become a bird and fly away from me . . . I will be a tree that you come home to," and then I can't go on, for Sarah's the tree, and she always has been. *What am I going to do without you? How can you leave me here alone?*

"Want me to read?" Rita asks, and I nod, because my vocal cords are rebelling now; any sound I make is in danger of becoming a howl. So, I listen to her read—unless she's just memorized the story—and realize that Rita's the little bunny and Sarah's the mother, turning herself into a fisherman, and a mountain climber, and a tightrope walker, and the wind. She will be hiding in every place, in every moment, only we'll never see her again. And then, I do start to cry, noiselessly, with shuddering shakes and clenched stomach muscles, as Rita leans her head into the crook of my neck, and flips the pages of the book. I'm grateful to be holding her right now in our little cave from the world, and for her clear, high voice, which never wavers.

ON THE SIXTH EVENING OF SHIVA, THE HOUSE IS BUSTLING WITH visitors offering condolences, and I am leaning against the kitchen doorframe, wearily watching my mother, wearing her *keriah* and shaking hands in the living room, when I straighten up and inhale sharply. Wearing a dark suit and his yarmulke, and holding a platter of meat and fish and dried fruits, Sol Rubinowicz is standing in the front room of the house on Beacon Street.

Quickly, I weave through the throng of guests, until we're face-to-face. His shoulders drop at the sight of me. "What are you doing here?" I ask, too flustered for hello. It's been ten months since we've seen each other last—and five since his last correspondence.

"I got your letter," Sol says. "I wanted to pay my respects."

"You shouldn't be here," I say, rescuing the platter and then rushing off, knowing that he'll follow me. Since the kitchen is full of my mother's friends—big bosomed, big-voiced, middle-aged women in aprons, doing dishes, refilling the trays—I slip the food onto the table and then keep going, out onto the back porch with Sol on my heels. The cold air hits me like a splash of water in the face. As per the custom, I haven't been outside in six days, and for a moment I'm taken aback by the weather. Is it really spring, when it's thirty-five degrees and the magnolia blossoms are blowing off the trees? In the kitchen behind us, the ladies pause, mid-conversation, like a stunned Greek chorus.

"Tzadok and I are engaged," I whisper.

"You can't marry your own cousin," he says, quickly slipping the yarmulke off his head, as if it's a force of habit now, looking like a goy.

"It's—we're—not related by blood," I say, flushing.

"Do you love him?" His earnest green eyes search mine, and my heart thuds painfully.

"I . . ." I glance down, thinking. "Does it matter?"

"Miriam?" Mama says from the doorway, and I startle and turn.

"Oh, Mama, this is—"

"Mrs. Lichtenstein, I'm Solomon Rubinowicz," he says, stepping forward and extending his hand. "I'm a friend of Miriam's from Texas—I'm so sorry," he adds quickly, mashing the phrases together as if it's meeting me he's sorry about rather than the loss of my sister.

"Thank you," Mama says, shaking his hand so warily that

for a moment I wonder if Sarah told her everything. But no, she wouldn't have; there wouldn't have been a reason, not when Sol and I had broken up months before I returned home.

"Sol's family was very nice to me in Texas. They took me to temple and had me over for Shabbat. He's in medical school in New York now."

"You're going to be a doctor," Mama says, approval seeping into her voice. "Well. That's wonderful. Has Miriam told you that she's getting married next month?"

"Next month? Oh." The way Sol keeps twisting his yarmulke in his hands reminds me of a man wringing out his own heart.

"I've already sewed her wedding gown," Mama adds.

I look at the broken floorboards of the porch thinking of the dress, the same one she married Papa in, which had to be hemmed just for me.

"Miriam, you're needed inside," Mama says. "Rita has eaten an entire basket of *rogalech* and knocked over a pitcher of cream. She needs a fresh outfit," she says, pushing me toward the back door, and I think, *This is my life now. This is the promise I made.* "Go on. I'll be there in a moment."

I have no idea what she says to him after I'm gone, but one moment I look through the window and see Sol nodding solemnly while Mama's head bobs and her finger points, and then I wrestle Rita into another outfit, and look up, and no one's on the porch.

"Please go be with our guests," Mama says as she shuts the back door and pulls down the shade to the kitchen window, lest I keep searching for him through it.

"You didn't let me say goodbye," I say, and she pushes past

me into the living room, into the throng of mourners. But I have to go look for myself. Cracking open the door to the back porch, I step outside and peek around. The backyard is still and cold, and, between the pockets of silence, there's a strange swishing sound. I look up and realize it's just the magnolia leaves falling around me, the sound of letting go. *This is your life. This is the promise you made.*

I think of the last time I saw him, the day we agreed to say goodbye forever. "What's the first thing you'll do in New York?" I'd asked on the ride back to base.

Sol shrugged. "Think about you. Unpack. Think about you some more."

"I wish . . ." I'd said, shaking my head, and he'd reached over and squeezed my hand.

"I wish, too."

"Miriam?" says a voice behind me, and I turn to find Tzadok stepping out onto the back porch. When I lean into his arms, he says, "Are you okay?" and I nod because now, finally, I'm crying on the outside, and it seems like the most natural thing in the world. *I wish, I wish, I wish.*

"The man who was here . . ." he starts.

"He's just an old friend from flight school," I say, wiping my eyes. It's a good thing all the mirrors are covered; I don't even want to imagine how awful I look right now.

"He asked me to give you this," Tzadok says, handing me an envelope.

I WAIT UNTIL MUCH LATER, AFTER THE VISITORS HAVE GONE, after we've put Rita to bed, when I'm lying in the room Sarah and I once shared, to rip open Sol's letter. Inside there's a short note, along with a one-way train ticket to New York, a subway ticket, a map of the Bronx, and a key. I turn the gold key over in my palm and think about how tomorrow begins the *sheloshim*, the reentry into society. We may clean ourselves up and leave the house and return to work. I can take off my black dress with the tear over the heart, comb my hair and wear my nice shoes, even put on a little makeup if I feel like it. And I can walk.

Dear Miri,

I am so sorry about Sarah. I want you to be well and find happiness, and I hate to think of the pain you must be in right now. I know that your family needs you now more than ever, but if you ever need to fly away for a little while, here is all that you'll need to come find me in New York.

As I'm reading, I imagine myself packing up my suitcase, including my retired uniform and flight jacket, and leaving a note for Mama—promising that I'll be back for Rita—and one for Tzadok, too. I see myself waiting on the platform, and the light as the train pulls toward me in the station; I feel my feet as I step aboard and the flutter in my chest as I scurry to find a seat.

When you reach Grand Central Terminal, you'll have to transfer to the number 6 subway train for the Bronx and get off at East 143rd Street and St. Mary's. Then keep walking northeast on St. Ann's Avenue until you reach Westchester Avenue. My building is the third block down on the right.

*Along the way, you might run into a woman, Mrs. Prospero—
she's a yenta and runs into everyone. She'll call you Mary.
Just go along with it. She thinks you're my wife and that I've
just been waiting for you to join me for the last year, which
is half true. I've never stopped wishing I could see you again,
even after you told me to let you go.*

I imagine saying hello to a complete stranger, this nosy old
woman, and answering to a new name before making my way
with my bags to the fifth-story walk-up. I let myself inside the
apartment and then sit down on the sofa to wait for Sol, turning
those two words over in my mind: "my wife." How could ever
I belong to anyone else, when we already belong to each other?

*I know what you must be thinking—that if you come to
New York, everything we say and everything we do will only
be half true, but I promise you, Miri, this lie doesn't have to
last forever, but my love for you will.*

I picture him getting home from the library and dropping his
books on the table when he sees me. "You're here," he says, looking at me with such fondness and relief that I'm overwhelmed.

And then we're kissing, not like the chaste kisses in
Sweetwater, but long, lingering, groping ones, where he
presses me against the sofa cushions and runs his expert hands
through my hair and over my breasts and back—and finally
grabs me from behind to pull me closer. Suddenly, he stops and
says maybe we should look for a justice of the peace, maybe we
should do it before nightfall, so that he can take me to bed a
married woman. But if I'm not Miri anymore, maybe it doesn't

matter whether I'm married or single, a Jew or a Christian or nothing at all.

After refolding the letter, I carefully place the tickets in the envelope along with the key. For the first time since I landed in Pittsburgh, the future exists, with a face and a destination. I lean back and close my eyes, knowing then that I'll go to him, no matter where we end up, no matter what name we're called. *I'll go.*

CHAPTER 22

Burial at Sea

T he best part about a death in the family," Mom said, "is
that people are always a little nicer, at least for a little
while." We were in the cab on the way to Grandma's
house from the Key West airport. The air was humid and the
trees dripping with water, but at least the hard rain had temporarily stopped. I was squashed in the middle of Mom and Aunt
Andie, who was turned in the direction of the flapping palm
trees out the window. I wondered if she was even seeing them.

The plan, Mom had told me, was that we were going to
bring Grandma back to Pittsburgh, where the funeral would
be. There was going to be a service at the temple my grandparents belonged to, a processional out to the cemetery, followed
by a nondenominational lunch with cocktails back at the country club for seventy-five of Grandma's "closest" friends. Dad
was staying behind with Toby and Huggie, but I'd insisted on
coming. It seemed like one of us should support Mom. Besides,
I kept thinking that Grandma would've left me a message or a

clue that I was supposed to discover—some sort of sign to let me know that the world was not as chaotic and random as it seemed. But as we drove past the aftermath of Hurricane Claudette, I suddenly had second thoughts about coming. Power lines were tangled along the sidewalks, and mailboxes had been felled like trees. A row of familiar houseboats along Route 1 had been blown apart, and I stared at the shards, feeling like one of the pieces. If I'd stayed in Pittsburgh, I could pretend Grandma was still happily living in a little pink bungalow in Key West; now there was no imagining away the truth.

We turned up the palm-tree-lined street toward Grandma's, which Mom was already claiming dibs on as our vacation home.

"By the way, I talked to Rabbi Horowitz," Mom said to Aunt Andie. Mom had been channeling her shock over Grandma's sudden death by making funeral arrangements with the precision of a party planner. "He said the eulogies should really go on no longer than twenty minutes. I've gotten in touch with a few of her friends from the old neighborhood, both of whom want to speak, so that's five minutes each—unless you don't want to get up there, in which case that'll be about seven a person—or maybe I'll take ten and both of them can have five."

"What about Ray? What if he wants to speak?" I asked, and Mom kind of rolled her eyes at me.

Aunt Andie turned from the window and said, "Mom changed her mind about a funeral after all. She wants to be cremated and buried at sea."

Startled, I looked from Aunt Andie to my mother, who blinked.

"She doesn't like eulogies because it's not an accurate portrayal of the person. 'No one's perfect—until the funeral!'"

Aunt Andie added, quoting Grandma with the same la-dee-dah inflection.

"What the hell did she have in mind? We just dump her over the side of Ray's kayak?" Mom snapped.

"We'll go out on the powerboat and make a day of it."

"Is there anything else I should know?" Mom asked.

Aunt Andie hesitated. "She made me the executor of the will."

"*You?* Oh, that's just . . . why pick the lawyer?" Mom shouted at the ripped ceiling of the cab.

"And Ray gets the house."

WHEN RAY ANSWERED THE DOOR, HIS BLUE EYES IMMEDIATELY welled at the sight of us, and he gave us all hugs. Mom hadn't wanted him to pick us up from the airport because she thought he'd sounded drunk when she'd called him from Miami to say our flight was delayed, but he seemed more sober than I'd ever seen him, even as he was offering us all strawberry-banana smoothies.

"Only if there's rum in it. That was one hell of a flight," Aunt Andie said, setting down her bag.

"Jane? You look like you could use one," Ray said, moving toward the blender. "Elyse? Smoothie?"

"Only if there's rum in it," I echoed, which earned a chuckle from Ray and Aunt Andie. *Maybe that's why I've come,* I thought.

While Ray went to work in the kitchen, I glanced around the small living room, half-expecting to find Grandma curled up on the sofa. The furnishings always struck me as tacky: the rug was long and shaggy, the lamps were metal and angular, and the bar stools were covered in some kind of faux animal print—leopard, maybe. When Grandma lived in Pittsburgh with my grandfather, they'd had "a library" with built-in bookshelves holding hundreds of novels, but since moving here, she read everything on her Kindle. Why had I assumed she'd leave me a clue, when Grandma had "downsized" her secrets a long time ago?

"Here you go, kid, a virgin smoothie," Ray said, handing me a drink moments later, and my cheeks flushed with embarrassment just to hear an adult use the word *virgin* in front of me. It reminded me of Holden Saunders and his asshole friends, stuff I didn't really want to think about, so I opened the sliding glass door and stepped out onto the back patio, where a speedboat was motoring past. From where I was standing, I couldn't see where the lawn dropped off into the canal, and with the backdrop of bushes, and the green grass in front, the boat looked like it was driving across the land.

I sat down on the patio furniture, realizing belatedly that the cushions were soaked, and now it would look like I wet my pants. I imagined Grandma sitting next to me, watching the boats zip by. *Was* she sitting next to me in some ethereal, invisible form? I sort of believed it, but at the same time, I sort of didn't.

I wondered what Mrs. Browning would say about the afterlife. Whenever I thought of her ditching her religion for love, it reminded me of Mom and Dad keeping up a few traditions for us kids and tossing out everything that required more commitment. "A lot of the time, I just . . . feel so lost," I'd admitted to Grandma when we were in Miami.

"Oh, honey. You may be lost, but God knows exactly where you are," she'd said, patting my knee. "He knows where I am, too."

"But then why—" I'd said, and then stopped, because the question I was going to ask, *But then why are you suffering?* had made my throat constrict.

"You are one of God's chosen people, too. It's in your birthright."

I blinked. "It is?"

"You already *are* one of us."

"I am?" I'd wiped my eyes.

Grandma had smiled. "You are."

I'd remember that moment forever, and it was all thanks to Mrs. Browning.

"Elyse," Aunt Andie said, and I jerked my head up to see her beckon me to come back inside. I hurried back up the patio steps, startling a green gecko.

Inside Ray led the way across the hall to Grandma's bedroom, which had a queen-size bed, a dresser, and a little TV. Palm leaves were slapping against the window as the ceiling fan twirled overhead, but it took me a moment to get what he wanted the three of us to see: a box of ashes sitting on the dresser. *Grandma.*

"This is what she wanted," Ray said, opening the box.

I stared into the wooden container, trying to comprehend that this gray dirt was the person who'd made jokes in the hallway of the hospital and said, "You remind me of me!" This dirt had given birth to my mother, who'd given birth to me.

"I'll let you three sort out the jewelry and the clothes later," Ray said, nodding toward Grandma's open closet. It was strange to see her scarves and dresses hanging there; her shoes neatly paired on the floor. I felt like she should walk in and ask us why we were sipping smoothies in her bedroom. "Don't you dare sit down on my bed, kiddo," she'd say, pointing at my butt, which was still sopping from the patio furniture.

Aunt Andie crossed the room to Grandma's night table, which was littered with medicine bottles. "What about the pain medication? Can we divvy this up, too?" she asked, which made Ray smile, but Mom only scowled.

"Here, kiddo—from Grandma," Ray said, handing me an old weathered book, whose fabric binding was embossed with the words *The Secrets of Flight*. "Your grandmother's novel."

"I haven't seen that in ages," Mom said, as I ran my fingers over the green letters.

"Mom wrote it about her aunt who died in the war. I think I lost my copy in one of the moves," Aunt Andie said. "Can I reread it after you?"

I nodded slowly and opened up the front cover, where the name *Margarita Schiff* was on the title page. Schiff was my mother's maiden name, but "Margarita"? "Is that a pseudo-nym?"

"Yes and no," Ray said. "Her parents named her after the actress Rita Hayworth, but later on, after they died, her grand-mother changed her name to Margot—she thought Margarita sounded like a Mexican floozy."

From between the pages, a black-and-white picture flut-tered to the floor. Gingerly, I picked up the photo of a little girl, dark hair in braids, sitting on the front stoop of a house. Ray squinted at it and then flipped it over so we could decipher the handwritten smear on the back.

" 'Margarita, 1945,' " I sounded out.

"She must've been about four." He passed the picture to Mom and Aunt Andie. "Margot was looking at a bunch of pictures just the other day," Ray said. "She must've stuck this one in here for Elyse."

"It's kind of blurry," Aunt Andie said.

"It's disintegrating," Mom said, curling her lip.

"Look closer," Ray said, handing it back to me. "You might even recognize her smile."

IT RAINED THE WHOLE NEXT MORNING, SOME SORT OF REMNANT of Claudette, and it wasn't until later afternoon that we packed a cooler of sandwiches and motored out toward the pinkish horizon for the burial at sea.

"Is there gonna be a storm?" I asked Ray, who followed my finger where the thunderheads were gathering in the distance.

"Nah. I checked the weather maps before we left. Might get a little wet, though."

Once we'd cleared a succession of buoys and the island itself looked small and distant, Ray cut the motor, and we bobbed up and down on the whitecaps in the humid breeze. The sea was unexpectedly greenish rather than the usual aqua, and stingrays kept darting just below the surface like little black omens. It was hard to relax when the life preserver that Mom made me wear was chafing around my neck.

"I'm assuming you got the permits for this, Ray?" Mom asked right away.

"Permits?" he asked, wiping off an icy beer from the cooler with his hand.

"It's illegal to dump human waste, including dead bodies,

in the ocean. The Coast Guard may have a problem with us disposing of the ashes this way, if not the Key West boating authority," Mom said.

Before I could ask if she was just making stuff up, Aunt Andie snapped, "Are you fucking—?"

"I got the permits, Jane," Ray interrupted, putting a staying palm on my aunt's shoulder. "I got the permits." Then he cracked open the Yuengling and handed it to Mom. "Now drink up."

We ate our sandwiches in silence, save for the crunch of Ray's chips, as the warm wind scudded across the deck and the thunderclouds grew closer, like a gathering army. We sat on opposite sides: Mom and me facing Ray and Aunt Andie, the wooden box of Grandma perched between us. As waves slapped the side of the boat, I thought how Grandma always said she'd fallen in love with the ocean when she fell in love with Ray. "How is it possible that I grew up landlocked?" she'd asked me once, and I felt a little bit bad for Pittsburgh, as if its crisscrossing rivers and endless bridges didn't even count.

"Is this what Mom wanted?" my mother suddenly asked, jerking her head toward the ashes. "That we just sit here in silence?"

"I brought a poem," I said, holding up a book with the one by W. H. Auden about stopping all the clocks and putting away the sun—we'd read it in Mrs. Kindlings's class earlier in the year. "And we could look for the green flash," I added. One time Thea had told me about the crack of green on the horizon when the last of the sun melts away, and I wanted to see it now, wanted it to be a sign from Grandma that she'd crossed over to the other side.

"I don't think Margot would have a problem with you girls sharing some memories," Ray said as he swigged some beer. "Hell, I'll start. I remember the night your mom and I met down on Duval Street. She was drunk as a skunk, and she was singing karaoke, and she had an unbelievable set of pipes, even if she always picked the most melancholy songs by Carole King."

"I'm sorry. I'm just—trying to understand something," Mom suddenly said to Aunt Andie, who glanced up from her sandwich. "Do you have a legal background that I wasn't aware of? Did Mom pay for a couple of 'Intro to Law' courses at your community college? Because I can't figure out why she would've made you the executor of her will."

"Margot figured it would be easier for Andie to help me out, since you're such a busy lady."

"What's that supposed to mean?" Mom asked, and Ray shrugged as he swigged his beer.

"Did you ever call her back?"

"Maybe we should do this another day," Aunt Andie said, setting down her sandwich. "It's not what I imagined . . ."

"That's funny, it's not what I imagined, either," Mom snapped. "If I had known we were—scattering *Mom,* I would've brought the boys."

Easy, people, Grandma would be saying right about now. *It's my funeral. Can't you all just relax?* I stopped flipping through my book of poems. Trying to read on a lurching boat was making me queasy.

"Margot said she wanted to be scattered in Key West, and she didn't want to wait. She's Jewish," Ray added with a shrug. "They bury their dead right away."

"Yeah. We *bury* our dead. In the ground."

I wished they would stop arguing almost as much as I wished the boat would stop rocking but neither seemed like it would be happening anytime soon. The sea kept rising up, threatening to swallow us, and soon the debate about what to do with Grandma would be pretty much beside the point after we'd drowned.

"Oh, Jane." Aunt Andie rolled her eyes. "This isn't about what you want; it's about what Mom wanted. So don't be such a martyr."

"Do you even know what it's like to work hard?" Mom asked. "To not have Mommy and Daddy pay for everything?"

"I've supported myself for years!"

"You can't even pay the rent on freezer space for your god-damn eggs!"

"Stop it!" I shrieked, bringing my hands to my ears. The book of poems slid off my lap and hit the deck, literally. "Stop it! Stop it! Stop it!"

There was a moment of silence, most likely of the stunned variety, before my mother said, "Elyse, honey—"

"If you don't have anything nice to say just shut. The fuck. Up!" I screamed.

The beer in Ray's hand seemed frozen halfway to his lips, and for a second I wasn't sure if there was a wave about to break over my head. I glanced behind me, at the rolling, dark water, and then back at Ray, still watching me with a silly grin on his face. Then he raised his beer bottle, as if in salute, and said, "Here, here."

Aunt Andie stood up and began pacing the deck—or more like stumbling the deck, as the boat kept up its nauseating roil.

The breeze had escalated to a full-fledged, wet wind, and my stubby ponytail was whipping in the air.

"Watch it!" Mom said, when another lurch sent Aunt Andie tripping into her lap.

"I *am* watching it!" Aunt Andie said, untangling herself.

"Ladies, I'm just gonna toss this out there, but seeing the two of you together right now, you're actually a lot alike." They turned and fixed their eyes on Ray, who was pointing back and forth between them with his beer bottle. "You both do this thing when you're concentrating where you look like you could kill whatever it is you're focusing on." They continued to stare at him, until he slowly lost his smile. "Maybe I'll . . . go check on those permits."

Mom waited until he'd ducked down below to say, "Elyse, I'm sorry. I know this is hard—"

"Don't apologize to me, apologize to each other!" I shouted, trying to make myself heard in the rising wind. With each pitch of the boat, my stomach bobbed up in the back of my throat.

"She's right." Aunt Andie slumped onto the cushion across from Mom and exhaled. "Look, Jane, I'll pay you back as soon as I can."

"This isn't about the money!" my mother said. "This is about Mom loving you more than she loved me!"

Aunt Andie craned her neck forward. "Are you—kidding?"

"You think if *you* had a baby, and your husband was diagnosed with cancer, Mom would've moved over a thousand miles away to party in Key West? I don't think so. She would've stuck around and helped you raise it. She would've been there for you. She was always there for you."

"I'm a mess. I've always been a mess. You've always had your shit together. She knew you'd be okay."

I was relieved they'd switched from fighting to talking; now if only I could push a button and make the boat stop its roller-coaster ride. The shore seemed so far away.

"Have you ever heard that story about the Prodigal Son?" Mom said. "There's the irresponsible son, who goes out and blows through his parents' inheritance partying like a rock star? And then there's the other son just working the farm, sweating in the hot sun and doing the right thing, and then his little brother gets home, and he's broke, and they throw him a goddamn party? It always seems like the wrong brother gets the fatted calf."

"I think the point is that God always welcomes you back, no matter what you've done," Ray said, coming up from down below.

Mom blinked. "Is that the point?"

"Jane, your whole life is the fatted calf," Aunt Andie said. "You got the guy, the house, the kids, the career."

"I have a little bit of everything," Mom agreed. "And I am in pieces."

When my mother began to weep, Aunt Andie put her arms around her shoulders and squeezed, murmuring apologies into my mother's ear, only the wind was taking away Aunt Andie's words, as the boat kept rising and falling. I wished Holden would've held me like that and told me he was sorry. I wished Daddy would come back home, and Grandma were still here. Sobs started to well up inside me, but when I opened my mouth to howl, the only sound that came out was vomit, spewing all over the deck.

"Whoa! Man down! Man down!" Ray said, quickly setting down his beer.

I hurled again, only this time the wind blew it back in my face. Aunt Andie and Mom—showered with stomach acid rain—shrieked from somewhere behind me.

"Oh my God! Elyse! Are you all right?" Mom asked, all concerned. Brownish, yellow puke was splattered everywhere; Aunt Andie was wiping it off the box of Grandma. "Oh, sweetie . . ." Mom said, smiling in spite of herself.

"I'm not feeling so good," I said, woozily, stumbling back and forth with the boat. My front felt sticky with puke, but when Ray handed me a towel, I automatically started wiping off the deck cushions.

"Aw, buddy, that towel's for you. If you feel like you're gonna throw up again, maybe don't aim right into the wind."

"You feel better now?" Aunt Andie asked, as Mom scooted next to me and wrapped me up in a new, fresh towel, and I nodded, feebly. "Wow. I haven't been puked on since Emmett Socoletti drank too much at prom," Aunt Andie added, and I felt Mom's shoulders shaking with laughter, even while she was hugging me.

"He drank something red—grain alcohol and Kool-Aid, right? You should've seen the front of her dress. Grandma thought she'd been stabbed," Mom said, and she and Aunt Andie cracked up, giddy tears rolling down their cheeks.

It seemed hard to believe this was the miraculous reunion designed by Grandma when my eyes stung and my throat burned. But then again, it had been years since I'd seen Aunt Andie and Mom laugh at the same time.

"What do you say we head back, kiddo?" Ray asked me.

"What about Grandma?" I asked, just as swell of wave sent the bow of the boat crashing down and the box of Grandma toppled right off the side and into the ocean.

Mom jumped up with a yelp, and Aunt Andie made some weird sort of utterance—almost like a moan—and even Ray stood there, his mouth sagging open as he scratched his head. I joined them at the rail and peered into the green water. It was amazing how quickly the wooden box had been swallowed. The ashes made tiny explosions under the surface of the sea. The four of us stared at the water for a long time as if the ocean were one of those Magic Eight Balls, and we were waiting for an answer.

"Can we go home now?" I finally asked.

Ray nodded slowly. Then he moved back to the steering wheel and fired up the engine.

CHAPTER 23

The Bronx

1945

Five months after leaving Beacon Street, I am in New York hanging clothes to dry on the fire escape outside my window and half-watching the children playing stickball in the street when I notice Mrs. Prospero, a perpetual fixture on the stoop of our building, chatting with a woman on the street below. I squint and then gasp, realizing belatedly that the woman in the checkered dress with the velvet hat who's been talking to Mrs. Prospero for the last five minutes is none other than my own mother.

"Mama!" I call, but she doesn't seem to hear me. Mrs. Prospero nods her head and opens the door to our building, so I climb back in the window and slam it shut. I have eight flights. Eight flights until Mama crosses the threshold into my new, married life; eight flights to hide everything. Suddenly frantic, I toss clothes into the closet and dishes into the sink. In the

bedroom, I slip off my penny loafers and then bounce across the mattress to reach for the crucifix hanging over the bed. After shoving the wooden Jesus into a drawer of my night table, I rush back into the kitchen again, where Mrs. Prospero's voice is trailing in from the hall. She's saying something about what a fine couple we are, so nice to have as neighbors, how proud of us Mama must be—a son-in-law who's going to be a doctor! I unlatch three locks and then stop, take a deep breath, and push my little gold cross under my ruffled blouse. Then I fling open the door and smile and thank Mrs. P before quickly pulling Mama—who's still panting from the steps—into the apartment.

"You're here!" I say, hugging my mother before latching the door behind me. Her face looks older and wearier than when I left last spring, and her hair more gray. "Why didn't you tell me you were coming?" I add, breathless.

"I sent you a letter." Her dark eyes dart around like dragonflies, looking for a lovely place to rest on, as she unbuttons her wool coat. I would tell her that the letter just arrived yesterday, that I'm still in the middle of writing her back, proposing I visit her in Pittsburgh rather than put her up in our tiny apartment right now, but Mama keeps peering about as if searching for something. I show her the tiny space like a real estate agent hoping to make a sale. It's a one-bedroom apartment with a bathtub in the living room. The entire tour takes about a minute.

". . . And this is where Rita will sleep," I say, cracking the door to our bedroom and then quickly closing it again, suddenly self-conscious about the unmade bed, the impropriety it represents rather than sloppiness. Since we eloped last spring,

I still have the feeling that Mama doesn't believe Sol and I are actually married.

"But that's your room," Mama says. "She can't stay in there."

"Sol and I will sleep in the living room," I say.

"Where? In the bathtub?" she asks, and I manage to laugh as if she's joking.

Moving back toward the stove, I put on the kettle without even asking if she wants tea. "Once Sol has finished his training, we'll be able to move to Wakefield—still the Bronx, but there are three-bedroom houses with yards. I already saw where she'll go to grade school. And I put in an application at Queens College. When I finish my degree I can get a job teaching English." This is my new, practical plan since piloting is no longer an option.

Mama sinks into a kitchen chair, slides some bobby pins out of her hair, and removes her hat. When she doesn't say anything for a while, I wonder if she's still thinking about the unmade double bed in our room or how we will all fit. Sol has half a mind to ask if Rita can stay with Mama and Uncle Hyman a few more years, just until we move out of the city, but I'm afraid that if we put it off, she'll never let my niece come join us.

"Where *is* Sol?" Mama finally asks, glancing around.

"The library. He has to study all the time," I say, slipping my hands into my pockets to hide their sudden trembling. "He's really looking forward to having Rita come and live with us. He wants to have a big family." I turn and meet her eyes. "How is she?"

At least that gets her talking. She chats about Sarah's daughter, who loves to read and draw and wants to be a writer some-day. Frankly, I'm distracted. At any moment Sol might come striding through the door, and I want to warn him up front that Mama is here. She might wonder why his old clothes are spattered in paint and Sol, never inclined to lie, might tell her he's been helping the Lutherans paint their new fellowship hall, which still strikes me as odd: enlisted to work for the church on their Sabbath? When do they rest? I sit down next to my mother and let go of the breath I didn't realize I was holding.

"You look well," Mama says, without a trace of scrutiny in her voice, which makes me relax for a second, until she adds quietly, "Your neighbor, the woman in the hall . . . why did she call you Mary?"

"I—don't know." The kettle starts to howl, so I jump up to take it off the burner. "I introduced myself when we first moved in, and she must've misheard me, and—I keep meaning to correct her but it seems too late now. She's been calling me Mary for months." From the cupboard, I take the saucers down before rattling the teacups into place on top.

"And Sol? Has she been calling Sol 'Thomas' for months as well?"

My heart seems to stall in my chest. I swallow and turn.

Mama reaches down into her pocketbook then and takes out a letter—addressed to her and Uncle Hyman—which she hands to me. It's from Sol's mother and in it, she reveals every-thing: how Sol changed his name to get into medical school, how ever since we eloped and moved to New York we have been acting as gentiles, and how they are in despair. Sol is dead to them; they have lost their only son, and Hannah, the older brother she looked up to. "Is this true?" Mama asks, and finally

I understand why she's shown up unannounced: she wants to catch me in the lie of my life—unless it's the opposite, and she's here to reassure herself that there isn't a bit of reality in that letter. Either way, she has to see for herself.

I shake my head, but my eyes are giving me away, wide with fear and guilt and shame.

"Because I can't have Rita wrapped up in your lies."

"Nothing's changed," I say. "It's just a name on a paper to get around the quotas."

"They're lifting the quotas now!" Mama says, which makes me think of Sol telling me just last week about the clinical trial for streptomycin. *What good is a cure when she's already gone?* "You do read the newspapers, don't you?" Mama adds, reminding me of my sister. "You realize the Jews were kept in camps, marched into—"

"I don't want to hear about it! I don't want to talk about it!" I say.

"Who are you?" Mama says, leaning forward. "What is your name?"

"You know who I am," I say, looking down at my hands.

"Think of Papa," Mama says, her voice quiet and pleading.

I think of my father. In my mind, he is young again, building the *sukkah* for the festival of Sukkot, working outside in his undershirt. How young and strong he looked, wielding his hammer for hours in the hot sun. When he finally finished, we drank lemonade under the flimsy roof covered in green branches, and I showed him the story I'd just written about a little girl who could fly through the seasons without a plane. He read without pausing and then looked up from my pages.

"I built a flimsy little hut," he said, pointing to the walls of the *sukkah*. "But you, Miriush—you've built a whole house with your words."

I tell Mama that I think of Papa often. "I imagine them together—Sarah and Papa. I'm sure they're together." Then my cheeks burn when Mama glances up at me. She knows. She knows there's a cross under my shirt.

"I don't want you taking this road," she says, and her eyes are shiny with tears, which reminds me of the last time she almost cried—in the weeks after Papa died, when she'd found a library book that I'd drawn a picture in. "Look what you've done, Miri," she kept repeating, her voice breaking with disappointment. "How are we going to pay for this?"

She never loved Uncle Hyman, I realize now. She married him so we would still have a home after Papa's death. Then she gave up her own dreams, whatever they were, to send me to college and then to flight school. Surely she wanted more out of life than a clean house. *Look what you've done, Miri.*

I want to cry in her arms and be held. I want her to promise me that I will be safe no matter what my name is. But of course I don't, and she can't.

"This is just a means to an end. It won't last forever." I don't tell her the whole truth, which is that I don't even know what I believe anymore. I am caught in the shadow of two worlds, feeling cold and uncertain.

"Some choices are irrevocable," Mama says.

I DON'T FULLY APPRECIATE THE WEIGHT OF HER STATEMENT UNTIL after she's gone back home and the envelopes, scrawled with my

own handwriting across the front, start to arrive one by one—
unopened and marked "Return to sender." It must be Uncle
Hyman's idea to cut me off, I decide, which makes me more
determined. Every Wednesday, I send out another letter like a
heartbeat, letting her know I'm still alive. I imagine Rita prying
open the mailbox and the thrill of seeing her own name, so I
address one to Margarita Glazier. Inside, I write that I love her,
and I can't wait for her to live with me, and for two, whole glorious months the letter doesn't come back, but then a box arrives
from Pittsburgh. In it I find my beloved Patsy doll, every card
I've ever made for Mama, the letters I sent to Sarah from flight
school, and the last eight weeks' worth of correspondence. The
letter I wrote to Rita is right at the top of the stack, still sealed.

I WAIT UNTIL JUNE OF THE FOLLOWING YEAR, 1946, TO TAKE THE
train back to Pittsburgh. Sol offers to go with me for moral support, but I need to go alone, to make Mama forgive me and to
claim Sarah's little girl for my own.

Walking from the trolley on Forbes to Murray Avenue, I
pass the candy store, and the butcher, and the five-and-dime,
noticing glances and smiles along the way from the shopkeepers
and pedestrians, anyone who likes the sight of a young pregnant woman in a sundress. I smile back as if I'm still wearing
the uniform, hoping that motherhood is what I've been missing
and not just the sky.

My last flight took place a year and a half ago on a sunny
day in Houston. (How often is life like that, where it's only
after you look back that you realize it's over—that no matter
how many times you walk outside on a clear day and think,
Today is a good day to fly, you've already taken that final flight?)

I round the corner of Beacon Street where boys are playing stickball and swinging their yo-yos and mothers are walking their baby carriages, and girls are playing hopscotch and then I huff and puff up the hill toward the narrow, falling-down, three-story colonial that, in my mind, is still home.

After unlatching the metal gate, I make my way down the sidewalk to the front porch, when a harried blond woman sees me and gasps.

"Miriam?" she asks, stricken, as she lays a hand over her heart.

"Mrs. Byrd?" I ask, equally startled. Have I wandered into the wrong yard?

"You're . . ." she trails off, speechless, looking me up and down.

My hands fly up to my pregnant belly. "Almost six months along—I'm married now," I quickly add. "We just had our year anniversary in May." It occurs to me that is the longest conversation I've had with my former next-door neighbor.

"Congratulations," she sounds out slowly. When she nods, her hair swishes back and forth. "I was just leaving some ginger bread for your mother," Mrs. Byrd adds hastily, as if I've just caught her leaving some Christian literature wedged in the screen door. "Is this a surprise?" she says, finishing her descent down the front porch steps.

"A—surprise?" I ask, with a glance at my belly, before I realize she's talking about my visit. "A bit of one, yes." *On both accounts.*

"Well, it's wonderful to see you looking so—*well!*" She rushes past me, down the walk. "Tell Rina I'll stop by another time. I didn't want to wake her up."

Since when is my mother "Rina"? I wonder, glancing at my watch. And it's ten in the morning.

Inside, the house is shockingly quiet, save for a multitude of clocks measuring out their discordant ticks as I step from room to room. "Hello? Anyone home? Mama?" Still clutching Mrs. Byrd's ginger bread, I make my way up the stairs to Mama's room thinking, *She's sick, she's dying, she never got my letters—it was Hyman who sent them back.* Except that inside her room, the bed is empty and neatly made, and her night table is free of medicines; there's only a deck of cards for playing solitaire. Fanning myself in the stuffy air, I move across the hall and push open the door, as thoughts of Sarah come flooding back. "This was our room," I whisper to the baby inside me. It's still set up for a girl: the pink carpet, Sarah's Patsy doll on one of the bedspreads, the paintings of rainbows and horses. I think of our nighttime whispers in the dark, during the air raids, and the secrets we exchanged and kept. I consider leaving the journal and stuffed bear I've brought for Rita on one of the beds, until the sound of footsteps overhead startles me into leaving.

I head back to the hallway, just as Mama comes down the attic steps. Even in her housecoat, I can see that she's thinner than the last time I saw her. She stops short when she sees me. *"Miriam?"* she asks, unmistakable horror in her voice. "Did anyone *see* you?" It's only then that I understand why Mrs. Byrd was so shocked: she must've been told I was dead.

"No one except Mrs. Byrd," I say, holding up the ginger bread. "She seemed to think you'd be sleeping."

"Sleeping, ha! I don't have time to sleep."

"Where's Rita?" I ask, and then—thinking she's going to

hit me with the broom in her hand—flinch as Mama moves toward me.

"That's none of your business now, is it?" she says, hurrying past.

"I brought her something—I'd like to give it to her," I say.

"She's at day camp," she says, over her shoulder, taking the second flight of steps, and I rush to keep up. "Keep your treats, Miri. And you need to leave before anyone gets home," she says.

"Mama, look at me, please. This is your grandchild I'm carrying," I plead, breathless, and she stops on the landing and finally turns to meet my eyes.

"You don't exist to me anymore. That baby does not exist to me," she says, jerking her head toward my belly, and never have I heard her so cold.

"But Sol says as soon as he graduates, we can move to Wakefield and raise her Jewish—"

"You joined a church, Miriam. A *church!*" Mama says in a scary hiss. "You made your choice. Don't call. Don't write. Don't *confuse* Rita. Leave her alone, Miri—leave *us* alone."

EVEN WHEN I GO, WEEPING INTO MY HANDS, I DON'T REALLY believe it's over. But three months later, when the baby I've carried for nine months emerges lifeless and blue, with a cord wrapped around its beautiful neck, I think of my mother's words and give up. I made my choice, and these are the consequences. My baby doesn't exist, and Sarah's daughter will never be mine.

For a long time, I don't exist to me, either.

CHAPTER 24

Miri, Found

It was amazing how quickly the transformation had occurred: in one moment I'd walked in, fully dressed, to the preoperative holding area and less than a half an hour later, I'd been stripped—my Mary Janes replaced by socks with treads, my clothes by a checkered gown, and my dignity tucked into a plastic bag and placed somewhere out of reach. Thank heavens I possessed my own teeth. Climbing aboard the gurney as if it were a rowboat being cast out to sea, I felt different suddenly, lost and uncertain. I was a patient now.

"Retired?" asked a young woman, after confirming my insurance information for her computerized records.

"Retired pilot," I said pointedly, mostly just to get her to look up. It worked. Her typing fingers paused, and her rosy face finally met my own for the first time since she'd scooted over to my gurney on her rolling stool.

"No kidding! How cool!" she said, with a genuine smile before quickly reassuring me that it would be just a few more questions, and then she could let my friends and family back to wait with me.

Friends and family, I thought with a sigh, as I rearranged my blankets over my legs. I'd been trying not to fret about Elyse's silence since her return from Key West the Monday before and trying not to think the worst when she'd skipped last week's meeting of the writers' group. I even felt foolish for packing her a gift, simply because, weeks ago, she'd promised to be here. Surely, between her parents' divorce and her mother's shaky career, the girl had more important things to worry about than me.

At last, the young woman finished typing my demographic information into the computer, at which point a nurse popped her head in to ask for my preoperative paperwork to pass on to the anesthesiologist. As I handed over the forms, I couldn't help thinking of my uncomfortable conversation with Gene Rosskemp the night before, when I'd asked if he would be willing to act as my medical power of attorney.

"That's what you've got Dave for," Gene reminded me, and, with great reluctance, I admitted that Dave couldn't be my power of attorney, because he had actually stopped speaking to me over a slight miscommunication.

"Who is Hannah Bergman?" Dave had asked me during our final conversation. He was calling with news from Seattle: Baby Tyler had cut two teeth and was just learning to walk, Carrie was almost finished her first year of teaching, and Dave had just gotten a job with a start-up company doing computer software.

"I don't know. You tell me," I'd said, as if it were a game. "Who is Hannah Bergman?"

"Some lady who wrote me a letter. She says she's Dad's sister." I had inhaled sharply, as if stabbed in the gut, when he added, "Her maiden name was Rubinowicz."

"I have no idea," I said, my voice off-key.

"She wrote a bunch of stories about Dad that sounded legit—stuff he told me about growing up in Texas, and his father's mango tree in the backyard. She knew he hadn't gotten into medical school three times . . ."

I'd clutched the phone harder, as if it might steady me.

"She says Dad's name wasn't Thomas. She says it was Solomon, and that he changed it to hide his religion. Is this true, Mom?" Dave had asked, and for a moment, I just stood there swaying, my heart rattling inside my rib cage. "Am I really Jewish? Is that my last name?" Dave added.

"Your last name is Browning. Check your birth certificate," I'd said sharply, my teacher-self returning.

"What about the 'secret love language'?" he asked after a moment. "What was that really?"

I should tell him it was Yiddish, I thought. "I told you. Just something Dad and I made up," I heard myself say.

"An entire language." Dave's voice was grim.

"That's right."

"Why won't you tell me the truth?" he'd shouted, startling me. My son was never a shouter.

"The past has nothing to do with you," I said.

"How can you say that? I'm your son! Your history is my history!"

I told him I wouldn't be spoken to that way, that I was deserving of his respect, and that if he continued to yell—

"I want to know who I am!" he'd shouted again, and with hands trembling, I hung up the phone. After three weeks of silence, before I could apologize, before I could tell him why we told the lie that became our lives, Dave and Carrie and Tyler were gone.

Remembering this now, alone in the preoperative holding area, made my throat clench and my eyes blurry. How could I have explained? We abandoned the past for the sake of our dreams, which included Dave's limitless future, unmarred by hate. But that didn't change the fact of my cowardice.

"Mrs. Browning?" asked an uncertain voice from somewhere behind me. I looked over my shoulder to see none other than Elyse herself, peeking from behind the curtain that surrounded my bed. I sat up straighter, wiped the corner of my eye, and managed a watery smile.

"How *are* you, my dear?" I said, reaching out a hand to her. I could hear the flush of delight in my own voice.

Elyse answered with a shrug. "Better than you, I guess, right?"

But she didn't look better than me. There were circles under her eyes, and her shoulders were hunched again. Perhaps she was cold, I decided, in her thin jersey shirt and jeans, so I offered the present I'd brought along specifically to give her—my leather flight jacket. I pointed to a plastic bag on the lower metal rungs of the bed. "Go ahead. I brought it for you," I said. I watched her mouth gape a little, when she realized what it was, and then I smiled as she slipped it on. "Check the pocket," I remembered, and she pulled out the Dictaphone and snapped it open.

"No tapes?"

"Oh dear. I must've forgotten them. But here, let me see you,"
I added, and she stood up straighter, the jacket transforming
her hunched posture into a straight-backed, self-assured pilot.
She could've been a fly girl, right then. She could've even been
me. "It's perfect. You keep it."

Her eyebrows went up in alarm. "I don't want to keep it.
It's yours."

"Well, it can't stay mine forever," I said, and her hazel eyes
filled with tears.

"My grandma died last week," she finally said. "I left on
Sunday, and she died on Thursday."

"Oh, my dear . . ."

"We went back to Key West last weekend and scattered her
ashes. Thank you," she added quietly. "If you hadn't sent me, I
never would've seen her again."

I sighed and rubbed my temple; a headache was gathering
like a storm behind my left eyebrow.

Elyse shoved her hands back into the pockets of the jacket.
"My mom and my aunt are in shock that Grandma died. She
was only diagnosed with cancer a month ago."

"And you must be in shock, too, I gather."

"I don't know what I am. I feel like . . . I'm not a kid anymore."

"Oh, my dear," I said again, looking up at her heart-shaped face.

A nurse yanked back the curtain. "Your brother-in-law's
here. Is it okay to let him back?"

"Brother-in . . . ?"

"I hope it's okay," Elyse said. "I saw Gene Rosskemp in the

hallway and told him to come on back. I thought only family were allowed."

"Oh goodness," I said, inwardly groaning, but smiling and nodding my okay to the nurse, who mistook my yanking up the blankets around my neck as a sign that I needed more warm blankets—bless her—before scurrying off to retrieve Gene. Honestly, I was surprised he'd shown up at all.

"What happened with the flour baby?" I asked Elyse, as we waited for Gene.

"Oh. He died, too." God only knows what my face did, because she rushed to console me: "It's okay! Really. Now that I'm not worrying about *him* all the time, I've been thinking about my novel again—how you said the half sisters need to be united against something, once they find each other? I figured out that they want to make their school part of the Civilian Pilot Training Program, but the headmaster doesn't think girls can fly. And so they secretly apply to FDR's program anyway, but the headmaster's *evil son,* who tries to seduce all of the girls at the school, keeps thwarting their flight plans, and the only way to succeed is to *kill* him and *burn* him and scatter his ashes at sea."

"My word!" I said, massaging my temples again, as Gene appeared, looking a mite sheepish.

"Hey, Mary. Thought you could use a little cheering squad here," he said, and then I smiled, surprised, because he was actually right. "You just ask for the good stuff, you hear? So you don't go waking up in the middle of surgery."

"That happens?" My neck craned forward in a spasm of disbelief. "People wake up before it's over?"

"Only very rarely," Elyse said, with an authoritative nod. It wasn't until Gene nudged her and she smiled that I realized they were teasing me.

"Tell 'em you want the hammer," Gene insisted. "And while you're off in la-la-land, Elyse and I will hang out in the waiting room."

It was heartening to imagine two people simply being there for the sole purpose of awaiting news of my recovery. My shoulders dropped with relief. "It's supposed to just take forty-five minutes. I'll be home tonight."

"Forty-five minutes or four hours, don't matter. I've got my dirty magazines"—he held up *Car and Driver*—"and Elyse's got . . . ?"

"Oh!" she remembered, reaching into her backpack to pull out a hardback book. "I brought this for you. It's my grandmother's book, about a Women Airforce Service Pilot, so I thought you'd like it, even if it's not very literary."

"Why do you say that?" I asked, running my fingers over the cover of the old and yellowed book. The dust cover, if there had ever been one, was long lost, and instead it was just a brown binding with the words *The Secrets of Flight* embossed in green.

"That's what Grandma said. The girls in the story are all beautiful and sexy, and they're always talking about boys more than the war, while they do their hair. And they always say, 'Yee haw!' when they take off. But I couldn't put it down," she added sheepishly. "I finished it in a day."

It sounded like drivel, but naturally I was curious. Perhaps the author was related to someone I might've known in flight school, someone who'd only imagined us to be glamorous pilots, rather than the hard workers we really were. I looked at the binding.

Margarita Schiff, I thought, perplexed by the name and still wincing from my headache when the anesthesiologist arrived, a young man with a doughy complexion, who forgot to introduce himself before launching into the potential side effects of general anesthesia, including death. I glanced at Elyse, who gulped, and then to Gene, who smiled and nodded at the form. *Let the man do his job.*

After shakily signing my life away, I watched as the anesthesiologist stuffed the clipboard with my papers into a slot at the end of the bed.

"I have a terrible headache," I said, but he left without a backward glance.

"Mary, in a few minutes, you won't even know you have a head," Gene said with a wink, and when I shot him a skeptical look, he added, "You gotta give yourself over to these people. It may not seem like it, but they know what they're doin'."

When Dr. Khaira stopped by next, I could almost believe it. He shook Gene's hand, and knocked his fist against Elyse's before thanking her for sending him such an interesting and delightful patient. I remembered how tempted I'd been to reveal my name to him that day in his office, just by way of apology. It seemed like he would've understood that when I left Miri Lichtenstein behind, I was giving up much more than a Congressional Gold Medal.

Dr. Khaira listened attentively as I gave him a bit of advice that my husband, the late Dr. Thomas Browning, always said:

that treating older people is like driving on ice. "Do not make sudden, large movements." He laughed and squeezed my shoulder and promised to be very precise.

"Ma'am, your family is going to have to come with me now," said the nurse, peeking behind the curtain again. "They're ready for you in the OR."

Elyse reached over and gave my hand a squeeze, while Gene flashed me two thumbs-up, before they both ducked out behind the nurse. It occurred to me then that somehow Gene hadn't made a single pun in the last half hour, which made me wonder if it was a sign of my own dire condition.

I looked down at the book on my lap, *The Secrets of Flight*, which, after a few unsettling moments, I cracked open. It wasn't as if I were expecting to hunker down and read for a while, but I was anxious, and it was there, and sometimes the only comfort one will know in a time of uncertainty is a book—even a very bad one, about women pilots styling their hair.

The author did, at least, have enough sense to choose an intriguing quote for the title page:

> *Time is but the stream I go a-fishing in . . .*
> *Its thin current slides away, but eternity remains.*
> *I would drink deeper; fish in the sky,*
> *whose bottom is pebbly with stars.*

Ah, yes, Mr. Henry David Thoreau—always a winner, I thought, as I flipped one page back, to the dedication: *To Miriam Lichtenstein, my "Aunt Miri," who made every sky seem like someplace worth fishing.*

"Uh oh—let's put that in here with the rest of your belongings," said a bubbly woman in scrubs, slipping the book from my hands. My mouth opened to protest, but the words were trapped inside me.

It is I—I am she—

"Look at you, tach'ing away," the girl added, pointing at the heart monitor on the wall, where my startled and desperate heart was on display for anyone to see.

"Rita?" I finally managed, wondering how it could be true: How could I have inspired that little girl, when she knew nothing of me, nothing except that I'd left to fly? How could Sarah's daughter have written me a book?

"No, honey, I'm Stephanie, the nurse anesthetist." The other anesthesiologist had gone for coffee, she explained, but she'd be taking over, and in fact she was giving me Versed that very minute. "It's going to feel like you've had a couple of glasses of wine."

The last thing I remember was Sol's face, leaning over me to kiss me. He whispered that he loved me. His lips were very soft. And then I was gone.

CHAPTER 25

Complications

The first time Dr. Khaira came out to the waiting room after Mrs. Browning's surgery, I was sitting all by myself reading a *Glamour* magazine. "Everything went beautifully, buddy," he said, sitting down beside me, and I quickly shut the article I was reading, thinking how Gene was right: as soon as he left to go to the bathroom, someone would come and tell us what was going on. "Her vital signs are perfect—and her gallbladder was about to rupture, so it was a good thing we got it out," Dr. Khaira said. "We're just waiting for her to wake up from the anesthesia, and then you can go see her."

"Great!" I said.

Dr. Khaira gave me a fist bump. "Stay out of trouble, kiddo."

A half an hour later, the anesthesiologist came out from the recovery room. Gene was back from "the can" (his word) by then, so the doctor told us both that Mrs. Browning had a minor reaction to the anesthetic that they'd given her to relax her muscles, but that it would wear off in no time—anywhere from eight hours, up to a day.

"What kind of side effects are we talking about here?" Gene asked, rising to a stand, since the doctor never sat down.

The anesthesiologist shrugged and said, "Temporary paralysis of all her voluntary skeletal muscles. We'll be admitting her overnight, obviously."

"Are her eyes open yet?" I asked, and he looked down at me like I was a tool before telling me that eyelids *are* voluntary skeletal muscles, so obviously hers were paralyzed shut.

"So basically, you can't be sure she's not awake inside that head of hers?" Gene asked. "'Cause I don't want her to know nothin'."

"She'll be kept sedated," the anesthesiologist said. "Instead of waking up five minutes after surgery, it might just be tomorrow."

I felt kind of weird collecting my things in my backpack and leaving knowing she was still on a ventilator and that she couldn't move any muscle in her entire body and that she'd practically predicted this. I thought about the conversation that we'd had the day after I'd sent her to Dr. Khaira, when she'd said that if she went ahead with the surgery and she couldn't "resume regular life as I know it now," she'd rather not be anywhere at all. I had just stared at her, thinking about my grandma and how her regular life as she'd known it had gotten all fucked up, when Mrs. Browning added, "I would rather meet my maker than face the inside of a nursing home, if you catch my drift."

I could tell Gene felt sort of uneasy about leaving her behind, too. He'd rolled up his *Car and Driver* magazine and paused just beside the sliding doors of the hospital to tell me that we should just meet up the same time tomorrow and pretend that nothing bad had happened and that it was still Tuesday. "That way Mary doesn't get to be right—she was so sure something would go wrong," he'd said, hovering on the gray mat, which made the doors keep opening and closing, blasting me with cold air and then warmth. I had already cut an entire day of school, but I'd told him I'd find a way to get there.

It wasn't until the next day that I heard anything about Mrs. Browning naming me her decision maker. I should've been in first period study hall, listening to the sound of student's text alerts, but instead I was sitting in a different waiting room this time, a smaller, more private one just outside the double doors of the Intensive Care Unit, when Dr. Khaira came out to talk to me. The skin under his eyes looked puffy, and, for once, his mouth wasn't smiling.

"The muscle relaxant is out of her system, but she still hasn't opened her eyes yet," he said. "She's losing a lot of blood from somewhere, and I'm going to have to take her back to the OR to find out where." Then he showed me the form that had my name on it in Mrs. Browning's shaky writing. "Do you know anything about this?"

I read the top of the form and said, "What exactly is a medical power of attorney again?" and Dr. Khaira kind of threw up one of his arms as if that was his answer.

"Without an exploratory surgery, she might die. I need the power of attorney to sign a consent form for the surgery . . . but you can't when you're only fifteen years old." Dr. Khaira ran his fingers through his hair like he might want to pull it out, clump by clump, and said that since she was a "full code"—

meaning she'd authorized him to save her life—he was just going to do the surgery and call in the hospital lawyers later.

"Should we page Gene?" I asked. "He's probably in the cafeteria. He would know what Mrs. Browning would want."

Dr. Khaira looked up from his hands. "Is Gene eighteen years of age or older?"

I thought of how Gene's even got vertical forehead wrinkles, as if eroded by years of standing in the rain. "I'm guessing he's like . . . eighty-five?"

"How's Gene related to Mrs. Browning?"

"He's not," I said. "He's just in the writers' group, too."

"Find him," Dr. Khaira said.

When Gene made it up to the waiting room ten minutes later, he listened to what Dr. Khaira had to say about the emergency surgery. "I'd say go ahead and do whatever you need to do," Gene said.

ONCE DR. KHAIRA HAD LEFT, GENE SAT DOWN NEXT TO ME AND shook his head, like he still couldn't believe it. Finally he said, "She called me the night before the surgery, said she had a favor to ask of me—the whole power of attorney thing. And I told her I've been through all of this once before, and let me tell ya, once is enough . . ." he trailed off, still shaking his head, probably thinking of his wife, Lucille, who was starring in his story about saving the bottles of wine during the war—it had all been for her, his quest to come home alive with a souvenir. Then he seemed to remember that I was still there. "Looks like when she wakes up tomorrow we're gonna have to pretend it's yesterday," he said instead, and I smiled at the idea of Mrs. Browning waking up, and everything going back to normal.

LATER THAT AFTERNOON, I STOPPED BY MRS. DESMOND'S CLASS-
room, even though we don't have psychology on Wednesdays.
I'd been married to Holden for over three weeks by now, and
Henry had been dead for six days. She was sitting behind her
desk, which was covered in papers, but she put down her red
pen as soon as she noticed me. "Can I talk to you?" I asked,
shifting my slipping backpack up onto my shoulder.

"Of course!" she said, and her face lit up like she was wishing for any excuse not to have to grade another paper. "Please—
have a seat! Is this about the Marriage Project?"

"About that . . ." I said, pulling up chair. "I want a divorce
from Holden Saunders."

Mrs. Desmond frowned and her eyebrows furrowed, and
I wondered if it sounded dramatic, considering that after
Friday—the day we were supposed to turn in our sacks of flour
to get full credit—we could pretend we'd never met anyway.
Mrs. Desmond was probably older than Mom, but her hair reminded me of Aunt Andie's: brown and frizzy, which made
it easier to keep talking, so I told her the story of Henry's
demise—the abbreviated version, minus the public ridicule.
Finally, she said, "I have to tell you, Elyse, that in all my years
running the Marriage Project, I've never had a student divorce.
I'd hate for you to be the first couple unable to work it out."

"Don't we automatically fail if the kid gets killed, anyway?"
I asked.

"Not necessarily," she said, with encouragement in her
voice, as if it were just my grade that I'd been worried about.
"If you and Holden write an informative essay about what
you've learned regarding teen pregnancy, you can still get a C.
After all, that's the point of the project, isn't it?"

"What if I expand the paper to include divorce statistics after the death of a child, and I write it alone?"

Mrs. Desmond sighed before picking up her pen again. "Elyse, I think you two need to find a way to work this out."

AFTER SCHOOL, I WAS ROOTING THROUGH MY LOCKER WITH MY backpack on my knee when Holden Saunders walked toward me wearing jeans and my favorite navy sweater of his that makes his eyes bluer, but his face was serious, so I knew he must've heard from Mrs. Desmond about the divorce. It was easier to peer into my backpack and search for my ringing cell phone than to meet his eyes. Dr. Khaira was calling to tell me that Mrs. Browning's second surgery went great. "Did you get the bleeding stopped?" I asked, and he said yes. When I asked if she was awake, he said, "Not yet, kiddo; she's still sedated from the surgery." Holden just stood parked next to my locker and watched me talk to Dr. Khaira.

After I hung up, Holden said, "Wow. Go, Dr. Strickler," as if I'd had an incredible promotion from hospital volunteer. I shrugged and zipped up my backpack. "You really rocked that physics bridge," he added.

"Thank you. I know." I slammed my locker shut.

"What was that—like, the Golden Gate?" he asked, shoving his hands in his pockets.

"We live in a city with four hundred and forty-six bridges, and you think I'm gonna pick one from San Francisco?" I started walking.

The corridor was empty, which was probably why he said, "Elyse—wait. I'm sorry," instead of avoiding me in front of his friends like he had all week. "This Homecoming thing with

Karina isn't, like, exclusive or anything." I turned around and asked him what he was saying. "I'm saying she's not my girl-friend. No one's my girlfriend. Me and you can hang out again. I had fun—I still think you're cool."

It wasn't fun; I thought I might love you; and it's "You and I" not "me and you." I turned and started walking again.

"Don't you care about your psychology grade?" he called after me.

"Not if you fail, too," I said over my shoulder. It was almost scary how I could convert all that love into hate.

OUTSIDE OF SCHOOL, I WAS WALKING BY THE TENNIS COURTS when I heard a familiar half cackle/half shriek and turned to see Thea, running back and forth between two different courts and swinging a racket. It was probably forty-five degrees, but she wasn't wearing tights and the skin between the bottom of her miniskirt and the top of her combat boots looked red and cold. I guess she was taking her fashion tips from Carson Jef-fries, perpetual wearer of shorts, who was sprinting between two courts on the other side of the net and yelling at her to "keep it going!" They were playing our game, the one we made up in the summer before sixth grade, where the only rule is to hit the ball no matter where it lands—even if it's three courts away. I buttoned up the top of Mrs. Browning's flight jacket and watched them through the chain-link fence until Mr. Glansman, the tennis coach, called to them that the courts were reserved for the team and they would have to leave. Carson was collecting their balls, and Thea had just grabbed her back-pack off the ground, when she glanced up at me and kind of gaped and then scowled. I waved but she didn't wave back, so I walked over to the door in the fence, their only way out.

"Can I talk to you?" I asked, once she and Carson had come through the exit. Thea hesitated and glanced at Carson as if he were her real husband.

"I'll meet you in the library later," he said before walking away. A few paces later, he whirled around and asked where their flour baby was.

"In my locker," Thea said, like, *duh.*

"As long as our little bundle of joy is safe," Carson said, and Thea rolled her eyes.

"I'm sorry," I said, once he was gone. Thea and I walked through the grass and away from the courts, where the tennis team was starting to assemble for practice. "I'm sorry I ditched you for the physics bridge. I'm sorry I haven't called or texted you lately . . ."

"And where the hell have you been at lunch? It's like you disappeared off the fucking map."

"I've been kind of . . . busy . . ."

"Yeah, I heard. How's *Holden*?" she asked, and the sound of his name made my cheeks redden.

"I'm such a tool."

"No, you're not," Thea said with a noisy exhale. "He's the asshole."

"Yeah, but . . . I was really into him," I said.

Thea put her arm around me. We sat on the hill and watched Karina Spencer run across the court. I wished my legs were as long and as perfect. I wished I knew for sure that saying "I'd prefer not to" had been the right thing to do. I wished part of me still didn't want to be with him, which reminded me of Mom and Dad, loving and hating each other at the same time.

"My parents might be getting a divorce," I said, realizing all at once that if I said it out loud, I was afraid it might make it come true.

"That *sucks*. Which one of them cheated?" Thea asked. Ever since her mom moved to California with Rocco, she thinks there's only one reason people split up.

I hesitated, wondering whether to admit that I'd seen a drug rep's pen and underwear at Daddy's apartment. "Neither. It's . . . complicated," I said, echoing Daddy.

Thea hugged her knees and stared ahead at the tennis team, making it look so easy to keep all the balls within the lines. Finally, she glanced at me. "Your bridge was fucking insane, dude."

"My dad has the steadiest hands in the world," I said, remembering the way he'd just held them there, waiting for each toothpick to dry, whereas I had accidentally ripped down one of the arches when a clump of wet toothpicks had stuck to my thumb. Even then, at four in the morning, he hadn't gotten mad. "And patience," I added. We were both quiet for a minute, as Mr. Glansman blew his whistle and told everybody to switch sides. Then Thea stood up and brushed the grass off the back of her skirt. I stood up, too, and slung my backpack over my shoulder again. "I'm sorry I disappeared," I said. "All this stuff happened. My friend from the writers' group got her gallbladder out, and my grandma died . . ."

"Oh, no. I'm really sorry," Thea said.

"Thanks," I said, as we started to walk toward the parking lot. I was about to ask her if she still hated me, but instead found myself asking her if she still respected me—for wearing skinny jeans, for cutting my hair, for . . .

"—not giving Holden Saunders a blow job?" Thea suggested.

I nodded, slowly. "Everyone's calling me a prude."

"People are assholes. Haven't you heard the rumor that we're gay for each other, or that Carson Jeffries and I are hooking up?"

I smiled. "I thought the last part was true."

"Oh, you're gross," Thea said, shoving me. "He's such a spaz."

"So are you," I said, and she didn't argue; instead just asked me what was up with *my* mock marriage. I told her about my meeting with Mrs. Desmond, how I was going to write a term paper by myself and see if she accepted it.

"Can I ask you a question?" Thea said, and I nodded. "What the hell is a gallbladder?" she asked, and for some reason that made us both crack up.

I DIDN'T MAKE IT BACK TO THE HOSPITAL UNTIL SATURDAY, AND by then, all the doctors making rounds had stopped talking about how quickly they were going to get Mrs. Browning off the ventilator. Dr. Khaira had consulted some hospital experts on "Ethics" to help make the decisions. I repeated the one thing that she'd told me: that if she couldn't go back to regular life as she knew it, she'd rather not be anywhere at all.

Over the next week, Mrs. Browning looked less and less like Mrs. Browning, and it wasn't just because her eyes were shut and her top curl was gone. When she was on the ventilator, she looked like the Pillsbury Dough Woman. Her wrists were swollen and her feet were even fatter; they reminded me of bear feet, the kind in cartoons and toilet paper ads. At first she didn't move at all, but after a while she started to twitch and sometimes her hands would fly up and the lines would get dislodged and alarms would start bonging, so then they tied down her wrists. The doctors making rounds kept acting like she was getting better, though: the cardiologist checked the catheters in her neck and some numbers on the screen above and said they were looking good; the pulmonologist checked the chest X-ray and said it was getting better; the kidney doctors looked at the urine that was hanging in a bag and said urine was a good sign. Everyone kept agreeing that she was making tremendous progress.

Friday night, Mom was in the kitchen pulling dinner out of the oven when I came in through the back door. It was weird—she'd made what I always pick for my birthday dinner: chicken piccata, and rice, and steamed artichokes. In fact, it was kind of bizarre that she was cooking at all, since lately all she'd been doing is lying in bed and telling us to fend for ourselves for dinner. We'd been eating a lot of Velveeta mac-'n'-cheese.

"The boys are at the hockey game tonight with Dad," Mom said. "It's just us girls." When I jammed my hands into the pockets of my leather bomber jacket and told her I'd already eaten at the hospital, she said, "Oh, really? Where do they have you working now?"

"ICU," I said, without skipping a beat.

"That's funny." Mom pulled the rattling lid off the artichoke pot, which let off a plume of steam. "Because when I called the hospital today, they said you're not a volunteer there. They said you haven't even applied."

I glanced at the floor. "I'm not—not really."

"Then why . . . ?"

"Because you really wanted me to, and I thought it would make you happy."

"It was just a suggestion," Mom said, her voice baffled, as if she couldn't imagine why I thought lying about it would've made her happy. "Where'd the flight jacket come from?" she added, and I felt myself shrinking inside of it. "What a funny little gremlin," she added, touching the patch of Fifinella and her blue wings.

"My friend from writers' group gave it to me."

"The writers' group that Thea's in?"

Startled, I glanced up. "Thea's not . . . actually."

"And where did you sleep the night before your toothpick bridge was due?" Mom asked, folding her arms across her chest. "Because I ran into Gordon Palmer at the grocery store, and he said you didn't even *do* the toothpick bridge with Thea."

"I was at Daddy's apartment."

"Oh, really—just like it was Daddy who bought you the tickets to Florida?" Before I could answer, Mom blurted, "I know you have a boyfriend."

"I-I don't."

"Cut the crap, Elyse. You haven't been volunteering, you've been 'hanging out' somewhere with your boyfriend. You slept over at his house, and you—"

"Call Daddy and ask him! I was there! We stayed up all night."

When I thrust my cell phone into Mom's hands, she seemed startled, as if she wasn't sure she wanted to dial Daddy's number. But then she looked down and squinted at what I really wanted her to see: my home screen, a picture of the Hulton Bridge made entirely out of toothpicks. It had the same cables tethering the five archways, the same railing halfway up, and you could just imagine the Allegheny River rushing beneath it. I watched Mom staring at the picture of Dad, who was grinning wildly, as he stooped over our masterpiece. "Wow . . . that's . . . made of toothpicks?" Mom asked, and her blue eyes were shiny with tears.

"And glue. It won 'Most Aesthetically Pleasing.' And it held forty pounds." I took the phone back and slipped it into my pocket. "Daddy was psyched."

"Why did you lie to me?"

"I didn't want to answer any questions about his love life." Mom's eyes widened, and I expelled a breath of air. "Thank you," I said. "For not asking me."

My cell phone beeped: a text from Thea, who was running late to pick me up for the movies. "Almost there," she'd written.

"Do you want to at least take off your jacket and stay a while?" Mom asked. "I want to hear all about this boy . . ."

"Mom, I don't have a boyfriend," I said. "I—he—it's over."

"Oh, honey . . ." Mom said, reaching out to touch my sleeve again.

"Don't," I snapped, pulling my arm away.

"Why can't I . . . ?"

"Help? Now? After you wouldn't let me see my own grandmother for five years because—why? You wanted to punish her for moving far away? After you refused to send me to see her when she was dying? And you wonder why I started making stuff up?"

The cordless phone started ringing, and Mom swiped it

off the counter before I had a chance. "Satinder Khaira?" she asked, reading the caller ID aloud.

"That's for me," I said, but Mom just shot me a look before pressing the TALK button.

"Jane Strickler," she said, like she was at the office. "Rich isn't here, Satinder. You want his cell?"

I looked at my watch and glanced out the kitchen windows for car lights in the driveway. "Does he need to talk to me?" I whispered to Mom, and she furrowed her eyebrows and shook her head.

"Just a moment, please," Mom said, her voice kind of stern, only she was talking to Dr. Khaira, not me.

"I'm going to the movies with Thea," I said, and she covered up the receiver.

"Elyse, I—trust you," Mom said, which was probably meant to be an apology for everything she'd just accused me of, but it didn't make me feel any better.

THE NEXT MORNING BEFORE MOM GOT UP, I RODE MY BIKE TO the hospital and met Dr. Khaira in the ICU. Mrs. Browning was supposed to get a trach that day, which meant that they were going to cut a hole in her neck so they could suction the crap out of her lungs. Dr. Khaira and I were sitting side by side on the chairs in her private room, and he was explaining why this procedure would get her off the ventilator faster, when Selena Markmann walked in and gasped. I was surprised to see her, too—dressed in black for a change, like we were already at a funeral.

I watched as Selena went up to the bedside and looked at Mrs. Browning with all those tubes going in and out of her and picked up one of her swollen hands and said, "Oh, Mary," in a small little whisper. That was when I knew I wasn't imagining it that Mrs. Browning wasn't Mrs. Browning anymore. Then Selena whirled around and asked us where Dave was.

"Dave's dead," I said, and her face kind of collapsed, except for those McDonald's arched eyebrows, and her hand flew up to cover her mouth. Her fingernail polish was lavender, I saw then, which gave me a weird little hope. "So is her grandson Tyler," I added. "He died when he was a baby. There's nobody else."

"Oh, God. Dave was *real*? I always thought—he seemed like just a story . . ." Selena glanced at Mrs. Browning again and then back to Dr. Khaira and me. She straightened up. "Gene sent me. He said he couldn't be here—he couldn't handle seeing her like this, but he wanted to be sure, she wasn't . . . suffering . . ." she trailed off. "May I ask who exactly is making her decisions?"

"We have a committee of experts on ethics, who are committed—" Dr. Khaira started.

"Bullshit. 'Experts on ethics'?" Selena repeated. "She told me herself that she never wanted to be resuscitated. You were there, weren't you, Elyse? After one of Jean Fester's godawful stories?"

That was when Mrs. Browning's neck started to move, sending her head swishing back and forth and back and forth on the pillow. It was almost spooky, like a cadaver coming back to life.

"Mary? It's Selena," Selena suddenly called, squeezing one of her fat hands, like a little hug, and I swear it looked like Mrs. Browning's fingers gripped back. "Do you want us to tell them to stop?" Mrs. Browning's head went from side to side again. "Do you want us to tell them to keep going?" Her head repeated the same. So, what did it mean?

"We have every hope that she's going to be fine, as soon as we can get her off the ventilator," Dr. Khaira said, but Mrs. Markmann just glared at him as she pulled up a chair beside the bed. Dr. Khaira touched my arm and jerked his head toward the nurses' station, so I followed him outside the room, over to the white counters where all the computers sit, and all the doctors and nurses oversee the patients like operators in an aircraft control tower.

"What if—we're doing the wrong thing?" I said, choking on the words.

"Kiddo, listen, I promise I wouldn't . . . oh, no," he said, looking at my frowning face and the tears starting to drip out of my blinking eyelids. The thing was, I wasn't quite crying over what we had done, but over what I hadn't done: I hadn't held Mrs. Browning's hand, or spoken her name, or done anything but sit in a chair and read a book and watch the ebb and flow of the Intensive Care Unit.

"Oh, geez . . . come on . . . keep it together . . ." Dr. Khaira added, glancing around like he wished someone would save him, when I started to cry harder. That was when the double doors of the ICU swung open, and Mom walked through them, dressed up in one of her power lawyer suits: pencil skirt, blazer and blouse, heels. She looked better than I'd seen her in weeks, better than before Daddy left, except maybe too thin. When a nurse pointed her my way, I mopped my face on my sleeve. It wasn't until her face met mine and I saw her exhale with relief that I realized how glad I was that she'd found me. The suit made her look strong and powerful again, and I wanted to fall into her arms and let her take over.

"Jane," Dr. Khaira said, his voice sounding as relieved as I felt, and I didn't know if the relief was because now he wouldn't have to comfort the weeping teenage girl or because she looked like she meant business. It seemed like since this whole thing began, he wanted someone else to tell him what to do.

"Satinder," Mom said with a sharp nod, all businesslike, and he turned and explained to me that he'd called my mother last night to ask for her opinion on the trach.

"You seemed pretty mad. Unless maybe you didn't mean to hang up on me?" he added.

"As I told you last night, I've never heard anything about this *Mary Browning*"—Mom narrowed her eyes at me—"which is why I suggested you make her a ward of the state and leave my daughter out of it."

"Mom!"

"But this morning I woke up and had my coffee and thought a little more about your phone call. I'd like some information about the case," she said, folding her arms across her chest, and I exhaled.

So, we followed Dr. Khaira into the "family room" off in the corner of the ICU, which is different from the waiting room, because it has just enough chairs for one family at a time, a single phone and no TV. Mom and I sat across from him and listened while he summarized everything about Mrs. Browning's last week, about her lungs and her kidneys and her heart, and how two days ago they'd stopped the medication to keep her asleep on the ventilator, but Mrs. Browning still hadn't woken up.

"But she shook her head a little earlier when Selena Markmann asked her if she wanted us to stop," I said, ignoring the part where she also shook her head when Selena asked if we should keep going.

"We did send her down for a CT scan of her brain, and there is no sign of a stroke," Dr. Khaira said.

"Well, you shouldn't keep doing procedures on a woman who has no chance of meaningful recovery," Mom said.

"I wouldn't be doing this if I didn't think she was going to pull through," Dr. Khaira said. When he added, "I'm not trying to torture her," he seemed to be pleading with Mom like she was a judge.

"What I can't understand is, well . . ." I started to say and they both turned and looked at me like they'd forgotten I was there. "The heart guy says her heart is fine and that the fluid on her lungs is from the kidneys, and the kidney doctor says the kidneys are okay, but the reason there's fluid there is from the heart, and the lung specialist says the fluid is from both the kidneys and the heart but that the lungs are okay, and the neurologist says she's not waking up because of the kidneys and the heart and the lungs but that nothing is actually wrong with her brain."

"What you have witnessed, my friend, is a pissing war, called Not My Organ System," Dr. Khaira said. "You want to know what I really think? I think that the anesthetic threw her for a loop, which started a cascade of badness. She is eighty-seven years old."

"Is she going to be able to go back to her apartment again?" I asked.

"That's my intent," Dr. Khaira said. Then he looked at Mom again, who clasped her hands together on her lap as if she were about to say grace and said she wanted to be sure we're doing this for all the right reasons—that we weren't "moving forward with aggressive interventions because we can." And I couldn't remember what the right reasons might be: because Gene and Dr. Khaira and I wanted her to be all right?

"Give me three days," Satinder said. "If I can't get her extubated by Tuesday, we'll stop everything and let her go."

MOM AND I DROVE HOME IN SILENCE, WITH MY BIKE IN THE back of the station wagon. I knew I should've thanked her for coming, but I didn't want her to think that just because I was proud of her back in the ICU, I wasn't still mad about everything to do with Grandma—and everything to do with her and me.

"Elyse, I really don't know what to say," Mom finally said. "How well do you know this woman?"

I didn't know how to answer that, so I confessed instead that Mrs. Browning was the person who'd bought my tickets to Florida. "I was typing her memoir, but we didn't get to finish . . ."

"Why on earth would she name you as the power of attorney? I mean, she had to be *desperately* lonely . . . and just plain *desperate* . . ."

"I was nice to her. And she was so nice to me." Then I started to cry again, thinking of everything I'd told her about my plot, and my parents and my life, and everything I hadn't told her but that she'd known anyway.

"Honey, I'm sorry. I can't imagine what you've been going through," Mom finally said. "You're *fifteen*. And I want to protect you—"

"You're too late," I said, folding my arms across my chest. My tears were gone now; there was just a hard lump in my throat. "*I* didn't ask you to come today."

"I know," Mom said, her voice quiet. "I'm sorry you didn't feel you could tell me about something so important." I watched as she turned back onto the road leading into the Regal Estates. "Let's go home and get the boys. We'll all go out for pancakes," Mom finally decided, injecting her voice with false enthusiasm. The last place I wanted to be on a Saturday morning was at a diner, surrounded by a bunch of happy families, but then she added, "It'll be my birthday treat."

Oh God. How had I forgotten her birthday—how had we all forgotten? It seemed too late to wish her a happy one now, after Grandma was dead and Daddy was having sex with a drug rep. There wasn't another car on the road for miles, but Mom put on her blinker when she turned into the driveway. I waited until she'd parked in front of the garage to tell her I was sorry for not having a present. She stared at me for a beat, like she was waiting for me to apologize for something else, but then she just shrugged and said, "All I really want for my birthday is to be with the three of you."

THE HOUSE WAS EMPTY WHEN WE GOT INSIDE.

"Toby? Hugh?" Mom called, as we came in through the kitchen. "Boys?"

"We're going out for pancakes!" I yelled, and then, when there was no reply, I ran upstairs to check their rooms. The only signs of my brothers were Toby's chess set—paused midgame with a queen dangerously close to checkmate—and a torture bed of Legos on Huggie's floor.

Coming back downstairs, I could hear Mom calling, *"Huggie?"* her voice growing frantic. She whirled around and startled when she saw me in the doorway of the family room. "When I left they were watching TV. And now they're gone!"

"Maybe Daddy—"

"Daddy is at a continuing medical education conference today!" Mom shrieked, just as I heard the door in the foyer open followed by scampering feet.

"Hello?" I heard Aunt Andie call. "Anybody home?"

We hurried into the front hall, where the boys were shedding their coats on the floor, as if it were the mudroom.

"Mama!" Huggie said, rushing at my mother's legs.

"They showed up at my condo," Aunt Andie said. "I thought it would be best to bring them back before you freaked out."

"Too late," I mouthed behind Mom.

"We walked down the hill and took the bus from Waterworks Mall," Toby explained.

"You took *public transportation*?" Mom said, stooping to cradle Huggie with her arms, as if he were still a baby with a squishy head.

Toby fished in his pocket and held up a little bottle. "I made him Purell."

"Would you believe he found Great-Aunt Miriam?" Aunt Andie said. "The one Mom wrote the book about?"

"Wait," I said. "You *found* her? How?"

"Google Books."

"Mom had been told her aunt Miri was killed in a plane crash, but there was another rumor in the neighborhood, which she'd never wanted to believe, that Miri had abandoned the family and was alive and well in New York," Aunt Andie said.

"You asked me for more information, right?" Toby said to me, since I'd come to him curious about Grandma's real-life inspiration for *The Secrets of Flight,* the story of a Women's Airforce Service Pilot and her sister, a Broadway actress. "So I typed in every family member's name in the family tree, and 'Sarah Glazier' came up in the ninth essay of this book, *Miss Bixby Takes a Wife*. It's about a girl who dies of TB the same year that the cure is invented," he said. "The author's name is 'Mary Browning.' Only she and Miriam Lichtenstein were both from Squirrel Hill, Pennsylvania, and they both were pilots, and they were both born on September the first, 1922."

"How long did it take you to come up with this?" I asked.

Toby shrugged. "About five minutes."

"Are you all right?" Mom asked me, so my eyes must've been getting as big and crazy as they felt.

"We have to go to the hospital right now," I said.

CHAPTER 26

The Secrets of Flight

I wake up the first time to an electric shock on my left lower leg—the sort police officers use to silence unruly college students. At least that's what I imagine. I try to jerk my leg away, but my leg won't move.

"Still nothing," I hear the anesthesiologist say, before he zaps me again.

A great force is pressing upon my lungs, and my arms are frozen to the mattress. Meanwhile, my eyelids are inexplicably sealed shut, no matter how hard I try to open them. A catastrophe has occurred. My body is a cadaver, and I'm trapped inside.

The nurse calls from the end of the bed, "Don't worry, Mary, you're just having a reaction to the medication. It's going to take some time to wear off."

My chest is like an expanding balloon on the verge of an explosion. If I could just raise my arms. Shrug my shoulder. Lift a finger.

"Is she sedated?" I hear Dr. Khaira ask.

"Giving her Versed right now," the nurse says.

"Her count is dropping," he adds. "I might have to take her back to the OR."

Oh no, I think. *Please, God, don't let me—*

I AM NOT AWARE OF ANYTHING FOR CLOSE TO A WEEK. I AM KEPT intentionally unconscious by the team of doctors and nurses, and for that, I am grateful. When I finally become aware of my surroundings once again, I am in a different sort of pain than before—deeper and gnawing—and I'm unable to pinpoint the source. My limbs are no longer paralyzed, just profoundly sleepy, and it doesn't occur to me to try to move; I am too weak and tired. I can hear people talking, though. I become a floating brain, absorbing the conversations around me, the voices between the beeps.

Doctors make their rounds and discuss my remarkable progress, but I assume, having no idea that I'm in a private room, that they are referring to the patient in the next bed. I hear the residents chitchat as they place an intravenous catheter in my groin. The third-year male resident coaches the intern ingénue through the procedure. I feel the bee sting at the start, and the pushing and pulling, but it is nothing now, this pain, and it doesn't compare to what I've been through. I listen to the younger one, who says that she finds this ICU stuff depressing, that she's thinking of switching specialties to ophthalmology, where "nobody gets naked," and I think, *Am I naked?* I am not dead, but I am not alive; I hover somewhere in between.

My nurses are truly gifts from God. They talk in my ear, and call me "Mary," and tell me what they are doing as they do

it, even when they are just rolling me over in the bed. Sometimes they tell me to relax, other times they tell me that I'm
doing just fine, and they always let me know that it's *me* they
mean, not the lady in the next bed.

I hear Satinder Khaira, too, and I can tell that despite his
confidence, he is beside himself because of whatever unfortunate turn of events has led me here. In fact, whenever the team
of surgeons comes by, it's his voice I can pick out, the only
person who doesn't just speak of me in regional segments of
my anatomy. When the chief resident reports my urine output
and my level of inspired oxygen, I hear Satinder say, "Did
you know this lady was a pilot, and she wrote a book?" and
the shuffling stops; I hear these young doctors remember that
whatever I am now, I was once a human being, too.

I listen to his voice when he's not on rounds, as well, when
he's telling a woman—possibly one of the nurses?—that she's
too thin; she ought to eat more, and when the woman swears
she is, he says, "What exactly do you eat? I want a calorie
count, lady."

"Tree bark and kitty litter. Food, Satinder. I eat food."

"Well, you look worse than she does and she's been in a
coma for the last week," he says. Then he adds, "Happy birthday, Jane," and this Jane, whoever she is, replies, "You remembered."

I SLEEP, TOO. STRANGE, DRUG-INDUCED DREAMS THAT ARE IN-
terrupted by periodic jerks of my muscles, and I startle awake,
only to find myself running through another long, dark corridor, where I am opening stadium doors, and searching for
Dave—not grown-up Dave, but Dave as a young boy—and

each door that I open reveals more darkness, and more strangers, and more terror. I want to cry out for help, but the sounds won't come out of me, and nearby voices mingle with my nightmares until I realize that I am awake again, listening to the cadence of my hospital room, and its telltale sign of background beeping and breaths going through a hollow tube, as if someone were snorkeling nearby, and I am eavesdropping on a conversation underwater.

"Still unresponsive," I hear a woman say. "They're going to take her off the ventilator and see what happens."

"God, it's all so surreal," says another feminine voice. "Just imagine if Mom knew . . ."

"What kind of stuff did she tell you—near the end?" the woman asks, with an unmistakable catch in her throat.

"Mom?" There's a pause. "She told me not to buy Pottery Barn furniture."

I hear a snicker of laughter. "Classic," the woman says.

"She told me she wished we would just enjoy our lives and stop trying to rule them."

"But it's so hard to let go."

"Okay, folks, time for Mary to get a bath. You'll have to wait outside," the nurse says.

And I'm sorry for the woman in the next bed, that her daughters must be moved from the room all on account of me.

I DREAM THAT I AM FLYING THROUGH THE SEASONS—WITHOUT a plane, without an engine—the wind lifting me through the air and over the autumn trees. I drink up the glorious color of each flapping leaf, and then I dip down, as if the air were water, and the first flakes begin to fall, and I am flying through the glimmering, snowy forest, and I am laughing because it's so beautiful, and then the trees open up to a clearing, and the sun gets brighter, and I push my arms back and soar upward to the blue sky, and then I hear Sol, whispering in my ear, *Miriam Lichtenstein, wake up.*

I open my eyes. The sky is gone, and the beeping is back, and I am sitting in a hospital room. There's a curtain drawn over the window, while the one closest to the door reveals nothing but bustling chaos outside it: people in scrubs and white coats rushing past. In the chair beside my bed sits a girl with mounds of wiry brown hair, drawing on a pad of paper, and I wonder if she could be my daughter-in-law, except that Carrie is petite and blond and never wears jangly jewelry. The girl yawns and shifts in her seat, shoots me a glance, and then startles and stands up.

"Miriam Lichtenstein?"

I smile and nod. "Hello, my dear," I say. "I'm embarrassed to say that I can't quite remember how you and I might've met before . . ." but the girl is squinting at me, unable to read my lips. I haven't figured out yet that the snorkeling sound is coming from my own neck and there's a breathing tube still connected to the ventilator. *Who. Are. You?* I slowly mouth the words.

"I'm Andie," she says, and my eyebrows furrow.

Do you know my son Dave? I want to say. I've lost him at a baseball stadium.

"I can't believe you're actually awake . . ." this Andie person says, collecting her things in a little cloth bag with handles: her sketchpad, her colored pencils, her erasers. "I've gotta go make some calls. Just—stay right here, okay?" she says, and I smile at the eagerness of her nod and try to convey with my open-palmed shrug, *Where else would I go?*

But I wait, and she never returns, and I suppose I probably doze off, but try as I might, I never return to the sky. The next time I open my eyes, there is a young doctor—a girl, really, with a ponytail and glasses and a long white coat—at the foot of my bed taking inventory of my vital statistics for her clipboard. *The poor dear,* I think. Her eyes are so tired. I watch as she checks the ventilator, then the bag of urine, then the heart monitor, making notation after notation. Then our eyes meet, and she gasps and takes a step back. "You're awake!" she says. "Mrs. Browning, you're awake! Holy sh—" She clamps a hand over her mouth, and her laughter sounds so startled and amazed that it makes me smile. "Mrs. Browning, your family will be so happy. Your family has been waiting for you!" And she clasps my hand, for just a second, before pulling away. "I'll be right back!"

No! Wait—

But thankfully, she doesn't go far. I can see her standing in the doorway of my room and looking down the hallway at someone whose footsteps are approaching. The intern is pointing at my bed—pointing at me. "Go. Look," she says to someone, an order, and I think how interesting it is that bad news requires a preamble, but good news needs only a witness. How curious it is that *I* am the good news.

A woman with short blond hair and a visitor's tag on her jacket squeezes past the intern, and I recognize her right away, even though we've never met before. Her name tag says "Jane Strickler" but somehow I know she must belong to Sarah.

"Miriam Lichtenstein?" she says, rushing toward me with

an outstretched hand, and I nod and smile and mouth, *Hello.* Even though she's laughing with disbelief, I can see the tears invading her blue eyes. "I'm Jane—Margarita's daughter; Sarah's granddaughter," she says, and I squeeze her hand back and then pull it to my cheek, and mouth, *Hello, Jane.* "Elyse!" she calls, over her shoulder, and I open my eyes again and lean over to see the girl rushing in the room, and she's wearing my flight jacket. It's not until then that I remember that we met on my birthday, and she was my present.

Elyse leans over and gives me a hug. "I'm so sorry this happened to you," she says in my ear.

Me, too, I mouth and nod, squeezing her back. And when she pulls away, I wonder for just a second about the day we met, and the phone call from the doctor about my bone density test, before I left for writers' group . . . Jane must see me trying to work something out, because she leans over and asks, "Yes, Aunt Miri? What is it?"

Did I break my hip? I slowly mouth, pointing to my own anatomy, and that makes them look at each other and smile.

"You had your gallbladder out," Elyse says.

"Your hips are fantastic," Jane adds. "You could dance a rumba."

No, thank you, I mouth, and when they laugh, their giddy joy makes me smile.

IT TAKES ME EIGHT WEEKS TO GET BACK TO MY APARTMENT, AND five months before I return to the writers' group. In the hospital ICU, I am disconnected from the ventilator and transferred to a step-down unit, and from there to a rehab center, where I attend physical therapy sessions twice a day, and try to convince myself that despite the plethora of older people in wheel-chairs and the foul smells, this is not a nursing home. I try to convince myself that despite the healing hole in my neck and my difficulty walking to the bathroom without assistance, I am not the tragedy that I feel like, but that I am, as Jane keeps insisting, a miracle.

What she still doesn't understand is that she is the miracle—they all are, these nieces of mine—but especially Jane, who stops by the rehab center every day of the week, usually while her children are in school and sometimes after hours with Elyse. Jane is unemployed these days and still trying to figure out what kind of law she wants to practice or if she even intends to return to it at all. For now, she seems content to sit at my bedside and encourage me to eat and to talk. I'm tired, but she coaxes out the answers to her stream of questions about my growing-up years, about my impressions of her mother—"She was a whiz at hopscotch and reading picture books," I say—my time as a fly girl, and how Sol and I fell in love.

"Why didn't you ever pilot again, later on?" she asked me one day, and I remembered how Sol had offered to buy me flight time on a Beechcraft Bonanza F-35 for my birthday one year. I'd refused, telling him I didn't want to take the risk when we finally had Dave.

"The truth is, it just wouldn't have been the same," I said to Jane.

She seems to want some advice on what to do with the rest of her life, which I can't possibly give her, but I can tell her to enjoy the one she's got now, to enjoy her children, because she'll wake up one morning and wish she could do it all over again.

ELYSE PAYS ME VISITS AS WELL, SOMETIMES WITH HER MOTHER and sometimes alone. Now that she's running indoor track and volunteering at the hospital—"for real this time," as she says— and going back and forth between her parents' homes on the weekends, Elyse is a typical busy teenager, although she still, thankfully, likes to hear what I have to say—unless it has to do with my surgery; then she seems to think it's her job to distract me. Whenever I say, "I just can't figure out why on earth this happened to me," she'll change the subject: to her own novel, to her parents, to her new experiences as a member of a team. It's the same way when she sees the scar in my neck: she always glances away. But the day she brings me lunch along with the last of the chapters I gave her to transcribe, Elyse looks me in the eye and says, "You know, my grandma was told you were dead."

"If I could go back and choose again . . ." But what would I have chosen, an entirely different life without Sol—or Dave? I shake my head and say, "I'm so sorry," because that much is true.

"I know you are," she says, still watching me. "I'm glad it was just a lie—the 'plane crash' that took your life."

"Ah, heavens, as am I," I say, realizing as I say the words that I actually mean them. "How lucky am I that it turns out you're my great-niece?" I add.

Elyse frowns. "I'd still be here even if we weren't related," she says, and then I feel even luckier.

SELENA MARKMANN IS MY OTHER FREQUENT VISITOR. THE FIRST time she arrives at the rehab center, we stand there and hug and cry in each other's arms like we were the old friends we should've been for the last ten years. Then she helps me get back into bed and sits on the side instead of on the chair, the way Jane and Elyse do. It's very sisterly, and I'm grateful for it. Selena gathers herself back together and wipes her eyes and takes a deep breath and then tells me the bad news, that Gene is dead.

"*Gene?*" I say, shocked. Just a few days before, he'd sent an orchid, and now he's gone? "What happened to him?"

"The other Jean. Jean Fester," she says quickly. "A heart attack, they think. Her son found her."

"Good God. Jean," I say, equally shocked. "Despite all evidence to the contrary, I never thought she'd really die but that her terrible stories would keep coming forever, and she would outlive us all."

Selena laughs, in spite of herself. "She wasn't the best writer," she admits, "but she was a good critic. She knew the right questions to ask of an author. And she meant well."

"She will be missed," I say, and it's actually, strangely, true.

THESE DAYS, I HAVE A COMPULSION TO TELL THE TRUTH. I TELL Elyse that I won't be contacting the president about my Congressional Gold Medal, because I'd burned all the records with my real name on it, and she doesn't bat an eye. I tell Selena that there are no twins, and she just shrugs and says, "Oh, Mary, I wasn't born yesterday." I tell Gene, when he finally comes in person to show me his hangdog face, that it's all right that he couldn't do what I asked of him. The fact is, it was my own fault for not getting my affairs in order years ago, my own fault for putting him on the spot at the last minute. The real truth is, until the very moment of his confession in my apartment, I never noticed he wasn't there.

"But . . . I haven't slept in months about this," Gene says. "I went to confession to ask for forgiveness, and I'm not even Catholic, and then I had to be forgiven for that, too. Didn't you wonder about my card?" he adds, meaning the card that arrived with his orchid, which read "I'm sorry, Mary," instead of "Get Well."

"I assumed you were sorry that things had not gone according to plan," I say.

"Well, that, too," he says, so glum that I have to reach over and pat his hand, and he looks grateful but unconvinced. "I almost forgot; I brought you a present . . ." He suddenly remembers, handing me a rather large, flat gift.

I feel the raised, square edges through the paper and then unceremoniously tear it off. Inside the wrapping is a framed copy of the newspaper article from last July's *USA Today*. Grace, Murphee, and I smile into the wind under the banner: "First women to fly American military aircraft served courageously, blazed trails during WWII."

"Oh my word. Gene," I say.

He taps on Miriam Lichtenstein, beaming at the center of the frame, and says, "A little birdie told me that this is you." His use of the present tense brings tears to my eyes. He's the president now, handing me my Congressional Gold Medal.

"It is me," I agree with a watery smile. "Gene. Thank you."

My eyes linger longer on Grace, lost to cancer years ago, and then Murphee of the bottle-red hair. *Whatever happened to*

Murphee? I wonder, and then decide if anyone could track her down, it would be Toby. *A project for tomorrow.*

"When are you coming back to group?" Gene asks.

"As soon as the snow is over," I tell him, and feel as if I've become another old woman, afraid of the winter.

Andie's visits may be the least frequent, but are often the most entertaining. She has a funny way about her, acting as if she has known me her whole life, while telling me random stories about people I've never met, with great animation, as if I've known them forever, too.

"So, Gordon Palmer asked me out, at least I think he did; I mean, he really just invited me to have coffee in the cafeteria at work. He's kind of a gloomy Gus, but I mean, wouldn't you be if your daughter was on a reality TV show, and you had to sit in a dark room for a living looking at pictures of people's insides? Mom would probably say I should give him a chance," Andie says.

"She'd probably say, 'Thank goodness, you're not marrying Blane,'" I add, having heard the whole story about the pillow salesman.

Andie's head snaps up to look at my smile, and then she bursts out laughing. "So true, Aunt Miri, so true," she says, slapping her knee, and I find myself chuckling, too. How wonderfully odd it is to reclaim my old name—and yet somehow I am still Dave's mother Mary, too. I am grateful to be both.

A FEW WEEKS LATER, ELYSE TURNS UP AT MY DOOR TO SAY THAT this is the warmest winter Pittsburgh has had in ages, and that she's coming by next Tuesday to walk me to the writers' group, so that I can see it for myself—the clean sidewalks, the green grass, the hints of spring, maybe even a crocus. I can tell that Elyse is afraid I've become a bit of a shut-in, which I have. If it weren't for Selena Markmann's steady stream of groceries, and Jane's tuna casseroles, and Andie's borscht, which she freezes in small portions for me, I may have actually had to sign up for Meals on Wheels. "Everyone agrees that you should pass something out next time," Elyse adds. "What about the memoir? I can look and see where we left off."

"I think I want to write about when I got sick," I say instead, realizing it all at once. Perhaps this is why Jean Fester had always felt the need to put the horror on paper—to get it out of her and to let it go. But then I remember how painful it was to take on her discomfort as a reader. "I just don't want it to be . . ."

"A downer?" Elyse suggested. "Just write like no one will ever read it."

"What good advice," I say with a smile.

And so, I begin to speak as Elyse types my words: *I wake up the first time to an electric shock on my left lower leg—the sort police officers use to silence unruly college students. At least that's what I imagine. I try to jerk my leg away, but my leg won't move.*

THE GROUP IS ALL THERE FOR MY RETURN: HERB SHEPHERD, Victor Chenkovitch, Gene Rosskemp, Selena, and Elyse, and there are hugs all around. There's even a "Welcome Back, Mary!" cake, and it feels like my birthday. When I hand out my first submission in ten years, Gene cheers.

When I get back to my apartment that night, it looks different, more cramped, the apartment of an old lady with too much furniture in too small a space. I feel a strange sense of surrender these days, maybe even hopefulness, and I'm not sure if it's because I am worn out from what I've been through, or if it's because after so many eras of regret, I finally got to apologize. Now when I climb into bed and shut my eyes and think about My End, my heart doesn't flutter in panic. Instead, I think about my family, lost and found, and the grace of forgiveness. I remember my vision of the sky, and the way I sailed over the trees. Maybe tomorrow I will open my eyes and find myself here, where the windows won't open and the radiator forces heat even as the weather begins to break. Or maybe I will unlock the door and fly.

Acknowledgments

I am so grateful to my agent, Brianne Johnson, an early champion of this novel back when it was over a hundred pages longer and every character had a point of view—thank you so much for believing in this story. I am equally grateful to Amanda Bergeron at HarperCollins for her enthusiasm and exquisite editorial advice. I couldn't have hoped for a better editor.

I am so thankful for my sister, Katherine Brown, who provided me with reading material, encouraged me after rounds of rejections, critiqued multiple drafts with complete insight into the characters, and basically made this a better book. Thanks also to my little brother, Brad Lincoln, who read and commented on the third draft, and to my brother Chris Leffler, for urging me to get the novel out there. Thanks to my stepsister, Sarah Carpenter, whose great name I borrowed for Miri's sister.

I'm incredibly fortunate to have spent the last decade of Tuesday nights dissecting fiction with an amazing group of writers: Cindy McKay, Mike Murray, Jennifer Bannan, Scott

Smith, Anjali Sachdeva, Eric Ruka, and Joe Balaban whipped this manuscript into shape over bottles of wine (*Snippets!*). Let's keep meeting forever.

Thanks to my surrogate sisters, Shannon Perrine and Elizabeth Finan, along with Ellen Sarti, Dedee Wilson (my fellow night owl), Wendy McCorkle, Amy Nevin Martin (my pseudo-sister-in-law), Susie Hobbins, and Joy Lynn, as well as medical schoolmates Ernie Lau (the man, the myth) and Jay Lieberman for your friendship.

Thanks to Women Airforce Service Pilots Lucile Wise, who answered all of my emails regarding the WASPs, and Florence Shutsy-Reynolds, for discussing her experiences during WWII, conversations that truly brought Miri's story to life. "Shutsy" encouraged me to take a demo flight on an antique plane, a suggestion that did not mesh well with my fear of heights. Instead, I watched United States Navy training films: "Flying Sense" produced in 1944, as well as "Advance Flight Training with AT-6 SNJ, Take Offs, Approaches and Landings." In addition, I read *They Flew Proud*, by Jane Gardner Birch, a history of the Civilian Pilot Training Program, which was where I came across the "Ten Commandments for Safe Flying" from the Piper Cub Owner's Manual. Conversations with commercial pilot Grey Hobbins also helped tremendously. I'm sure I got things wrong, and the fault is entirely mine. Thanks also to Danielle Marcus, for sharing with me everything I needed to know about Jane's career as an asbestos attorney.

Portions of Mrs. Browning's medical crisis were inspired by my own experience with anesthesia, which I wrote about in an essay for the inaugural issue of the University of Iowa Carver

College of Medicine's *The Examined Life Journal*, titled, "The Other Side of the Stethoscope." Thanks also to Dr. Chris Bartels for making a reluctant patient better.

My mother-in-law, Sue Martin, gave me a copy of an article written by Elmer Puchta, LTC AUS, a retired army Captain who commanded the 3360th Quartermaster Truck Company in 1944. The article included an intriguing paragraph about a convoy of trucks sent to Paris to obtain the French liquor that had been taken by the Germans. "The security for this convoy was greater than any cargo we carried," Puchta wrote. He also mentions a surviving bottle of champagne drank on his wedding night. This anecdote, which is part of the Veterans History Project in the Library of Congress, inspired Gene's writer's group story about the captain of a truck company.

The article "Tuberculosis sanitorium regimen in the 1940s: a patient's personal diary," was a fascinating account of life in a TB sanitorium written in 1944 by a young mother who had to be separated from her husband and baby after her diagnosis. Her diary, published in the *Journal of the Royal Society of Medicine* in 2004 by Raymond Hurt, FRCS, DHMSA, inspired Sarah's time spent battling TB in the pre-streptomycin era. Piero Scaruffi's "A Time-Line of World War II" on the web was extremely helpful to my research as well.

I am grateful for my mother, Dr. Martha Leffler Lincoln, whose spirit I have felt pushing me through this story, and my father, Dr. Allan "Ted" Leffler, who pulled an all-nighter many years ago to help Kristie Burke Murray and me construct the most aesthetically pleasing toothpick bridge in the history of Atholton High School. Thanks to my stepmother, Melissa Leffler, who has always kept the family together despite all of our losses.

To my sons, Jacob Martin, a budding writer who thought of the title to this novel back when he was seven years old, and Owen Martin, who was two when I wrote the first chapter—thank you both for putting up with the writing of this book. I am so lucky to be your mother. Eternal gratitude to my husband, Tim Martin, without whom there would be no book. I love you more.

About the author

About the book

Read on

Insights,
Interviews
& More . . .

Meet Maggie Leffler

MAGGIE LEFFLER is an American novelist and a family medicine physician. A native of Columbia, Maryland, she graduated from the University of Delaware and volunteered with AmeriCorps before attending St. George's University School of Medicine. She practices medicine in Pittsburgh, Pennsylvania, where she lives with her husband and sons. *The Secrets of Flight* is her third novel. ᮁ

The Women Behind
The Secrets of Flight
An Essay

IN 2009, I set out to write a multigenerational saga about family, lost and found, envisioning a teenager, Elyse, inadvertently showing up to a senior citizens' writers' group and having an instant connection with a woman in the group. I already knew that the elderly woman, Mary, was hiding a distressing secret, and that it was up to Elyse to save her, but I wasn't sure what Mary's backstory was until I read an article about President Obama honoring the World War II Women Airforce Service Pilots (WASP) with Congressional Gold Medals. Having been fascinated with flight since I was little (probably since I read *Ballet Shoes*, where Petrova Fossil becomes a pilot instead of a dancer), I knew then that that was part of Mary's history—she'd left her family behind when she dared to go fly, fell in love, and made a life-altering decision she'd been haunted by ever since.

I started learning about the Women Airforce Service Pilots at www.WingsAcrossAmerica.com, an amazingly helpful website with interviews, articles, photos, an interactive timeline, and everything a person might want to know about the contribution of these remarkable women. There was even a part of the website, "Contact a WASP," where I could choose a former pilot to write to. With excitement, I emailed Lucile ▶

3

Wise and told her about my novel, and, over several emails, she graciously answered all of my questions. "I hope you will not portray us as glamorous," Ms. Wise wrote. "We worked hard and had little time to worry about our hair or make-up." (I'm sorry, Ms. Wise, but I just kept seeing Miri in that red dress.)

Originally the novel had more points of view, including Elyse's mother Jane's as well as Aunt Andie's, until I realized the story really belonged to Elyse and Mary, and that young Miri needed a voice of her own. I rewove letters between Miri and her sister Sarah from the 1940s into Miri's first-person narrative. Four drafts had been completed, yet still something was missing—more details about a woman pilot's life during the war. Just as I was coming to the conclusion that the chances of randomly bumping into a WASP to interview were slim to none, my friend Joe Balaban randomly bumped into a WASP to interview—at a work function honoring veterans. "I got her phone number," he said with a smile. "She said you can call her." It was kismet. Over several conversations and emails, Florence Shutsy-Reynolds generously answered all of my questions, and Miri's time in the air force came alive.

It was Shutsy (pronounced "shoot-see") who told me her first impressions of flight, how she'd gotten to Texas in the first place—after learning to fly by competing with forty-five men in her class for a government flight scholarship—and what happened at Cochran's Convent once she arrived. From the sleeves of the enormous flight suits, which would get caught on the seat belt levers and accidentally unbuckle them, to the captain who informed her that he hated women pilots just before her check ride—Shutsy shared detail after detail and invited me to use them all.

She told me about the WASPs who, while away ferrying aircrafts, had arranged for the fueling of aircraft and were on their way to dinner when they were promptly arrested on charges of solicitation since it was after 9 P.M. and they were wearing slacks. "Eventually, they got a hold of Nancy Love, and she threatened the sheriff with court-martial if he didn't let them go." And it was Shutsy herself who had to land unexpectedly in a storm and stay at a hotel, where she and her fellow WASPs, in their leather jackets without insignias, were told to say they were a baseball team rather than admit to being pilots. "We were one of the best-kept secrets of the war," Shutsy said to me.

I read the account of WASP Lorraine (Zillner) Rodgers, whose rudder cables were cut, forcing her to have to eject from the plane before it crashed, and wondered if there were other forms of sabotage that, for purposes of my plot, would allow the plane to get up before the engine would fail. Both Shutsy-Reynolds and Wise separately told me about sugar in the gas tank as a means of sabotage. "You have to understand, this was a period of time when a cockpit of a military aircraft was a man's sanctuary," Shutsy explained. Each time there was a WASP crash, Jackie Cochran was sent to investigate, and more often than not it was written up as "pilot error" after she left, which Cochran usually did not contest. "We were on thin ice," Shutsy said, even before the congressional hearings where they ruled to disband.

Short of combat, these inspiring women flew every type of military aircraft and performed every job in the air, flying "solo, in all types of weather, all times of day or night, in aircraft in perfect condition and in some that were hardly holding together. . . . [W]e were pilots. . . . Being a female was not a consideration," Shutsy wrote to me once. "We wanted to learn, improve our skills, fly solo to the ends of the earth, fly better than anyone else." She asked me to portray the WASPs the way they really were: independent, argumentative, opinionated, "a fiery bunch" who were "extremely loyal." Unlike those in Miri's history, the friendships Shutsy made during her time as a WASP have lasted forever.

The Secrets of Flight took five drafts over four and a half years before it was acquired—and then another few drafts after that— but it was the Women Airforce Service Pilots themselves who made this a richer story. I just hope I have done the WASPs justice with this novel, as they deserve far more than that. ∽

Reading Group Questions

1. Did you know about the Women Airforce Service Pilots program before reading this novel? What do you think it must have been like to be one of these women? Would you have applied at that time?

2. Mary and Elyse form an unexpected bond. What does each bring to the other? In what ways are their coming-of-age stories different and in what ways are they similar?

3. Miri and Elyse both get "makeovers" to fit in with those around them. Is this a positive change? What are the possible repercussions when you change your appearance for the approval of others?

4. Do you think Mary was justified in hiding her heritage? Why or why not? Would you ever change who you are to achieve your dreams or help someone else achieve theirs?

5. Jane seems to epitomize the woman who "has it all" until everything falls apart. Is this a possibility for women or is it a myth? How do you think Jane would view it?

6. Why is Miri so drawn to flying? What does it represent for her? Is she rushing toward or away from something? Do you think she succeeded?

7. During one of her last flights, Miri thinks that the only role for her in the sky after the war would be as a flight attendant. What do you think it was like for women who had taken on unexpected roles during wartime? In what ways do you think that shaped where we are today?

8. Elyse dreams of becoming a writer, following in a family tradition that she's not completely aware of. Are there talents or desires that are intrinsic in some people's DNA? Have you ever experienced this?

9. How does Elyse help her mother and aunt accept Margot's death? How does Mary finally come to terms with the death of her son? ❧

Further Reading

Books on Maggie Leffler's Night Table

Franny and Zooey, J. D. Salinger
The Things They Carried, Tim O'Brian
Love in the Time of Cholera,
     Gabriel García Márquez
Catch-22, Joseph Heller
To the Lighthouse, Virginia Woolf
About a Boy, Nick Hornby
The Bell Jar, Sylvia Plath
Possession, A. S. Byatt
The Hours, Michael Cunningham
The Wonder Spot, Melissa Bank
A Visit from the Goon Squad,
     Jennifer Egan
The Family Fang, Kevin Wilson
The Beautiful Ruins, Jess Walter

Bibliography

Birch, Jane Gardner. *They Flew Proud*.
     Nappanee, IN: Evangel Press, 2007.
Dubner, Stephen J. *Choosing My
     Religion: A Memoir of a Family
     Beyond Belief*. New York:
     HarperCollins, 1998.
Ehrlich, Elizabeth. *Miriam's Kitchen*.
     New York: Penguin Books, 1997.
Gay, Ruth. *Unfinished People: Eastern
     European Jews Encounter America*.
     New York: Norton, 1996.
Kolatch, Alfred J. *The Jewish Book of
     Why*. New York: Penguin Compass,
     1981.
Lindbergh, Charles A. *The Spirit of
     St. Louis*. New York: Charles Scribner's
     Sons, 1953.

Squirrel Hill Historical Society. *Images of America: Squirrel Hill*. Charleston, SC: Arcadia, 2005.

Trillin, Calvin. *Messages from My Father*. New York: Farrar, Straus & Giroux, 1996. ᵔᷢ